The Time Seekers

The Time Seekers

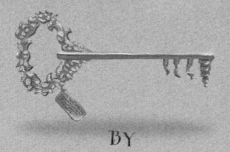

BY

D. A. SQUIRES

ILLUSTRATIONS BY KELLY ARNOLD

THIS BOOK IS INSCRIBED

TO

Children everywhere . . .

■ ◆ ■

They are the stars in our midst.

And in memory of Loretta Barrett, who believed in this story.

CONTENTS

✷ x ✷

✶ ◆ ✶

THE TIME SEEKERS MAP

The Time Seekers

PROLOGUE

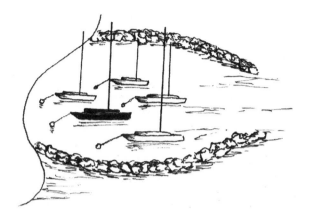

I f you drive the winding coast road in Maine, eventually you will come to a village called Dark Harbor. The small harbor is protected by two rock jetties that curve outward like arms, sheltering the sailboats from the harshness of the open ocean. Taut anchor lines strain in the unending wind and tides, the boats pulling like wild horses wanting to be set free. In the summer, sails are unfurled and sleek hulls ride the waves of the navy-blue Atlantic. When winter arrives, Dark Harbor appears frozen between the icy black harbor and a cascade of snow-laden pines, the village shuttered and the sailboats battened down, silently and bravely riding out the winter at anchor.

Just past the village, there is a sharp curve in the road. Rounding the curve, you will see a rocky promontory cliff jutting far out into the Atlantic Ocean. Towering pine trees cover much of the rugged peninsula. At land's end, and looming high above the ocean, stands an imposing Victorian mansion. Built in the late eighteen hundreds by a wealthy ship captain who made his fortune with a fleet of whaling ships, the once elegant mansion is now old and weathered. Buffeted by harsh New England storms for so many years, the grand façade is gray and fissured, resembling driftwood strewn along the Maine coast.

Long ago when the captain died, having no family of his own, he left his home to be used as a private school for young children.

As this story begins, The Pine School is where Alexandra St. Germaine is about to begin her sixth year. A wide covered porch, always empty, wraps around the perimeter. Black wooden shutters cover the windows. From the second floor, a narrow spiral staircase leads to a rooftop turret and widow's walk. On nights when the moon is full, two ghostly figures can sometimes be seen walking together, their dusky shadows traversing the rooftop in a somber march . . . or so it is said.

And whenever the thick Atlantic fog rolls in or a nor'easter brings winter snow squalls from the ocean, The Pine School disappears altogether.

ALEXANDRA'S ROOM

Alexandra awoke precisely at 7:00 a.m.

She opened her eyes and smiled as she looked across the room. Her alarm was not a buzzer or radio, but instead was the quite distinct voice of a South American blue and gold macaw parrot named Taco. In his very large brass cage, standing in one corner of her room, Taco was spreading his wings and watching the bed intently with his beautiful, painted eyes.

"GOOD MORNING, PRINCESS! Wake up! Can't be late! Can't be late! First day of school! First day! FIRST DAY!"

"I know, Taco. I'm getting up."

Alexandra yawned, stretched her arms, and pulled a feather pillow over her face. Grinning, she peeked at him from under the pillow.

"I have plenty of time, Tacoooo." She liked to add the *o*'s because it sounded funny.

Tossing the pillow aside, she stared at the canopy above her. By habit, she reached for her necklace, found the gold disc, and rubbed it between her fingers. It was her mother's necklace, with her first initial 𝓔 for Elisabeth. The 𝓔 was carved in elegant script, and from the bottom of the letter, a delicate swirl swept upward to a small diamond. Fine lines were etched around the glittering stone, making it look like a starburst. She gazed around the room. It had been her mother's bedroom years ago.

"I don't want to get up, Taco. I never wanted this morning to come. How did the summer disappear so quickly? Here I am again, the same old uniform to wear, nothing new except a new teacher. I've got Miss Blueberry this year. Did I tell you? She's not only round as a blueberry, she *really* is blue, I mean her skin and hair are bluish. It's really quite disgusting."

With a deep sigh, Alexandra finally got out of bed, walked slowly to the large armoire that held her clothes, and opened it.

"Disgusting. Disgusting," Taco echoed her as he often did.

Alexandra sometimes found it annoying that he repeated the same word, yet other times it made her laugh. He had a large vocabulary for a parrot, but this habit of repeating certain words was apparently unbreakable.

"Taco blue?"

His head was tilted to one side and the white skin on either side of his large curved beak had turned a very pale pink, which happened whenever he was embarrassed or upset. Alexandra looked over at him affectionately.

"Yes, Taco, it's fine that you're blue. You're a blue macaw, perfectly normal."

She tried to sound reassuring, as he was quite sensitive and his feelings could easily be hurt.

Alexandra turned her attention back to the open armoire, standing with her hands on her hips and shaking her head.

"Black and white, everything in here is black and white . . . oh, and gray, how could I forget, the one other color allowed—if you can call gray a color it's so ugly and boring."

She looked over at Taco. He was shaking his head slowly from side to side, mimicking her with great precision.

"Ugly, boring, ugly, boring, ug—"

"Oh, Taco, stop it!"

As she admonished him, she was laughing. He was the funniest bird.

With a sigh of resignation, she pulled out the black pleated skirt, crisply starched white blouse, and gray bow tie, lifted her nightgown over her head, and dressed quickly. She stood in front of the mirrored doors of the armoire and adjusted the bow tie, brushed her long blonde hair straight back, put on a black headband, then pulled on black knee socks and stepped into the ugliest pair of black-tie shoes you could ever imagine.

Finished, she walked over to Taco's cage to say good-bye and reached in to rub the sides of his head near his ears, which he liked so much he would almost fall off his perch in utter relaxation.

"Well, bye, Taco. I'll see you this afternoon, if I live through the day. Think of me with Miss BLUEberry."

Taco blinked contentedly and said softly, "Blue, Taco blue."

Alexandra smiled.

"Yes, Taco, you are, and the most handsome blue and gold macaw ever."

Then she turned and walked to one corner of her room where there was a shiny brass pole, and a round hole in the floor. She casually grabbed on, swung her legs around the pole, and disappeared with a swooshing sound.

The bedroom was now quiet. Taco tucked his head under one long blue wing and was soon asleep, snoring softly.

Beneath a beautiful embroidered canopy, the bedcovers were rumpled and one chenille teddy bear with a red bandana was nestled between the bed pillows. On either side of the bed, floor-to-ceiling murals of different seasonal scenes covered the bedroom walls. (One was a frozen pond with skaters under a moonlit sky, the other a summer beach scene.) At the end of the room, a large bay window and window seat framed a tall maple tree. In the fall, afternoon sun illuminated the colorful leaves and cast a soft orange glow throughout the room.

Next to her bed, a nightstand held a lamp, books to read, and a single framed photograph. It was the very last thing Alexandra looked at every night.

Inside the silver frame was a black and white photograph of her parents on their wedding day.

They died when she was one year old.

BREAKFAST AT CHADWICK MANOR

The kitchen was brightly lit, and the smell of bacon filled the room. It was a very large kitchen over which Evelyn presided, who was the cook and housekeeper.

Gleaming copper pots hung from a pot rack, and a fire in the kitchen fireplace crackled away. Burnished oak cupboards, drawers of all shapes and sizes, and thick marble counters that looked like slick snowpack wrapped around the walls. Adjoining the kitchen was a walk-in pantry the size of a small room, stuffed with canned goods, preserves, bins of fruits and vegetables, dishes, and glassware. At one end of the room, there was an enormous white porcelain kitchen sink, and hanging over the sink window was a smiling Man in the Moon face. He had greeted Alexandra every morning since she could remember.

Soon, breakfast was being hungrily consumed by one girl who sat alone at a large round oak table in the center of the room. (It had been a bit startling when Alexandra realized *blueberry* pancakes were stacked on her plate. When she first looked down, she thought she saw Miss Blueberry's face looking up at her, suspended in a blue cloud hovering over the stack of steaming pancakes. Thankfully, the blue haze—and the face—had quickly disappeared.)

"Evelyn, this is so good. Your breakfasts are the best."

"Ah, lovely, my mouse," Evelyn replied, using the name she had always called Alexandra.

Alexandra looked into the kind face she knew so well. Evelyn had cheerful green eyes and attractive red hair, always wound up in a neat bun. She typically wore small pearl earrings and a floor-length dress with long sleeves and crisp white cuffs (the fabric was white and navy or white and green pinstripes). A long, white pinafore apron tied at her waist covered most of the dress. She loved the scent of gardenias, a heavy, tropical fragrance, and the only perfume she wore, which usually preceded her into a room. Evelyn was efficient and organized, and kept the Chadwick household in very good order. She was always bustling about, but never too busy to give a hug or sit and talk at the kitchen table.

"Breakfast is the first proper meal of the day, sets the day right if it's good, or crooked if it's not. That's what I say."

Alexandra smiled. Evelyn was British and had all kinds of odd expressions, even some Alexandra had adopted over the years having heard them so often. She liked the word "crooked" to describe when things were not as they should be.

"Your grandmother's having her breakfast in bed today, so when you're finished, go and give her a quick good-bye. She will miss you today, after having your company all summer. But don't dillydally! Hurry back so Blackie can get you to school before the first bell. First day, you can't be late! Can't be late today, my mouse!"

Alexandra was reminded of Taco for a moment. Evelyn sometimes repeated her words, and Taco had said exactly the same thing.

She finished her pancakes and the last of the milk, and was about to hurry down the long hall to her grandmother's rooms when Evelyn reminded her to take her vitamins. Every day, the cobalt-blue glass bottle with the large gold V emblazoned on it was sitting on the table at breakfast, and every morning she swallowed a large spoonful of the contents. When first poured on the spoon, a rainbow of colors with tiny gold flecks ran through the liquid, but just as she would put the spoon to her mouth, it would change to a single color and flavor. It was always delicious and did seem to keep her very healthy, because she could not remember ever being sick. She double-licked the spoon this morning (the purple color had a delicious grape taste), said good-bye to Evelyn, and was quickly out of the kitchen, through the swinging door.

A very long, wide hallway extended the length of the back of the house from the kitchen. The inside wall was dark cherry wood with raised panels. A bank of leaded-glass windows lined the outside wall facing the backyard of Chadwick Manor. The window panels were nearly the height of the wall, each with a clear glass border of diamond shapes. Within each panel were intricate scenes and designs made from thousands of shards of colored glass. Growing up and spending so much time alone, Alexandra had studied each stained-glass window and she knew every detail. There was a hunting scene with horses in midair over fences, the red-jacketed riders holding tight to the reins, chasing a single red fox, and seasonal scenes of snow-covered mountains and frozen lakes, pumpkin fields and brilliant fall foliage, spring flower gardens, and sailboats riding white-capped ocean waves. Other scenes were of Maine wildlife: a raccoon family traveling single file across a rocky stream, deer grazing in a meadow, moose and black bears roaming in a snowy forest. She had spent countless hours lying on the thick oriental rugs that lined the hallway gazing at the colorful panorama, the sunlight wrapping her in a cocoon of warmth while throwing dazzling displays of rainbow prisms on the ceiling and walls.

It was one of her favorite places to daydream.

However, today she hurried along the long hallway. So many thoughts were rushing through her head as she made her way to the large double doors leading to her grandmother's rooms. As she reached the doors, almost breathless, she heard her grandmother's voice.

"Come in, my dear."

Alexandra paused, and the thought occurred to her, as it had so many times . . . *how does she know I am here?* It was something she could not put into words but had always felt, as though there were secrets not yet shared. Alexandra opened the doors and stepped into a small sitting room, as her grandmother called it, then through another set of double doors leading into the bedroom. There, nestled among ruffled pink pillows, was the person she loved most.

Her only family.

"My dear, come and give me a quick hug before you are off with Blackie. So, Alexandra, it is the first day of your sixth year, how excited you must be!"

Her grandmother's blue eyes were bright and her small face lit up with happiness.

However, it was not excitement Alexandra was feeling; still, she tried to look happy and thought quickly of what to say.

"Well, Grand Mama, it's always hard going back after the summer and I have a new teacher. I'm not sure how it will be, well, you know . . ."

Her voice trailed off. She could not think of anything else to say.

"I'm sure you will feel comfortable in no time. Your mother and father were students . . ." Her grandmother paused and then continued.

"Well, anyway, Alexandra, darling, it is a very fine private school."

Her grandmother's smile was not as strong, and the edges of her mouth changed, as they always did when she spoke of them. If a smile could be sad at the same time that is what it was.

"Yes, Grand Mama, I know. I'm sure I will have a good day. Don't worry about me."

Alexandra leaned over and kissed her papery cheek, which already had a soft hint of rouge. As she breathed in the faint rose perfume, she could see the pale blue eye shadow in the fine creases at the edges of her grandmother's eyes, and the soft pink lipstick on her lips, and remembered their joke when she was little. Her grandmother would always say, "I must put on my face!" to which Alexandra would respond, "Your face is already on, Grand Mama!" Her white hair still had streaks of pale blonde and was wound up in a perfect French twist. She was still beautiful. As was her name, Silver Chadwick.

Good-byes were said, a last hug shared, and then Alexandra was off.

BLACKIE AND MAX

Blackie was waiting for her in front of the garage and carriage house where he and Max lived. Blackie, wearing a chauffeur's cap and uniform, was in the driver's seat of the long black antique touring car. Sitting next to him was Max, his brown and white border collie. The car had a black convertible top, one of the first ever, Blackie had told her, and on nice warmer days, it was always down. On this early September morning, the top was down, which Blackie knew Alexandra liked. There was a rumble seat in the far back where she and Max would sometimes ride, but it was very hard to talk from that distance, so Alexandra typically rode in the front.

"Hello, Blackie! Hello, Max!"

Alexandra slid in next to Max and hugged him. She *always* looked forward to driving with Blackie. Max was usually riding along in the front seat, and she loved riding with him, but most of all, she liked their car rides because she could tell Blackie whatever was on her mind. He would listen thoughtfully, never interrupting, and sometimes give her advice, which she usually agreed with. Blackie was special.

Alexandra felt he was like a father and a grandfather and a good friend, all combined.

"So, Alexandra, how do you feel about going back to school? Probably wishing it was still summer? Am I right?"

He smiled at her. He had thick white hair and blue eyes that seemed to twinkle. Blackie always looked happy. When she was little, he told her he went to sleep with a smile on his face each night, and so should she, and whether it (the smile) stayed on her face all night did not matter.

"Oh, Blackie, I *really* don't want to go back. You know how I feel. It's not the school Grand Mama remembers. I have asked her to visit so many times, but she always says she can't because it reminds her too much of my parents. The Pine School is like a prison . . . we cannot even talk to each other, so we have to pass notes. Do you think it's that way in all schools, Blackie?"

She was staring at the brilliant blue sky, stroking Max's head.

"Your school wasn't like The Pine School, was it?" Alexandra asked, turning to look at him.

They were out the winding drive of Chadwick Manor and going down the coast road that led to the school. She could easily walk to school and had suggested it, but her grandmother would not hear of it.

"Well, Alexandra, 'twas a long time ago. Back in England in those days, the young ones did not go to school for long. They learned the trades. When I was a lad, I only went to school for a short time before I worked as a stable hand . . . and the horses seemed to like me, jolly good luck . . ." He paused, looking at her with a gentle smile, and then continued, "I know your mother liked going to The Pine School. She would tell me about playing basketball in the gymnasium, and she always brought home stacks of books from the library. Your mother loved to read, just like you, lassie."

"Well, Blackie, *everything* has changed since my mother was there. I know I have told you there is no, what did you call it, gymnasium, or library. My books are all from Grand Mama's library. They are not from school. There is no fun at The Pine School. Ever."

Blackie's brow furrowed slightly.

"Can't say why it is the way it is, lassie . . . but we play basketball in the drive, and your grandmother probably has more books than the school ever had. So try to think about the fun you have at home. And let's not forget your crazy parrot, Taco. I would bet all the tea in China no one at The Pine School has a macaw parrot," he said with a smile as he winked at her.

Looking at him, she felt how much she loved him. Blackie and Evelyn were like family even if they were not *real* family. Blackie always tried to find a way to cheer her up and usually did. He had known her mother her whole life and over the years had told her many little things—that her mother loved strawberry ice cream the best and had tiny freckles, like sugar, sprinkled over her nose and cheeks. It was the smallest details that seemed most important to know.

They were approaching the school—the ride was never long enough—and she could see the massive black gates with the tarnished gold *P* in the center. Her fist had tightened around a clump of Max's fur, but he did not flinch. She kept hold of him until they arrived under the portico and then Blackie leaned across Max and squeezed her arm.

"'Twill be all right, Alexandra, don't you worry. Now, go along and see your friends."

Alexandra looked back at him solemnly, saying nothing, then let go of Max, who licked her cheek, and slowly got out of the car. She stood on the first step leading into the school. It felt like she was glued to the spot. Her feet and legs did not want to move. Behind the grimy windows of the main door, she could see Headmaster Green peering at her, and a shiver ran down her back. She waited and watched until Blackie and Max had disappeared from view, and then her gaze fell upon the grove of towering pine trees in the front lawn. Pines . . . The Pine School . . . the pine trees had always looked scary to her, somehow menacing. As she was lost in thought, she heard the creaking hinges of the door opening and the unmistakable raspy voice calling to her.

"Come in, Miss St. Germaine. We are waiting for you."

She turned and with a very deep sigh, slowly walked up the steps of The Pine School.

THE PINE SCHOOL ~ SIXTH YEAR

As the door opened, Alexandra felt the summer fade away and then instantly disappear. The vague, familiar smell of mildew met her nostrils. It was as though she had never left. Just inside the door stood Headmaster Green. His skin was the same pasty yellow (which actually matched his teeth), and his suit was the same ugly pea-green color. Even his shoes were green. He was smiling at her, and she instinctively moved away.

"And how are you after your summer vacation, Miss St. Germaine? I hope you had a good rest and are well prepared for the rigors of your sixth year."

Alexandra remembered how frightened she was of him when she started going to The Pine School her first year. She had never actually cried but many of the little children did.

"I am fine," she said quietly and then swallowed; her throat seemed to have become quite tight and dry. She was thinking *perfectly fine until I got back here*, but then felt she should say something polite in response.

"I hope you had an enjoyable summer, Headmaster Green."

She was looking into his eyes. They were the same putrid green color as his suit with flecks of luminous yellow, and it suddenly felt like she would throw up then and there. All over his green shoes. However, the nausea passed as quickly as it came.

"Yes, thank you."

His voice was always raspy, and he looked quite unhappy as he answered. Alexandra was thinking there was no way he could possibly enjoy anything—except punishing students. She could imagine he would enjoy watching them cry or squirm.

"Your room is Classroom #6, up the center stairs and to the left."

He pointed with a long knobby finger down the large hallway and turned to greet the next arriving student. Alexandra did not need directions and began walking very slowly down the dimly lit hallway. The same black and white tile floor met her footsteps, dingy and grimy looking. As she walked, oblivious to the other students around her, she began to hear a young girl's voice singing. The voice was very faint. "Miss Mary Mack, Mack, Mack, all dressed in black, black, black, with silver buttons, buttons, buttons, all down her back, back, back . . ." Then she realized it was her own voice she was hearing in her head, and a memory from long ago returned. She was in her first or second year, hopscotching from one large black tile to the next singing the clapping song, only to have Miss Citrine or was it Miss Indigo, she couldn't remember, stop her with hands clamping down hard on her shoulders, admonishing her to be quiet and "*Never, never* do that again." At home, the foyer floor had the same large, square black and white tiles, but they were always polished and gleaming. Growing up she had hopscotched all over them, singing, but not at The Pine School.

She looked up and saw the same giant cobwebs draped over the large chandeliers. The chandeliers were probably once beautiful but were now tarnished and dusty, many bulbs were missing, and thick cobwebs clung to every tier. Then, very reluctantly, she began to climb the flight of stairs to the second floor. She remembered the beginning of her fifth year, when going to the second floor for the first time was exciting, one of the only times she could remember feeling that way at school. (The second floor was reserved for the older students, in the fifth through eighth years. The first floor was for the younger children in the first through fourth years.) Her legs felt heavy as she started to climb. She knew there were exactly twenty steps on the first staircase, then the landing, then another twenty. Maybe it was her mood, but her legs really did feel like they were filled with lead. As she stepped onto the second floor, straight ahead was the door marked "To the Turret." Then she turned left and saw the sign hanging out from the wall, "Classroom #6." As she approached the classroom door, she saw another door she had never been through, and it said, "Boarders Only." She shuddered involuntarily.

Standing just inside the classroom door was Miss Blueberry.

Alexandra remembered her very well. She had seen her from a distance for many years knowing that one day she would be her teacher. Up close, she was truly a sight to behold. From her tiny round head with faint bluish hair and skin, to her perfectly round body, to her little tiny legs and feet, she looked as if she would topple over with the slightest jostle. If it were to happen at the top of a hill, Alexandra was certain she would roll like a beach ball down to the bottom. Her dress was deep purple with swirls of turquoise-blue peacock feathers, and a necklace of purple and blue beads was wound in a thick web around her neck. She wore her bluish-gray hair pulled tightly back from her face in a neat knot on top of her head. Her dark blue eyes were too small for her face (but so was her head compared to her body), and they moved like a bird of prey's, intense and darting.

"Hello, Miss St. Germaine, welcome to Classroom #6," she said in a squeaky, high-pitched voice, which was instantly annoying. Her small lips were now in a contorted smile, as if smiling was something difficult for her to do.

"Hello," Alexandra managed to reply, wanting to turn and run all the way home.

"Your name is on your desk, in alphabetical order, starting at the southwest corner of the room. Please find your seat, take out the notebook in your desk and begin the writing assignment on the board at once. Of course, *no talking*, and remember—questions are limited to two per student per day, so choose your questions *wisely*."

The last word seemed to hang on her tiny pursed lips, lingering there for effect. Alexandra also observed Miss Blueberry's mouth was so small it seemed almost miraculous any words came out.

Alexandra entered the room slowly, taking the longest time she could to get to her desk.

Not that there was anything of interest to look at. All classrooms in The Pine School were nearly identical. There were five students already in the room, so another nine would be arriving soon. Each class was limited to fifteen students, and no exceptions were ever made. She expected she would know most of the students; there were rarely any changes. Some of The Pine School students in years four through eight were "boarders," which meant they lived at the school. She knew from her friend Theo, who was a boarder, about the attic room where the metal beds were lined up along the walls and mice ran rampant, and you could see your breath in the winter it was so cold. The boarding students all came from England and only occasionally received letters from their busy parents who never came to visit. When Theo first arrived at The Pine School for his fourth year, there were eight boarders. Last year, only three. Alexandra wondered how many there would be this year. She always felt sorry for them and begged her grandmother to let them live at Chadwick, especially Theo. However, her grandmother told her it was against the "bylaws" of the school, something like rules, she had explained, only more important. It was the one thing Alexandra had to admit Headmaster Green was very good at—making rules.

As usual, the classroom was without color. The desks were in three perfectly straight rows, five desks in each row, facing the long blackboard. Hanging on one wall was a yellowed world map that looked like it had been there for a hundred years, and a few bookshelves held old textbooks. The walls were otherwise bare except for one large clock and an American flag hanging in one corner. It, too, looked ancient, faded and thin, maybe from the Revolutionary War, Alexandra thought.

The windows—there were four along the outside wall—were darkened by shutters latched shut on the outside, and the lighting in the classroom was not bright enough to make up for the lack of sunlight from the windows. So it was into a drab, dull room that Alexandra walked looking for her desk. The only good thing was no one else had a last name that began after *S*, so she was the farthest from Miss Blueberry's desk, which she felt definitely had its advantages.

The other students were busy working on the assignment written on the board: *Describe what you enjoyed most about your summer vacation.* The directions said: 1) *Be specific and use detailed imagery,* 2) *Include all ten spelling words listed,* 3) *Spelling and grammar count,* 4) *Five paragraphs minimum.*

Alexandra reached into her desk, pulled out the writing notebook, and opened it. The blank page stared at her. *As blank as this room,* she thought. The classroom was like a prison cell—empty and cold. She picked up her pen and found herself writing, "My summer vacation was wonderful because I wasn't here." Then she put down her pen and closed the notebook. She was finished. There was nothing more to say. She thought about the possible punishments for not following instructions and not making an effort, all required in something she had had to memorize from the third year called "The Code of Behavior." Nevertheless, Alexandra decided it would be worth it just to see Miss Blueberry's face.

It was at this moment Alexandra knew, with absolute certainty, that she and Miss Blueberry were destined to do battle. For some reason she did not understand, she realized she wanted this to happen and the years of always doing what she was told and following every rule were in the past. However, she also knew there would be *consequences*. The peculiar thing was the fear of punishment that had always stopped her before did not seem to frighten her anymore.

As the other students were filing into the classroom, she was aware of the high-pitched drone of the same instructions being repeated over and over again. She caught the eyes of some of her classmates and could tell they were bursting to talk, to share summer stories, but no one dared utter a word. Then she saw coming toward her, her best friend, Theodore Eddington—Theo (or "T" as he had always written on the notes secretly passed between them over the years). His desk was right next to hers, the last seat in the next row. Alexandra smiled. That was at least *one* good thing.

Theo looked thinner than ever and very pale compared to her summer tan. His red hair was quite straggly. Round, wire-rimmed glasses sat somewhat bent on his nose. He wore black pants, a white shirt, and the black tie that all the boys were required to wear. However, his uniform, unlike most students', was always rumpled and never pressed. Theo was the only boarder whose parents never even wanted him home over the summer, so he had to live at the school year round. For the last two years, as summer approached, Alexandra had begged and pleaded with her grandmother to invite Theo to live with them, but once again, she heard the same answer. It was not permitted under the "bylaws"—boarders were never allowed to leave the school and there would be no more discussion.

As she was thinking about how miserable his summer must have been, wondering what he did for two long months, and what he could possibly write about a summer vacation he did not have, Theo sat down in his chair. *Very oddly*, a puff of fine, silvery dust rose around him. His face turned quite pink and he looked down in obvious embarrassment, but she was the only one who had noticed. Just as Alexandra was puzzling over what she had seen, Miss Blueberry slammed the door shut.

The first day of the sixth year was about to begin.

THE FIRST DAY IN
MISS BLUEBERRY'S CLASS

Everyone sat very still and watched with restrained amusement as Miss Blueberry made her way, ever so slowly, to her desk. She listed from side to side like she was about to fall to the floor any minute, and made small grunting noises, as though it was very hard to put one tiny foot in front of the other. Her breathing was labored, and very strangely, a faint bluish tint could be seen coming from her tiny nostrils as she exhaled. She finally reached her desk, where she collapsed in a chair that looked like *it* would collapse any minute.

Then the crackle of the loudspeaker could be heard and the raspy voice of Headmaster Green slowly repeating, "Testing one, two, three. Testing one, two, three." It was the one moment of every school day that was actually funny. He repeated the same thing every morning without fail, even though the intercom system *always* worked.

"Good morning, students. Welcome back to our returning students and a very big welcome to our new students."

He paused and breathed loudly. Alexandra scanned the classroom. There were no new students this year. She knew them all.

"This will be another good year at The Pine School if all students abide by 'The Code of Behavior.' Your teacher will pass out 'The Code' this morning, and you are required to memorize the rules if you are in classrooms three through eight."

He paused and again breathed heavily. It was a very creepy wheezing sound, amplified by the microphone. Then he made some strange noise as if he was trying to stop a sneeze mid-sneeze. Alexandra looked at Theo. They both were dying to laugh and had to look away from each other or they would have. Then he continued.

"If any rule is broken, the punishments are as follows. For the first offense, you will be required to come to my office and then write an apology for what you did wrong one hundred times on the blackboard during the lunch period. Any student who is foolish enough to break the rules a second time will spend the day in the Turret *without lunch*. Now, please stand for the Pledge of Allegiance, and then we will begin another *exciting* day of learning at The Pine School."

He put great emphasis on the word "exciting," but the word should have been "horrible" or "awful."

Miss Blueberry told everyone to stand for the Pledge. She could not get up easily, and it took three or four times of rocking back and forth for her to be propelled to her feet. Then it appeared she might lose her balance and fall forward. She rocked slowly on her little feet another three or four times before she finally came to a stop. Her blue breath was getting darker from the exertion. Everyone was trying very hard not to laugh. With the Pledge finished, she told them to be seated.

"Katherine Briggs, please distribute 'The Code of Behavior' to your classmates."

With that, the girl who was always "The Most Favorite" (or "TMF" in their notes), and whose desk was always closest to the teacher's desk, sprang up and with a smug smile began handing out "The Code." Alexandra had never liked her. This year, in spite of her grandmother's rule, "Never use the word 'hate,' Alexandra," she knew how she felt. She *hated* Katherine Briggs.

Katherine Briggs always wore her hair in neat braids tied with black or gray ribbons. As she placed "The Code" on Alexandra's desk, she gave her usual phony smile and Alexandra could see she had gotten braces over the summer. She seemed to want everyone to notice, because she never stopped smiling as she handed out the papers.

"Now, class, your attention. We will review the rules by repeating each one in unison. I am sure there will be no violations this year."

Miss Blueberry again attempted to smile. She was holding "The Code" in one hand and with the other hand was adjusting the beads around her neck, pushing them in a slightly upward motion over and over again. Alexandra wondered if she would do this all the time. It was very distracting.

With somber, reluctant voices, the students of Classroom #6 repeated "The Code":

1. We, the students of The Pine School, will always be on our best behavior.
2. We will not speak unless spoken to by a teacher or the headmaster, and we will not laugh aloud.
3. We will always make our best effort to achieve 100% in all subjects.
4. We will always do what we are told without question.
5. We may ask no more than two questions each day by raising our hands.
6. If asked about our school, we will tell the truth, and say our teachers are wonderful, and we have fun-filled days of learning.

Alexandra felt her throat tighten as she barely spoke the words, which of course, she knew by heart. They all did. She glanced at Theo, who was hardly speaking either. Rule number six was the worst—lies.

"Now, class, we will proceed with reading aloud your summer vacation essays. We will begin with Alexandra St. Germaine."

With her beady, birdlike eyes, Miss Blueberry looked expectantly at Alexandra, who stared back at her but did not open her book.

"Miss St. Germaine, did you not hear me? Please stand up and read your essay to the class."

Her small mouth was pursed as though she were about to whistle. Alexandra was thinking how funny that would be when Theo kicked her foot and whispered urgently, "*Answer her.*"

Alexandra slowly stood up, staring at Miss Blueberry, and said clearly and steadily, "My summer vacation was wonderful . . . because I wasn't here." Then she sat down.

The silence was as if the air itself had been sucked out of the room. All eyes were on the front of the classroom. There was a moment when everyone thought Miss Blueberry was going to tip over because she started to sway back and forth. Then there was a sound like air coming out of a balloon when it's pricked. Alexandra thought maybe she was filled with air and was going to deflate and all that would be left would be a puddle of bluish purple and some beads to match. Next, someone giggled, which made the whole class go into fits of snickers and laughter. Then it happened. A scream filled the room that made everyone cover their ears because it was so piercingly high and horrible. The face that had a faint bluish cast when normal had become red over the blue, making it purple, and the eyes that were small and beady popped out like they were about to leave her head and roll down the aisles between the desks. The mouth that had looked as small as a bird's was open wide enough to fit a tennis ball. Then the scream became a name—her name—but it was said in slow motion, "AAAA—LEXXX—ANNN—DRAAAAAA!" Then Miss Blueberry fell back into her chair, her eyeballs receded into her head, her eyes closed, and her body, still rotund, went limp.

The next few minutes were somewhat blurry in Alexandra's mind even though the moments leading up to the fainting were extremely vivid. Theo seemed to take charge. He ran up to her, and while holding her wrist, said he thought he felt a pulse and she was probably still alive. Then he pressed the buzzer on the microphone, which connected each teacher to the Headmaster's Office. Everyone gathered around Miss Blueberry, some talking and some still snickering. Most were silently staring at Alexandra. It was a very strange sensation. She remembered looking back at them and seeing their disbelief and horror but not feeling anything like that. She actually felt very calm.

The speaker crackled to life with the usual static and then it was the familiar raspy voice.

"Yes, Miss Blueberry?"

"Well, sir, it's about Miss Blueberry. She fainted or something."

"What? Fainted? Who is speaking?"

"This is Theo, Theodore Eddington, sir. I tried to feel for her pulse, and I think she's alive. But I'm not sure. She's very purple."

"Very purple? What do you mean? She is always a bit bluish. That is normal for Miss Blueberry. Young man, can she talk? Are her eyes open?"

The voice was now very raspy, and there was a loud wheezing sound with each breath.

"Her eyes almost came out of her head, and she's not breathing and she—*she looks dead*!!!"

It was none other than Katherine Briggs screaming into the microphone.

"And it's all because of Alexandra St. Germaine!!!"

She added the second statement for good measure, smiling at Alexandra like the cat that swallowed the mouse.

The static got worse. Then the connection went dead.

Miss Blueberry's eyes suddenly fluttered open as she began gasping and licking her lips. Even her tongue was bluish. Alexandra felt like she was an observer, somehow removed, as though she was passing by and happened upon this awful scene. Katherine Briggs was wafting papers in front of Miss Blueberry's face like a fan, saying repeatedly with overly dramatic breathlessness, "It will be all right, Miss Blueberry . . . everything will be all right! Headmaster Green is coming. He will be here right away. Don't worry . . ."

Soon, the classroom door opened and Headmaster Green shuffled in followed by Miss Pomegranate, his secretary. Miss Pomegranate was dressed in hues of orange and red; even her hair was orange, which matched her fingernails and shoes. Alexandra had seen this from her first year—the teachers all had last names that were fruits or vegetables or colors and they dressed in those same colors; even their skin and hair took on that shade. Whenever she mentioned it to her grandmother the response was always, "I am sure it is not as exaggerated as your mind is making it, Alexandra. People do not come in colors of fruits and vegetables. It is your overactive imagination, nothing else, my dear."

Over time, Alexandra had stopped talking about it and had given up asking her grandmother to visit the school. Whenever she asked, the response was the same. She always apologized and said it was just too painful a reminder of Alexandra's parents, who were working at the school before the accident. Her mother had taught sixth-year students. (She had wondered over the summer if her mother was still alive how it would have been to have her as a teacher—would they have allowed it, and if not, where would she have gone?) And her father . . . well, as hard as it was for her to imagine given his replacement, he had been the headmaster. Headmaster St. Germaine. When they died, the ancient Mr. Green, who had been teaching eighth-year students, replaced him and Miss Blueberry replaced her mother. It often felt like a nightmare, where if she just waited long enough, it would magically change back. The spell would be broken. But it was also true she had grown beyond the age of believing in fairy tales. Alexandra already knew that life did not have happy endings for everyone.

The scene in the classroom was somewhat calmer, as it was clear Miss Blueberry was reviving. She was able to speak a few words, and Alexandra heard her say she needed some water, which Theo brought to her in a small paper cup from the hallway fountain. They were told to return to their seats and begin reading their geography books. The books were opened, but all eyes remained glued on the front of the classroom. With Headmaster Green holding her by one elbow and Miss Pomegranate by the other, together they tugged and pulled with much exertion and were finally able to lift Miss Blueberry out of her chair. Very, very slowly, they made their way out of the classroom.

Miss Pomegranate took her place for the remainder of the day.

But nothing that happened after Miss Blueberry barely squeezed through the door could even be remembered.

DAY TWO IN CLASSROOM #6

The ride home with Blackie and Max was filled with laughter as she told the whole story, blow by blow. Even Max seemed to understand. The border collie had the most amazing eyes; they were intelligent, almost human looking, and the color of amber gold. Each eye was outlined with what looked like thick black eyeliner. With his dramatic eyes and long nose, Max actually looked more wolf than dog. After the last detail was shared, Blackie became serious and seemed to be mulling everything over. As they pulled into the drive at Chadwick Manor, he said it would be best not to tell the story to her grandmother "in case there are any repercussions." Asked what that meant he said, "Until you know Miss Blueberry will recover." Alexandra felt somewhat deflated by this advice; after all, she had just told the truth. She could not be responsible for Miss Blueberry's reaction. The summer had been wonderful: sleeping late, playing with Max, picnics with Blackie, having no strict bedtime, and best of all, finding out about the sailboat. Going back to The Pine School was like going back to prison after being free.

However, not surprisingly, after giving it more thought during the afternoon, Alexandra decided to take Blackie's advice. So nothing was said about what had happened on the first day in Classroom #6.

The next day Headmaster Green was waiting behind the grimy glass, greeting each student as he did every morning. This time, after saying good morning, he asked Alexandra to wait in the hallway until the last student had passed through. Her stomach flip-flopped. Had something worse happened to Miss Blueberry? Was she going to be blamed?

In his low raspy voice he said, "Miss St. Germaine, come with me," and placing a long bony finger on one shoulder, he firmly propelled her toward his office door. She was surprised that she did not feel scared. She actually felt somewhat curious. The door she had never been through in five years was opening. Just before it opened, she was looking at the glass door—it was right in front of her nose—and in the grimy glass, she saw it. The name in gold foil, "GREEN," was directly underneath "HEADMASTER" and placed above a ghostly outline that could still be read, "ST. GERMAINE." She sucked in her breath. Her father. Her name.

She noticed the smell first. It was faint, but she knew it immediately. Pipe tobacco. Blackie had always smoked a pipe. She had grown up accustomed to the smell; it was a safe, comforting aroma. Her father had also smoked pipes—she had seen photos of him with a pipe in his hand or mouth. It occurred to her that maybe the whiff of pipe tobacco was from her father because she could not imagine Headmaster Green smoking a pipe. Alexandra gazed around the small room, then at Miss Pomegranate's desk (she was nowhere to be seen), realizing this room had seen her father and heard his voice. All of a sudden, she felt jealous of the furniture and file cabinets. He had been in this office when she was a baby, too young to have any memories of him, or remember his voice, or his face.

Alexandra soon found herself seated in his office, staring across the desk into the yellowish face and the green eyes with bright yellow specks. It was not easy looking into his face at such close proximity, so she looked away, glancing quickly around the room. It was very plain, nothing on the walls, no windows. On the desk, a single reading lamp with a green glass shade only dimly lit the office, casting a greenish glow. Thick piles of paper were scattered across the top of the desk making it look most disorganized. In the center of the desk was the large pewter-colored microphone used to broadcast the morning announcements.

Alexandra looked back at him as he started to speak.

"Miss St. Germaine. We have an eyewitness. Well, let me say we actually have a classroom full—fourteen, to be exact. As this happened in front of all fourteen students, I have to assume the events were exactly as Miss Katherine Briggs told me. Her accounting of the unfortunate events is as follows."

Alexandra was not listening as he began to recite the "unfortunate events." Instead, she was trying to imagine her father sitting at the desk and then began looking around the room for anything that might have been his. Headmaster Green was droning on about the infractions of "The Code of Behavior" and the punishments when she saw it on a small table in a far corner, partially hidden by a very old-looking world globe. A single pipe was hanging from a small pipe stand.

"Excuse me, Headmaster Green."

He stopped talking and winced, as if he had been stung by something sharp.

"*Miss St. Germaine*, surely you have learned by now that it is not polite, in fact, it is *rude* to interrupt when someone is speaking."

He glared at her. The yellow specks in his eyes seemed to be glowing. She swallowed hard. It was difficult to look at him so closely. His sallow skin, sunken cheeks, scraggly eyebrows, and the worst, his crooked yellow teeth, were just a few feet from her across the desk.

"Yes, sir, I know that, but I have to ask you something . . . important."

He sighed and then his expression brightened, just a bit.

"Something about what happened to Miss Blueberry, which you are personally responsible for having caused?"

"Well, no. I was wondering if you, if you . . . smoke pipes?" Her voice was close to a whisper.

He was silent for a moment. She could see from his expression he was surprised, but that quickly disappeared.

"*Miss St. Germaine*, how can you be so, so . . . *impertinent?*"

Before he could speak again, she jumped up and walked over to the small table, gently lifted the pipe from the stand, and then returned to her seat.

"Was this . . . my father's pipe?"

She could see the pipe was layered thick with dust. It had not been used in a long time. Headmaster Green's eyes closed shut as he inhaled deeply, making a raspy, rattling sound. Then his eyes opened into slits, which reminded her of a snake's. Even the yellow specks seemed to have coalesced into vertical luminescent pupils. It felt like she was looking into the eyes of a venomous snake. She shivered and her stomach felt queasy.

"Have you no respect, *Miss St. Germaine*, for property that is clearly not yours? Do you know no bounds? How dare you interrupt me, then stand up, and pick up something in my office? Most of all, for causing *lovely* Miss Blueberry such serious distress? I have to say that I am *terribly* shocked by all these bad behaviors. I know your grandmother will be as well."

Then it was Alexandra's time to be silent. She thought quickly about what he said—that her grandmother would be told about Miss Blueberry. Somehow she felt stronger holding what she knew was her father's pipe and decided what to say.

"All I did was tell the truth about how I felt coming back to school. My grandmother has always told me to tell the truth."

His eyes widened, still snakelike. It was obvious he had not anticipated her response. He seemed to be considering everything, and his shoulders sagged ever so slightly. Apparently, what she said worked. Then he reached for a very large and very old-looking book, which was sitting to one side of his desk.

"This is the most important ledger kept at The Pine School. Do you know what it is?"

She shook her head no.

"It is *The Code of Behavior Infraction Record Book*," he answered, enunciating each word slowly and with great precision.

"It has been here from the first day this school opened many, many years ago. Every student who has ever broken one of the six rules is listed in this book. Let me see, Elisabeth Chadwick . . ." He had opened the book and one bony finger was slowly tracing names as he scanned one of the pages.

Her heart almost stopped—her mother. Her mouth felt dry, and she felt anger rising up in her throat.

"Hmm. No entry. Not one. Moreover, as I recall, a very good student. However, your father. That is another story. He came here from another school for his eighth year. I remember him quite well. He was in my classroom. There were many infractions. Let me just say he was *difficult*, like his daughter. Not respectful of authority. He laughed often and loudly. From the first day he walked into my class I knew he was going to be a problem. I never understood how he was selected to be headmaster of this prestigious school. He was so . . . so . . . young, far too young for such an important position."

Then he quickly added, "However, I am sorry for your loss."

He did not sound sorry. At all.

"I would nonetheless suggest you model yourself after your mother, not your father. Now, for your punishment . . ."

Then, lifting a quill pen out of a dusty inkwell, he very carefully turned the antique pages and began writing and reading aloud as he wrote.

"Miss Alexandra St. Germaine. Sixth-year student. Rude and disrespectful, causing *severe* physical and emotional distress to her teacher, Miss Blueberry. Violation of rules number one and number four."

He paused, looking up at her, clearly expecting his careful enunciation of the violations and the grave seriousness of the offenses to weigh heavily upon her. Shoulders slumping, tears perhaps. However, seeing no such response, he continued with the punishment.

"As this is your first infraction, Miss St. Germaine, the punishment will be to write one hundred times on the blackboard during lunch, 'I am very sorry and will never be disrespectful again.'"

Finished, he closed the book carefully and with that, a small puff of dust flew out of the pages, briefly hovering in the air above the desk. His long yellowed fingers gently caressed the cover as he studied her. The awful smile had returned to his face, and the luminescent specks were once again dispersed in his green eyes, no longer vertical and reptilian looking.

"Now, you may return immediately to your classroom. Let us hope you take my advice, Miss St. Germaine. Remember, like your mother. Not your father."

She nearly flew out of the office and up the stairs to Classroom #6.

Headmaster Green was not the only one smiling. Clutched in her hand and then put safely in a deep pocket of her skirt was the pipe. He had forgotten about it, and she had reclaimed it, part of her father.

No lunch that day. She didn't care. They always had the same food, baloney and cheese or peanut butter and jelly sandwiches on white bread. A few carrot and celery sticks and a carton of white milk, never chocolate, and an apple for "dessert" that was never crisp or cold. However, the worst part was not the food. They could not even talk to each other during lunch. (But many notes were passed.) And they could not go outside. First- and second-year students went to lunch first at 11:00 a.m. followed by third and fourth at 11:20, then fifth and sixth at 11:40, and last, seventh and eighth at noon. Each group would walk single file into a very large room, located at the end of the hall on the first floor, and sit at long tables with lunch trays at each place. Headmaster Green and two teachers would circle the tables while they ate in silence, watching them like hawks the entire time.

Over and over again, she filled the blackboard with the required apology. Miss Pomegranate sat at the desk grading papers and occasionally turned to look at her progress. She said nothing, but nodded in approval now and then. Alexandra noticed she had a cold and every time she blew her nose, it became a darker orange.

Alexandra's hand began to ache, and her fingers felt cramped from holding the chalk so tightly. She was finally done when the other students filed back into the room. Theo winked at her as he sat down and carefully passed a note.

ARE YOU OK? WAS IT TERRIBLE? T.

She wrote back, "yes" to the first question and "not that bad" to the second. Then she wrote, "I have my father's pipe. It was still in his old office. I am so glad. A."

He read it quickly and smiled as he stuffed the note in his pocket.

That night at bedtime, Alexandra placed the now well-polished pipe next to the photo of her parents on her nightstand. She had put the pipe to her nose, and even after so many years, there was still a faint aroma of tobacco. When she pulled the pipe out of her skirt pocket to show Taco, he had squawked with excitement and bobbed up and down exclaiming, "Graham's pipe! Graham's pipe!"

Taco had never spoken her father's name before, and he had not seen this pipe for many, many years.

Parrots, it seems, have an excellent memory.

DAY THREE IN CLASSROOM #6

The loudspeaker crackled to life as Headmaster Green said, "Testing one, two, three. Testing one, two, three," and then gave the morning announcements, complete with raspy breathing, some long pauses, and the sound of shuffling papers. As he was finishing, he said he had a very sad announcement to make. Alexandra and Theo immediately exchanged worried glances. It seemed Miss Blueberry had "decided to retire for health reasons" and not return to The Pine School. Everyone turned in their seats and stared at Alexandra, especially Katherine Briggs. Her look was smug and mean, both at the same time. Theo looked at her with concern and worry. The rest just seemed to be gawking, as though they expected she would be led away to the gallows that very moment. Alexandra breathed deeply. Relief. She had actually expected to hear Miss Blueberry died.

Miss Pomegranate was speaking in her nasal, monotone voice directing the class to open their math books and had called Theo to the board to do a division problem (Theo was very smart in "maths," as he called mathematics) when the door of the classroom opened slowly. The first to enter was Headmaster Green. Right behind him was someone new and yet somehow so familiar to Alexandra even from a distance. When she turned and looked directly at the class Alexandra felt her heart begin to pound, and she gasped loudly. Headmaster Green swiveled and gave her a withering glare.

"Sixth-year students, I would like to introduce you to your new teacher who will be taking Miss Blueberry's place, given her *unexpected*"—he looked directly at Alexandra with the same glare—"early retirement. Please say 'Welcome' to Miss White."

The students all said, "Welcome, Miss White," in unison.

All except for Alexandra, who was mute and transfixed, staring at the new teacher.

She looked identical to the photos of her mother, only older. The shape of her face, her green eyes, her smile, her black hair. From photos, Alexandra had memorized her parents' faces from the time she was very young.

Instantaneously, she was brought back to the moment when her grandmother told her about the accident. It was her second year at The Pine School. She had come home from school crying because everyone else had mothers and fathers, but she just had a Grand Mama. Why?? Her grandmother had led her outside to a glider and held her tightly as they swayed back and forth. Alexandra could still remember crying so hard it was difficult to breathe and her grandmother's thin, strong arm around her, not letting go, and the smell of roses.

They had drowned while sailing in a bad storm. No one witnessed what happened, so it was pieced together from the facts that were known.

The summer of her first birthday, her parents decided to sail their sailboat, *Windswept*, from Dark Harbor to Cape Cod. They loved to sail and bought the sailboat as their wedding present to each other. Her grandmother told her they both had tears in their eyes as they kissed her good-bye, her father hoisting her high in the air to hear her laugh, and they waved good-bye all the way down the long driveway.

Her parents arrived safely at Cape Cod. On the second day, they headed out for what was to be an afternoon sail. The storm had come quickly and lasted well into the night. It could never be known, but it was thought that one of them was swept overboard, and the other dove in attempting a rescue, and the sailboat was carried away from them in the rolling seas and strong winds. After the storm, another sailor came across the drifting, empty sailboat.

It was just this summer she found out their sailboat had been brought back to Maine after the accident and was moored at Dark Harbor. Blackie told her—he had sailed it back to Dark Harbor after it was found.

The same day Alexandra wanted to see the boat.

Blackie rowed the dinghy from the dock to the mooring. As they approached the red sailboat, she could see the gold lettering, still brilliant, glinting in the sun, *Windswept*.

They did not sail that day. Alexandra just wanted to explore the boat, searching for something, anything that would connect her to them. Below the top deck, there was a cozy cabin with red-and-white striped curtains, two small bunk beds, a miniature galley for cooking, and the tiniest bathroom she had ever seen. She climbed back up to the top deck and around to the bow of the boat, finally settling into one of the bench seats in the stern. That was when she found it. Carved into the weathered wooden tiller were three initials, "G, E & A." She looked over at Blackie. The afternoon sun was on his face. He was smiling and she could see tears in his eyes. As her fingers went back and forth across the carved initials, she knew . . . he had wanted her to find it on her own.

The night she learned about the storm and what happened to her parents, her grandmother reached into a pocket and pulled out her mother's necklace. The necklace had been left behind in a small tray of jewelry the day they left on the sailing trip. Her mother had never taken it off before that her grandmother could recall. Alexandra could still remember lying in bed that night and rubbing the small gold disc in her fingers, thinking she would never, ever take it off.

She came back to the present with a thud, realizing she had not heard anything, and was again staring into a face that looked so familiar.

One hand was resting on her chest.

She could feel the necklace under her blouse.

MISS WHITE

The day Miss White arrived in Classroom #6 was a blur in Alexandra's mind. She had no memory of any lessons that day, nothing. Miss White left shortly after she was introduced. The class was told she needed to get settled, having just moved to Dark Harbor from Boston. Alexandra wondered about this. Why did she move, and how did she find The Pine School exactly when she was needed? And why did Headmaster Green choose her? Miss White was the first normal-looking teacher Alexandra had ever seen at The Pine School. She was wearing a white dress with a red belt, and a red silk flower was pinned to the lapel of her dress. Completely normal, with no odd hues to her hair or skin. And very pretty.

However, all Alexandra could think about was she looked so much like her mother.

All day at school, she thought about it. She knew her mother had died. It could not be her, so how could she possibly look almost identical to her mother?

She spent the afternoon lying on her bed, looking at the wedding photo, thinking and wondering about everything. When Evelyn called for dinner, she was still lost in thought, but slowly got up from the bed and Taco flew to her shoulder. He dug his feet in (she always winced but was used to this), then she swung her leg around the pole and down they went together.

She and Blackie were having tacos, which was a tradition once a month—and this was how Taco got his name. Blackie had told her this story many, many times as she was growing up. Her mother loved spicy foods, especially tacos, and one day began calling him Taco.

His name was actually "Winston," named after Winston Churchill by her grandfather, Thaddeus Chadwick. However, upon hearing it, the beloved macaw had announced, "Name is Taco! Name is Taco!" Her grandfather did not think the name was appropriate or funny and continued to call him Winston. However, her mother loved that he had chosen the name for himself, and forever after he was officially Taco.

"I looove tacos," Alexandra said as she bit down on a fat, sloppy taco. Chopped tomatoes dribbled down her chin onto her plate.

"Love Taco?"

He looked demure, almost bashful. His head was turned slightly to one side and his white cheeks were the palest pink. He was sitting on his kitchen perch, and had paused between slurping chunks of watermelon and pineapple from the attached food tray. It was just too funny, and everyone laughed.

"Yes, Tacoooo, everyone looooves you!!" Alexandra smiled at him.

He bobbed his head up and down.

It was at that moment she suddenly decided to ask the question.

"Grand Mama, I know this is going to sound crazy, and I'm sure you would have told me, but . . ." She paused and took a deep breath. "Did my mother have a twin sister?"

Alexandra noticed Blackie immediately looked serious and dropped his eyes. Evelyn nervously asked who wanted more to eat, but no one answered. Taco had stopped eating and was staring at her. Her grandmother put down her cup of tea and briefly closed her eyes. Alexandra began to feel sorry she had asked.

"Why do you ask, Alexandra?"

Her grandmother's voice was soft, almost a whisper, but the tone was factual, not emotional. Her eyes, however, looked very sad.

"Well, I . . . I had a dream . . . that she had a twin . . ."

CHAPTER EIGHT

It was not a very good answer, but it was all she could think of. "A dream."

Her grandmother repeated the words, and from her tone of voice, Alexandra felt she had accepted it as the reason for her question.

"Yes. She did have a twin sister. However, she died shortly after birth."

Alexandra could not believe what she heard.

"She died when she was only one week old, just before we moved here from London. She came down with pneumonia and died at the hospital. They could not save her. Her name was Olivia."

Her grandmother drew in a deep breath and then continued.

"I never even told your mother. There did not seem to be any need to tell her . . ."

Alexandra was not feeling hungry anymore. She slowly stood up and went to her grandmother. With tears in her eyes, she told her she was so sorry and hugged her. As she turned to get Taco, she saw a tiny tear run down his painted face. She had never seen him cry before and did not know parrots could cry. Gently placing him on her shoulder, she slowly walked out of the kitchen and up the stairs to her room.

That night she had a hard time falling asleep. If Olivia had died as a baby, it could not be her. Yet, it seemed hard to believe anyone could look so much like someone else.

"Olivia," she said the name aloud and then heard the distinctive echo.

"Olivia, Olivia."

Alexandra finally fell asleep. The room was quiet.

Taco was settling in for the night. As he tucked his head under his wing and closed his eyes, the blue macaw whispered, "Olivia . . . Olivia White."

CLOSE CALL IN CLASSROOM #6

For the first time ever, Alexandra was excited about going to school. She would swish past Headmaster Green, run up the stairs, and arrive at the classroom door expectantly and breathlessly, because every single day there was something new in Classroom #6. The first day there was a beautiful red rose on Miss White's desk. The next day, a new American flag and new world map appeared. A floral fragrance soon infused the classroom from the perfume she wore, and the musty smell of something old and mildewed was gone. New textbooks *and* library books filled the bookshelves. One day, the shutters were open and sunlight streamed into the classroom. No one knew how she had done it, because the shutters were latched shut on the outside of the windows.

It seemed like a magical spell had been cast over Classroom #6. Without anything being said, it was understood by everyone, even Katherine Briggs, that nothing should be said about any of it—to anyone—lest the spell be broken. Every day, once all the students arrived, the classroom door was closed and locked by Miss White. Occasionally, there would be a rap on the door by Headmaster Green, and he would ask to come in. She would hold a finger to her lips and then say, "We are testing right now, Headmaster Green, so another time would be better for a visit." He would cough and mutter, saying he would be back, but each time he was turned away. Everything seemed so perfect.

The day had started like any other.

The students in Classroom #6 were now swept into a classroom filled with everything interesting and colorful. Plants were growing from seeds that had sprouted under the bright sunlight. There were piles of library books to read and large pillows scattered across a colorful, thick rug Miss White called the "Reading Rug," where they could take a book and read. Mobiles were hanging from the ceiling of the solar system and sea life, and Miss White and some of the students had painted murals on the walls. Theo painted one mural, and the entire class had been astonished at his artistic ability, most of all Alexandra. He drew scenes of London—Big Ben, Parliament, Windsor Castle, and Alexandra's favorite—the red telephone booth with Alexandra inside (and it did look just like her). Two guinea pigs appeared one day, a black and white male named Boris and a brown and white female named Natasha. There were fresh flowers on Miss White's desk each day and delicious candies in a dish that you could take *whenever* you wanted, and she always wore colorful dresses with matching scarves and glittery jewelry. A note passed by Theo one afternoon said simply, "Snow White." It was true. The new teacher in Classroom #6 did look hauntingly similar to the fairy tale character, a resemblance Alexandra had noticed many years ago looking at photographs of her mother.

However, on this day, beginning with a loud and insistent knocking on the classroom door, it seemed like the magical spell would end.

It was Headmaster Green; they could hear him wheezing and coughing. All the students stopped what they were doing and were quiet as mice as Miss White answered in the usual manner. However, this time he did not go away.

"Miss White, *you must let me in.* I have the parents of one of your students here. It is an unexpected visit . . ." He coughed and then continued, "A . . . *surprise.*"

Alexandra wondered if he had ever said that word before, because he seemed almost to choke saying it.

Everyone was perfectly still, staring at Miss White. She did not seem upset or nervous as she whispered, "Return to your seats, quickly."

Then she whispered again, "Close your eyes."

Alexandra felt anxious and afraid. She closed her eyes and wondered what could possibly happen next.

"When you open your eyes, say nothing. You may open your eyes."

Alexandra opened her eyes. She was staring at the old faded flag, the old world map, the shuttered windows, the plain dingy walls. As they were all looking around the room in disbelief, Miss White opened the door, and Headmaster Green shuffled in. Trailing behind him was an old couple who were looking at all the students until their gaze finally settled upon . . . Theo. Theo's parents. Alexandra looked at Theo and knew he was in shock. He usually saw them just once a year when he went home for Christmas. She studied them more closely. Their coats looked a bit worn and ragged, and they looked very nervous. However, they did not look mean or nasty, as she had pictured them. They actually looked nice, but much older than she would have thought.

Theo got up and walked slowly to them. They hugged awkwardly and then filed out of the classroom behind Headmaster Green.

Alexandra wondered where they would go to visit; there was no place with comfortable chairs to sit and talk. Most of all, she wondered why they had come. There had to be a reason. No parents had ever visited any classroom in all the years Alexandra had been at The Pine School.

The classroom was silent. All the students were staring at Miss White, who was leaning back against her desk, which looked exactly like Miss Blueberry's old desk. Her expression was very serious. It was the first time Alexandra had seen her look this way.

"I have something important to say, which I will ask you to respect," she said, pausing as her gaze swept around the room.

"I must ask that you not question what you have seen or tell anyone. Please trust me . . . sometimes in life it is best to accept what happens without understanding. A kind of leap of faith that things are as they should be, even if you do not understand why. Will you do this for me?"

The answer came at once, in hushed, serious voices.

"Yes."

It was a pledge, an oath that would not be broken.

THEO'S DILEMMA

For the rest of the day and into the next morning, Alexandra could not stop thinking about everything—the unexpected visit by Theo's parents and the shocking change in the classroom. The room had been slowly transformed, with everything secretly brought in by Miss White, something new each day—or at least this was what everyone had assumed. Now, thinking about it, how could she have gotten everything, including two guinea pigs in cages, past the Headmaster's Office? And the instantaneous change back to the old classroom—which had remained the same throughout the rest of the day, no one daring to ask why, but worried looks were frequently exchanged—there were no reasonable explanations. Theo had returned to the classroom, but he was obviously preoccupied and had not passed any notes to her about why his parents had come.

The drive to school was silent with Blackie, and even Max, casting sidelong glances at her. She felt more nervous than she could ever remember. It was the longest walk down the grimy corridor and up the two flights of stairs. When she saw her other classmates, they all looked like she felt—scared of what they might find when they reached the second floor. Alexandra even wondered if Miss White would be gone and Miss Blueberry would be back.

Alexandra stepped onto the second floor and immediately looked down the corridor to Classroom #6. Miss White was standing outside of the classroom door, smiling. Her dress reminded Alexandra of Taco; it was a gorgeous "blue macaw" blue with a bright yellow scarf draped across one shoulder.

The dream was not over, at least not yet.

As Miss White closed the heavy wooden door and bolted the lock, it once again felt like all the good was locked inside and all the bad shut out. The classroom was exactly as it had been before, shimmering with color, and everyone was grinning. Everyone except Theo.

Alexandra whispered to him during the morning announcements.

"What happened, Theo? Why did they come?"

His hair and clothes looked more rumpled than ever, and his eyes were red-rimmed. He pushed his crooked glasses up on his nose, looked down at his desk, and swallowed hard.

"I will have to leave at Christmas and not return. There is no money left for me. And . . ."

His voice was thick, as though he was holding back tears.

"And I found out they are my aunt and uncle. Not my parents." His voice cracked with emotion.

"They told me my parents died in a plane crash when I was a baby. I am an orphan. Just like you."

Alexandra felt weak, and her stomach seemed to knot. An orphan. She had never really thought of herself as an orphan because she had her grandmother. But Theo was right. They were both orphans.

"All the money is gone. I hated this school from the start, but not now . . . now with Miss White . . . I don't want to leave."

His voice was trembling, and his knuckles were white as he gripped his pencil hard.

Alexandra felt all the warm, good feelings disappear and her eyes filled with tears.

THE LETTER

Theo was never far from Alexandra's mind as she struggled with what she could do to help. She talked to Blackie about it and asked what he thought the chances were she could convince her grandmother to let Theo live with them and pay whatever it cost to go to The Pine School. He thought maybe yes, so they talked about when and how to bring it up to her grandmother. They were getting ready to . . . when the letter arrived.

The mail was delivered to Chadwick Manor every afternoon around three o'clock, slipped through a large brass slot in one of the front doors. Evelyn would retrieve the mail and place all the letters on a silver tray, which sat on a long table under one of the staircases. Later, at four o'clock, she would take the tray to wherever Silver Chadwick was sitting and bring her afternoon tea. On this particular day, the mail was still on the silver tray when Alexandra arrived home from school. She had finished her snack in the kitchen and was rounding the corner under the staircases when she stopped in her tracks.

One letter was suspended, *in midair*, above the tray.

Alexandra stood frozen, staring at the letter, and after a few moments began walking slowly and cautiously toward it. She was close enough to reach out and take it when Evelyn suddenly came from behind and rushed around her, quickly grabbing the letter and the tray of mail.

"Never mind that, my mouse, never mind that."

Evelyn's face was beet red. She was more flustered than Alexandra had ever seen her before. Alexandra watched as Evelyn flew down the hallway toward her grandmother's rooms. Then she turned and ran down the hallway in the other direction, out the door, across the lawn, and up the stairs of the carriage house.

Blackie sat in silence as she told him exactly what she had seen. He was smoking his pipe and Max was lying on the rug at his feet. She was sitting on the rug next to Max, leaning up against the chair, absently petting Max, her mind elsewhere.

"Blackie, how could this happen? How is it possible? How does a letter hang in midair all by itself?? How??"

A cloud of pipe smoke enveloped his head. Blackie seemed to be staring into space, and when he spoke, he did not look at her.

"Not explainable, lassie." He paused and took a deep breath. "Unless the letter is from your uncle."

"My uncle? I don't have an uncle."

"S'pose I will get into trouble for telling you, but you do have an uncle."

His smiling eyes were now serious as he looked back at her.

"He is your grandmother's son. She never told your mother she had a stepbrother and never told you that you have an uncle." He paused and then continued.

"Your grandmother was married before she married your grandfather and they had a son, Philippe. The marriage did not last, and his father wanted to raise him, which he did. There has been little contact between them over the years. Philippe is . . . different. He has some . . . some . . . let me call them, powers. They have been carried down through generations in your family."

Alexandra felt as if the room was spinning, and she laid her head against Blackie's knee. This could not be true, not possibly. All these secrets. . . . Her mother's twin sister who died as a baby, an uncle who was alive, and . . . powers? What kind of powers? To make an envelope float?

Blackie patted her head.

"It will be all right, Alexandra, 'twill be all right."

There was a long silence between them.

"Do I have them, Blackie? Do I have powers?"

Alexandra felt light-headed and weak.

"Don't know, lassie. I don't know."

MYSTERIOUS MYSTERIES

S he woke up very late. It was Saturday so Taco was off duty, but he was watching her as she opened her eyes.

"What time is it, Taco?"

She had no clock in her room because Taco always knew the time.

"High noon, twelve sharp, zero hour, twelve hundred hours military time."

Then he mimicked the gong of an old-fashioned clock twelve times. Like an echo, she heard the twelve chiming bells of the grandfather clock in the downstairs living room. Taco was exactly right, as always. Alexandra was surprised it was so late; she could not remember ever sleeping this late before.

She began to giggle, but noticed he was swaying back and forth on his perch, which he would only do when he was excited or nervous.

"Taco, you are the smartest parrot ever."

"Taco very smart. Very smart."

Alexandra laughed again, but Taco was now moving even faster back and forth.

"Taco, is anything wrong?" Alexandra stretched while watching him.

"Letter. Taco saw letter."

Alexandra sat upright and scrambled to the end of the bed to be closer to his cage.

"You saw it, too?"

Taco bobbed his head up and down.

"From Philippe. Philippe Merle. Parlez-vous français?!!"

It was obvious he was very agitated.

"Taco, you must know him. You have been alive for over fifty years, and why are you speaking in French? Does he live in France, Taco? Does he have powers?!"

Everything was tumbling out, all the questions coming back into focus from what Blackie had told her the day before.

"Blackie told me . . ."

Taco slowed his movement and suddenly became completely still. Like most birds, he had highly sensitive hearing and knew someone was outside the room. At that moment, there was a light tap on the bedroom door and the door opened.

"Well, you are a sleepyhead! We wondered when you were coming to breakfast, but now it will be lunch!"

Her grandmother had appeared, as she sometimes would do, quietly surprising her. Alexandra never heard her footsteps on the marble stairs. As she was speaking, she was looking sternly at Taco, and her expression did not match her tone of voice. Her blue eyes were very serious. Taco scurried to the far side of his perch and tucked his head under his wing.

"Grand Mama, you've upset Taco. What is the matter, Taco, my love?"

She got up and went to him, but he would not respond.

"He will be fine, my dear. Now get dressed and come downstairs quickly. I have something important I want to talk with you about. Once you have had something to eat, come and find me in the garden."

Alexandra got dressed and tried to talk to Taco. But her words were not acknowledged, and he would not take his head out from under his wing, so she went over to the pole and grabbed on.

With a swish, she was gone.

Evelyn was waiting with pancakes ready. Alexandra finished quickly, swallowed the strawberry-flavored vitamins, and headed to the garden.

Her grandmother was sitting on the glider, and she patted the seat next to her. The glider was in the middle of a large flower garden that was fading quickly with the early fall weather. It faced a large multi-tiered marble fountain with an angel on top. When Alexandra sat down next to her grandmother, the memories of that day many years ago came flooding back. They always did.

The sun was shining, and there was a cool breeze coming from the ocean. The water in the fountain made a soothing sound as it slipped from tier to tier.

"Now, my dear Alexandra. Blackie has told me that you came to him quite upset yesterday about something you had seen. He also told me that he told you about your Uncle Philippe."

She was wearing a large-brimmed straw hat so her face was somewhat shaded, but her voice was solemn and her small hands were clasped tightly in her lap. Her eyes seemed focused on something far away.

"Alexandra, this is not easy for me. Some of what Blackie told you is true. I do have a son. I married at a young age and I was very unhappy. When the marriage ended, his father wanted to raise him, which I agreed to. I know that is hard to understand . . . but it was for the best. Later I met your grandfather, Thaddeus, who was the love of my life."

She breathed deeply and then continued in the same subdued tone.

"Philippe has a son who is two years older than you. His name is Nicolas. He also has a daughter, Jaclyn, who is a year younger than you are. I have known of them, but have never met them. Philippe was brought up in France where he also raised his children. Their mother left when they were very young. I have never understood why."

She paused, still staring into the distance, and then continued.

"Philippe has written to me—the letter you saw. He has some business to attend to, which will require much of his time, and has asked if the children may come and live here for the school year and attend The Pine School. I have decided they may, so I wanted to tell you that your cousins are coming to stay with us. I hope this makes you happy, my dear. I know you have always wanted more family, so I hope this is good news."

Alexandra sat quietly, almost in shock, trying to absorb everything she had heard. Before she could say anything, her grandmother turned to look at her.

"About the other matter, which I know you were puzzled by, I will only say this. Blackie may have said some things that are not true, Alexandra. I am sure the letter was swept up by a draft when you came upon it. Letters *do not* float in the air. So best to put those thoughts out of your head and start thinking about your cousins."

She paused again, her gaze returning to the fountain.

"They should arrive in about two weeks. Let me see, what else? Oh yes, they speak English very well. And their father asked if they could bring their pets. I said they may, even though he did not say what kind of pets they are. So that will be a surprise for all of us."

She looked back at Alexandra with a quick smile, patted her arm, then got up from the glider and walked back to the house. Leaving Alexandra to ponder . . . everything.

An uncle, two cousins, Miss White, the classroom . . . and a letter that *was* floating in midair.

PREPARATIONS

As the days passed since the conversation with her grandmother, Alexandra began to feel excited thinking about the arrival of her cousins. Anticipation was in the air. It was also true her grandmother had become more relaxed and happy, and Blackie was once again his typical jovial self. On their drives to school, he never brought up Philippe, or what he told her, and neither did she. Alexandra felt it was a mystery that would eventually be solved, in time.

Each night at dinner there was talk about the imminent arrival of Nicolas and Jaclyn and all the preparations that needed to be done. Taco was also excited and seemed most relieved to hear Philippe was not coming, just his children. When he heard they were bringing their pets, he asked, "Parrots? Blue macaw?" Alexandra laughed and said maybe, but she knew that was the remotest of possibilities.

Alexandra's bedroom was in one wing of the second floor of Chadwick along the front of the house. There were many other bedrooms on the second floor, off the long back hallway. However, she had never seen them—the rooms had always been locked. So, it was very exciting when two rooms were opened in preparation for her cousins' arrival.

Their rooms faced east toward the ocean.

Jaclyn's bedroom was decorated in blues and greens, ocean colors. The pale blue walls were stenciled with creamy white seashells and starfish. A puffy striped valance ran across the top of a large picture window, and drapes made from layers of sheer white organza, which looked like wedding veils, cascaded to the floor. The furniture in the room was painted white, twin beds with canopies and matching quilts in seashell designs, and a mirrored armoire for clothes. A plush rug the color of sea foam covered much of the wood plank floor. Best of all, there was a small fireplace in one corner of the room, and Evelyn said it still worked.

The room next to Jaclyn's was going to be Nicolas's bedroom. It was a dark, masculine room. The wallpaper was navy blue with tiny white anchors. Against one wall was a large canopy bed made from mahogany with four massive posters. A navy-blue velvet canopy covered the top, and floor-length velvet curtains hung from the canopy frame on each side of the bed. As soon as she saw the room, Alexandra jumped on the bed and closed all the velvet panels. Inside it was completely dark, even in the daytime. A pair of brass nautical lanterns hung on either side of the bed, one red, the other green. The mirror above the chest of drawers was made from a brass porthole, and an old wooden ship's wheel hung on one wall, mounted so that it could still be spun. Alexandra thought the room looked like it belonged on a ship.

A large picture window faced the ocean, just like Jaclyn's room. However, the picture window in Nicolas's room also had smaller windows flanking each side, with hand cranks so they could be opened. What was most surprising was the drape across the windows—it looked like the sail of a sailboat—putty-colored fabric with a stiff, almost waxy feel, and in one corner, stitched in red, were the distinctive letters and numbers she had seen on the sails in Dark Harbor. The large red letters were "JYS 12." The drape was attached by brass hooks to a thick white rope running across the top of the window. Alexandra wondered if the sail could possibly have been from the *Windswept* and asked Evelyn. It was. Evelyn told her when her parents bought the sailboat it needed a new mainsail, but her father wanted to keep the original, so they had worked together to make it into a curtain for the "nautical room," as her father had called this room. Alexandra ran her fingers across the hand stitching along the hem. Just like his pipe and the tiller of the *Windswept*, it was something she could hold that his hands had touched.

It was while they cleaned and prepared the rooms that Evelyn told her what she had somehow always known. When her mother was growing up, friends from England often came to visit, but after her parents' accident, there were no visitors. All the rooms had been closed and locked. Yet it was still very hard for Alexandra to imagine the bedrooms filled with people and voices. It had been just the two of them, herself and Taco, on the second floor for as long as she could remember.

All the preparations were at last complete. The bedrooms were ready, and a large bathroom she had used by herself was now stuffed with stacks of thick towels and creamy soaps in large glass jars. Alexandra decided this was the time to ask about Theo. There were other rooms on the second floor.

They were having dinner when she brought it up.

"Grand Mama, could you think about something that would make me very happy? It's about Theo. I know I have asked before, but could you just think about this? Please don't answer right away. Could Theo come and live here when Nicolas and Jaclyn arrive? It would just be three instead of two. If we don't help him, he will have to go back to England and leave The Pine School. He just found out his parents died when he was little, and he thought his aunt and uncle were his parents . . . but they aren't, and there's no money left . . ."

She was talking very fast and had hardly taken a breath when she was interrupted.

"Alexandra."

The kitchen was silent except for Taco, who was slurping a piece of watermelon and making a soft "mmm" sound. (He loved watermelon the most.) However, he was clearly aware of the conversation. When he finished eating the watermelon, he was listening closely for the response.

"I am aware of the situation. It came up when I called Headmaster Green about enrolling your cousins, and I must say, it was *most kind* of him to make an exception to policy and accept two new students mid-term. He told me about Theodore's plight, and said he would like Theodore to stay on as a boarder. However, there are no funds, as you know. I have decided I will provide his tuition so he may complete this school year. Nevertheless, Theodore will continue to live at The Pine School as the headmaster prefers."

"But, Grand Mama, he *hates* it there. Theo told me he is the only boarder this year. He is *all alone* on the third floor."

"Alexandra, if it were so dreadful, no parent would send their child to board at the school year after year. I am sorry Theodore is alone. However, I am certain there will be some new boarders next term. That will be the end of the discussion."

Alexandra looked at Blackie. He looked disappointed, but she knew from a quick raise of his eyebrows he felt it would be difficult to change her mind, and nothing more should be said, at least for now.

THE NECKLACE

Things had returned to normal in Miss White's classroom. The room was alive with colorful artwork, and even drab subjects like math seemed interesting. The raspy, boring morning announcements were made each day and, occasionally, Headmaster Green would rap at the door, but he would always leave, grumbling, without coming in.

They were studying early colonial times, the mid-to-late sixteen hundreds in New England, and everything they were learning related to that period. The math lessons were from a schoolbook from the colonial period, and some of the tests were the actual tests given to students back then. (Calculating bushels of wheat from crops harvested was one question.) Spelling words were also from the late sixteen hundreds. (It was hard to believe it was English, the words were so different.) They were reading *The Witch of Blackbird Pond*, and Miss White asked one student to read a chapter aloud to the class at the end of each school day. Alexandra was fascinated by the Salem Witch Trials—and all things "witches"—but it seemed more like fiction than history. It was very hard to believe innocent women, even young girls, were found guilty of witchcraft and some were hanged at Gallows Hill.

One day there was a delicious surprise. When they arrived in the classroom, there was a large table filled with food from the colonial period. Miss White told them they would be having a feast and would not go to lunch.

Amazingly, Headmaster Green did not even rap on the door when the students from Classroom #6 did not appear for lunch. There was cornbread (delicious with lots of butter), chutney (not so delicious), turkey soup (wonderful), and apple pie (everyone loved this the most).

Theo ate and ate and ate. Everyone wondered how Miss White did everything, but no one wanted to ask. No one wanted it to end.

While they were eating, Theo told Alexandra about some "jolly good news." Grinning, he told her Headmaster Green said he would be able to stay for the rest of the year, due to a "benefactress." Theo said he asked what that was, and Headmaster Green told him it was someone who heard about his dire circumstances and offered to pay his school tuition, but the person wanted to remain anonymous. Of course, he had no idea it was Alexandra's grandmother or that Alexandra wanted him to move to Chadwick Manor. He seemed completely content to know he could stay for the rest of the year, no matter what his living conditions were, and even if he was alone. Alexandra smiled as she listened, but she was determined not to give up.

It was later that same afternoon when time seemed to stand still.

"Please finish up your work for the day. Alexandra, I will ask you to read the next chapter to the class."

As everyone was putting away their textbooks and papers, Miss White brought the book to Alexandra with a bookmark marking the next chapter. As she opened the book and handed it to Alexandra, the bookmark fell out and fluttered to the floor. Miss White was still standing near Alexandra's desk and leaned over to pick it up. As she did, Alexandra saw a flash of gold. When Miss White stood up and placed the bookmark on her desk, Alexandra was looking at a necklace with a small gold disc.

She could see the letter ⊘ in elegant script. There was a swirl from the bottom of the letter leading up to a small diamond with a starburst around it.

TACO'S SECRET

The words had come out of her mouth, somehow. She never understood how she actually read the chapter aloud, and she did not even look at Miss White as she left. It was all too overwhelming. Alexandra had not stopped thinking about the resemblance between her mother and her teacher, but knowing her mother's twin had died at birth made it impossible to believe there could be any connection. The ride home from school was silent, and Blackie's attempts to make conversation were not even acknowledged.

There was only one conversation Alexandra wanted to have.

Taco was napping when she ran into her room. His head was tucked underneath one wing and he was perched on one leg, the way most parrots sleep, keeping one foot close to their body for warmth.

"Taco, wake up, Taco!!!"

Alexandra ran to his cage and gently shook it. His head shot up, and he blinked rapidly, looking very surprised.

"Taco, I have to ask you some questions. Taco, you know this was my mother's necklace."

She quickly pulled the necklace out from under her blouse. Taco was blinking and trying to wake up.

"You know Grand Mama told me my mother had a twin sister who died when she was a baby. *But I have just seen the same necklace*!! Taco, my teacher, who looks so much like my mother, has the same necklace! I saw it today, Taco, I saw it—it is identical, with an ⊘ instead of an &. *How is that possible*??"

Taco began swaying back and forth, and his head was bobbing up and down at the same time. He appeared to be agitated and quite shocked. Slowly, his movement stopped and he became very still. After a few minutes, he looked at her with a very serious expression.

"Olivia . . . Olivia White," he answered softly.

Alexandra was standing in front of the large brass cage staring into Taco's painted eyes.

"Is she my aunt?? Taco, she is *alive*??!!"

Alexandra felt like she did not even want to breathe.

Taco suddenly flew out of his cage, landed on the window seat, and began walking back and forth on the long seat cushion. It made Alexandra smile in spite of everything. There was something funny about it when he walked. He listed slightly from side to side (he was a very large bird with very long tail feathers), and always reminded her of a somewhat portly person who thinks as they walk, with their hands clasped behind their back. And it was obvious Taco was in deep thought.

"Taco, what happened? Grand Mama told me she was taken to the hospital in London where she . . . died."

Taco kept up his somber pace but finally began to speak.

"Taco followed car to hospital. Taco outside window day and night, night and day, day and night . . . doctors, nurses in and out, in and out. One day Dr. White covered Olivia with sheet. Taco so sad, so sad."

Taco stopped walking and was perfectly still. His head was hanging down.

"Dr. White took Olivia . . . Olivia . . . lived."

She had lived.

Olivia White was her aunt. Her mother's twin sister.

Alexandra walked over to the window seat, sat down next to him, and began stroking his long feathers. So many emotions swirled through her. Shock, disbelief, happiness, it was so incredible that she could not speak. They sat in silence for a while, and then Taco slowly began to tell her what happened so many years ago at that London hospital.

Taco had stayed near the hospital after seeing Olivia covered with a sheet. He was sitting in a nearby tree when he noticed Dr. White leaving the hospital carrying a small wrapped bundle in his arms. Taco watched as he got into his car and decided to follow him, flying high above, as Dr. White drove home. He had perched on the far side of a windowsill and watched as Dr. White handed his wife the small bundle. The doctor's wife was crying. Then he heard her say she was so happy they finally had a baby to adopt.

When he finished telling the story, Taco flew to one corner of the window seat and stared out the window. Alexandra thought about asking him why he had not told her grandmother, but felt she should not ask. Looking at him, with his back to her, she wondered how he had kept this secret for so long and her heart ached knowing how hard it must have been for him. It seemed far too heavy a burden for such small, feathered shoulders. She did ask about the necklace. He answered quietly, still staring out the window. He told her both Olivia and Elisabeth had their necklaces put on the day they were born. So the small round disc had been around Olivia's neck when she was taken from the hospital, and after so many years, it was still there.

Alexandra rubbed the gold disc around her neck and lay down on the window seat. How had Olivia White come to Dark Harbor and to The Pine School? It seemed completely impossible. Looking at Taco, she realized he had to be wondering the same thing.

Then she thought—*maybe the tiny diamond star finally led Olivia home.*

ALEXANDRA'S SECRET

It was very hard to go to school the next day.

She had barely slept. The familiar nightmare had returned, calling desperately for her mother and father in strong wind and rain. She could never see anything, but it always felt like the rain was real, stinging her face and eyes, and there was always a feeling of being scared and completely helpless.

Oblivious to Evelyn's fussing, she hardly ate any breakfast and kept thinking, *how do I tell her?* And what about Grand Mama? Overwhelmed with all her thoughts, she was unaware of the ride to school, or Max licking her face, or Blackie telling her to have a good day.

At the classroom door, Alexandra was greeted by the usual warm welcome, but nothing else—and why should there be? Olivia could not possibly know what she knew. This was going to have to be her secret until she could figure out what to do. She knew it would take some time because it was so complicated. Alexandra sat down at her desk and tried to concentrate on the history lesson, but she could not stop staring at her. Her mother's twin sister—*her aunt*. She looked the same as her mother would have, had she lived. It was so strange, so incredible, but most of all, so wonderful.

Because it really felt like her mother had come back to her.

Alexandra knew Olivia White lived somewhere in Dark Harbor, and was thinking about going to Dark Harbor by herself and trying to find her. After that, she could not really imagine what would happen next. What would she say? Why was she there? How would she even begin to tell what was so unbelievable? She wanted to have Theo with her, but how would that be possible? He could never leave the school. So many thoughts and emotions were swirling through her mind that she really could not focus on her work.

She was jarred from her thoughts when Miss White rang a small bell on her desk. It was the signal to stop talking and return to their desks. Everyone returned to their seats and quieted down.

"I have something very exciting to tell you. We are going to leave school for one day to go on a field trip. It will have to do with the early colonial period we have been studying."

There were gasps, and everyone looked at one another in disbelief. Theo looked at her and smiled, then tilted his head back, grinning broadly. This was just too wonderful. Leaving school? Alexandra had never heard of a field trip—no one had.

"We will be back before the end of the school day. We'll be going in a few weeks, and I will let you know more as it gets closer. I will have to ask that you keep this a secret as no other classes are going."

She paused and then added, "I can tell you it will have to do with the Salem Witch Trials." Her eyes twinkled and then she looked directly at Alexandra, smiling.

Where were they going?

And how would they be able to walk out of school right past Headmaster Green's office?

A DARK AND STORMY NIGHT

C hadwick Manor was ablaze with lights.

A storm had come up and was blowing in from the ocean, bringing pelting rain and strong winds. The night Jaclyn and Nicolas were to arrive had finally come. Blackie was picking them up at the airport in Boston in the afternoon, and they would arrive in Dark Harbor in the early evening. Between school, Olivia, and the anticipation of her cousins' arrival, Alexandra felt like she was riding on waves of emotion with new surprises and mysteries rolling in with the dependability of the tides.

Taco was also nervous and excited. He had been asking every day for the last two weeks, "Today? Coming today?" Each day Alexandra told him their arrival date but as smart as he was, he did not understand the concept of the future. It was either the present or a past memory (and he did have an excellent memory). When the day finally came, he kept saying all day, driving Evelyn crazy, "This is the day! This is the day!" Then, "Bringing parrot, blue macaw?" After Taco asked this question more than once, Alexandra finally realized what he really meant. He wanted his own bird friends. However, she knew there was little chance a bird would be coming from France. It would be a cat or a dog, but not a bird. (She had worried about the possibility of a *cat*, but felt Taco would be able to keep his distance, and he was a very big bird and could fly to high places.)

Alexandra could not eat any dinner, nor could Taco. They paced the front foyer floor together, Taco walking behind Alexandra, listing slightly to the right then to the left, and when he got tired, he rode on her shoulder. Together they walked and waited, peering out into the darkness, each lost in their own thoughts.

The entry hall of Chadwick Manor was enormous.

A huge crystal chandelier hung from the high ceiling. Prisms of light reflected on the walls, ceiling, and floor from thousands of dazzling crystals. Crystal wall sconces were softly glowing, casting slivers of rainbows on the forest-green walls. Elegant, curved staircases hugged each wall, with burnished cherry handrails and white marble steps cascading down to a black and white marble tile floor. Two life-size porcelain tigers sitting on square pedestals flanked the base of each staircase, their emerald gemstone eyes staring at the front doors of Chadwick Manor. As a young child, Alexandra had been terribly afraid of them. The tigers were large and very lifelike, especially their shimmering emerald eyes, and it had taken many years before she dared to venture up or down the stairs unaccompanied by Evelyn or her grandmother. The imposing statues were why she preferred to use the brass pole to get to the first floor even as a very young child, because it dropped off near the kitchen, far away from their intimidating eyes.

Evelyn was peering out a window when she suddenly exclaimed, "I see the lights of the car. They are here! They're here!"

At that same moment, her grandmother appeared at the top of the staircase farthest from where Alexandra was standing. She often wore long dresses in the evening, so it was difficult to see, but it always appeared she floated just above the stairs as she descended. No footsteps were ever heard. Alexandra wondered why she was on the second floor, but then realized she was probably checking their bedrooms one last time before they arrived.

They heard Blackie's voice above the wind just as the large double doors of Chadwick Manor flew open. At that exact moment, all the lights flickered and went out, but within seconds went back on. Taco and Alexandra shivered at the same time. Somehow, it seemed an ominous sign. Then, as though blown in by the storm with a loud whooshing sound, three rain-soaked figures were standing in the elegant foyer of Chadwick Manor.

"What a night, what a night! Goodness gracious, 'tis a stormy night, but this brave lad and lassie have arrived safe and sound!"

Blackie huffed as he pulled two large trunks into the foyer. When Alexandra looked at her cousins, wet and windblown, they reminded her of the name of the sailboat, *Windswept.* It was what they looked like.

Her grandmother stepped forward to greet them and Alexandra could see tears on her cheeks. These were her grandchildren whom she had never met before.

"Welcome, welcome, Nicolas and Jaclyn. I am so, so happy to meet you both, *at last.*"

Alexandra never realized how small her grandmother was until she was hugging Nicolas, who appeared stiff and uncomfortable, and he did not return the hug.

Nicolas was tall and wearing a black cape that went almost to the floor. A hood was covering his head, and when he pushed it back, she could see dark brown hair and eyes and a pale face. He looked—she was trying to think of a word—all she could think of was "dark."

"It is nice to meet you, Grand-Mère."

His voice was deep. The tone was somber.

Jaclyn was much shorter than Nicolas and very petite. She was wearing a lavender cape, and her dark blonde curls were windblown and dusted with raindrops. Perched on her tiny nose were round wire-rimmed glasses with very thick glass lenses, somewhat fogged up from the weather. It was obvious she did not have good eyesight. In one hand, she clutched a tiny suitcase with a wire cage door. As she set the small suitcase on the floor, Alexandra could see the face of the smallest dog she had ever seen peering out at everyone.

Silver then hugged her granddaughter and Jaclyn grinned, hugging her back, obviously delighted to be meeting her grandmother for the first time.

"I'm so happy to meet you, Grand-Mère. I could not wait to get here! It felt like we were flying on the plane forever!"

Jaclyn's voice was soft, almost musical.

"Well, my dear Jaclyn, it is so, so wonderful to finally meet you and Nicolas! Now, come and meet Alexandra, your cousin," her grand-mother said as she gestured toward Alexandra.

Jaclyn picked up the suitcase and followed by Nicolas, they walked slowly toward her. As they walked by the tigers, Jaclyn looked askance at them, but Nicolas paid no attention. As Jaclyn approached, Alexandra quickly extended her hand because in that instant she realized she could not imagine hugging Nicolas. Jaclyn's eyes were a gorgeous green color and magnified by the thick lenses. She was grinning from ear to ear. They both giggled nervously as they shook hands. However, Jaclyn's gaze was obviously torn as her eyes moved back and forth from Alexandra to what was perched on her shoulder.

"This is Taco. He is a South American macaw parrot and a member of our family. He's actually quite old, but doesn't look it, and he's very friendly and *very, very smart*. And he loves to talk!"

When Alexandra said "old," she felt his feet dig into her shoulder.

"It's nice to meet you, Taco! This is Biscuit. He's called a teacup Yorkshire terrier because he's so tiny!"

She tried to hold the itsy-bitsy suitcase up high, so Taco could see him better. Taco leaned down and peered into the cage.

Alexandra put her hand to the tiny whiskered face.

"Please, let him out. He must be dying to run around!"

As Jaclyn put the case down to open it, Taco said very politely, "Nice to meet you, Biscuit, nice to meet you."

Alexandra reached up to stroke him. She was not sure how Taco would react, but this was better than she could have expected. Biscuit was soon free, running and sliding across the black and white checkerboard tiles, and with Evelyn chasing after him, he ran toward the kitchen, sniffing and exploring.

Then Nicolas approached her, and they shook hands. His hand was cold, not warm like Jaclyn's, and he did not smile as he said hello. He was taller than she was by four or five inches, and his dark brown eyes were stormy looking and unfriendly. She had felt Taco's body tense as Nicolas stepped closer to shake hands, and then suddenly without warning, Taco spread his wings and screeched. The piercing sound echoed off the floor and walls. Never before had Alexandra heard it. The sound was earsplitting. Nicolas immediately stepped backward, quite startled. Everyone was staring at Taco, who was glaring at the left side of Nicolas's cape. Alexandra could now see there was something noticeably protruding from that side of his cape.

Then, as though performing some kind of magic trick, with his right hand Nicolas reached over and flung back the left side of his cape. In his left hand, he was holding a domed, antique-looking birdcage.

Inside the cage was the biggest black bird Alexandra had ever seen. He had a long, thick, black beak and beady black eyes that were glaring at her and then Taco.

Taco's feathers seemed to be standing on end. His large curved beak was open, and he was making a hissing sound. Then she felt his feet dig into her shoulder as he pushed off. He flew toward the stairs, his expansive butterscotch wingspan in full display, then up to the center section of the banister that looked down from the second floor to the foyer below. He landed in the center of the railing and spread his wings again. As shocking as it all was, at that moment Alexandra thought he looked more powerful than any American eagle—and there were no arrows in his beak.

"Taco! That is no way to behave. I am *ashamed* of you!"

Her grandmother glared up at him. Following her admonishment, he *very slowly* folded in his wings, but his painted eyes never left the cage Nicolas was holding.

For the first time Alexandra could ever remember, Taco looked fierce.

"It is all right, Grand-Mère. I am sure Taco was not expecting another bird, and birds are territorial. His name is Noir. It means black in French. He is a common raven. Noir is also highly intelligent. Many believe the raven to be the smartest of all birds."

Nicolas looked directly at Alexandra as he was speaking, not at her grandmother, and in his eyes she could see an intensity and superiority that was both unfamiliar and uncomfortable, something she had never seen before. He spoke authoritatively, and his last remark felt like a challenge, as though a gauntlet had been thrown.

Both Nicolas and Jaclyn spoke perfect English, but his French accent was unmistakable. The inflection was very pronounced and could be heard with every word, unlike his sister's. He then spoke to

Noir in French, nothing Alexandra could understand except for the tone. It was kind and comforting, not the tone of voice she had just heard.

Alexandra was at a loss to say anything. She kept looking at Taco and then at Noir and then at Nicolas.

How was this going to work?

Two birds who obviously hated each other from the first moment, living in the same house?

GETTING SETTLED

Blackie hauled the trunks up the stairs and down the hall to their rooms.

Everyone followed in silence.

Alexandra quickly took Taco to their room, where she placed him on his perch in his cage. For the first time ever, she closed the cage door and latched it shut. His face was so expressive, and as she looked at him behind the wire cage, it was obvious his feelings were hurt—never before had he been locked inside his own cage. It was also clear he was still in shock the black bird would now be living with them, and she felt the same disbelief. However, she wanted to prevent him from doing anything he would regret. This was his home and his first reaction to Noir was obviously territorial, just as Nicolas said. She had never seen Taco behave this way before and now understood it was his instinctive behavior to protect his home from any perceived invader. Fight or flight, she remembered this from something she read, and fighting had to be avoided—at all costs. With a deep sigh, and knowing there would be a protest, she threw a blanket over his cage. Unlike most birds, he did not have his cage covered at night to sleep, and much preferred it that way.

"Taco wants to see. Take off!!"

"No, Taco. It will help calm you down. I will be back soon. See if you can sleep. You have had too much excitement."

"Taco no sleep. Black bird bad. Noir bad bird. Bad black bird."

The disgruntled voice was coming from beneath the blanket, which made Alexandra smile. She had never before heard his voice without seeing him.

"Taco, he's just a common crow, or raven, I guess . . . and he will have to stay in his cage. I will make sure Nicolas understands that. Anyway, this is your house, Taco, not his. Now try and get some rest."

She could hear the perch swaying back and forth.

Alexandra set off down the hall. It was very strange to hear voices and see people on the second floor. She could hear Jaclyn's voice as she approached her room.

"I love my room, thank you, Grand-Mère. It is so beautiful!"

Jaclyn was twirling around looking at everything and smiling. Her cheeks were pink from excitement as she ran to greet Alexandra and hugged her. Alexandra hugged her back. As new as they were to each other, it actually felt like Jaclyn was someone she had known a long time—someone like a sister.

"I am so glad, my dear Jaclyn. Evelyn and Alexandra did all the work and preparation, so they both have all the credit."

Her grandmother now looked genuinely happy. It almost seemed like the earlier incident had never happened. With that, she turned and went to the next room, and they followed.

Nicolas had closed his door, so her grandmother knocked and he said to come in. He was sitting on the bed with Noir on his shoulder. Both seemed to glare at everyone gathered in the doorway. Only the ship's lanterns were lit, so there was an eerie red and green glow to the room.

"And how do you like your room, Nicolas?"

"It is nice, Grand-Mère, merci. I am very tired from the trip, and I want to go to sleep now."

It seemed to Alexandra he emphasized the word "I." He was clearly used to doing what he wanted to do.

"Yes, I am sure you are very tired, both you and Jaclyn. So, sleep well, my dears, and I will see you in the morning."

CHAPTER EIGHTEEN

As she turned to leave, Alexandra spoke to her grandmother.

"Grand Mama, don't you think it would be a good idea if Noir stays in his cage? I'm afraid something could happen. Taco was obviously very upset."

Alexandra was casting glances at Nicolas as she spoke. He was glaring at her, as was Noir. Before her grandmother could answer, he did.

"I do not think that will be necessary, Grand-Mère. Noir is used to having freedom, and he will stay in my room. That is what he is used to."

His voice was now softer, the same tone he had used to speak with Noir, but his eyes were not. Her grandmother was studying her grandson and his bird, and then she nodded.

"That will be fine, Nicolas. Just be certain he cannot leave your room, as we do not want anything to happen to Taco or Noir. However, when you leave your room with Noir, he must be in his cage."

He was obviously pleased with the answer and maybe it was her imagination, but Noir seemed to have the same look—smug. Nicolas had won. Alexandra felt like this was the beginning of something that would be difficult, some kind of battle.

They all left, closing the door behind them, and Alexandra went with Jaclyn back to her room. Evelyn had already unpacked Jaclyn's trunk and stowed her clothes in the armoire. Biscuit was snuggled in the blankets Evelyn put next to the floor radiator where the heat came up, and he was sound asleep. Jaclyn sat down on one of the twin beds and Alexandra sat on the other, facing her.

It was like a miracle. Alexandra thought she had no family other than her grandmother and suddenly, she had two cousins.

And an aunt.

There was so much to talk about and so many questions to ask that

Alexandra was suddenly at a loss for words. Looking at her cousin, she could see how tired Jaclyn was and got up to leave. Alexandra knew there would be days, weeks, and months to talk. She stood at the door for a moment smiling back at a very sleepy face.

"Good night, Alexandra . . . I'm so glad to be here. And I am really, really glad you are my cousin." Jaclyn's voice was heavy with sleep.

"Me, too, Jaclyn," Alexandra whispered as she closed the door, "me, too."

When Alexandra opened the door to her room, she could hear the soft snoring. Poor Taco, what a terrible surprise it had been. She wondered if he would have nightmares. As she got ready for bed, she was thinking about all that had happened. What were the chances her cousin would have *a pet raven*? They were obviously a pair, Nicolas and Noir. Even their names seemed to go together.

She shivered and closed her eyes and tried to go to sleep.

THE NEXT MORNING

The next morning Alexandra was awake early. Taco was still snoring softly under the blanket as she crept out of bed, put on her bathrobe, and went quickly down the hall. She could hear Biscuit at Jaclyn's bedroom door, his tiny nails pawing against the door, and hesitated, but decided she would tap very lightly in case Jaclyn was awake.

A soft, sleepy voice answered, "Come in."

Alexandra gently opened the door, and there was Jaclyn, almost lost amongst the quilts and pillows, rubbing her eyes and smiling.

"I hope I didn't wake you up. I know it must feel strange to be waking up here, so I thought I should come by your room. Do you want me to take Biscuit downstairs?" Alexandra whispered while watching a still sleepy Jaclyn.

Then she realized Biscuit had already left the bedroom and was heading down to the kitchen. She could hear him going down the stairs all by himself. They both smiled. Biscuit was already making himself at home.

Jaclyn stretched and sat up, putting her glasses on. Alexandra sat on the edge of her bed. They just looked at each other without saying anything. It was still so new to both of them. Cousins.

"Do you want to go downstairs and have breakfast? Evelyn is always up very early. Are you hungry?"

"Yes!"

Jaclyn quickly hopped out of bed and found her bathrobe, hanging on the back of the door.

"Would you want to see my room first?" Alexandra asked, feeling happy and excited.

The answer was a wide grin, and with Alexandra in the lead, they ran down the hall and around the second-floor banister to Alexandra's room. When Jaclyn walked through the door, she put her hand to her mouth. It was a very large room for a bedroom, with an unusually high ceiling. Painted murals covered the length and height of two opposite walls. They were colorfully detailed and so realistic you could think you were actually at the beach on a beautiful summer day or skating on a frozen pond on a moonlit winter night. Jaclyn slowly walked along each mural, silently studying each one, and then skipped over to the bay window, climbed up on the window seat, and looked out.

"This is all so beautiful, Alexandra!" Jaclyn exclaimed as she gazed at the colorful maple tree and then turned back to look at the room.

Jumping down from the window seat, she walked over to Taco's cage just as Alexandra was lifting off the blanket and opening the cage door.

"Good morning, Jaclyn."

Taco's voice was warm, and his eyes were soft.

"Good morning, Taco!"

Taco was looking around the floor of the room.

"Biscuit here? Biscuit here?"

CHAPTER NINETEEN

"Oh, no, he went downstairs for breakfast already," Alexandra explained.

"Black bird?"

His eyes became serious, and he looked nervously around the room.

"I told you, Taco. Noir will be in his cage. He cannot fly free. Grand Mama told Nicolas last night that Noir must stay in their room if he's out of his cage."

Just then, Jaclyn spied the brass pole in the corner of the room and ran over to it.

"What is this?! Where does it go?! Do you slide down this, Alexandra?!" Jaclyn asked, her green eyes dancing with excitement.

Alexandra walked over to the pole.

"Are you ready to have breakfast now?" Alexandra asked, smiling like a Cheshire cat. She was having fun watching Jaclyn's reaction to everything.

"Does this go to the kitchen? How far down is it?" Jaclyn was on her knees, peering down through the hole.

"It's not far at all, it's just one floor—there's the black and white tile floor downstairs—it drops off right outside the kitchen door in the back hall. It's so easy, Jaclyn, you just hold onto the pole, wrap one leg around and then the other, then let yourself slide down."

And with that, Alexandra disappeared with a swish through the hole.

"But I'm too scared!!"

"Don't be scared, don't be scared!"

Taco was watching Jaclyn from the bed and could see she was afraid.

"Watch Taco!"

Like it was the most natural thing for a bird to do, he flew to the pole, wrapped his huge wings around it, and with his feet braced against the pole, down he went. It was the funniest thing to watch; after all, he could just fly down through the hole in the floor. Alexandra had never seen him do this before—he was either clinging to her shoulder or flew down himself. As she watched him unfold his wings and step away from the pole, she realized why he had spontaneously thought to do this . . . he wanted to give Jaclyn the courage to try and not be afraid. Once again, Alexandra was reminded of how special Taco was. He was sensitive and kind, and nicer than many people. (The face of Katherine Briggs momentarily loomed up in her mind.)

When Jaclyn peered down, she could see Taco was now on Alexandra's shoulder. They were both looking back up at her, expectantly.

"Here I come!!"

Jaclyn grabbed the pole, swung her legs around it, and in seconds she was sitting on the floor, still holding onto the pole.

"Good show, good show, Jaclyn! Jolly good show!!" Taco sometimes used expressions he had learned from Thaddeus Chadwick years ago.

"Thank you, Sir Taco, for showing me, and I can't wait to go down again!"

They were laughing as Alexandra helped her cousin up and then she pushed open the swinging door to the kitchen.

Which is when the second macaw screech in two days filled the halls of Chadwick Manor—and might have been heard all the way to South America.

There, sitting at the kitchen table, was Nicolas with Noir on his shoulder.

He was feeding the raven a piece of muffin.

Taco opened and closed his wings repeatedly, but Noir kept

eating as though nothing had happened. He occasionally looked over at them with his beady black eyes as if he was bored by the whole display, and certainly not the least bit intimidated. Alexandra realized she had seen beady eyes like his before. They reminded her of Miss Blueberry's. She was shocked at the sight of them sitting there, casually eating breakfast; however, the shock quickly turned to anger.

"Nicolas, Noir is supposed to stay in your room or be in his cage. That is what Grand Mama told you last night."

Alexandra looked at Evelyn, who was wringing a dishtowel in her hands, looking very flushed and obviously upset.

"I did not think you would be up this early, so I thought there would be no problem with Noir having breakfast with me. As he always has."

Nicolas's voice was controlled and steady. It appeared this did not upset him—at all.

"And we are finished, so I will leave. Perhaps we should let them get to know each other. They could become friends?"

He looked at Alexandra with a smug coolness. Taco dug his feet into her shoulder. Alexandra knew that would never happen.

"That will never happen, Nicolas. Never," she answered, working to make her voice steady and even, just like his.

Nicolas got up and left the kitchen with Noir on his shoulder. As they passed by, Taco's beak was wide open, his eyes glued to Noir, but neither Noir nor Nicolas looked at them.

It was quiet in the kitchen as Evelyn prepared breakfast. Taco went to his perch and slowly ate some fruit but kept his eyes on the swinging door. His blue feathers looked like he had been through a wind tunnel; they were all tousled and raised up. Jaclyn held Biscuit in her lap, her face etched with concern as she looked at Alexandra, who was obviously lost in thought.

"I'm sorry my brother upset you and Taco. He loves Noir, and I don't think Noir would do anything bad. Nicolas found him in the woods when he was a baby bird. He was hurt, and Nicolas fed him with a dropper and took care of him. Noir has been his pet for many years . . ." Her voice trailed off, and she looked very sad.

Alexandra looked at her cousin and smiled weakly.

"Don't worry, Jaclyn. Somehow, we will work this out, but Taco and Noir will never be friends. Never."

EXPLORING CHADWICK MANOR

Alexandra felt the second incident with Noir was a bad omen. It was not going to be easy to keep the peace. The raven had to stay in Nicolas's room or be carried in his cage if they left the bedroom. Her grandmother spoke to Nicolas about it again, after hearing what happened at breakfast, and told him he must respect this rule. Alexandra was already coming to the conclusion that neither could be trusted—the bird or her cousin.

However, she put those thoughts aside and turned her attention to showing Jaclyn around Chadwick Manor. Without any real enthusiasm, she asked Nicolas if he wanted to join them, but he declined and did not appear to be the least bit interested. When the invitation was rejected, Jaclyn told Alexandra all her brother liked to do was read books, and that he preferred to be alone. Hearing this, Alexandra thought, *Nicolas would be the perfect student at The Pine School.*

After getting dressed, Jaclyn came to Alexandra's room and sat on her bed, studying the murals.

"I love your room, Alexandra! It feels like the set of a play with winter and summer scenes. But most of all, I love Taco," she said while looking at the blue and gold macaw with obvious affection, who was asleep in his cage, snoring quietly. It had been a very stressful morning.

Alexandra smiled, looking around at what was all so familiar to her.

"Thank you. This was my mother's room . . . and Taco is very special. He was my grandfather's and then my mother's . . . macaws live a very long time."

Alexandra hesitated and then went to the nightstand and picked up the photograph of her parents and gave it to Jaclyn. Jaclyn studied the photo and then gently handed it back.

"This was taken on my parents' wedding day . . . they died when I was one year old. Maybe your father told you. They died in a storm. Their sailboat was found, but they were never found. Just this summer, Blackie told me he sailed their boat back here after the accident and it was moored in Dark Harbor. The first time I went on the sailboat I found our initials carved in the tiller, 'G, E & A' for Graham, Elisabeth, and me . . ."

Alexandra stopped talking. It was too hard. She was staring at the photo and suddenly thought of Olivia, but knew she did not want to say anything about that, yet. She looked at Jaclyn and could see tears in her eyes.

"I know. My father told us before we came. He told us so much we did not know . . . that he was your mother's stepbrother and your mother and father died when you were a baby. And he told us our grandmother was still alive, and we would be coming to the States to live with her and with you, our only cousin. It was all so hard to believe . . ." Jaclyn's voice trailed off to a whisper.

"What happened to your mother?"

As soon as she asked the question, Alexandra realized maybe she should not have and looked worriedly at Jaclyn.

"She left us. When we were very little. I don't remember her at all. Nicolas said he does. He said she was very beautiful. I have never even seen a photo of her. My father never told us why she left, and we did not feel we could ask him. We don't know where she is or if we will ever see her again. I think it would be easier to know she . . . died."

The last word was whispered and barely audible.

Alexandra climbed on the bed, and then they both lay down, staring up at the canopy.

"Were you sad to leave your father and come here?"

"Not as sad as I thought I would be. He has always traveled a lot. We were raised by a nanny. Her name is Chantal. It was harder for me to say good-bye to her than to my father, but not for Nicolas. He did not want to come here at all. My father and Nicolas are very close."

They lay on the bed in silence. After a while, Alexandra reached for Jaclyn's hand and pulled her up.

"Let's go, Jaclyn, I want to show you your new home!"

Alexandra walked over to the pole, wrapped her legs around it, looked back questioningly at Jaclyn, then down she went.

"I'm right behind you!"

* ✦ *

Alexandra first took Jaclyn through a large archway from the back hallway into the formal living room.

The expansive living room was filled with oversized pillowed chairs and couches, all upholstered in robin's-egg-blue and ivory velvets. Brocade drapes framed a large window overlooking the front lawn. There were lamps of all shapes and sizes with beautiful fringed shades, fancy embroidered pillows, and coordinating oriental rugs. The walls were pale blue and stenciled with elegant designs of ivy vines, trellises, and bird silhouettes in creamy white. At one end of the room was a fireplace so large Alexandra could still stand up in it. A heavily gilded mirror hung above the fireplace mantel, and standing next to the fireplace was an antique grandfather clock. The chimes rang on the hour and the half hour, deep and reverberating, and echoed throughout most of Chadwick Manor. Exotic palms and flowering plants, small round tables with chess and checker sets, and a grand piano completed the décor. The room had a warm, inviting feeling even though it was a very large room with very high ceilings.

"Every Christmas, Blackie goes into the woods and brings back the biggest pine tree he can find. It's always huge and goes right here in front of this window. This Christmas you will be here to help decorate it!"

She twirled around to look at Jaclyn, who had settled into one of the overstuffed couches.

"I can't wait for Christmas."

Jaclyn's voice seemed to float like a snowflake in the air.

Alexandra smiled, realizing it would be the first Christmas she would not be the only child. Then she walked over and pulled Jaclyn up from the couch, leading her by the hand to a door in one corner of the living room.

As they walked into her grandmother's library, Jaclyn drew in her breath. There were *thousands and thousands* of books. They went from the floor all the way to the far reaches of the high ceiling around the entire room. Each wall had a polished wooden ladder mounted on wheeled tracks so the books on the highest shelves could be reached. In the center of the room were more fluffy couches and chairs, all in peach velvet, and in one corner was a small fieldstone fireplace. Along one wall in front of the bookshelves was a large reading table with some chairs and table lamps, and in the middle of the table was a very thick dictionary. Jaclyn ran to one of the ladders, pushing it along the runner, then stopped and climbed up quickly to the very top and waved down to Alexandra.

"Have you read all these books, Alexandra?"

"Of course, I have!"

They both started laughing.

Then they went back through the living room and down the

hallway—slowly, as Jaclyn wanted to look at the stained-glass windows—to their grandmother's rooms. Alexandra knocked, but there was no answer, so she opened the door, and a faint fragrance of roses greeted them. The rooms actually looked like a rose garden: there were paintings of roses on the walls, real roses in crystal vases, and the bedroom was decorated entirely in shades of pink.

Suddenly, a door that looked like it was part of the wall opened, and in came their grandmother holding cutting shears and some deep pink roses. She was dressed in periwinkle-blue slacks and a matching sweater. Her cheeks were flushed.

"Well, hello, my dears! I see you are getting the grand tour, Jaclyn! Do you think you will like staying here?"

"I love Chadwick so much. I never want to leave . . ." Jaclyn was looking around the rose-filled room, smiling.

"Well, my dear, that day is a long way off. Alexandra, I'm sure Jaclyn would like to see the conservatory," she said, gesturing to the doorway she had just come through.

They ran through the secret door and were instantly enveloped by moist, humid air. The conservatory was a rectangular glass building with sunlight streaming in. The air smelled like earth and vibrant green was everywhere. Flowering plants in moss-covered baskets hung from beams and large tropical plants covered much of the slate floor. Ivy wound its way from large clay pots, clinging to the glass walls and climbing up to the highest point of the glass roof, where delicate tendrils hung down. Lush rosebushes provided bursts of color. Water splashed and gurgled in small fountains, and here and there, timeworn stone angels were standing, kneeling, or sitting, watching over.

Alexandra loved going into the conservatory in the wintertime the most. Maine winters came early and stayed late. Going into the conservatory was like opening a door and finding spring or summer on the other side. Even on the coldest days, the air was warm and humid as massive heaters and humidifiers pumped in warm, moist air. Tucked between the plants, Adirondack chairs with soft cushions were perfect for reading or stargazing at night.

Taco *adored* the conservatory.

He had his own perch nestled in the foliage and spent hours looking at the world beyond the glass. Even though he could see birds flying freely, he always seemed content to be inside looking out. However, there was another important reason why Taco loved the conservatory. In one corner, a large, round showerhead with a chain was positioned directly over another perch surrounded by palm fronds. About every three days, Taco would take a much-needed shower, pulling the chain himself and spreading his wings, making sure his entire body was exposed to the warm water. (Although feathers are mostly self-cleaning with powder down, which forms naturally and falls off, carrying the dirt away, residual dust attaches to feathers and must be rinsed off. In the wild, this is taken care of with rainfall—and parrots *love* rain.) Watching Taco shower was something Alexandra always found entertaining. He danced along the perch, lifting his wings with great gusto, and just like a person, was usually heard humming or singing some song he liked (off-key). His showers often lasted for quite a while, and when he was finally finished, he would pull the chain again, shake off the excess water, then sit on his perch looking like a puffed-up Buddha bird, his feathers all tousled and ruffled, waiting for the conservatory heaters to dry him out. When Alexandra was little, Taco perched on the rim of the large footed bathtub and occasionally would jump in with her, floating on the surface with his wings spread, and taking up most of the width of the tub. (Parrots cannot really swim, but they can float because their bodies have air sacs similar to lungs that extend the length of their bodies, making them quite buoyant.) What Alexandra found very funny was watching him happily float around amidst the mountains of soap bubbles that would cling to his head and wing feathers—most unusual for a macaw parrot to love a bubble bath, but Taco *was* most unusual. After having a shower or bath, Taco always spent time preening and scraping his feathers with his beak, making sure every feather was in its correct place. (All birds instinctively know how important this is, because even one feather out of place can make them a target for predators in the wild, as their flight would be less stable and more noticeable in a flock.)

For all these reasons, Alexandra knew the conservatory was Taco's favorite roost in Chadwick, and it was always where she looked first when he was not in their room. The truth was, the conservatory was the closest experience to a rainforest the South American macaw would have on the rocky coast of Maine, and somehow Taco knew it, too.

Then Alexandra and Jaclyn were outside and running. . . .

The backyard of Chadwick Manor was extraordinary. Great expanses of green, manicured lawn intermingled with rose gardens, a marble fountain, a giant maple tree with a rope swing, a boxwood maze, gardens of vegetables and herbs, and a gazebo, all leading to the cliff's edge, where the Atlantic Ocean stretched as far as the eye could see. Far below, waves crashed against the rugged coastline, the ocean's white-capped army relentless and powerful.

The air was salty and there was a brisk breeze blowing. It felt like they were soaring on the wind like the seagulls as they ran from one thing to the next, their laughter and words swept up and away by the ocean breezes. When she saw the maze, Jaclyn's eyes were as wide as her grin.

"A real maze?! Can you find your way out?! Have you ever been lost in it, Alexandra? Can we go in? Please!!"

"It's actually not that big and I have never been lost because I always take Max with me and he knows the way out, but let's wait. I want you to meet Max first!!"

As Alexandra ran toward the carriage house and garage, Max suddenly appeared around the corner and bounded toward them. He ran to greet Alexandra but stopped short when he saw Jaclyn. His wolf eyes became darker and he was staring at her, warily, with his head cocked slightly to one side. Alexandra talked to him as she walked toward him, and then gently led him by the collar to Jaclyn, who was looking equally wary. Max looked more wolf than dog. However, that was all it took. He sniffed her quickly, wagged his tail, and ran happily back toward the garage.

"Well, here are my two lassies! How are you today, Miss Jaclyn?"

"Oh, Blackie, I love Chadwick. I never want to leave. Everything is so . . . beautiful . . ."

"Well, Miss Jaclyn, we are so glad you . . . and your brother are here. It is good for all of us, but mostly for Alexandra, who has been by herself for so long. You two lassies must have worked up an appetite by now! There must be some sweet treats in the kitchen!"

He grinned at them, his eyes soft as he studied Jaclyn. It was obvious to Alexandra he felt the same way about her—Jaclyn belonged with them. But she also noticed the tiny pause when he said, "and your brother," and realized Blackie sensed what she did, that Nicolas was very different from his sister.

As they ran toward the house, it felt to Alexandra as if life suddenly held so much possibility.

THE NEW STUDENTS

The weekend flew by and then it was Monday morning.
Jaclyn did not sleep well; she said her stomach was too
nervous. She was dressed identically to Alexandra, and Nicolas wore
his black cape over black slacks, a white shirt, and a black tie. No one
talked at breakfast or on the ride to school. It felt very strange to
Alexandra that two other people were in the car, and all she could
think about was what their reaction would be to Headmaster Green—
and to their teachers. Jaclyn would have Miss Rhubarb, the fifth-year
teacher, and Nicolas would have the dreaded eighth-year teacher,
Mr. Gingerroot. Jaclyn had told Alexandra they were tutored at home
in France, explaining she learned English before French, unlike
Nicolas, who was taught French first—the reason her brother spoke
with a French accent and she did not. Alexandra had been shocked to
find out her cousins never attended school in France, and wondered
how she could possibly explain The Pine School.

Alexandra had thought a lot about this over the weekend and had
not been sure what to tell them ahead of time. In the end, she decided
Jaclyn needed some advance warning. So, on Sunday night, she told
Jaclyn that Miss Rhubarb always dressed in shades of red and green—
even her hair had traces of both colors—and that it would probably
take time to get used to her, especially when she got angry. (Unfor-
tunately, this was often, which Alexandra did not tell her. Whenever
Miss Rhubarb was "provoked," as she would say, her faintly greenish
skin became covered with splotches of blood red. Her eyes were deep
green and when she was very angry, the whites of her eyes would turn
red.) Alexandra decided not to tell Jaclyn how she looked when she

was mad, just that it was scary at first, but after a while, you got used to it.

Mr. Gingerroot was both feared and repulsive. His face and neck actually looked like an orange-brownish root vegetable, oddly shaped with bumps here and there. Even his hair looked like the fine, wiry tentacles of a root pulled from the ground. Nicolas had been distant the entire weekend, staying in his room with Noir most of the time, so Alexandra had not told him anything about Mr. Gingerroot ahead of time. However, Nicolas had gone for one walk around Chadwick by himself. Blackie told her, and said he tried to introduce Nicolas to Max, but Max had backed away, growling, and would not go near Nicolas. Alexandra felt this was another bad omen. Dogs could tell about people.

On the ride to school, they rode as they always had, with Max in the middle between Alexandra and Blackie. Nicolas sat in the back seat with Jaclyn. It was obvious Max was nervous. He was panting heavily, with his ears pricked, and often turned his head sideways to look back at Nicolas with one eye.

They soon arrived under the portico and all walked up the steps together under the watchful eyes of Headmaster Green. He was peering through the glass, smiling more broadly than Alexandra could ever remember, his crooked yellow teeth on full display.

"Welcome, welcome to our two new students. Wonderful to have you at The Pine School, just *wonderful.*" His raspy voice greeted them as they walked through the grimy doors, and then he stepped closer to them.

Jaclyn looked shocked and immediately took a step backward. Nicolas was calm and showed no reaction.

"Follow Miss St. Germaine to the stairwell and she will see that you find your classrooms."

He seemed so pleased, almost happy. *Two new victims*, Alexandra thought.

They climbed the stairs to the second floor. Miss Rhubarb was outside of Classroom #5, just as Alexandra had described her. Further down, Miss White was outside Classroom #6. Across the hall, Miss Mango stood outside Classroom #7, in shades of red (hair), orange (sweater), and yellow (skirt). Standing outside Classroom #8, Mr. Gingerroot was wearing a dark brown suit, looking, well, just like a root vegetable.

Alexandra squeezed Jaclyn's arm and whispered she would be fine, not to worry, but it did not seem to help. Jaclyn looked very scared as she walked slowly toward Miss Rhubarb (who could have been in a Christmas window; even her shoes were glittery red). Alexandra watched as Nicolas approached his classroom. His face was expressionless. He did not even seem to notice the strange appearance of Mr. Gingerroot. They were soon inside their classrooms, and the classroom doors were all shut tight. (The door to Classroom #6 was locked—from the inside.)

At the end of the day, Nicolas and Jaclyn were already on the portico when Alexandra pushed open the grimy door, not even glancing at Headmaster Green, who was standing at his usual post. Nicolas looked the same as he had in the morning, cool and calm. However, Jaclyn's face was flushed, and there were fine beads of sweat across her nose and forehead. She whispered anxiously to Alexandra, "Miss Rhubarb was *provoked* so many times! I couldn't look at her . . . I thought blood was going to come *spurting out of her eyes*! I saw your teacher from a distance. She looks normal??" Alexandra whispered back they would talk about it when they got home. Blackie tried to make conversation, but no one was answering him. Alexandra thought about Nicolas as they were riding home. From the moment she met him his face had been expressionless. It was as if he was wearing a mask, his true feelings hidden from view. Max was watching him again, just as he had on the morning ride, sitting sideways in the front seat, so one wolf eye could watch him all the way home.

After a quick snack, the two girls were lying on Alexandra's bed and that was when it all spilled out about Miss Blueberry (Jaclyn loved that story) and then about Olivia White. Jaclyn's eyes were wide and magnified by her thick glasses—they looked enormous.

"She is your aunt? Your mother's twin sister? Does that means she is my aunt, too? I cannot believe it! Taco saw her *kidnapped* from the hospital, *by the doctor*? Have you told Grand-Mère? How did she come to The Pine School?!"

Jaclyn was now sitting up with her knees close to her chest, her hands clasped around them, rocking back and forth.

"Yes, I think so, but I don't know for sure, so I can't tell Grand Mama . . . I don't know how she came to The Pine School. It's all so incredible that it doesn't seem real, but what should I do? I really don't know what to do . . ."

"Tell Olivia."

They both looked at Taco, who had quietly awoken from his afternoon nap.

TO DARK HARBOR

Taco's words echoed in Alexandra's mind.

It was, of course, what had to be done. She had not wanted to go alone, and Theo could not go with her. Now she had Jaclyn.

Thinking about it made Alexandra's heart race. What if there was some other explanation, and she was not her aunt?

The plan took shape over the next few weeks. Jaclyn and Alexandra talked through every idea, how, when, where. They decided to ask if they could bicycle to Dark Harbor with Blackie following behind them in the car. Jaclyn had not seen the village of Dark Harbor or the *Windswept,* so there were many reasons to go. However, there were some parts of the plan that could not be worked out ahead of time. They would have to be improvised.

Their grandmother had happily agreed to the plan, as long as Blackie would be with them. The bicycles required Blackie's help and mechanical expertise. Alexandra's own bike was now too small for her, and they needed two, so Blackie hunted through the far reaches of the garage and found some old bicycles that were the right size. They were pretty sad looking when he rolled them out—dusty, with flat tires and rusty chains. Nevertheless, Blackie loved working on anything requiring tools, and soon both bikes were greased, polished, and working perfectly. He even attached a wicker basket to each bike.

The day finally came, one Saturday in mid-October . . . and they were off.

Blackie and Max followed behind them in the car, very slowly. They were pedaling on a bike path that followed the coast road right into Dark Harbor. It was exhilarating. Alexandra had never done this before, and it gave her a feeling of independence and freedom as they flew down the coast road, passing The Pine School and winding their way toward Dark Harbor. The fall air was crisp and the sun was shining. *All a good omen*, Alexandra thought as she glanced down at the wicker basket.

There, wrapped carefully in a scarf, was the photo of her parents.

The ride did not take very long. Dark Harbor was only a few miles from Chadwick Manor. They arrived in front of Weston's Market with cold faces and windblown hair, hopped off their bikes, and slipped them into a bike rack in front of the market, which was when the improvising was to begin. However, when Alexandra turned to Jaclyn to say something, it appeared Jaclyn had completely forgotten about their mission. She was staring across the street at a small cluster of shops.

Dark Harbor was the only town Alexandra had ever known. The small village teemed with tourists and vacationers each summer; however, they all disappeared as fall became winter. That was when Dark Harbor became a frozen ghost town, the white clapboard buildings blending in with huge snowdrifts, icicles a foot long hanging like stalactites from roof gutters, the village shuttered and insulated. The market, bank, and tiny post office remained open, but most of the shops closed until late spring when they came to life again, like flowers pushing through warm soil.

In a row were Moo Bar, The Moose's Closet, Sweet Blooms, Quill & Parchment, The Book Nook, and Chadwick Bank & Trust Company. Each shop had a colorful wood sign with gold lettering and a coordinated striped awning. Along the sidewalk, there were buckets of fall flowers and pumpkins on hay bales and cornstalks tied to the street lamps. The fall decorations reminded Alexandra that Halloween was coming. Later in the month would be the nighttime costume parade. She smiled as she thought about it.

A bit further down from the shops, on a large wharf, was a restaurant Alexandra knew very well called The Claw & Tail. It was where her grandmother brought her, Evelyn, and Blackie for special occasions like birthdays. The sign on the roof was of a large lobster dressed formally in black tie and tails, standing somewhat precariously on his red-fanned tail, and balancing a silver tray on one large, raised claw. On the tray was a much smaller lobster. Draped over his other large claw, folded neatly at his waist, was a white linen napkin. One of her earliest memories growing up was hearing her grandmother tell her before each special occasion, "The Claw & Tail is a white-tablecloth restaurant, requiring proper dress and proper manners."

In the summer, the wharf was filled with picnic tables covered with red and white checked tablecloths because for some reason Alexandra did not understand, so many people loved to eat lobster. She had not yet acquired a taste for lobster, even though her grandmother assured her on every birthday she would. Luckily, The Claw & Tail also served delicious roast turkey.

"What is Moo Bar? And The Moose's Closet? Can we go in?! Alexandra, is that *your* bank?"

Jaclyn's eyes were shining with excitement and surprise.

"That is the bank my grandfather opened when they came here from England. We'll go into the shops soon, but not today. We have— *we have other things to do today . . .*"

Jaclyn suddenly remembered why they had come and nodded seriously, and then Alexandra turned to Blackie.

"Blackie, we want to take our time picking out the penny candy. Can we meet you at the end of the dock when we're done? It may take us a while . . . it's always so hard to choose."

Her heart was pounding in her ears as she watched his face for signs of the slightest frown, but there were none.

"Fine, lassies, take your time. Alexandra knows I'm partial to anything licorice," he replied with a wink and a smile at Jaclyn, and then swung the big black car toward the dock.

The little bell attached to the old wooden door rang as they pushed it open, and the wonderful Weston's Market aroma of coffee, pipe tobacco, pine scent, and firewood burning in the potbelly stove greeted them. The older man behind the counter was wearing a long white apron tied around his waist and a black and white checked flannel shirt with red bow tie. His white hair was naturally curly and thick, and horn-rimmed glasses framed his blue eyes.

"Hi, Mr. Weston."

"Well, hello, Miss Alexandra! And this must be your cousin from France, I understand?"

"Yes, this is Jaclyn. She and her brother are living with us for this school year."

"Well, welcome to Dark Harbor, Jaclyn! So, you are going to The Pine School with Alexandra. What a fine school, fine school."

Alexandra and Jaclyn looked at each other and tried not to show any expression.

"I bet you girls are here for some penny candy. You know where the bags are, Alexandra."

"Yes, thank you."

She took a deep breath, and trying to sound as casual as she could, continued, "I was wondering, Mr. Weston, if you . . . if you know where my teacher lives? Miss White, Olivia White. I know she lives in Dark Harbor. I thought we might surprise her and say hello."

She was watching his face intently. He was smiling and nodding.

"Well, as a matter of fact," as he pointed with a finger to the ceiling, "she rents the apartment right upstairs. She's probably there now. I haven't seen her leave today. So you can go up the stairs on the outside of the building once you've picked your candy."

Alexandra ran to the penny candy counter, pulling Jaclyn by the sleeve, and grabbed two small paper bags. They quickly tossed candy into them, without even looking at what they were choosing, and were back at the counter in what seemed like seconds. Mr. Weston looked very surprised.

"I don't think I have ever seen you pick your candy that fast, Alexandra. Did you get Blackie's licorice?"

Alexandra felt her cheeks turn hot. She had not even thought of Blackie and quickly ran back for the red licorice, and then handed Mr. Weston a crumpled dollar bill. Some change was placed on the counter and they were on their way out the door.

"Bye!! Thank you, Mr. Weston!"

Alexandra tossed the candy bags into the bike basket, picked up the scarf-wrapped photo, and then they hurried up the outside stairs. She heard her heart pounding in her ears again. They got to the landing, and above the doorbell on a small brass plate was her name, "O. White."

Alexandra looked at Jaclyn and then pressed the doorbell.

It seemed like the longest moment. Then the door opened and there she was. She was wearing brown slacks and a white blouse. An emerald-green cable sweater was draped over her shoulders and around her neck was the necklace. Alexandra could see it very well. The gold disc was glinting in the sunlight.

"Alexandra, what a nice surprise! I suppose Mr. Weston gave you directions. You can see that I do not have to go far for the candy I bring to the classroom! Come in, come in!"

Her expression almost looked as though she was expecting them, Alexandra thought. She really did not look surprised.

Then they were standing inside her apartment. The walls were pine paneled, and to the right was a very small living room. There was a multicolored, braided rug on the floor and pine furniture with green and red plaid cushions. Pots of ferns and ivy hung in front of a bay window that looked out on a steep slope dense with pine trees. To the left was a tiny kitchen, and a small fireplace was between the living room and kitchen. The apartment had a snug, cozy feeling.

Alexandra turned and looked at her. Her aunt. Her mother's twin. She did not know if she could speak but then heard her voice. It felt as if someone else was talking.

"This is Jaclyn, my cousin. She's from France. She and her brother are living with us this year. Their father is my Uncle Philippe . . . I never knew I had cousins or an uncle until just recently . . ." and as her voice trailed off she thought, *or an aunt.*

"Well, that is most interesting . . . and from France! I know that is far away. I'm from England but came to the States for school when I was very young. How do you like living here, Jaclyn?" Olivia asked, looking surprised as she studied Jaclyn thoughtfully.

Alexandra clutched the photo more tightly to her chest . . . *England.*

"I love it. I'm so happy to be here," Jaclyn answered softly.

"How wonderful you and Alexandra have finally met! Did you girls come to Dark Harbor on your own?"

The question hung in the air until Jaclyn answered and told her about their bicycle ride and about Blackie and Max, and that he had followed them in the car and was waiting at the dock. Alexandra seemed unable to speak.

Olivia turned to Alexandra. Her expression was suddenly more serious as her eyes fell, questioning, to what Alexandra was holding.

"What did you bring with you, Alexandra?"

Her voice was gentle and kind, as though she knew it was something very special.

Alexandra's hands were trembling as she slowly unwrapped the scarf. She looked at the wedding photo for one second and then handed it to Olivia. With a questioning look, Olivia took the photo. Alexandra felt tears well up in her eyes as she reached inside her sweater and pulled out the necklace she had never taken off since the day her grandmother had given it to her. Olivia looked from the photo to the necklace, and then to Alexandra. There were tears in her eyes.

The next thing Alexandra knew, she felt her aunt's arms around her, and felt her kiss her forehead. Then she led both girls to the couch and sat in the middle with her arms around them. Alexandra leaned her head against Olivia's shoulder. Olivia was the first to speak, and as she did, she stroked Alexandra's head gently. The morning sun was streaming through the windows, warming the room. A feeling of deep peacefulness seemed to wrap around them like a soft blanket.

"I only found out myself very recently when my father, Dr. White, was dying. My mother had already died. I was teaching school in Boston when I learned he was not going to live, so I went back to England to be with him. That is when he told me . . . everything. He told me I had a twin sister and what he had done . . . and he asked me to forgive him. I was in complete shock, but I loved him very much. He was the only father I had ever known . . . and I did forgive him. He told me what he could remember, most importantly the names of my real parents, Thaddeus and Silver Chadwick . . . and he told me they had moved to the States, to Maine, shortly after they thought I had died. He also told me my twin sister's name was Elisabeth . . . he even told me about the identical necklaces."

Olivia reached for the round disc with the letter &, rubbing it gently between her fingers, studying it.

"After he passed away, I returned to Boston and started research-ing the Chadwick name, which led me to Dark Harbor. When I arrived, it almost felt as though I was expected . . . the first place I went was Weston's Market, and for some reason I do not even understand myself, I asked if there were any rooms for rent in town. Mr. Weston's answer was handing me the key to this apartment. I just reached out and took it." Olivia shook her head, smiling, and then continued.

"That's when he told me I could be the twin of a woman who had grown up here, Elisabeth Chadwick, but he said she died in a sailboat accident many years ago. I could not believe it . . . that I would never know her, my own twin sister. I think he found it odd, but I asked him if Elisabeth's mother was still alive, and he said she was—he told me Mrs. Chadwick lived just up the coast road. Finding out my mother was still alive was so, so wonderful. Then, without knowing anything about me, Mr. Weston suggested I inquire about teaching positions at The Pine School. That same day I called the school, and Headmaster Green told me he needed a teacher for sixth-year students right away. It was as though I was brought here . . . that it was meant to be. And I believe it was."

They sat in silence and then she continued.

"When I was given the class list, Headmaster Green told me about you, Alexandra. He said you could be quite disruptive!"

Olivia laughed and squeezed Alexandra's arm.

"And he told me I looked so much like your mother, who was teaching at the school before the accident . . . it was the most amazing and wonderful surprise to find out I had a niece! However, I have to admit, I had no idea how I would tell you or my mother, so I decided to wait and see what might develop . . . I expected you would see the resemblance and I think you did, on the first day? I remember when you gasped out loud!"

Alexandra nodded.

"I knew you looked just like my mother from the photos, but I couldn't understand how that was possible. It wasn't until Taco told me the story . . ."

"Taco? Who is that?" Olivia asked with great interest.

"Taco is my parrot. He was my grandfather's and then my mother's . . . he's a blue and gold macaw, and he told me the whole story because he was there . . . Taco was outside the hospital window. He saw what happened. He saw Dr. White take you and followed him. Poor Taco, he didn't know what to do. He never told Grand Mama. It was his secret until I asked him. When I saw your necklace the day you picked up the bookmark, I felt certain Taco had to know something . . ."

Olivia was looking intently at Alexandra.

"Taco is the most intelligent parrot I have ever heard of . . . and I assume your grandmother, my mother, does not know anything?"

"No. No, she doesn't. I had to find out first if it was really true."

Alexandra was thinking about her grandmother. How would they tell her? How?

"Well, we certainly have a lot to think about. In the meantime, we have to keep this a secret. Now, you girls need to get to the dock before Blackie is knocking at my door!"

Alexandra did not want to leave. She had not thought this far ahead, about what would happen next if it were true, but saying good-bye did not feel right. She wanted her aunt to come back to Chadwick that very moment. However, the tone in Olivia's voice was unmistakable, there would be no further discussion.

"We will figure out the right thing to do, I promise," she said, pulling them both up from the couch and leading them to the door.

Olivia's voice was firm and resolved, like her voice in class.

"Soon?"

"Yes, Alexandra, soon," she answered with a smile and a hug. "It has been uncomfortable to be stared at by so many people in Dark Harbor, and some have told me I could be the twin of a woman who died . . . so, yes, very soon!"

"Are you my aunt, too?"

Jaclyn's voice was no more than a whisper. It was as if she was afraid what the answer would be.

"Well, I think so, don't you, Jaclyn?! And one day I hope to meet your father . . . it was an incredible surprise to find out today that I have a brother, another niece, and a nephew!" Olivia replied, hugging Jaclyn.

Alexandra carefully wrapped the photo back in the scarf, and they were out the door with a wave and a blown kiss.

They wondered if Blackie suspected something, but he never asked any questions as they ate their candy and explored the *Windswept*.

It was the *best* secret.

However, secrets are hard to keep.

LOOSE LIPS (OR BEAKS) SINK SHIPS

As soon as they got home from Dark Harbor, they had gone to Alexandra's room and told Taco *everything*. He bobbed his head up and down, and his eyes were sparkly and bright. They immediately began talking about how, where, and when the reunion could take place.

"Surprise party! Surprise party!" Taco kept repeating, "With balloons and cake! Surprise! Surprise! *It's Olivia!*"

As he said her name, he bowed his head slightly and put one wing folded in front of his body, then opened it straight out to one side, as though he was introducing her.

Alexandra and Jaclyn both giggled. He was so animated and excited. It was as though the secret that had weighed on him so heavily for so many years was finally lifting. Soon, Evelyn was calling them to dinner, but before going down the pole, Alexandra swore them all to secrecy. Taco nodded his head "yes" with great solemnity.

Dinner was a delicious roast beef with mashed potatoes and gravy, homemade rolls, and an assortment of salads and vegetables. They were all seated around the large oak table in the kitchen. The conversation was about their day trip to Dark Harbor (leaving out, of course, the visit). Alexandra and Jaclyn had saved some penny candy for Nicolas and gave it to him at dinner. Although he seemed completely disinterested, Alexandra noticed he glanced in the bag after putting it on his lap. Noir was not allowed to come to dinner—he had dinner in Nicolas's room—so Taco ate in peace. On his food tray were some small carrots, broccoli, sliced apples, chunks of watermelon, and a bowl of fresh water. He had water with every meal for drinking, and sometimes dunked his food in it before eating, something macaws in the wild will occasionally do, cleaning their food in fresh water. He also had a small dish of assorted nuts (hazelnuts, almonds, and walnuts) for dessert. They were finishing their dessert, Evelyn's delicious chocolate cake called "Mississippi Mud and Gravel" with vanilla ice cream, when it happened.

"Well, I am so glad it was a fun day for you girls. Next time, perhaps you will join them, Nicolas?"

Her grandmother was looking at Nicolas seriously. She clearly did not approve of his solitary nature.

"Perhaps, Grand-Mère. But there is nothing very interesting about Dark Harbor from what I have heard."

"Oh yes, oh yes, sailing and ice cream and penny candy . . . and Olivia!!"

There was silence. Blackie and Evelyn looked at Taco and then at Alexandra. Her grandmother was staring at Taco, as was Nicolas.

"Who is Olivia?" Nicolas asked, his dark eyes swiveling to Alexandra, studying her face.

"She is—she is my teacher. Her name is Olivia White, Miss White. She took Miss Blueberry's place when she retired . . . she had just moved to Dark Harbor from Boston—I think I told you, Grand Mama," Alexandra answered, trying to sound casual, turning to look at her grandmother.

Alexandra heard her heart pounding in her ears for the third time in the same day.

Her grandmother looked thoughtful.

"I did not know her first name. It is not common. It is a surprise to hear . . . that name. Did you see her today?"

Alexandra looked quickly at Blackie, who was looking at her with a questioning expression.

"Well, yes, for a few minutes. She lives above Weston's Market. We found out by accident from Mr. Weston. He mentioned it when we were getting the penny candy, so we just stopped in to say hello . . ."

"Why did you not mention this when you told us about your day?" her grandmother asked.

All eyes were on Alexandra. She looked at Taco, who had put his head under a wing.

"I guess I just forgot, Grand Mama. It was only to say hello and then we left."

"Well, my dear, I am sure she appreciated your visit. After all, she is new to The Pine School and to Dark Harbor."

Her grandmother smiled and told them they were excused.

Alexandra was relieved, but not happy with one blue and gold macaw.

She got up and held out her hand for Taco, who hesitated before stepping on, and then placed him firmly on her shoulder. She was through the swinging door in seconds and bounded up the stairs with Jaclyn right behind her.

They shut the bedroom door and Taco immediately flew to the window seat, burying himself as quickly as he could underneath the pillows.

"Taco, how could you say her name? How could you?? You kept that secret for years and years. You promised not to say anything, remember?"

Alexandra was scowling at him and watching as he tried to bury himself deeper under the pillows. Soon, only his very long blue tail feathers could be seen.

"Don't be mad at Taco, Alexandra. He didn't mean to break his promise. He was just too excited and happy about Olivia, just like we are. Taco kept that secret for so long . . . I don't think Grand-Mère suspects anything. She believes Olivia died when she was a baby and many people have the name Olivia . . ." Jaclyn's face was filled with concern, as she looked at the pile of pillows with one long blue tail visible.

Alexandra considered all of this and had to agree. It was just a close call.

She went over to the pillows and gently pulled them away, one by one, until he was uncovered, still facing the corner.

"Come here, Taco. It's okay. I know Grand Mama doesn't suspect anything. Jaclyn is right. I'm not upset with you anymore."

She stroked his back and then reached around and rubbed around his ears, which he loved, and then gently put him on her lap. He nuzzled against her. She leaned over and kissed him on the green luminescent patch on the center of his forehead.

"Taco sorry. Taco keeps secrets . . ."

"I know you can, Taco. You can keep secrets better than anyone I know."

Alexandra scooped him up and lay down on the window seat cushion. He snuggled on her chest, his beak almost touching her chin, his eyes closed. Jaclyn curled up in the other corner of the window seat. They all were lost in their own thoughts.

What they did not see was one black eye peering through the keyhole of the bedroom door.

NOIR

Nicolas seemed to be observing the rules. Noir stayed in his bedroom or, if they ventured out, Nicolas carried him in his cage. Everyone was aware Taco and Noir had to be kept apart, most of all Alexandra. However, keeping the birds separated was not really a problem, because it had become quickly apparent Nicolas and Noir were happiest when they were alone together. Other than Nicolas's bedroom, the only place they would spend time was the library.

It was clear that Nicolas was used to a solitary life and clearly preferred books to the company of anyone. He would spend hours in the library, climbing the ladders to the highest point, pulling out books, deciding which ones were of interest. Alexandra had seen piles of books in his bedroom.

Late one afternoon, Alexandra had finished her homework but Jaclyn was still working on a book report, so Alexandra went by herself to see if Evelyn needed help with dinner. From her earliest memory, Alexandra could remember going through the swinging door into the kitchen and smelling the aroma of delicious food that made her mouth water instantly. There was a small fireplace in the kitchen, and a fire was lit every evening except in the summer. On this fall evening, the fire was crackling away as Evelyn was making buttermilk biscuits to go with roasted chicken. Nodding appreciatively, Evelyn said she only needed the table set for dinner. When Alexandra finished, she wandered out of the kitchen and decided to see if Nicolas was in the library.

The door from the living room, which was the only door into or out of the library, was open just an inch or two. Alexandra peeked through the opening. Nicolas was sitting in one of the peach velvet chairs. Noir was on his shoulder, not in his cage. For a moment, Alexandra just stood there watching. She had not been seen or heard. Nicolas was wearing a black turtleneck and black slacks, what he always wore when he was not in school. Alexandra thought it was like having another uniform, but she also could not imagine Nicolas wearing anything but black.

It was what she remembered most vividly about him the night he arrived—the black cape, the black bird, and the darkness of his eyes.

Noir was sitting on Nicolas's shoulder, looking snug and comfortable. Alexandra studied them. They looked like they belonged together, a matched pair, and the effect was quite dramatic, two black figures against the peach velvet. Nicolas was reading intently. What was most interesting was that it looked like Noir was reading along with Nicolas—his eyes were clearly focused on the open page.

"Nicolas, you are supposed to keep Noir in his cage all the time when he's not in your room. What if Taco was with me?"

She pushed open the door and walked in. Her voice was not as stern as she wanted it to be.

"I can see he is not with you, so why is it a problem? Noir lives here, too. He needs his freedom, just like your bird."

He scowled at her but did get up to put Noir back in his cage, which was sitting on the library table. Alexandra went over to another plump velvet chair and sank down among the pillows. They had never been alone since he had arrived, so she decided this would be a good time to try to find out more about her cousin and his bird.

"Jaclyn told me you found Noir when he was a baby . . . she said he had fallen out of his nest and was injured. She told me you fed him with a tiny dropper and saved his life."

"Oui, yes, that is what happened. It was fate. That is what mon père said when I brought him home. Our last name, Merle, means blackbird in French."

Alexandra could not believe it. Jaclyn had never mentioned this. It seemed to be more than a coincidence—a baby raven found and adopted by a family with that name.

"So, he is a raven. Isn't that the same as a crow?"

"Crows are their cousins, as we are cousins. They are the same family, called Corvidae, and the genus is Corvus. Other corvids are jays, jackdaws, and magpies. There are common ravens and thick-billed ravens. Noir is common. There is a legend that England would never fall to a foreign invader as long as there were ravens on the grounds of the Tower of London, so they keep common ravens there to this day. The English are a superstitious people."

This was the most she had ever heard him speak. His voice was husky, almost hypnotic. He spoke in a grown-up way, as if he was much older than fourteen, and he had obviously become an expert on ravens.

"That is very interesting, but I don't see how they can be as smart as a macaw?"

"The raven is the most intelligent. This has been determined over years of study. Their brains are the largest of any bird species. It has been proven that ravens can solve problems, and they can manipulate others to do their work. In the wild, they will call prey to a dead carcass so they can more easily eat from it. They watch where other ravens hide their food and later go back for it. Sometimes they pretend to hide their food, to deceive others who are watching them. Ravens can make simple tools from branches to retrieve food otherwise unreachable. They have been observed playing with twigs, tossing and fetching them. Very few species of birds play. This is a mark of high intelligence. And Noir likes games. I have even taught him some card games."

Nicolas paused and his eyes dropped to her neck.

"He especially loves shiny objects and likes to hide them so only he knows where they are. I have seen him look at your necklace."

Alexandra reached up and put her hand over the necklace, relieved knowing it would always be safe because she never took it off. As he was talking, she was thinking of Taco. He was also very intelligent and loved toys and games. Years ago, Blackie had taught her and Taco how to play penny poker. However, there was much Nicolas said that was disturbing. Ravens were obviously cunning and manipulative and not to be trusted.

"And they can learn to speak, just like a parrot. Noir has an impressive vocabulary. He speaks only French, not English, except for one word. When he was young, I used to read him a poem by Edgar Allan Poe. It is a famous poem called 'The Raven.' Maybe you have read it. In the refrain is the word 'nevermore.' It is the one English word Noir will speak."

Then she heard it again, echoing in the room, "nevermore." It was perfectly clear as though a person had spoken; the voice was flat, monotone. Alexandra had never heard of the poem. How did Nicolas know so much? He had been taught at home, not even in a school, and it was a shocking revelation that Noir could speak. The black bird had been silent from the moment he arrived, at least when he was with others. "Nevermore" . . . a word she could not remember ever hearing, it sounded haunting and sad. Yet there was something about it that made you want to say it over and over. When would you say "nevermore?" Then the answer came to her. When you would never see your mother or father again. *Nevermore.*

Nicolas was looking at Noir with pride, and his expression had noticeably softened.

"Noir can make many vocalizations, and he is an excellent flier. Ravens are known for amazing aerial acrobatics, and unlike any other bird, they seem to do it for their own pleasure. They have been seen flying on their backs for some distance—no other bird has ever been observed doing this—and they can fly to great heights. Noir needs to fly, to soar, as he did at our home in France. He cannot be housebound like your macaw. I take him to the edge of the cliffs behind Chadwick. He has flown out over the ocean and back to me."

Alexandra was speechless. Nicolas had been such a mystery and had suddenly told her so much. She had never seen him take Noir outside and wondered when he did this. At the same time, she felt something else that was unfamiliar. She realized she felt inadequate. She did not know very much about macaws and had never studied them. Her gaze fell on Noir, who seemed to know the conversation was all about him. His black feathers had faint traces of deep purple and greenish blue, iridescent and gleaming in the lamplight, and the thick, shaggy feathers under his throat had fluffed up. He was look-ing at her, his black eyes intense and judgmental. She had to admit that Noir did look exceptionally intelligent. Alexandra looked back at Nicolas, wanting him to keep talking. In her silence, he seemed to understand.

"There are many myths and legends about the raven. One legend is that Noah sent a raven to look for land during the great flood. Before leaving, it was pure white, like a dove. The raven did find land but never returned to lead Noah to safety, so his feathers turned to soot. Another is from Norse mythology. The god Odin had two ravens named Thought and Memory. They flew around the world every day and would come back to tell Odin all that was happening. Ravens have symbolized life and death, good luck and bad. Many people are afraid of them and fear they will bring death and diablerie—black magic. I do not. I think the raven is bonne chance, good luck."

Alexandra got up and walked over to Noir, looking at him more closely than ever before. He looked strong and powerful, but she felt it was a force of darkness, not good. His black beak was exceptionally long and thick, and for the first time, she could see there were tiny black feathers covering his nostrils from the base of his upper beak. It made him look exotic but in a dark and mysterious way. She wondered if any other birds had feathers on their beaks. There was something else: she felt he could not be trusted. Looking into his eyes, she knew it. He seemed to be studying her as well, and she found herself feeling almost intimidated by his dark stare.

"How old is Noir? How long do ravens live?"

Alexandra was certain it could not be as long as a macaw.

"He is only six years old and ravens live in captivity as long as forty or fifty years. So Noir will be with me for a very long time."

"Taco is between fifty and sixty years old. We don't know for sure when he was born. Macaws can live to over eighty, so Taco will be with me for a long time, too."

That she and her cousin had something so unusual in common was hard to believe. She realized there was a kind of equality; both birds were formidable and exceptionally intelligent.

They heard the dinner bell ring. Alexandra walked to the door, and then turned back toward Nicolas.

"I enjoyed learning about Noir, about ravens, and I don't think they are common . . . at all."

She could see his eyes soften just a little when she said this.

"I like talking about them. Ravens are solitary by nature, as am I."

He paused, lost in thought, looking into space.

"And it is said they can fly to the *back of beyond* . . . and return." He barely whispered the last two words, so she did not hear them.

Then he turned to look at her, his dark eyes now almost mischievous.

"But, their *cousins,* the crows, are not solitary. They live in large groups. I bet you do not know that a group of crows is called *a murder?*"

He looked amused as he said this, clearly enjoying her surprised look. As she was puzzling over why a group of crows would be called "a murder," he picked up Noir's cage and quickly swept by her.

Alexandra stood there pondering.

Flying to the *back of beyond* . . . where was that?

THE FIELD TRIP

The routine at Chadwick Manor with two new children was becoming more comfortable for all of them, not as strange as it was at first. After their conversation in the library, Alexandra felt somewhat more relaxed around Nicolas. There was a little more conversation at breakfast and dinner, but he clearly preferred to be alone with Noir, and that was how it was going to be. Noir and Taco did not cross paths, but Taco was ever on the alert for the "bad black bird" as he called him. Alexandra had told Taco some of what Nicolas told her about ravens, but it was very clear Taco was not impressed. When she told him the raven's brain was the biggest of all birds', Taco had shrieked in protest, and shook his head "no" for what seemed like an hour. Finally, Alexandra had to calm him down, so she told him intelligence was not based on the size of the brain and macaws were the smartest of all birds—that it was scientific fact. She realized from what Nicolas told her it might not be true, but then again, she did not see how it could ever be proven the raven was *the* most intelligent bird.

School days were very hard for Jaclyn. She was terribly afraid of Miss Rhubarb. All she wanted was to be in the same class with her cousin and her aunt. They had talked about it a lot, but Alexandra did not see how it was possible. Jaclyn was a year younger and belonged in the fifth-year classroom.

However, one day something unexpected happened.

Miss White left the classroom, which she rarely did, explaining she had to speak with Headmaster Green. She returned quickly and with her was Jaclyn. With a wink to Alexandra so fast that no one could have seen it, she propelled Jaclyn to the front of the classroom. Jaclyn was beaming.

"I am delighted to introduce our newest student. This is Jaclyn Merle. She was in Miss Rhubarb's fifth-year class, but she will now be with us. She is Alexandra's cousin from France, and her brother, Nicolas, is in Mr. Gingerroot's class. In France, students are taught at a faster pace, and Jaclyn was not challenged enough in Miss Rhubarb's class. She is ready for sixth-year work, so she will be joining us."

Alexandra could not believe it. Their desks were now in a large circle (having been changed from rows soon after Olivia arrived), and she had noticed there was a new desk next to hers when she arrived that morning—everyone had. In seconds, it was no longer an empty desk. Jaclyn was sitting in it, still grinning. Theo was on one side of her and now Jaclyn was on the other. It all felt perfect.

Later that day came another surprise, but this one they had been anticipating. They were at last going to hear about "The Field Trip."

"May I have your attention? Everyone, please come over to the Reading Rug, I want to speak with you about the trip we will soon be taking."

Olivia was sitting on a small hassock in the center of the rug and everyone gathered around her.

"As I have told you, we are going on a field trip. We have been studying the period of the late sixteen hundreds in New England. As you know, during that time, in the year 1692, the Salem Witch Trials took place. Jaclyn, I will give you some books to read as quickly as you can before our trip. We have been reading about what happened, but it is hard to understand what it was really like from reading history."

She paused, looking at everyone. Her expression was very serious.

"The best way for you to understand what happened is to witness it. I am going to take you to the sentencing of a young girl. Her name is Mercy Disbrow. She is about your age, twelve, and she was accused of putting a spell on her neighbor's livestock. All the cattle and horses died. She was tried as a witch, and found guilty."

Never before had there been such a deafening silence in Classroom #6. No one even moved. They were staring at Miss White. No one could believe what she had just said.

"I know what you are all thinking. How can we see what took place hundreds of years ago? We are going to time travel. We are going back in time to the date of her sentencing and we will, hopefully, change history . . . because if we do not, she will die."

There were loud gasps. Then Miss White opened a small book on her lap and began reading.

"Mercy Disbrow, age twelve, was found guilty of casting spells over the livestock of Farmer and Goodwyfe Warren, resulting in the death of all livestock. Chief Judge William Stoughton sentenced Mercy Disbrow to death on October 23, 1692, by hanging at Gallows Hill on October 31, 1692." She paused, looking up from the book.

"Are you brave enough to do this—to go with me?"

She looked at each student and waited to hear the answer from each one.

One by one and with great solemnity, the whispered answer was spoken, "*Yes.*"

The only student who asked a question was Theo.

"Miss White, could I ask one question? How, how do we do this— time travel? How is that even possible?"

Theo looked very pale, as always. But his eyes were dancing.

"It is possible, if everything goes perfectly. You will have to trust me, and you will have to do exactly what I say. *Exactly.* We must go tomorrow because it is October 23rd, the date of her sentencing. We have to be witnesses for her innocence. I will give each of you a short script as you leave today and the name by which you will be called. Memorize what is written and then rip it up in tiny pieces. When you are called to be a witness, you must recite what was in the script. Does everyone understand?"

All heads nodded.

"We will leave from this classroom and return to it before the end of the school day. We will be together all the time. There is nothing to be afraid of. You will not feel or see anything while we are traveling, except you may have a little dizziness when we begin, but it will pass. When we arrive, it will feel like a second has passed. That is all. You will have on the clothes of children your age in that time period. I will also be wearing appropriate clothing for the period. Now, for the most important part. To do this, *no one else may know*. You cannot tell *anyone*. Not your parents or brothers or sisters—*anyone*. If any one of you tells someone else, it will not work. We will not be able to go, and we will have no chance to save her. Is that under-stood?"

All heads nodded again.

"So, there will be no homework tonight, except to memorize your name and script, *and to keep this secret*. You may now return to your seats. Headmaster Green will be dismissing you shortly." She paused.

"And no, he does not know."

Her face was serious, but her eyes seemed to twinkle as she said this.

As they all filed out of the classroom, Miss White handed each student a small envelope. When she gave Alexandra her envelope, she leaned to her ear and whispered, "We must save Mercy, Alexandra. We cannot fail."

A shiver of fear went down Alexandra's spine.

Saving Mercy Disbrow was obviously very important to Olivia. Why?

How would they possibly save her . . . and what if they did not succeed?

A SALEM WITCH TRIAL

They were told to gather around her on the Reading Rug in tight circles.

Olivia was in the very center, and she selected who would be in each concentric circle. Jaclyn was chosen to stand with Olivia. Around them was a circle of four students, then five, and the outermost circle was six students. They were instructed to hold hands, and Olivia told those standing in the outermost circle they must not—under any conditions—let go. She said the outer circle could not be broken, or they would not succeed in getting back to 1692 and might find themselves anywhere between that year and the present. Alexandra was holding Theo's hand on one side and Katherine Briggs's on the other. They were in the outermost circle. Her hands were cold and clammy with sweat, as were theirs. The door to Classroom #6 was bolted shut and the entire class of sixteen students waited nervously to see what would happen next.

Olivia told them to close their eyes and keep them shut until she said they could open them. They heard the faint sound of wind, which quickly became louder, and then strong gusts were swirling around them like a hurricane. Their feet left the ground and they began spinning, seemingly pushed up and spun around by the force of the winds. Alexandra did not feel scared, just dizzy, and remembered that was normal.

Then, as quickly as it began, it ended. The spinning stopped and they were standing still. They had arrived; everyone knew it. The air was damp and cold, and Alexandra could hear the sounds of horses nearby . . . clump, clump, clump. The chill in the air seemed to come through her clothing, and the fabric felt prickly and stiff on her skin. She knew she was wearing a cape with a hood and had some kind of close-fitting bonnet tied under her chin.

"Open your eyes. You are in Salem, Massachusetts. The date is October 23, 1692."

They were holding hands so tightly Alexandra wondered if her fingers would unfold. Slowly, they all looked around. They were standing in a long narrow alleyway between brick buildings. It was shadowy and they were alone; no one else was in the alleyway. At one end, the alley simply ended with another brick wall. At the other end, in the distance, was the street. People were walking by, and horse-drawn carriages were moving along at a brisk pace. The sound of the horses hooves echoed in the alley as they clip-clopped along.

No one spoke. It was all too amazing. Alexandra could now see what she had felt and looked down at a long navy-blue wool cape and black buckled shoes, which were already uncomfortable. The boys were wearing wide-brimmed black hats, gray wool jackets, and white shirts with large black bows tied at the neck. Their pants were dark brown and went only to the calf, meeting thick white leggings that continued down to the same black buckled shoes. The girls were all wearing long wool capes with hoods, with white cotton bonnets tied under their chins. As they looked at each other, they began to giggle.

"Shhh!"

Olivia stepped out of the circle and held her finger to her lips. She was wearing a black cape, but it was not plain like theirs. Made from heavy velvet, not thin wool, her cape was elegant and regal. Black satin embroidery in an elaborate design covered the neck and shoulders, and the luxurious velvet hood had tiny crystals, like small diamonds, sewn into the red satin lining, illuminating her face. On one side of her cape was a coat of arms embroidered in red, and in the center was the letter *O* in gold. It was obvious to all of them she was wearing a cloak that signified something of importance, like the braids and medals worn by a decorated soldier. Only hers was not for military distinction. Alexandra felt her heart beating fast . . . the velvet cape and insignia were identical to the cape worn by her grandmother every Halloween for the parade in Dark Harbor, only with an *S* for Silver. What did this mean? It was overwhelming and too much to think about—the only thing Alexandra could think about was that she had *traveled through time*. She was standing, breathing, and looking around, and the year was 1692. As she looked at Theo and everyone else, she knew they were thinking the exact same thing.

Casting furtive glances down the alley toward the street, Olivia began speaking to them in a hushed, urgent voice.

"I know this is very odd and a funny sight to see yourselves in seventeenth-century clothing. However, we must remember why we are here. We need to get to the courthouse right away. Stay close behind me and walk in small groups. Do not talk and keep your heads down. If anyone speaks to you, I will answer. When we get to the courthouse, follow all my directions, exactly. It is most important that we stay together. However, if anyone should become separated from the group, listen very closely. Watch the way we go to the courthouse from this alley. It is not far. Return the same way to this alley. I will come back for you. Do not be afraid, I will return for you, and do not leave the alley. Now we must go. As we are walking, think about your scripts and practice silently."

Alexandra looked around and caught Jaclyn's eye. She knew Jaclyn was thinking the same thing. Becoming separated from each other in the year 1692 and perhaps never getting back to the present was the scariest thing imaginable.

They were soon hurrying down the side of the cobblestone road, keeping their eyes low, but never taking them off the flowing black velvet cape that was leading the way. Silently, Theo and Jaclyn joined her, and they huddled together in a small group as they walked.

All of a sudden, Alexandra noticed they did not have their glasses on—the glasses had been on their faces in the alley just moments before.

"Where are your glasses?" she whispered.

"I don't know . . . they just disappeared . . . I cannot see very well," answered Jaclyn in a hushed voice.

"I cannot see well, either. Maybe they didn't have glasses in 1692?" whispered Theo.

No one had thought of that possibility or knew the answer—the glasses had simply vanished. Alexandra gripped their hands.

"Just follow me."

Alexandra was trying to think about her script, but it was hard. She wanted to look around and stop and stare at everything—the buildings, the horses, and most of all, the people. With her head lowered, she was also trying to glance here and there for landmarks, just in case.

They were now turning off the road they had been on and began walking down a wider street filled with horses, carriages, and people. The air was heavy with the smell of wood burning, and a slight haze from the smoke was in the air. Some straggly dogs were running around, apparently on their own. As they hurried down the cobblestone road, Alexandra glanced sideways and she could see men and women with children bustling in and out of small shops that lined both sides of the street. Whenever she glanced up, she saw people looking at them. It gave her a chill. What if they were stopped and questioned?

Olivia slowed and turned back to them, giving a nod to the columned building on their right. Many people were arriving and going through the large doors. It was now very clear they were being stared at, most of all Olivia. They made their way up the stone steps to the front doors and were inside quickly. Alexandra was relieved; it felt safer to be inside than outside. They were soon huddled together in a far corner of a very large room. In a whispered voice, Olivia told the boys to take off their hats and the girls, their capes. As she pushed her hood back, everyone could see her black hair was now in a neat bun. There was a table against the wall where she told them to put their hats and capes, and then she covered everything with her own cape. Olivia was wearing a dress similar to what Alexandra and the other girls were wearing, a long gray dress with long sleeves and a simple white collar. (Very, very plain and a little itchy.) Next, she reached into the pocket of her dress and put on the same close-fitting bonnet the girls were wearing. Then she turned away from them for a moment. When she turned back around, there was the necklace, the gold disc shimmering against the plain gray fabric. Alexandra immediately put her hand to her chest in panic, relief flooding through her as she felt it under the dress. The glasses had been lost, but not her necklace, thank goodness.

The courtroom was noisy and very crowded and seemed disorganized. Some dogs galloped in and then out and some chickens waddled in, but were quickly sent scurrying back outside. People were milling around talking and most were casting curious glances at the group in the corner.

Suddenly, they heard a gavel pound three times and the court was called to order. A loud, deep voice was pronouncing something about the Year of our Lord and the King and Queen of England. They could not see who was speaking or any of the judges at the front of the courtroom—too many people were standing in the way. So they did not see Mercy Disbrow as she was brought into the court. The crowd was all straining to see her and talking amongst themselves.

"Order, order in the court. The reading of the sentence shall now be heard."

The crowd hushed. The deep voice resonated throughout the room.

"To George Corwin, High Sherriff of County of Essex, greetings: Whereas Mercy Disbrow of Salem, County of Essex Sawyer, at a special Court of Oyer and Terminer held at Salem on the fourteenth day of June last past, before Chief Justice William Stoughton and his Associate Justices and was arraigned upon several Indictments for using and practicing Witchcraft upon the livestock of Farmer and Goodwyfe Warren, whereupon all died, to which said Mercy Disbrow pleaded not guilty, and for Tryall thereof put herself upon God and Country, whereupon she was found guilty of the felonies and Witchcrafts whereof she stood indicted. A Sentence of Death is now accordingly passed against her as the Law directs, Execution whereof yet remains to be done. These are therefore in the Name of their Majesties William and Mary, now King and Queen of England, to will and command that upon Friday next being the thirty-first day of this instant month October, between the hours of eight and twelve noon, be safely conducted from Salem Prison to Gallows Hill, and there be hanged by the neck until she be dead. And hereof, not to fail at your peril, this shall be sufficient warrant given under my hand and seal this twenty-third day of October in the year of our Lord 1692 in the fourth year of the Reign of Our Sovereigns, King William and Queen Mary over England. So writ by Chief Judge William Stoughton."

The crowd erupted in cheers. The gavel came down again three times.

Then there was a woman's voice, firm and strong.

"Your Honor, I come here today as a witness for Mercy Disbrow."

Olivia had disappeared and was now at the front of the courtroom.

"Step forward. State your name."

"Olivia White. I am a teacher and mistress to orphans. There is a small schoolhouse and lodging for orphan children on the old Putnam Farm, bequeathed for this purpose in Farmer Putnam's last will and testament. My students and I can bear witness to Mercy Disbrow's innocence."

The crowd was straining to see Olivia and the courtroom had become very quiet. There was some whispering amongst the judges and then the Chief Judge spoke.

"Putnam Farm is not known to me nor to any of the Associate Judges. No matter, doth thee not know the Law of the Court, Goody White? You are in contempt of court. No witness may swear testimony on behalf of the accused nor there be legal representation for those accused of witchcraft and sorceries. Mercy Disbrow spake only for herself ag'n the sworn depositions of many good citizens of Salem. Spectral evidence proved the accused to be a witch. Upon proper examination, witch's marks be found on her body."

He paused for a moment. The voice sounded old and rather weak, but the tone was clear. He was becoming angry.

"Mercy Disbrow was seen casting horrible spells upon the animals, her face and body contorted as something unnatural had taken hold of her, and that be Satan. Others swore oaths having seen the accused flying with other witches through the winter mist o'er Oyster Pond. The jury found her guilty at Tryall. Gallows Hill awaits Mercy Disbrow."

Alexandra could hardly breathe.

"I will witness, as will the orphans I teach, that Mercy Disbrow is, too, an orphan, and she lived with us and attended my school during this time. She was never at Warren Farm. The good witnesses must be mistaken. It could not have been dear Mercy. Mercy Disbrow never worked for Farmer Warren and his Goodwyfe. *These facts, Your Honor, must be heard.*"

Alexandra realized the way Olivia had said the last few words was somehow different. It sounded like a command. The silence was deafening.

Alexandra's heart was pounding. She looked around at Theo, Jaclyn, and the others. They looked as scared as she felt and they all huddled closer together.

"Call the orphans to speak to the Court."

The crowd was stunned; some gasped loudly. After a few seconds, there were loud yells, protests, and demands that Olivia be arrested. Then the deep booming voice was heard again.

"Quiet in the Court, all be silent! The Chief Judge has so ordered. All ye who be orphans come forward to state ye names and what ye know to be the whole truth and nothing but the truth."

Alexandra knew she had to lead. She whispered to the others to follow her, and then wound her way through the angry crowds not looking at anyone, just straight ahead, and found her way to Olivia's side. Her aunt looked strong and powerful and not the least bit afraid.

"Orphan One. State ye name and what ye saw."

She felt Olivia touch her shoulder, so she stepped forward.

"Alexandra Brimley. As God is my witness, Mercy Disbrow lived with us on the old Putnam Farm. We milked the cows together every morning and she never missed one milking. Not one."

Alexandra added the last two words just for good measure. They were not in the script.

"Orphan Two. Step forward."

"Theodore Adams. As God is my witness, Mercy Disbrow helped with plowing the fields. She is very strong for a girl and can drive the plow horses as best as I."

"Orphan Three. Step forward."

"Jaclyn Pratt. As God is my witness, Mercy Disbrow helped me wash the clothes every day. She is the best clothes scrubber and nary a spot would be left."

"Orphan Four. Step forward."

"Katherine Bishop. As God is my witness, Mercy Disbrow helped me pick the summer vegetables and set up the pantry for winter."

One by one, they all stepped forward, standing tall and speaking bravely and clearly, until the last of the sixteen had spoken. They were lined up, eight on one side of Olivia and eight on the other side, facing the four Associate Judges and the Chief Justice William Stoughton. They had each ventured a quick look at Mercy Disbrow. She was sitting in the defendant's box, to one side of the judges, looking very scared and very frail. It was shocking to see because she was just a child.

Mercy had pale white skin and jet-black hair that reminded Alexandra of Olivia's, except it was very long and unkempt. She was wearing a tattered, stained blouse, and her hands were bound together with cloth strips. Her eyes were red-rimmed and she looked as though she had not slept in a long time. When Alexandra had given her statement, she looked straight ahead into the fat face of an old man with bushy eyebrows who was wearing a fake white wig and a fancy ruffled shirt. She had not dared to look at Mercy. However, when she stepped back next to Olivia, she had looked again, and Mercy was staring back at her.

For some reason Alexandra did not understand at all, she felt a connection to her, as though Mercy was someone she knew. Her eyes were hazel colored, more green than amber, and her face was pale but quite beautiful. As she studied her face, Alexandra realized Mercy looked similar to Olivia, and then she thought of her mother. She had seen photos of her mother when she was a young girl, and Mercy strongly resembled her. As she was thinking how odd it was that Mercy Disbrow looked so much like her mother, her thoughts were interrupted by the voice of the Chief Justice.

"The Court will consider each of these statements, separately, as to truth and veracity or bearing false witness."

Alexandra saw Olivia slowly move her hand to her chest and hold the small disc between her fingers. She began rubbing the round disc very discreetly; however, the movement was hardly noticeable.

"The statements of each will be considered in their order of testimony. Orphan One, the Court finds . . ." the voice trailed off and the silence was almost unbearable to Alexandra.

". . . the statement to be true. Orphan Two, true. Orphan Three, true."

There were again loud gasps from the crowd, but no one yelled out. They all seemed mesmerized. As Alexandra watched Chief Justice William Stoughton state his findings, she noticed that the word "true" was not the word he wanted to say. He appeared to struggle, his mouth looked formed to say "false," yet each time the word "true" escaped his lips. Alexandra looked at Olivia and could see the faintest hint of a smile at the corner of her mouth. Mercy Disbrow had collapsed forward on the rail of the box, weeping.

He droned on until the sixteenth and with the last utterance of "true," it actually looked like he would collapse. Weakly, he ordered Mercy Disbrow be set free. The sheriff cut the cloth bands around her wrists and immediately escorted her out through a back door for her own safety. The Chief Justice then addressed the crowd, his voice and physical demeanor noticeably weakened.

"The sentence found earlier today hath no merit. The new testimony proves to the Court Mercy Disbrow could not have committed these evil acts and she be . . . not a witch."

What happened next was somewhat blurred as things were happening so fast. Olivia told them to come with her and forged a path through the crowd to the back corner telling them to *quickly, quickly* put on their hats and capes and follow her back to the alley—*at once.*

The crowd in the courtroom was still in shock, so making their way to the corner and leaving the courthouse was not difficult. There was much whispering and muttering and everyone was staring at them, but there was no outburst. They were outside and well down the street when it happened. There was a loud yell from someone in the crowd on the steps of the courthouse.

"That woman be a witch!! There be no farm for orphans, all lies!! She be rubbing a witch's talisman 'round her neck, a spell she cast over the Chief Justice. *Stop her*!!"

They began to run, this time looking straight ahead, following the black cape as it swished and flew. Olivia was moving very fast. Alexandra, Jaclyn, and Theo were at the back, closest to the gaining crowds, who were yelling, *"Stop them*!! *All be witches*!!" Jaclyn and Theo were on each side of her and Alexandra immediately grabbed their hands, but it was difficult to run fast while holding hands. Theo immediately realized the dilemma, whispering they would be fine running together as a group, and Jaclyn said she could see Olivia's cape, so Alexandra dropped their hands and they ran.

It was all a blur. Running as fast as they could, gasping for breath, scared to death, never losing sight of the black cape that seemed to fly through the streets, and finally making their way back to the alley. Without saying a word, they quickly formed their circles, clasped hands with eyes closed, and the winds came . . . and then the spinning and lifting.

Just as the spinning began, Alexandra opened her eyes for one second, turning quickly to look at Theo and then at Jaclyn in the center of the circle.

Her screams could not be heard above the howling winds.

THE RESCUE

They were back in Classroom #6 wearing their regular school uniforms. As the spinning and winds stopped, everyone heard her screams and all eyes were on Alexandra.

"Alexandra, what is it?!"

Olivia had come to her and was holding her shoulders.

Alexandra gulped for air.

"Jaclyn, Jaclyn's not here!"

Olivia spun around quickly, scanning all the faces, and then swiveled back to Alexandra. It was obvious in all the confusion Olivia had not noticed that Jaclyn was not standing next to her in the center of the circle.

"What happened, Alexandra, did you see? Did someone from the crowd grab her??"

"I, I don't know. She was running with Theo and me, and I thought she was right next to me . . . but when I looked, just as the spinning began, I didn't see her in the center of the circle . . . I . . . I dropped her hand when we started to run . . . her glasses were gone, but she said she could see your cape and we all started running as fast as we could . . ."

Alexandra started crying again. All eyes were on Olivia.

"I will find her. I promise. You have all trusted me with everything, and you must continue to do so. Jaclyn will be back with us tomorrow."

Olivia's voice was steady and confident.

At that moment, the dismissal announcement came across the speaker, raspy and wheezing as always. Very slowly, everyone filed out of the classroom, except Alexandra, who stood next to Olivia near the doorway. Theo was the last student to leave. As he passed by

Alexandra, his eyes were filled with concern, and he very reluctantly walked out. Looking at him, she realized his glasses had been recovered somehow . . . they were back on his face.

"I have to go back with you, I have to! Please, you must take me with you, please!"

Olivia began pacing slowly back and forth, thinking, and then turned to Alexandra.

"You will go with me. And so will Nicolas."

Alexandra could not believe what she was hearing. Nicolas did not know anything about Olivia, about time travel, about where they had been. Nothing.

"Alexandra, I have to tell you some things I think you already know to be true. Come with me."

Olivia led her to the Reading Rug, where they both sat on the hassock, and she wrapped her arm around Alexandra, holding her tightly.

"Today, you helped save your own family."

Olivia looked deeply into her eyes and held her quivering chin.

"Mercy Disbrow is our ancestor. We needed to go back to save her from Gallows Hill. *And we did.* Had we not succeeded, we would not have been able to come back through time today."

Her voice became a whisper.

"If Mercy had been hanged . . ." but she did not finish the sentence.

"And the fate of all my students—they would be living as orphans in the year 1692, never to be found again."

It seemed impossibly complicated and not at all real.

"Let me read to you what history now says . . ." and she reached for the same book she had read from earlier that day.

"Mercy Disbrow was acquitted of all charges, the only accused witch to ever have been freed, on October 23, 1692, as a result of witnesses who came forward in her defense and were granted permission to speak to the court by the Chief Justice. This was the only time during the Salem Witch Trials an accused witch was permitted to have witnesses testify in her defense. A group of orphans and their teacher vouched for Mercy as living with them, therefore proving she could not have killed Farmer Warren's livestock. After testifying, the orphans and their teacher, Goody White, were never seen again. Mercy Disbrow went on to live a full and long life. She died a peaceful death at age seventy. Four children survived her, as did six grandchildren."

She paused, stroking Alexandra's hair, and then continued.

"My dear Alexandra, this is very hard to explain and I don't expect you to understand. You will have to trust me. We have been living in a parallel universe, which was based upon Mercy living. That is how we are alive today, as her descendants. At this exact time, it was my challenge to return to Salem and save her from the gallows—*to change history*. If we had not been able to save her, well . . . that is best left unspoken . . . and Mercy Disbrow did have powers, but she never killed anything. As you now know, I also have them."

Alexandra felt limp and weak, like she would faint. She fleetingly thought of what Blackie told her. He had told her the truth. Then she felt Olivia pulling her up.

"Alexandra, *you must be strong for Jaclyn*. We must go back to 1692 and bring her home. All that I have told you we will talk more about, but right now, we must focus on one thing, getting Jaclyn back."

Just as she finished, there was a knock at the door. Olivia went to the door, and without hesitation, quickly opened it. Nicolas was standing there with a quizzical look on his face.

"Come in, Nicolas. I do not think we have met. I am Olivia White," she said as she extended her hand. He shook it, staring at her with great interest. Then he looked around the room and Alexandra could see his surprise.

"This does not look like my classroom. Where is Jaclyn? Blackie has been waiting for you both," Nicolas said, looking at Alexandra, but before she could answer, Olivia quickly responded.

"Nicolas, go and tell Blackie you are staying with the girls to work on a school project. Tell him to come back at 5:00 p.m. sharp to pick you up. He will not question this. Hurry, come right back."

Alexandra heard the same tone of voice she had heard earlier. It was a command. Without questioning her, Nicolas left. He returned quickly, and Olivia locked the door to Classroom #6.

"Nicolas, there is too much to explain to you now, but I promise I will, very soon. Right now, I need you to come with Alexandra and me to find Jaclyn. She is lost. She is lost somewhere in Salem, Massachusetts, in the year 1692."

Nicolas stared at Olivia with no outward trace of surprise or disbelief. Calm and cool, he was just like Noir, Alexandra thought, even upon hearing what was impossible to comprehend.

"Oui, tell me what to do."

Olivia led them to the Reading Rug. They stood in a small circle. She told them to hold hands, not let go, and close their eyes. Alexandra felt the coldness of Nicolas's hand, then the wind and spinning, lifting, and then stillness.

They were back in the same alley. Alexandra had on the same clothes as before and Nicolas was dressed as all the boys had been. Olivia was wearing the same magnificent black cape. Alexandra quickly looked up and down the alleyway. It was clear Jaclyn was not there, which made her stomach clench with fear.

"I will go alone to find her. I want the two of you to stay together,"

Olivia said in a whispered voice while looking with obvious concern at the empty alley.

It was getting dark very fast.

"She may be in Salem Prison. I am going there. It is right behind the courthouse. If the crowd got her, she is there, waiting for her trial as a witch."

Alexandra shuddered and felt her stomach twist again, but it also seemed like an impossible search—what if Jaclyn was not there?

"But if she was able to run away, we cannot know where she is. *How will we ever find her??* You said we should come here and wait no matter what, but Jaclyn isn't here?" Alexandra asked, feeling a wave of panic.

"She could have come here and left again if someone followed her. If she is able to, she will come back. One of you can go across the street and watch the alley, the other stays in this alley. Do not venture farther away. Keep out of sight and talk to no one. I will be back, hopefully with Jaclyn, very soon."

Olivia vanished into the twilight.

Nicolas seemed lost in thought. It was exactly how Alexandra felt. He walked slowly toward the street and she followed him. There was an old barrel at the end of the alley. He pointed to it and she slid down next to it. He nodded and then crossed the cobblestone street, tugging down on his hat. There was another narrow alley across the street. He leaned up against the inside wall. She could see him in the little crack between the barrel and the brick wall. The light was fading quickly and once it was dark, she knew she would not be able to see him.

There were far fewer people and carriages on the streets at this time of day. It was twilight and eerily quiet. When a horse and rider or carriage came by, the sound of the hooves on the cobblestones seemed to echo long after they had passed. Alexandra could see a sign above a door to the right of where Nicolas was standing that said, "Ingersoll's Tavern," and she could hear noise and laughter coming through the open door. To his left, another sign read, "N. Saltonstall, Esq." She knew that a tavern was for food and drink, but did not know what "Esq." meant. That was a mystery. It was getting darker and colder. Soon there would be no light in the sky. The smell of wood smoke filled the night air.

Alexandra had some time to think for the first time all day. However, it was very hard to think clearly, because there was so much jumbled together in her mind . . . finding Jaclyn, witch trials, Gallows Hill, parallel universes, Olivia's magical powers . . . and Mercy Disbrow. She had helped save her own ancestor. Looking out into the darkening street, Alexandra realized somewhere tonight Mercy was free and safe, and she would live a long life.

It was incredible, like some fantastical dream. She looked over at Nicolas, remembering their time together in the library. Chadwick Manor seemed like it was in another part of the universe and she realized at that moment it was. Now Nicolas knew about Olivia, or at least her powers, and there was more he would find out. He had seemed genuinely concerned about Jaclyn and he obviously loved Noir, so maybe there was a heart underneath the indifferent and cold exterior.

She was jarred from her thoughts by a long, low whistle. She got up and peered across the street. Nicolas was pointing to an elegant black carriage that had just pulled up a little above the entrance to the alley on her side of the street. Two gleaming chestnut horses were snorting and pulling at the reins. The small door opened and a petite figure stepped out wearing a dark cape with a hood.

"Thank you. You have been most kind, Mr. Saltonstall. I will be fine now. My teacher will come for me. She told me to wait here for her. Thank you, again, very much."

The carriage pulled slowly away and there she was—Jaclyn.

Alexandra cried out, but muffled most of the sound with her hand as she ran toward her. Nicolas was running from across the street and took them both by their arms when he reached them. His grip was very strong.

"It is not safe here, so close to the road, *vite, hurry!*" Nicolas whispered urgently, while leading them into what was now a very dark alley.

"Jaclyn, what happened today? Did someone grab you? I thought you were right next to me the whole time! Who brought you here in the carriage? Did I hear you say Mr. Saltonstall? His name is on a sign across the street . . ." So many questions tumbled out.

"Alexandra, je ne sais pas! I was running right behind you and fell down. I tripped on this long cape. When I got up, I could not see where you were without my glasses, but I knew you were far ahead. They were coming so fast, yelling that we were witches. J'avais peur! I didn't know what to do!"

Alexandra smiled in the dark. It was the first time she had heard Jaclyn speaking French.

"I jumped into the first door I saw, the one across the street. A man took my arm and led me to the back where there was a large trunk . . . he told me to get in and I did. Then he closed it, I could hear the key turning in the lock. He whispered, 'Do not be afraid. Make no sound. They will not find you here, and I will get you out as soon as they leave.' Then I heard him throw something heavy like a blanket over the trunk. They came in moments later, shouting, "*Where be the wee witch?!*" I could hear them pushing things, opening and closing doors, and then they were standing right next to the trunk! Then I heard someone sit down on it! I thought I was going to die, mourir, die! Thank goodness, they never suspected I was in the trunk! Finally the man, Monsieur Saltonstall, let me out and told me I would be safe with him . . ."

All of a sudden out of the darkness, Olivia appeared. Seeing Jaclyn, she looked hugely relieved and quickly hugged her, but her eyes were serious and darting back toward the street.

"I am so glad I did not find you in Salem Prison, Jaclyn, but we must leave at once! Some men who recognized me from the courthouse have followed me. Circle and clasp hands, *quickly*!"

They all looked toward the entrance of the alley. A group of men with lanterns had just turned into the alleyway, and were yelling and running toward them. As the wind howled around them, Alexandra looked at the small circle. *Her family*—and everyone was safe.

Then they spun around and around and up and up.

Three tired students were standing under a single dim light on the steps of The Pine School. There was no sign of Headmaster Green or anyone else. Headlights were approaching and soon Blackie and Max were right there in front of them.

"Well, right on time, 5:00 p.m. sharp. Dinner is waiting." Blackie's voice was warm and cheery.

They were going home, all together.

THE SECOND TRIP TO DARK HARBOR

Everyone in Classroom #6 was happy and relieved to see Jaclyn back the next day, just as Miss White had promised. What was most peculiar was their teacher did not talk about the field trip or Jaclyn's rescue during class, nor did any of the students. It was almost as if the trip to Salem had never happened.

However, Jaclyn had told Nicolas and Alexandra what happened after she got out of the trunk, and what she found out about the man who saved her.

Nathaniel Saltonstall was a lawyer and had served as an associate judge for the witch trials. Over time, he became convinced innocent people were being falsely accused. He realized the evidence against them was very weak, and he did not agree the accused could have no legal representation or any witnesses to speak in their defense. So he resigned from the court and returned to practicing law.

On the day of Mercy's sentencing, Nathaniel Saltonstall heard the angry crowds approaching his office and he saw Jaclyn trip and fall. He knew they were after her, so when she stumbled into his office, he helped her hide. Once the crowds dispersed and were nowhere in sight, he opened the trunk and helped her out, telling her he had sat down on it, as an extra precaution. Then he said he wanted to bring her to his home where she would be safe. Jaclyn told them she was too frightened to be alone in the alleyway, and trusted him because he had protected her, so she agreed to go with him. She described the exciting carriage ride as they flew through the countryside until they came to an entrance with two large fence posts. The horses slowed to a trot, and they headed down a long dirt road and into a red barn where a young stable hand helped her out of the carriage. Then the lawyer led her into his home. The ceiling was very low and there was a fire in the fireplace, and large black pots hung over the fire. The lawyer introduced his wife, who had a very kind face, and their two little children. They all sat at a long wooden table and ate some soup and bread. After dinner, the lawyer asked if he could help her get to safety, and before she could answer, he opened a door and out came . . . Mercy Disbrow.

Jaclyn said Mercy hugged her tightly, and told her she would never forget the angels who saved her from Gallows Hill. The lawyer explained he was taking Mercy to another town in Massachusetts, to friends who would protect her, and he was certain they would help her, too. He said he had helped many others escape what he called the "Salem Madness." Jaclyn said she thanked him very much, but explained she had been told what to do and that she must get back to the alley. He had reluctantly agreed. But before she stepped out of the carriage he told her if her teacher did not come, she could open a back window of his office and would be safe until he arrived in the morning.

Alexandra and Nicolas sat in amazed silence after hearing the story. Had she fallen into the hands of almost anyone else, she would not be sitting there with them. They would never have found her.

* ✦ *

On Friday, as they were leaving school, Olivia handed Alexandra a folded note. As they were riding home, she opened it.

> *Dear Alexandra,*
> *I would like you to come to my apartment tomorrow at*
> *2:00 p.m. Bring Jaclyn and Nicolas. Ask Blackie if there is a*

third bicycle for Nicolas, so you can show him around Dark Harbor.

Come by yourselves. I am sure your grandmother will allow this.

Love,

Aunt Olivia

Alexandra smiled reading the note, feeling a happiness that was still so new . . . *Aunt* Olivia. She was relieved that her aunt would be explaining everything to Nicolas. He had asked many questions about the trial and time travel, but Alexandra and Jaclyn told him Olivia needed to explain. It was clear he wanted to know the answers and his impatience was growing. And, Nicolas and Jaclyn would find out about their connection to Mercy Disbrow.

Just as Olivia wrote, her grandmother said it was fine, they could go by themselves, and in no time, the third bicycle appeared, polished, with plump tires. Their ride this time was faster as Nicolas obviously liked speed, and they wanted to keep up. It was not long before they pulled into Weston's Market and were parking their bicycles in the rack.

Nicolas was looking around Dark Harbor with mild interest, but no enthusiasm, so unlike his sister's reaction.

"We should go right up. It's two o'clock and she's expecting us."

Alexandra again found herself directing attention to where they needed to be. They followed her up the stairs. Olivia opened the door as soon as Alexandra reached the top step.

"Come in! Did you have a good ride?"

Her green eyes sparkled. She was wearing a heavy fisherman knit sweater and matching cream-colored wool slacks.

"Oui, it was enjoyable," Nicolas answered in a factual tone while looking around the tiny living room and kitchen.

The wonderful smell of fresh baked cookies had wafted through the open door as soon as they stepped in. Alexandra could see the small kitchen table was set with orange mugs and plates. A large pumpkin was in the middle of the table.

"Come over and sit down. I made you hot chocolate and cookies. The cookies are my own invention . . . I hope you like them."

They sat down. Mugs of hot chocolate with dollops of whipped cream and shaved chocolate were at each place. Olivia offered them cookies from a plate shaped like a maple leaf. They did not look like any cookie Evelyn had ever made. Some had large chunks of white and dark chocolate or pecans, covered with thick swirls of chocolate frosting, and topped with sparkling silver and gold sugar crystals. Others were covered with orange or purple frosting and topped with shimmering sprinkles. The sprinkles *changed colors* as you looked at them.

No one spoke for a few minutes. The girls were eating the delicious cookies and sipping the creamy hot chocolate. Nicolas seemed completely disinterested in the food. He was looking at Olivia intently.

"Well, I am so glad you were able to come to see me today. I want to talk to all of you," Olivia said, with a serious look on her face.

"This is all quite complicated. Some of this is known to some of you, so I think it would be best if I just start at the beginning."

Nicolas stared at Olivia, and his dark brown eyes shone with interest.

"I am the twin sister of Alexandra's mother. I was taken—kidnapped—when I was a baby. My mother, your grandmother, thinks I am dead because that is what her doctor told her. He told her I was the smaller twin, very weak, and that I died shortly after birth from pneumonia. I knew him as my father. His name was Dr. White."

She paused, looking around the table, and then continued.

"Just before he died he told me the truth about my birth. I traced the names of my parents to Dark Harbor and came here a few months ago. I was teaching in Boston so it was not that far, and when I walked into the market, Mr. Weston looked like he saw a ghost. He told me I looked very much like a woman who had grown up in Dark Harbor. He said her name was Elisabeth Chadwick and he told me she died over ten years ago in a sailboat accident. That is when I found out my twin sister was not alive. For some reason unknown to even me, I decided to rent this apartment and at Mr. Weston's suggestion, I called The Pine School about a teaching position. So suddenly and entirely unexpectedly, I found myself living in Dark Harbor and taking Miss Blueberry's place in Classroom #6. It all seemed to happen . . . as though it was meant to be."

She paused again and then continued.

"When I was given the class list, Headmaster Green gave me some background about each student and that is when I realized my sister had a daughter before she died, and my own *niece* would be in my class. Alexandra became suspicious when she first saw me, because I looked so much like her mother, and then there was the necklace." Olivia laid her hand on her necklace and Alexandra pulled hers out from under her sweater.

"They were put around our necks at birth, mine with an ☉ and my sister's with an ℰ. For some reason that will never be known, Elisabeth left hers behind when they went on their sailing trip." Olivia paused, looking at Alexandra. Her eyes reflected the deep sadness they shared, the loss of a sister and a mother.

"When Alexandra saw my necklace one day at school, she knew there had to be an explanation. That is when she asked Taco. Taco was outside the hospital when my sister and I were born, and he knew about the matching necklaces. Is everyone still with me?"

There were nods all around. Alexandra was relieved her aunt had not said anything about Taco witnessing the kidnapping. It was not something she wanted Nicolas to know.

"A few weeks ago, Alexandra came to Dark Harbor with a photo of her parents and that is when I met Jaclyn and learned about you, Nicolas. To find out I have another sibling—your father—was a complete surprise, and someday I hope to meet him. And to find out I am an aunt to all three of you makes me happier than I could ever explain."

She smiled, looking around the table at each of them, and then her expression became very serious again.

"Which brings me to the field trip. This is going to be a shock, so I will just say it. Mercy Disbrow was our ancestor. Had we not been successful in preventing her hanging, we would never have been able to return to the present because we would have died when she did. It is even more complicated . . . having to do with a parallel universe . . . but that is not something you need to understand right now."

Jaclyn gasped and Nicolas's eyes became almost black. Even though Alexandra already knew about Mercy, it was shocking to hear confirmed what she had suspected. They would now be dead, not sitting in this cozy apartment drinking hot chocolate.

"And there is something else."

She paused and looked at each of them.

"Mercy Disbrow was a witch."

The only sound was the soft ticking of a clock. The afternoon sun was streaming into the kitchen window, and the entire room seemed to take on an orange glow. They sat in silence.

"Because we saved her from Gallows Hill, Mercy lived a long life. She had four children and many grandchildren. Her powers have been passed from generation to generation but not to every descendent. As you know from our time travel to Salem, they were passed to me. I do not know if your grandmother has them or your father, Nicolas and Jaclyn. But the question I know you are thinking is, which of you may have them . . ." Olivia paused, looking at each of them.

The tension was nearly unbearable, each wondering what she would say next.

"You will not know until your fifteenth birthday. On that day, a letter *may* come to you. It will float in the air and land in your lap at midnight. If you receive the letter, it means you will have these powers, but if 12:01 a.m. strikes, and you have not received a letter, you will not. In the letter, there will be one challenge. In my letter, I was given the challenge of saving Mercy, and I had to wait many years until the precise calendar month, day, and year to travel back in time. And . . . you must succeed in your challenge."

"Or what happens?" Jaclyn asked in a hushed voice.

"The consequences of not succeeding with my challenge were very great, as you know."

The small apartment was again silent. Alexandra was thinking about another letter that had been floating in midair. Philippe must have powers. And Taco was afraid of him. Maybe these powers were not all good. She had never told Jaclyn about her father's letter; it had seemed best to say nothing.

"Nicolas, are you fourteen?"

"Oui."

"When is your fifteenth birthday?"

"Avant Noël, right before Christmas, December 23rd."

Alexandra felt her stomach twist . . . Nicolas with powers and she and Jaclyn with none. What if he could give powers to Noir? What could Noir do to Taco? It was all so frightening, and Christmas was only two months away. Jaclyn was obviously thinking the same thing as they exchanged grave looks. Alexandra looked at Nicolas. His expression was hard to read, but there was something different from just anticipation. He looked expectant but also worried, and she realized he was thinking what she was not—what if no letter came?

"Well, then, it will not be known until midnight of December 23rd," Olivia said in a matter-of-fact tone of voice.

It seemed to Alexandra as if her aunt was speaking about the date a package would arrive, or something else routine, not about something so momentous.

"In the meantime, I have something to suggest. I could come for Thanksgiving. It would be a surprise—we will have to tell Blackie ahead of time. There really is no easy way to do this. Do you have any other ideas?"

They did not.

No one could think about anything, except what might happen on December 23rd.

PONDERING EVERYTHING

T he next few weeks were uneventful and routine, apart from the amount of time Alexandra and Jaclyn were lost in their own thoughts. There was so much, too much really, to think about.

The time travel to Salem seemed to fade from their memories by the day. They noticed none of their classmates spoke about it, and no one suspected there was any relationship between their teacher and two of her students. So things were entirely normal, or as normal as they could be, at The Pine School. Daily announcements from the raspy, droning voice continued, but once the door was closed and locked, Classroom #6 was full of imagination and learning. Even math was made interesting by puzzles, challenges, and rewards. Theo usually won whenever there were problem-solving competitions, but he never acted as if he was smarter than anyone else. His cheeks became a little pink, and with eyes cast down, he would smile ever so slightly when his name was announced.

What had not faded at all was their meeting with Aunt Olivia. Would Nicolas receive a letter or not? Alexandra and Jaclyn tried to imagine what his powers could be like, what he might do with them, and what their grandmother knew. There were times when they could hear her speaking in French to Nicolas in his room with the door closed. Once, Jaclyn tried to eavesdrop, but as soon as she tiptoed to the door, Noir had cawed loudly. She had quickly scampered back, afraid of being caught. They tried to observe Nicolas whenever they were all together. He seemed his same somber self, but it was obvious he was preoccupied. At dinner, if someone asked him a question, he would have to ask that it be repeated. He spent even more time in the library and carried stacks of books to his room. They wondered if there were books about magic and witchcraft among the thousands of books in the Chadwick library. One day they spent hours pulling out antique books with no titles on the spines, but nothing about magic was found.

They also watched and observed their grandmother. There was nothing they witnessed that could be considered absolute proof she had powers, but both Alexandra and Jaclyn believed she did. And Alexandra decided not to talk about anything with Blackie, even though he had told her the truth.

Best kept as a secret . . . and to watch and wait.

HALLOWEEN IN DARK HARBOR

Halloween had always been very special for Alexandra.

From her earliest memory, she could remember feeling growing excitement as the calendar approached October 31st—of untold magical possibilities that seemed to swirl in the air on one mysterious and cold fall night. It was hard to sleep, as each night grew closer to what her grandmother called "All Hallows' Eve."

Even Taco would be restless with excitement, waiting for the annual Halloween parade. He had always participated, riding on Blackie's shoulder until Alexandra was big enough, and then on hers. His "costume" was some type of tiny hat Evelyn would make, secured by elastic like a birthday hat so it would not fall off. One year it actually was a birthday hat. Assuming it was his birthday, he sang, "*Happy Birthday, dear Taco*," throughout the Halloween festivities. Another year it was a tiny black top hat, first met with a very dubious look. However, once Evelyn explained it was the hat worn by United States presidents upon election to office—that was the charm. "*President Taco, nice to meet you!*" had echoed through the night.

As Alexandra grew older and with each passing Halloween, Taco's costumes became increasingly accessorized. When the embellishments were initially met with a doubtful look, she explained to her grandmother that *no one* wore just a hat for Halloween. Over the years, Taco had been transformed into Count Taco with a black cape and fake blood on his white cheeks, Indian Chief Taco with a long headdress and beads, and Dr. Taco with a surgeon's mask across his beak and stethoscope around his neck. He was usually enthusiastic, but sometimes not. The suggestion of being a ghost was quickly rejected—he definitely did not like the idea of being completely covered.

Her grandmother chose her Halloween costumes when she was very young; however, when Alexandra was in her second year at The Pine School and the choice was Tinker Bell, she told her grandmother she would only go to the parade dressed as Peter Pan. From then on, Alexandra decided on her own costume and was not particularly open to other suggestions. Fortunately, among Evelyn's many talents was also sewing, and upon request, the most amazing creations seemed to materialize from thin air.

The very best part was the transformation of Dark Harbor. Parents and shopkeepers worked for days hanging ghosts and goblins, bats, and black cats from every doorframe. Sheer swaths of black sparkling fabric hung from lampposts, becoming mysterious apparitions when swept up by the evening breeze. When darkness fell on All Hallows' Eve and the flames in the gas lampposts came on, it felt like the spirit of Halloween flew in and cast a magical spell over the little village.

Everyone wore costumes, and the small main street of Dark Harbor would fill with children and grown-ups, all transformed by costumes of every character imaginable. At seven o'clock sharp, those who wanted to be a part of the Halloween parade would assemble at the south end of the street. Alexandra's grandmother, wearing a black velvet cape (identical to Olivia's), always led the parade. She also wore an impressive black velvet witch's hat. Both her cape and hat had the same scarlet and gold insignia as Olivia's, but with the letter *S*. Alexandra had grown up seeing this, so it always seemed entirely normal.

It was just a Halloween costume.

Every year Blackie dressed as a mummy, wound up in long cloth bandages by Evelyn, and there was *always* an argument between them over whether the strips of cloth were wound too tight or too loose. Years ago, Evelyn had made the pale green bandages from bed sheets dyed green and then cut into long strips. Some were left hanging from his legs and arms and fluttered behind him as he walked, very stiff legged. Max was always the mummy's dog, with the same green cloth strips wound lightly around his torso and head. He wore a small sandwich board that read "I Love My Mummy" on both sides. Evelyn always went as Mary Poppins—she said she had all the props already (even an umbrella with a parrot-head handle, which always met with Taco's enthusiastic approval).

The Book Nook played scary music with Halloween sounds, as costumed grown-ups threw candy onto the street from sidewalks, and the children would scramble to get what they could. A hay wagon pulled by two old horses with special headdresses carried the youngest trick-or-treaters at the end of the parade. It was probably the shortest parade route ever, but no one cared because once they got to the other end of town, there was more fun to come.

Each shop was open with even more treats. The Book Nook always had candied apples dipped in green, orange, and purple caramel, and very realistic bloodshot eyeballs made from green, white, and red colored chocolate. The creepy witch standing behind the counter stirring a smoking cauldron unfailingly cackled, "Good food for the brain, the better to read by!" Moo Bar ice cream shop replaced their famous summer "red lobsicles" with purple and orange popsicles, and there was even black ice cream that tasted like licorice. The Moose's Closet offered bags of mystery treats with small toys and candy in each bag. At Weston's Market, Mr. Weston put out a huge black cauldron filled with penny candy and would say in a trying-to-be-scary voice, "One scoop per child. Cheaters will lose their heads." He always had some fake blood on his face and bad teeth and carried a long plastic axe, but no one was ever afraid of him. The Quill & Parchment stationery shop gave away pens made from peacock feathers to the girls, sword pens to the boys, and candy crayons to the littlest trick-or-treaters.

Chadwick Bank & Trust had ghosts and goblins standing behind each barred teller's window, and as each child approached, there would be sounds of screams from the large bank vault. The treat from the bank was always a netted sack of chocolate coins wrapped in gold foil and some Moose Money—a small wad of obviously fake hundred-dollar bills. In the center oval of each bill, there was a smiling moose. Underneath the moose's face it said, "Printed by the Dark Harbor Mint." However, the most fun was looking through the fake money because everyone knew ten lucky children would find one very real fifty-dollar bill mixed in with the Moose Money. Alexandra had never found one, but each year she still hoped.

The Claw & Tail Restaurant served drinks—warm and cold apple cider and hot chocolate—in paper cups that looked like bloody claws with a fake claw as the cup handle. Crowded with tourists eating lobster rolls during the summer, on Halloween night the picnic tables filled with ghosts and goblins eating candy and ice cream.

This year there would be three costumes to create—for the girls and Taco. Nicolas said he would not be going because Halloween was "pour bébés." Alexandra tried to describe the transformation of Dark Harbor and told him *everyone* went in costume, even the grown-ups, but he was clearly not interested. Jaclyn, on the other hand, could not wait.

There was, however, one very hard part for Alexandra each Halloween. Theo. Just like in the summers, she begged her grandmother to call Headmaster Green and invite Theo to come with them. Her grandmother always looked sympathetic, but said she could not be responsible for all the boarding students. Alexandra knew there could be no arguing, so she tried to put it out of her mind. This was not easy to do.

✴ ◆ ✴

There were many late-night conversations about who they should be. Finally, it was decided the best costumes would be pirates, especially with Taco—every pirate needs a macaw parrot on their shoulder. Jaclyn would be the pirate girl and Alexandra, the pirate boy. It was perfect, even their grandmother said so. Biscuit would be the pirate girl's dog and wear a teeny tiny cape that said, "Surrender the Booty," decorated with small dog bone treats instead of large crossbones. Evelyn got right to work. There were many fittings and decisions, which both girls took very seriously: fabric colors, boots, jewelry, pirate hats or bandanas, fake swords or knives. Jaclyn decided to wear tons of gold chains and big gold hoop earrings, a frilly blouse with a wide belt and colorful skirt, a purple bandana tied around her head, and *a lot* of makeup. She even wanted fake eyelashes (which did look amazing behind her thick glasses).

Alexandra also decided on a frilly blouse, along with a brown leather vest, striped pantaloons and white stockings, a tri-cornered hat, a fake mustache, and one round hoop earring. All pirates liked to wear jewelry and fancy clothes from what she had read. It was also decided that a large eye patch for Alexandra and a very small one for Taco would be essential accessories. When Alexandra told Taco about being a pirate, he bobbed his head up and down with great approval saying, "Aye, aye, matey! A pirate's life for Taco! Walk the plank, walk the plank!" As he said, "walk the plank," he pretended to do just that, covering his eyes with one long feathered wing, then setting one foot out in front of the other with great trepidation, as though the next step might be his last, even though he was walking on the floor.

They had all erupted in laughter at the sight.

However, when she told Taco he needed to wear an eye patch, he had looked at her with squinty eyes, as if to say, "Pardon me?" Then promptly shook his head "no"—many times. Alexandra finally persuaded him with a big—it had to be *very big*, he told her in no uncertain terms—bowl of watermelon upon returning home after the parade.

Proving parrots can be bribed, just like pirates.

✳ ◆ ✳

The magical night finally arrived.

Two pirates grabbed on to the brass pole and made a dramatic entrance into the large foyer where everyone was gathering. Biscuit took his time carefully going down one staircase, seemingly aware of his special role as the Booty Dog. Taco flew to the center rail and began to pace slowly back and forth, looking like the director of a Halloween movie set (who would also have an acting part), carefully studying his cast of characters assembling below. The "director" was most pleased with his own costume. He had immediately flown to the armoire mirror once Evelyn carefully put the tiny eye patch and miniature tri-cornered hat in place. She also made him a small leather belt with a tiny fake sword, so the entire ensemble made him the perfect parrot pirate. He obviously approved, strutting past the mirror many, many times, casting admiring glances while saying, "It's a pirate's life for Taco," followed quickly by, "Walk the plank! Walk the plank!"

The assembled group actually looked like they could be in a Halloween movie. The costumes were highly detailed and accessorized perfectly—each one was very authentic. And when her grandmother appeared under the double staircases, Alexandra thought, *the most authentic of all.* Everyone watched as the petite figure silently glided across the black and white tiles, the regal black velvet cape flowing behind her, carrying a broom in one hand. It was an unusually impressive broom: the long handle was made from twisted wood, polished to a gleaming mahogany, and the thick bristles were made of sturdy straw in every Halloween color—orange, purple, teal, black, and red—with sparkles that looked like shimmering diamonds scattered throughout the colored straw. The sparkles in the broom reminded Alexandra of the tiny crystals sewn into the scarlet lining of Olivia's hood. What had always been a Halloween costume now held an entirely different meaning—Alexandra and Jaclyn's eyes met thinking the same thing.

At that moment, Alexandra suddenly wondered if they would see Olivia somewhere in the crowd and if she would be wearing her identical cape. The thought sent a shiver down her spine. What if her grandmother saw Olivia? Alexandra had never told Olivia about the parade, and she now realized not telling her might have been a mistake.

Her gaze returned to her grandmother, who was now standing in front of her. She studied the intricate embroidery on the cape and the beautiful gold and scarlet *S* on the witch's hat and cape, and then looked into her grandmother's eyes. From her earliest memory, her grandmother's eyes looked like blue gemstones on All Hallows' Eve.

This night they were sparkling brilliantly. Her grandmother smiled and kissed her cheek, then Jaclyn's, and turned, leading the way to the front door.

Following behind was Evelyn, who could have been the real Mary Poppins, carrying a large carpetbag and parrot-head umbrella, and wearing a blue coat with silver buttons and high button shoes. Perched on her red hair, wound up in a neat bun as always, was a flat-brimmed straw hat with one real daisy. Blackie was next. He was a lifelike mummy, walking stiff legged, holding the mummy's dog by his leash with one hand and his pipe in the other. Because sitting was difficult—his legs had to be stretched out on the car seat—Evelyn always drove to town on Halloween. Only his eyes, nostrils, and mouth could be seen through the green cloth strips wound around his head. Alexandra knew that as soon as the parade was over he would walk around outside The Claw & Tail and smoke his pipe. The pipe smoke would billow around his wrapped head from the small slit that was his mouth. He made it look like it was completely normal for a mummy to be smoking a pipe. Everyone loved to see this. It was *very* funny.

Just as they were about to leave, two black figures emerged from the shadows on the upper balcony. The black bird on one shoulder let out a single long and sorrowful caw, echoing off the marble staircases and floor. Somehow, it seemed fitting. Crows and ravens have a long history with All Hallows' Eve.

Taco was perched on Alexandra's shoulder and glared up at the black bird. Then they all filed out the front doors of Chadwick Manor as two tigers watched with gleaming emerald eyes.

The foyer was now empty. Nicolas and Noir had returned to their room.

White mist began to rise from the black and white tile floor.

In the dim light, two tigers appeared to float on a surface of white clouds. Regal and imperious, the pair of porcelain statues had watched over the Chadwick family for many years.

Like a pool filling with water, the large foyer slowly filled with thick white vapor. Only the tigers' emerald eyes pierced the white veil.

Then something moved, sweeping away the white shroud for a mere second before disappearing again behind the thick fog.

Two orange and black striped tails were leisurely twitching in the shimmering mist.

＊◆＊

The town was ablaze with gaslight and the flames of dozens of flickering candles in all the shop windows. Ethereal black spirits were billowing in the chilly ocean breeze, and the air was filled with laughter and excitement. Promptly at seven o'clock, everyone assembled at the south end of the street, and Silver Chadwick raised her magnificent broomstick signaling the parade to begin. As they approached the first shops, parents and other onlookers began throwing candy on the street, met with shouts of glee as everyone scrambled to pick up all they could. Soon, Alexandra's ears were ringing with the well-practiced refrain, "Walk the plank! Walk the plank!" Biscuit was thoroughly enjoying himself, trotting along on his leash next to Jaclyn. Ahead of them, walking alongside a very elegant witch, Alexandra could see the mummy and his dog and Mary Poppins, who had put up her umbrella. *If only she could fly*, Alexandra thought and fleetingly wondered if her grandmother could make this happen with a spell or something.

As Alexandra looked at everyone around her, she felt

a burst of happiness. It was more fun this year than ever before because of Jaclyn. She realized how wonderful her life was now that she had Jaclyn *and* her Aunt Olivia. Just as she was thinking these thoughts, Jaclyn suddenly gasped.

"There she is!! Do you see her, Alexandra?" Jaclyn was pointing to the curb on the right side of the street.

Alexandra followed her pointed finger and saw her. She was standing at the edge of the sidewalk, in front of other onlookers. It was like looking at a real, living and breathing Snow White. Her aunt was in full costume, holding small blue birds cupped in one hand that looked very real—and Alexandra realized they probably were. She was wearing a blue, red, and yellow sequined mask around her eyes.

All at once, Alexandra realized her grandmother was also looking at her. They were not far apart. The front row of the parade had reached where Olivia was standing. At that exact same moment, her grandmother wobbled. She was obviously going to fall just as Blackie caught her by the arm. When Alexandra looked back to where Olivia had been standing seconds before, she had disappeared. There was no sign of her running or moving through the crowd. She was just—gone.

Blackie immediately wanted to take her grandmother to a sidewalk bench or home, but Silver told him she was fine and that the feeling of lightheadedness had quickly passed. However, everyone noticed her pink cheeks had turned ashen, and it was obvious she was shaken. Alexandra knew she had seen a ghost . . . the ghost of her dead daughter. And she wondered how they would ever be able to tell her about Olivia and what had happened in England so many years ago.

Much later that night they were sitting in the kitchen of Chadwick Manor.

While burning embers occasionally popped in the fireplace, one visibly tired Mary Poppins, whose straw hat was still on her head (although somewhat askew and with a now quite wilted daisy), was trying hard to stifle her yawns. Two bedraggled but very happy pirates were busy inventorying all their booty, and one parrot pirate (minus the eye patch) was busily slurping his watermelon reward, his tri-cornered hat and sword belt still in place. The tiny pirate dog was asleep in front of the fireplace, obviously dreaming with little quivers and yips, probably about all the scary creatures. The two pirates had already checked their Moose Money, having torn open the small packets and examined the bills while sipping hot chocolate at The Claw & Tail. Everyone always checked that first, but no luck again this year.

Taco's happy slurping suddenly stopped. He cocked his head slightly, looking intently at the kitchen door as it silently swung open. In walked Nicolas with Noir on his shoulder. He stood and looked at the table covered with candy and smirked.

"Why do you like this? If you eat all of this, you will be quite sick, malade. I will not feel sorry for either of you."

"We are not going to eat it *all at once*, Nicolas. *Évidemment.*"

Jaclyn looked at her brother with annoyance. Her eyelashes had come a bit unglued and were magnified by her glasses, so it was rather funny because she sounded so serious. Alexandra started to giggle, but then she looked at Nicolas seriously.

"Nicolas, Noir needs to be in his cage as Grand Mama has told you many times."

She looked at her cousin with disapproval. However, it was apparent her words had no effect on him.

"Noir and Taco need to get used to one another. They both live here now."

Alexandra stared darkly at her cousin and his black bird, and then looked at Taco. It was true he did not seem upset by Noir's presence. He had continued eating without any interruption.

"Well, we will have to see . . ." Her voice trailed off but the serious doubt was clear, and then she continued.

"You did miss all the fun, Nicolas."

Alexandra looked at Nicolas and then at Noir, giving them the same smug look they had often given her. She was rather enjoying the fact they had missed out. Then she returned to the serious job of sorting and counting her candy, which was actually the most fun, not eating it.

"Sooooo much fun! Candy! Ice cream! Eyeballs! Walk the plank! Walk the plank!"

Taco apparently could not resist rubbing it in either, and was looking directly at Noir with a rather superior look. He did not appear to be at all bothered by Noir's proximity and continued to calmly eat his watermelon. Both Nicolas and Noir glared at the macaw. Alexandra smiled at Taco, but realized he was probably braver because of his pirate costume.

"Well, I am glad you had fun with *les bébés*," Nicolas said, emphasizing the last word in a most dismissive tone, and then he turned to leave.

Suddenly, Noir swooped down to the table and grabbed a fake gold ring with a huge purple stone from one of the mystery bags. With the ring firmly secured in his black beak, he flew back to Nicolas's shoulder.

"Noir, retourne, tout de suite!" Jaclyn glared at the raven, who made no move to return it, and was staring back at her with equal intensity.

"It is only a cheap toy. Let him have it. Noir loves shiny objects, all ravens do. Surely you can spare one trinket, un jouet," Nicolas said, challenging his sister.

"Fine. He may have it. C'est un voleur. He is a thief, Nicolas. You should train him to ask and not to take things that are not his. I am sure Taco would never do that, never."

Jaclyn looked at Taco lovingly through one now very detached fake eyelash.

Taco seemed to preen at the compliment. He was obviously rather enjoying that Noir was getting into trouble.

Then they were gone as quickly as they had appeared.

Soon, everyone in Chadwick Manor was sound asleep except for one lone raven, whose black beady eyes shone with contentment as he gazed at the shiny purple ring now secure within his cage.

Ravens never sleep on All Hallows' Eve.

THANKSGIVING PLANS

November was a busy month.

There were exams early in the month for students at The Pine School, and they all had much more homework assigned every day. Afternoons were spent reading, studying, and watching the last leaves fall from the soon to be barren trees. Snow fell in Dark Harbor in early November, and Jaclyn and Alexandra were outside as fast as they could go, catching the first snowflakes with their tongues. Max and Biscuit joined them, running in and out of the maze many, many times. Both dogs seemed energized by the snow-laden gray skies and very cold air blowing in from the ocean. As they ran around and played with the dogs, Alexandra could see Nicolas standing at his window, watching. She waved for him to join them, but he shook his head "no" and walked away from the window. She could not understand Nicolas. Even Jaclyn had long since given up—she said, "C'est un vrai mystère," it is a real mystery. And it was.

One afternoon, a week before Thanksgiving, Olivia held Alexandra and Jaclyn back after everyone else had been dismissed.

"I think it's time for me to meet Blackie and tell him," Olivia said calmly, smiling.

Both Alexandra and Jaclyn looked at each other. They had known this was going to happen, but it still seemed shocking. Alexandra knew Blackie would think he was seeing a ghost.

It felt like a long walk from Classroom #6, down the stairs, then down the long grimy hall. Headmaster Green was standing guard by the doors, as always. He raised one scraggly eyebrow as they approached, and had just started to say something when Olivia interrupted him.

"I am going to review the homework that will be assigned for the Thanksgiving holiday with Blackie so he understands what is expected," she said smoothly with a smile.

Headmaster Green seemed to be at a complete loss for words as they sailed past him and out through the heavy wood door. There, idling under the portico, was the long black touring car. Blackie and Max were in the front, and Nicolas was already in the rumble seat where he liked to ride—by himself, of course. Nicolas's dark eyes widened when he saw Olivia with them. Olivia walked around the car to where Blackie sat behind the wheel. He looked completely shocked. His mouth was open but nothing came out.

"Blackie, I have heard so much about you from the girls. I am Olivia White. I am . . . Elisabeth's twin sister. Dr. White took me from the hospital—I did not die from pneumonia—and I was raised as his child. He told me just before he died that my birth name was Chadwick, and I had a twin sister, and the family had moved to Maine from London . . ." She paused and then continued.

"I did some research and found the Chadwick name in Dark Harbor and somehow—I do not really understand it myself—I became Alexandra's teacher when her teacher unexpectedly retired."

Blackie just kept staring at her. He obviously could not speak, so Olivia continued.

"I want so much to meet my mother, my real mother. I am sure you remember when she almost fainted at the Halloween parade . . . it was because she saw me. Even though I was in costume, I'm certain she thought she saw Elisabeth."

She paused, waiting to see if Blackie would finally speak. He did not, but he slowly opened the car door and stood. Then he put his arms around her. Everyone had tears in their eyes except Nicolas, who was just watching, with no obvious emotion.

"It's a miracle, a miracle, lassie. I cannot believe it. When I saw you come through the doors my heart almost stopped. I thought Elisabeth had somehow survived the storm and was alive, after all these years. This is going to make your mother happier than she could ever possibly have imagined."

Blackie wiped away his tears, and shook his head, studying Olivia's face.

"Well, well . . . how shall we break this wonderful news? We have to think about how and when. This will come as a tremendous shock so we will have to do this carefully. She is frail at her age . . ."

Then he paused, seeming to collect his thoughts.

"I will tell Evelyn. Let's see what we come up with, Olivia . . ." His voice trailed off, still in shock.

"Wonderful, Blackie, send me a note through Alexandra and let me know what you decide. I was thinking Thanksgiving might be perfect."

She stepped away, smiling, and waved good-bye as she opened the school door.

The ride home was silent. Everyone was lost in thought.

It was decided that Olivia would come to Chadwick Manor on Thanksgiving Day, around three o'clock, when they always had their Thanksgiving meal. It was always three o'clock in the afternoon because Blackie loved having a turkey sandwich with stuffing, slathered with mayonnaise and doused with salt and pepper on whole-wheat bread, late on Thanksgiving night. Over the years, Alexandra had joined him, just the two of them in the kitchen late at night, drinking apple cider, eating and talking. In some ways, she looked forward to the late-night sandwiches more than the formal dinner. It was cozy and comfortable (they always wore their slippers), and the house was hushed and quiet, except for the chiming grandfather clock.

Evelyn had taken the news very emotionally, and she was not able to hide her excitement and nervousness. Any number of times she was questioned by Silver Chadwick, "Evelyn, whatever is wrong with you? You seem more nervous than a beekeeper whose bees are loose!" (One of Alexandra's grandmother's favorite expressions.) To which Evelyn would mumble nothing was wrong, she was fine, and Silver would look at her *most* doubtfully.

However, there was yet another plan being hatched in an upstairs bedroom at Chadwick Manor.

Alexandra and Jaclyn decided Theo needed to be with them for Thanksgiving, that he could not be left in the attic of The Pine School by himself for another holiday. Once he was out of the school, they both believed that *somehow* they could convince their grandmother to let him stay.

This was going to require very good planning.

And some long and sturdy rope.

RESCUING THEO

It took everything they had to try to concentrate on school. There were more important things to think about—and plan for—as the days drew closer to Thanksgiving, and it was very hard to go to sleep each night. At last, the plan was set. One day in school, Alexandra passed a long note to Theo explaining the plan in detail. He pushed up his glasses a couple of times while reading the note—twice. Then he gave her the biggest grin, shaking his head in amazement. Next, he looked at Jaclyn, with the same broad grin and a thumbs-up.

Finally, the night arrived.

It was ten o'clock, the night before Thanksgiving. Both girls said good night to their grandmother, ran back upstairs to Alexandra's room and quickly changed from their pajamas to dark clothes—turtlenecks, hooded sweatshirts, warm pants, boots, and gloves. Alexandra tucked a flashlight into her sweatshirt pocket and draped a wool scarf around her neck, and then she signaled to Taco. He flew to her shoulder and down the brass pole they went. Evelyn was still in the kitchen, which they expected. They could hear her humming and the sound of dishes being stacked. Alexandra held one finger to her lips and gave Taco a stern look. He nodded as they tiptoed by the swinging door, and then they ran quickly down the carpeted hallway. Soon they were outside, enveloped by the cold dark night.

They ran to the garage.

Blackie's light was still on upstairs. Jaclyn quietly opened the side door into the garage and they crept in. The bikes were propped along the wall. From under a small tarp, Alexandra pulled out the rope and placed it in the basket of her bike, along with the flashlight. (Finding the rope had been the hardest part—they had looked around the garage so many times for rope and had almost given up when Jaclyn found it— just the right size, lots of it, neatly coiled inside the well of an old tire. When she first spotted it, Jaclyn looked like she had discovered hidden treasure, not some weathered rope.)

Silently, they pushed their bikes out the side door. Alexandra put Taco in Jaclyn's basket, which they had lined with a thick bath towel, to better secure him in the basket and allow room for his long tail feathers. Then she began carefully wrapping him in the wool scarf, and had already told him this would be necessary so he would not protest—he really did not like to be covered. (There had not been the slightest argument. Taco had listened to all their planning and was thrilled to find out he would help with the rescue.) Alexandra gently wound the scarf around his entire body, tying it off in a large knot so it would stay on securely. The very cold temperature was a big concern, because she knew macaw parrots were not supposed to be exposed to frigid temperatures. This part of the plan had worried her a lot, that even with the scarf he could become sick. However, the truth was, Taco was the most important part of the rescue plan—without him, there would be no way to rescue Theo.

Gazing at Taco in the moonlight, she almost wanted to giggle—he looked like a miniature mummy with a rather prominent "nose"—only his painted eyes could be seen. The image of a much larger, pipe-smoking mummy suddenly materialized, and she smiled at the thought of "Taco the mummy" riding on Blackie's shoulder for the Halloween parade. She would definitely suggest this costume next year—along with a very appealing bribe. Then, drawing in a breath and telling herself the scarf *would* keep him warm enough, she nodded to Jaclyn and they began walking the bikes down the long driveway to the coast road. Soon, they were on their bikes, pedaling fast under the light of a full moon, the cold night air sweeping over their faces. As they rode side-by-side, Alexandra and Jaclyn grinned at each other. *This was going to work.* And as she looked at the small, heavily wrapped figure in the wicker basket, so brave and focused on their mission, Alexandra knew it was a sight she would never forget.

Down the coast road toward Dark Harbor they sped, soon arriving at The Pine School.

What they had not seen was one lone raven flying high above them in the night sky, dipping in and out behind tall pines, never losing sight of them.

The gate to The Pine School was closed, but they did not need to open it. Their plan was to walk through an opening in a hedge farther down from the gate. They hopped off the bikes, pushing them deep into the snow-covered bushes. Alexandra grabbed the rope and flashlight and placed Taco on her shoulder, and they headed toward the pines on the front lawn.

The huge pine trees had always looked forbidding to Alexandra even during the day, and at night, they really were scary. They were very tall trees with thick curved branches that swept to the ground, so densely packed together the front lawn of The Pine School looked like a small forest. She drew in a deep breath, holding Taco with one hand for support, and they began to move quickly, darting from tree to tree toward the school. Fortunately, with the full moon reflecting off the snowy ground there was enough light to see, so they did not have to use the flashlight. They had not wanted to use it, fearful Headmaster Green, who lived in a small cottage next to the school, would see the light. A dim light was glowing in one of his windows. Luckily, he could not see the back of the school where they were headed.

They were about halfway to the school when Alexandra suddenly stopped, grabbed Jaclyn's arm and gasped loudly. She was staring at the roof of the school. In the light of the moon, two shadowy figures were walking the length of the roof together, arm in arm. Then they turned toward the back of the school, quickly disappearing from sight. The girls looked at each other in wide-eyed silence. Taco's feet dug into Alexandra's shoulder, but he did not make a sound. Alexandra had heard about the legend of two ghosts who sometimes walked the roof of The Pine School. However, she never believed it was true. She was jarred out of her thoughts when Jaclyn pulled on her sleeve, nodding toward the school. They had to keep moving.

As soon as they were under the portico, they began to run to the back of the school. Rounding the corner, they both immediately looked up. The roof was empty. Maybe, Alexandra thought, it had all been imagined.

Theo was watching for them from a small window on the third floor. He waved excitedly when he saw them, quickly opening the window. They waved back, both grinning at the sight of Theo perched on the windowsill. It had really been quite easy, Alexandra thought as she unwound the rope. The plan had worked perfectly, at least so far. Taco would fly one end of the rope up to the window, and Theo would tie it to his heavy metal bed frame that was right next to the window, and then slowly let himself down the rope. Of course, none of this would have been necessary if Theo could have left the third floor, walked down to the main floor, and let himself out through the portico door. However, Headmaster Green locked him in the attic every night. So they had known any escape was going to be more difficult.

With Jaclyn's help, Alexandra gently unwrapped the scarf around Taco. Then she gave him one end of the rope, which he clamped in his strong beak, and he immediately flew toward the window with the rope trailing behind. He landed on the windowsill in seconds. Theo took the end of the rope from Taco, tied it to his bed frame, and then gave them a thumbs-up. He was just starting to get positioned on the windowsill to lower himself to the ground when Alexandra suddenly thought of something she couldn't believe she hadn't thought of during their careful planning.

"Theo!" she whispered loudly. "Wait! Stop!! Taco, can you unlock Theo's door? Try to see if you can!"

Taco disappeared from the window, flying into the attic room.

"Alexandra, I can easily come down the rope. Why do you want Taco to unlock the door?"

Theo was sitting on the sill with the rope in his hand, looking quite confused.

"Because I want to go inside the school for a minute. I want to look at something . . ."

Taco flew back to the open window.

"Unlocked!"

"Great, Taco! Now go downstairs with Theo—we'll meet you at the portico door!"

Theo immediately jumped back into the attic room and they disappeared from sight.

The girls ran around to the portico, and minutes later, the front door opened. Standing inside was Theo, grinning from ear to ear, with

Taco on his shoulder. Even though parrots cannot smile, Alexandra could tell how happy Taco was to have accomplished his mission. As she looked back at Theo, she wondered if he was grinning about the success of the escape plan or because he had a gorgeous macaw sitting on his shoulder.

Probably both.

Alexandra flipped on the flashlight, putting her finger to her lips. It just felt like they should be as quiet as mice. Theo and Jaclyn nodded as she led the way down the main hallway to a door that was hidden by a heavy green velvet curtain. It was a door she had recently discovered when she brought the attendance to Headmaster Green's office. She had always been curious about what was behind the curtain. That day the hallway was empty so she quickly ducked behind the curtain, discovering a locked door with the word "LIBRARY" faintly visible.

They crept behind the curtain and Alexandra held Taco at the level of the doorknob. His curved beak was quickly inside the keyhole. With a couple of twists, the door unlocked. She opened the door, flashing the light around the room. It really was a library, and filled with many more books than the library at Chadwick Manor.

The air smelled musty and stale like something that had been sealed shut for a long time. Suddenly, Alexandra sneezed, which made everyone jump. They stopped to listen. All was quiet. Then she turned the flashlight on the main desk, where a very large book had been left open. They walked over. Alexandra shone the light on the open pages, thick with dust, moving the flashlight across the faded handwritten entries. Jaclyn and Theo were standing on each side of her and Taco was on her shoulder as the light illuminated the very last entry. She read the date aloud. It was just days before her parents died. Then she read further. The last book taken out was *Moby-Dick*. Her father's name was under the "Loaned To" column.

It read, "Borrowed by Headmaster St. Germaine for reading during a sailing vacation to Cape Cod. To be returned upon safe passage home. Call me Ishmael." Tears filled her eyes . . . *upon safe passage home.* It was the last entry. No books had been loaned after that date. The library had been closed at The Pine School. Why? And who was Ishmael?

Alexandra stood looking at her father's elegant handwriting, the last words he might have written, and with one finger, she slowly wiped away the dust. Jaclyn rested her head against Alexandra's shoulder. Theo lowered his head and gently patted her back. She felt Taco nestle close to her neck and reached up to stroke him. Then, with a deep sigh and a last lingering look at his handwriting and around the entombed library, she led the way out and down the hall to the room where they ate lunch—in silence—every day. She had wondered about this room. It was very large. Blackie told her years ago The Pine School had something called a gymnasium, where the students could play sports. As she shone the flashlight on the floor, moving some of the tables, she could see the ghostly outline of colored boundary lines in the wood floor. Blackie had put up a basketball hoop on the outside of the garage many years ago and had explained the rules of the game, so she knew these were the boundary lines of a basketball court. Then, as she was shining the flashlight on the white walls, over in one far corner they all saw the word "GYMNASIUM." Illuminated by the flashlight in the darkened room, the letters were very faint but still visible, as though they were lying beneath a surface of water and not paint, waiting to be seen and read.

Why had all of this changed? What had happened at The Pine School after her parents died? She was lost in thought when they all heard the sound of the front door slamming shut. Taco raised his wings in alarm, but thankfully did not squawk. Alexandra realized Headmaster Green must have seen the shadows of her flashlight through the shutters, because this part of the school was adjacent to his cottage.

Alexandra ran to one window, trying to open it. It would not budge. She ran to the next window—the same thing. Theo tried the others. They were all sealed shut. There was no place to hide and no way out other than the door to the main hallway.

They could hear him wheezing and then calling out, "Who goes there?"

His voice was faint and seemed distant. Alexandra opened the door to the hallway a crack. She could barely see, it was so dark, but he was not in the hallway. Maybe he had gone into his office. She beckoned them to follow her. Taco snuggled as close to her neck as he could get, Jaclyn and Theo followed, and clinging to the hallway wall they made their way very quickly back to the library.

They immediately ran to the back of the library looking for any place to hide. There were some empty lower shelves on adjacent bookshelves, and in seconds, Theo and Taco climbed into one bookshelf and Alexandra and Jaclyn climbed into another. They were facing each other. Moonlight was streaming into the library through very small windows along the upper wall near the ceiling. They had just gotten themselves squeezed in when they heard the door to the library open. Alexandra put her finger to her lips, looking at Taco, who nodded, but as he was nodding she could tell he was about to sneeze. She reached across the narrow aisle quickly, clamping her hand around his beak. Taco's eyes were wide with alarm and surprise, but he did sneeze, and even though the sound was muffled, they all knew Headmaster Green had to have heard something.

"Rapscallions you must be! Come out of hiding or I will find you! To the Turret you will go, for the rest of the school year!!"

His voice was quaking with anger and he began wheezing and

coughing. Then he sneezed very loudly and repeatedly. He left when his sneezing attack would not stop, never walking to the back of the library. They waited for what seemed like forever in their cramped hiding places. Finally, they heard the sound of the front door slamming shut.

Headmaster Green was gone.

It was the years and years of dust that saved them.

* ◆ *

When the small band finally arrived back at a darkened Chadwick Manor it was almost midnight. They had pushed their bikes most of the way because it was uphill, and Theo was walking, so it took longer to get home. As they walked, Alexandra told Theo about Olivia. She and Jaclyn had talked about this and decided he needed to know Olivia was their aunt and about the surprise reunion planned for Thanksgiving Day. Theo had been speechless, shaking his head in amazement as the story was told. Taco was again bundled in the scarf, sitting in the wicker basket for the return trip home. They were about halfway to Chadwick when he began to visibly shiver and shake. Alexandra immediately scooped him up, holding him close the rest of the way home.

Again, they did not see the raven following them, circling high in the night sky overhead.

Carefully and quietly, they rolled the bicycles back into the garage, and then headed to the main house. Alexandra reached into her pants pocket for the key to unlock the side door of Chadwick and they were quickly inside. (Remembering that Evelyn always made sure the doors were locked before going to bed and they would need a key to get back in was all part of a very detailed checklist they had written up, so nothing would be overlooked.) Theo was trying to take everything in, his head swiveling as they ran down the dimly lit hallway. He stopped in his tracks upon encountering the two large tigers standing watch in the foyer, his face full of surprise. At night, their green eyes shimmered and appeared to be illuminated from within. As they quietly crept up the stairs to Alexandra's room, Theo glanced back at the lifelike tigers more than once. They really did look like they could spring from their pedestals at any moment.

Taco immediately flew to his cage, tucked his head under one wing, and was soon fast asleep, snoring. Flopping on the bed, Alexandra, Jaclyn, and Theo started laughing at the same time. Even though their cheeks, hands, and feet were cold, they all felt warm inside. The plan had worked *perfectly*. Theo was *finally* out of that dreadful school. He was slowly looking around Alexandra's room when he got up to study the beach scene mural more closely. As he turned back to the bed, his gaze swept over to the corner of the room. He blinked in astonishment and walked over to the brass pole, whistling softly under his breath. It was obvious he wanted to try it. Alexandra grinned, nodding, and down he went with a whoosh. They peered down at him through the hole, trying not to laugh, not wanting to be heard. He was back up the stairs in no time, beaming, and went down a few more times. After the last run, he flopped on the bed, staring up at the canopy.

"Thank you . . ."

His voice was husky and emotional. They were silent for a while and then Alexandra told Theo where he would be sleeping—and staying—until the time was right to tell her grandmother. The girls had agreed it was best to wait until after Olivia arrived to introduce someone else to their grandmother.

One new person at a time.

They led Theo silently down the hall, heading to the staircase that went to the third floor. As they approached Nicolas's room they could see light from underneath his door, and then it was quickly extinguished. Alexandra fleetingly wondered if he had been spying on them, but she did not see how that was possible, and decided his light going out was just a coincidence. He often read late into the night. Cautiously and quietly, she opened the door to the third-floor staircase with another key "borrowed" from Evelyn's large circle of keys, which hung in the kitchen, and up they went.

It had been a surprise when she and Jaclyn first secretly explored the third floor of Chadwick. They found six small bedrooms, each with twin beds, a chest of drawers, two small desks with chairs, and a tiny closet. There were also two large bathrooms, each with a footed tub. Evelyn had told her many guests visited Chadwick when her mother was a young girl, so Alexandra assumed these were extra rooms for more guests once all the second-floor rooms were occupied. However, she thought it quite odd there were two desks in each room.

Together, late at night, Jaclyn and Alexandra had fixed up one of the small bedrooms for Theo. It was perfect. They found a small space heater in the garage that made the room toasty warm, made up one bed with sheets and blankets, and filled some of the drawers with clothes secretly taken from Nicolas's laundry (all black or navy blue, of course). They put some books to read and cards for solitaire on one desk. At night, with the lamps lit over the beds, the small room looked very cozy. One bathroom was cleaned and filled with towels, soap, shampoo, toothpaste, and a toothbrush. They even checked to see if the water did, in fact, get hot. It did. The last thing to figure out, which was all-important, was food. Secretly, they had taken some raisins, crackers, and cookies from the kitchen, but they knew Theo would need a lot more food if he had to stay hidden for a while. This posed the biggest problem of all—how to get food to Theo—and led to the best discovery of all. They discovered the dumbwaiter that went from the kitchen to the second floor also went to the third floor.

Alexandra had grown up knowing about the small elevator. She had wanted to ride in it since she was very little, but Evelyn always said no, "A dumbwaiter is for food, not people." On her birthday each year, Evelyn sent up breakfast in the dumbwaiter, but that was the only time it was ever used.

Still, she had always wanted to ride in it.

One day when Evelyn had gone to Weston's Market, they decided to go for a ride. Jaclyn's eyes danced with anticipation. She did not seem worried at all. As they were climbing in, she asked Alexandra why it was called a "dumbwaiter." It was a very odd name. Alexandra thought about it and then answered (guessing), because the elevator sent food to people without a real person delivering it. It seemed logical anyway, and Jaclyn nodded, seeming to agree.

However, Alexandra had thought about the possibility of being stuck somewhere between floors.

She figured if that happened someone would eventually hear them yelling, and Blackie would be able to get it running again. They barely fit in the box-shaped elevator, sitting with their knees pulled tightly to their chests and their heads lowered. There were three buttons labeled K, 2, and 3. Jaclyn pressed 2, and the door slowly shut. The dumbwaiter had a small round window in the door, like ships have, but once they began moving up, it was pitch-black inside. The motor had a low hum, slowly taking them to the second floor right across from Nicolas's room. It was nerve wracking when a soft bell rang as they reached the second floor and the door automatically opened. Nicolas's bedroom door was open and he was not in his room—which was very lucky—and they both breathed a big sigh of relief. Alexandra immediately pressed 3, and they slowly continued up to the third floor.

Grinning at each other as the dumbwaiter door opened, they knew it was *perfect* for their plan. Late at night, or when Evelyn was away shopping or in her room, they could send food, drinks, and notes to Theo. It was going to make it so much easier than trying to hide everything and carry it all past Nicolas's room.

All of their detective work had been well worth the effort—one small room on the third floor of Chadwick Manor was the perfect hiding place for one runaway boarder from The Pine School.

As they showed Theo everything they had done in his room and the bathroom (he was completely amazed), and were about to leave, Alexandra suddenly remembered the dumbwaiter.

"Oh, Theo, how could I forget what is most important?! This is called a dumbwaiter. It runs from the kitchen to the second and third floors. When the coast is clear late at night, we'll send you food and notes. You'll hear a bell ring and the door will open. Just take out the tray. When you're done, put the tray back and press *K* for kitchen. We'll get up very early in the morning, before Evelyn, to clean everything up."

"Just don't press *2*, because it would open right across from Nicolas's room!" Jaclyn quickly interrupted.

Theo nodded and grinned.

"Brilliant, a tiny lift!"

Both girls looked somewhat puzzled and he seemed to understand.

"A lift is what Brits call an elevator. This will be perfect!" Theo said, marveling at the small square opening in the wall.

"Well, we're going to send you a turkey dinner late tomorrow night . . . in the lift. It might be around midnight, so you'll have to stay awake," Alexandra replied smiling.

"I am sure my stomach will stay awake, so not to worry!"

"Oh, and I have to lock you in, Theo. I'm sorry to have to follow in

Headmaster Green's footsteps, but I don't want Nicolas to be able to open the door," Alexandra said, frowning a bit. She did feel bad about having to do this, but felt there was no choice.

"Being locked in is just fine with me. I could stay here forever . . ."

Theo was looking around smiling and pushing his glasses up on his nose, as though he was standing inside a beautiful palace admiring his elegant accommodations.

They whispered good night, crept down the stairs, and locked the door.

It was going to be an amazing Thanksgiving at Chadwick Manor.

A TURKEY IN THE DUMBWAITER AND A VERY SPECIAL VISITOR

Evelyn and Blackie were always up early every day, but on Thanksgiving, it was *very* early.

They always worked together to prepare all the delicious food for Thanksgiving. Blackie was in charge of the pies—apple pie, pumpkin pie, and pecan pie. He said the best dessert was a sliver of each along with a big scoop of vanilla ice cream. The grown-ups enjoyed all three pies but Alexandra always had just the apple. She loved watching Blackie roll out the chilled dough on the marble counter with the wooden rolling pin, periodically adding flour so it wouldn't stick, then trimming the edges for a perfect circle. (From the scraps of dough he made small tarts; once baked, he would fill them with raspberry jam for a midmorning "sweet treat.") Often, he would carve her initial, *A*, into the dough, surrounded by a heart, for the top crust of the apple pie.

There was so much to prepare for the dinner . . . butternut squash, fresh green beans, fluffy mashed potatoes, cranberry relish, celery, every kind of olive, sausage stuffing to go in the turkey, and a jellied salad made with pineapple and shaved carrots. The huge turkey was always fresh and had to be "dressed," as Evelyn called it, which had something to do with putting in the stuffing and then sewing it up with heavy string and long steel pins. It was the first thing they worked on, because it had to go in the oven very early so it would be ready by three o'clock. Alexandra still remembered the year Taco found out the turkey was a bird. He was sitting on his perch in the kitchen watching the preparations when Blackie referred to it as "the bird." Taco had looked at the cooked turkey, then at Blackie, and back again at the turkey in utter disbelief. He had raised his wings, and then flapped them ferociously with a look of both panic and shock on his face. It had taken a lot of explaining, and they were never entirely sure if he had stopped worrying that a parrot might be on someone's platter on Thanksgiving Day.

The gravy was last—also Blackie's job—and he was very fussy about it. He needed something called giblets, drippings from the turkey pan, flour, and lots of hot water. It always took a while and a lot of tasting before he declared the gravy was perfect. (And it always was.) Over the years, the preparations for the Thanksgiving meal had become well-orchestrated traditions in the Chadwick household, and quite simply, were not subject to change.

Soon, the sounds of a busy kitchen could be heard early on this Thanksgiving morning, with two cooks in the kitchen, both wearing frilly aprons. It always made Alexandra laugh to see Blackie wearing one of Evelyn's aprons, but he would wink and say it was better than ruining his shirt.

Alexandra was sound asleep when she heard Taco calling to her.

"Wake up, princess, Thanksgiving!"

She did not want to wake up. It felt so good to sleep because she had been so tired. As she slowly awakened, even before her eyes were open, she grinned. This was the day another family member would join them. Her stomach suddenly had butterflies just thinking about the excitement the day would bring. She opened her eyes, stretched, hugged her pillow, and then reached for the photo of her parents. For the first time she could ever remember, she felt herself smiling as she looked at them. Without realizing it, she had reached for her necklace and was rubbing the round disc in her fingers.

"Olivia . . ."

As she said the name aloud, she realized Taco heard her—he was staring at her, tipping his head from one side to the other. He had to be told before Olivia arrived. Alexandra got up and went to his cage.

"Taco, I have something to tell you. I know it will make you very, very happy. Olivia is going to come today for Thanksgiving dinner—to surprise Grand Mama . . ."

She stopped and watched him. He was staring at her, obviously surprised, so she continued.

"Taco, no one will ever know you saw her being kidnapped from the hospital. That will always be our secret. Grand Mama will never know. Olivia will tell her what happened . . . the whole truth. *Olivia found us,* Taco. She does not know you were there and saw what happened. And I will never tell her." (Alexandra knew this was a tiny lie she had to tell him.) "Everyone knows she's coming today except, of course, Grand Mama. It's going to be the most wonderful surprise, ever!"

Alexandra put her hand in the cage to stroke him. As happy as she knew he was about Olivia, she also knew he still felt burdened by the secret he had kept for so many years. Then he nodded. His eyes were very soft, and one tiny tear fell down his painted face.

In a whispered voice he said, "Olivia . . . coming home."

* ✦ *

The girls had the job of setting the very long dining room table. It was actually way too long for the small number of people who would be sitting down to dinner. The table had felt a mile long when there were just four of them for so many years. Her grandmother would sit at one end, Blackie at the other end, and she and Evelyn would be on either side in the center. It always felt rather ridiculous because they almost had to shout to talk to each other. However, it was what her grandmother wanted, so they always had Thanksgiving and Christmas dinners in the formal dining room.

Alexandra took out the silverware from a drawer in a large hutch. Placemats decorated with turkeys along with matching linen napkins were stacked at one end of the table. They had already talked about this, wondering if they should set a place for Olivia or not. It was decided they would—that it would actually be a part of the plan. So there would be Alexandra's, Jaclyn's, and Olivia's place settings on one side, and Nicolas's and Evelyn's on the other. Blackie and her grandmother would be in their usual seats at each end of the table. Olivia would sit between Alexandra and her grandmother. The placements were arranged and the silverware set, along with water and wine glasses for the grown-ups and heavy glass milk tumblers for the children. Jaclyn told her Nicolas had been allowed to have wine on special occasions, but Alexandra decided he should have milk. He was not a grown-up, even if he thought he was.

In a closet near the dining room, Alexandra found the two decorative feathered turkeys always placed on the center of the table for Thanksgiving. Pumpkin-colored candles in two crystal candelabras completed the table setting. She stood back and looked at the gleaming cherry table, set for *seven* people. Alexandra thought it had never before looked so inviting.

The aroma of turkey was starting to wisp its way from under the swinging door. Smelling the turkey cooking all day was one of the things Alexandra liked the most about Thanksgiving. The girls checked on the cooks periodically and shared their secret with silent smiles. One time they all huddled together in a big hug. It felt to Alexandra like her heart would burst if three o'clock did not come soon.

Around one o'clock, Alexandra and Jaclyn went upstairs to get dressed and wait.

As they sat in silence on the window seat, Alexandra was thinking about how waiting for anything you wanted to happen made it feel like time moved in slow motion. However, it was also true that time in Chadwick Manor was not a silent visitor. Instead, it was announced unfailingly and precisely. The antique grandfather clock in the living room marked every hour and half hour, all day and all night every day, the chimes echoing throughout Chadwick and up the marble staircases. Growing up, the ticking of the large clock and the reverberating chiming gongs had been a constant presence in her life.

Finally, there were two gongs and then one. It was two thirty. They looked at each other with excitement knowing she would arrive any moment. The plan was for Olivia to wait in her car until three o'clock, and then come around to the front door of Chadwick. Their gaze was fixed on the long stone driveway bordered by tall hedges and pine trees (the driveway eventually disappeared from sight around a curve). Then they saw the car. A small red sports car with a black convertible top came slowly down the drive. Alexandra instantly thought of her parents. They had left for their sailing trip in a small convertible, waving good-bye to her. She had imagined the scene in her mind countless times. Olivia was arriving in the same car she had imagined, even the same red color. It all felt like a dream.

Jaclyn jumped up first with Alexandra and Taco quickly following. They were down the brass pole and in the kitchen seconds later, the girls whispering excitedly to Blackie and Evelyn that she had arrived.

Suddenly, the swinging door opened and Silver walked into the kitchen. She was wearing an ice-blue floor-length velvet skirt and matching ruffled silk blouse, with long strings of pearls around her neck and pearl drop earrings.

"Well, there must be something afoot with all the whispering?" Silver asked smiling, with a quizzical expression on her face.

Before anyone could answer (all relieved no one had to), Nicolas strode through the door with Noir on his shoulder. Silver's expression changed as her eyes fell upon Noir, and she looked at her grandson disapprovingly.

"Nicolas, Noir must be in his cage. You have been forgetting this rule lately, it seems. Noir cannot be loose. We have spoken about this."

Nicolas frowned but did as he was told, striding back out of the kitchen in silence. Taco seemed quite satisfied hearing the admonishment, and then everyone filed out of the kitchen behind Silver, who led the way to the dining room.

Taco flew to his perch, which had been moved from the kitchen to the dining room. He would get a bowl of fruit and some palm nuts when they began to eat. The golden brown turkey was on a huge platter, "resting" as Blackie called it. (Taco had looked at the turkey somewhat askance, and clearly not without some lingering concern.) Gravy boats were filled, and the vegetables were in elegant covered dishes. Evelyn lit the candles and poured the wine and milk, and the cooks took off their well-used aprons. Blackie was wearing a white shirt with a red bow tie and a chocolate brown cardigan sweater. Evelyn's dress was a deep plum color, and a large gold turkey pin anchored a lavender-hued silk scarf.

Blackie held her grandmother's chair and then Evelyn's. Then Nicolas walked in and placed Noir's cage next to his chair and sat down.

Silver Chadwick had just draped her napkin across her lap when she noticed the extra place setting between her seat and Alexandra's. Her blue eyes were intense and questioning as she looked directly at Alexandra. Before she could say anything, Alexandra spoke.

"Grand Mama, could we let each person say what they are thankful for? I would like to be last." It felt like her voice was quivering, but she hoped it was not noticeable.

Her grandmother nodded "yes," while still staring at the extra place setting.

"Jaclyn, will you be first?" Alexandra asked, turning to look at her cousin seated next to her.

Jaclyn nodded, clasped her hands, and shut her eyes very tight.

"I want to say merci, thank you, to Grand-Mère and everyone here for making us feel like this is home for Nicolas and me. And for Biscuit and Noir, too. And to say j'adore, I love all of you."

Jaclyn opened her eyes and looked across the table at her brother, whose eyes were cast down.

Next, Alexandra nodded to Blackie.

"To the lassies and the lad at this table, thank you for making me feel I am part of this special family. I am grateful we can *all* be together today and for this magnificent tom turkey!"

Alexandra noticed he seemed to emphasize "all" and smiled at him. His blue eyes looked teary and he winked back at her, smiling.

Next, she looked at Evelyn.

"To my darlings, you have given me a family, too, just like Blackie. There is nothing in the world more important than family. My heart is full."

When she said "family" her voice broke, and she wiped a tear from her eye with her napkin.

Alexandra looked across the table at Nicolas, wondering what he would say. His dark eyes showed no emotion as he looked back at her. Then he looked down.

"J'aimerais vous remercier de votre aide, Grand-Mère. Et Noir."

His voice was very soft, and he kept his eyes lowered for a moment after he finished. Alexandra was not sure what he said, but thought it had something to do with aid or help from one word that sounded familiar.

There was sadness in her grandmother's eyes, even though she had smiled at him when he looked up, and then it was her grandmother's turn.

"Well, I think I have the most to be thankful for. I have the most wonderful grandchildren and two of the best friends and companions any person could ask for. These are all very great blessings for which I am deeply grateful. My dearest love to all of you and Happy Thanksgiving."

Alexandra was next. She looked at Blackie and he nodded. His eyes seemed to send her courage. She had memorized what she was going to say and knew her aunt was now waiting at the front door. Then she drew in a deep breath, hoping her voice would not tremble, and bowed her head.

"I am so thankful for all of you and that my family has grown. I never knew I had cousins. I'm so glad I do . . . and that you are living with us . . ."

She paused, turning to look at Jaclyn and then at Nicolas. Jaclyn looked up and smiled, but Nicolas was again looking down. Then she continued.

"I know there are tragedies in life. But miracles can happen and today there is a miracle I am so thankful for, and why there is a place next to me, Grand Mama."

Alexandra's eyes filled with tears as she looked at the person she loved the most. Her grandmother was now leaning back in her chair, her eyes wide with question and surprise, yet somehow also guarded. One hand was on her chest.

Blackie had gone to the front door and in seconds there she was, standing next to Blackie, her arm tucked through his. Olivia looked radiant. Her cheeks were rosy and her black hair glistened in the afternoon sunlight streaming in from the large window. She was wearing a long kilt skirt in blue and brown plaid and a heather-blue turtleneck sweater with a deep brown scarf. Alexandra could see the glint of the gold disc necklace and without thinking put her hand to hers.

Tears were falling down her grandmother's cheeks like tiny raindrops. Olivia ran to her, dropped to her knees, and then put her arms around the diminutive, elegant woman who was her mother.

"It is me, mother. It is *Olivia*. You lost me a long time ago, but I did not die. Now I have found you . . . and that is all that matters . . ."

Olivia reached for her necklace, holding the small disc for her mother to see. Silver gently took the disc in her fingers and studied it, then looked into the face she never thought she would see. At the same moment, as though rushing upward from watery depths and breaking through the ocean's surface, she saw an identical face appear and then the two melded into one, and she placed her hands on one face belonging to two daughters.

Silver slowly stood, and they held each other for a very long time. She was saying, "Olivia," over and over again.

* ◆ *

The rest of the dinner was a blur of talking and laughing and tears and just looking at this person who had been a ghost for so long, who was now real. Slowly, the delicious food was eaten as Alexandra,

Jaclyn, and Olivia told the stories: how Olivia became the new teacher in Classroom #6 when Miss Blueberry retired, about the bookmark falling and Alexandra seeing the necklace, their secret visit to Olivia's apartment in Dark Harbor with the photo of her parents, and the plan they had all worked on for Thanksgiving. And very gently, Olivia told her mother the truth about what had happened all those years ago in a London hospital. When she began, Alexandra got up and put Taco on her lap. She knew it was going to be very hard for him to listen.

At some point during dinner, Olivia was introduced to Taco. She had gotten up, stood in front of his perch smiling, and then reached out to stroke his long feathers. He had gazed at her with a very tender, loving look. Watching him, Alexandra realized how emotional this had to be for him—he was looking into the same face as her mother's, and she knew the memory of what happened so long ago still weighed heavily upon him. Olivia was also introduced to Noir. That was a very different kind of introduction. Noir had just glared at her through the wire cage.

After dinner, there was a tour of Chadwick Manor, and then Olivia and her mother went to the conservatory, sitting together for hours as darkness fell and the stars came out on a cold Thanksgiving night.

It was about nine o'clock when Olivia said good night to her mother, leaving her in her bedroom off the conservatory, and then came to the kitchen to say good night to everyone. Alexandra had wanted her to stay the night, but Olivia said she needed to go home after such a long and emotional day. There were hugs all around and she promised she would be back the next day.

Later that night, Blackie made some turkey sandwiches and they sat together around the oak table in the kitchen, just the three of them, Alexandra, Jaclyn, and Blackie, reliving the most amazing day. It had also been a very long day, and it was not over yet.

That there was another yet-to-be-introduced person in the house had not been forgotten.

Once they finished the last of the cider and sandwiches, Alexandra told Blackie they would put everything away and he should go to bed, "tout de suite" as Jaclyn told him, with a mischievous grin. Without much argument he had agreed, but told them they needed to do a good clean-up job or he would have to deal with the consequences of one unhappy Evelyn, then out the swinging door he went.

Lifting the heavy platter out of the refrigerator and then pulling off the dampened cloth, they could see the large turkey had been carved to the bone on one side, but the other side was untouched, including one plump turkey leg. They debated what to do. Jaclyn said they should put the platter with the entire leftover turkey on the dumbwaiter and send it up because Theo was probably starving, having only eaten raisins and crackers all day. Alexandra thought they should try to carve it up, but she had never carved anything with a sharp knife. In the end, Jaclyn prevailed, and the dumbwaiter was filled with the turkey on the platter, along with gravy, mashed potatoes, stuffing, and green beans, all of which they had reheated on the stove and then placed in small serving dishes. Tucked here and there around the platter were a tall glass of milk and a big piece of apple pie (but no ice cream—it might melt before he ate it), napkins, a plate, a carving knife, and utensils.

Last, a note. Alexandra wrote it as they decided together what to say.

Dear Theo,

We missed you at Thanksgiving and we are sorry you could not eat with us. It was amazing. Aunt Olivia met her mother and the reunion cannot be put into words. We will work on everything tomorrow. Hopefully you can come out of hiding.

Please eat as much turkey as you want and just send everything back when you're done. Press K for kitchen. We are getting up very early tomorrow before Evelyn to put it all away.

Alexandra & Jaclyn

P.S. We will send up more food when the coast is clear.

Alexandra folded the note and placed it under the utensils. She pressed the button for *3*, and they watched as the door slowly closed. They heard the quiet hum of the motor raise the dumbwaiter, now laden with a midnight Thanksgiving feast, as it slowly made its way to the third floor, both girls hoping Theo was still awake. Two content conspirators then crept out of the kitchen, knowing their third-floor stowaway was not going to starve.

Before getting into bed, as tired as she was, Alexandra woke Taco, who clearly did not appreciate it. She told him to wake her up at 6:00 a.m. *sharp*. He had blinked sleepily and nodded.

However, even parrots can oversleep.

THE DISCOVERY

The morning came early but not as early as Alexandra had planned.

There was a firm rapping on her door that woke her.

"Mouse, my mouse, wake up!"

She realized it was Evelyn as she pushed through her sound sleep and then sat up instantly, as if an electric shock had run through her. She had overslept. The door opened and in came Evelyn, quite flushed, holding a piece of paper she handed to Alexandra. Taco was also waking up with the commotion, and in a sleepy voice said, "Six o'clock, six o'clock, time to wake up, princess!" Alexandra looked at him quickly and in equal parts wanted to laugh and scold him. Then she read the note.

> DEAR ALEXANDRA & JACLYN,
>
> I HAVE NEVER HAD A MORE EXCELLENT MEAL. (NOR HAVE I EVER BEEN SERVED A WHOLE, OR I GUESS MORE ACCURATELY, HALF A TURKEY ON A PLATTER.) I WAS DOZING OFF BUT HEARING THE BELL, JUMPED UP TO FIND THE MOST AMAZING TRAY OF FOOD AS THE LIFT DOOR OPENED. JUST WISH YOU COULD HAVE SEEN MY FACE. PURE HEAVEN. I CAN LIVE LIKE THIS FOREVER, NO NEED TO HURRY. UNDERSTAND IT MAY TAKE SOME TIME. HOPE YOU WILL VISIT WHENEVER THE COAST IS CLEAR.
>
> THEO

Alexandra took a deep breath.

"I can explain everything, Evelyn. I was supposed to get down to the kitchen very early, but apparently my alarm clock was asleep," she said, turning to give Taco a stern look.

"Anyway, this note is from Theo, you know, my friend from The Pine School. You remember, Evelyn, he was going to be all alone again this Thanksgiving . . . he just found out he is an orphan and has no money, you remember. But we didn't ask Grand Mama about his coming to live here because so much was happening with Aunt Olivia, and she said he had to stay at school as a boarder . . ."

Alexandra looked into the kind face she knew so well, got out of bed, and put her arms around Evelyn. As always, she felt the hug come back.

"All right, 'tis all right, my mouse. Your secret is good with me. I knew 'twas the poor lad, Theo, and I sent him breakfast already, but no note," Evelyn replied, shaking her head and laughing softly.

"Not to worry, Theo won't starve. I'll put his meals on the lift until he comes out of hiding. But best tell your grandmother . . . and sooner rather than later. She has a keen sense of things, as you know, my mouse," she said with one eyebrow raised, and then hurried out the door.

Alexandra sat down on her bed and reread the note, smiling. Then she looked at her partner in crime who had missed his cue. He was looking most uncomfortable.

"Well, Taco, that was a close call. Thank goodness Evelyn found the note."

Taco put his head under his wing feathers and wouldn't look at her, and then she headed for Jaclyn's room.

Jaclyn's eyes were wide with concern. They were sitting on Jaclyn's bed after Alexandra had wakened her with news of the discovery.

"Taco ne s'est pas réveillé à temps, Taco overslept? Evelyn found the tray of food in the dumbwaiter?! Catastrophe!"

"No, it really wasn't a catastrophe," Alexandra replied, pronouncing it with the same inflection, smiling quickly.

"But thank goodness it wasn't Nicolas or Grand Mama who found it. Evelyn said she would send food up to Theo, and I know she will help us for a while . . . but we have to tell Grand Mama soon. If we don't, she's going to discover he's up there . . . somehow."

Alexandra was worried and concerned. She needed to find the right words to tell her grandmother about Theo, and it was not going to be easy.

"What if Grand-Mère sends him back? Headmaster Green will be furious and who knows what he would do. He might not give Theo any food—for days! Theo could freeze and starve, geler et mourir de faim!"

As she looked at Jaclyn's furrowed brow, her cousin's words hung in the air. Whenever Nicolas or Jaclyn spoke in French, she could hear the emotion in almost every word, making English sound dull and flat. French was more like listening to music, as if musical notes were attached to each syllable and she was hearing strands of music, not spoken words. Her thoughts returned to Theo. The musical refrain she was hearing now was not a melody but instead was a sharp horn, a warning sound.

"We will never let her do that, Jaclyn. Never. Theo must live with us from now on."

However, she had no idea how that would be accomplished.

* ◆ *

They dressed, ate breakfast, and then went to see their grand-mother, who was having her breakfast in bed.

"Come in, my dears."

Once again, the greeting came first before the knock at her door. Alexandra and Jaclyn looked at one another and in they went.

Her grandmother looked happier than Alexandra had ever seen her before.

"What a wonderful morning this is! My daughter is alive and has returned to me . . . and you girls and Nicolas have an aunt!"

"I know, Grand Mama. It's so wonderful. It almost feels like my own mother has come back. When she came into my classroom for the first time that is how I felt . . . as soon as I saw her."

"Yes, my darling, I am sure that is what you felt. It is a miracle, just as you said."

She took a sip of the steaming tea and closed her eyes for a moment.

"Yesterday was one of the happiest days of my life."

Her eyes opened, she put aside the breakfast tray, and pulled away the covers.

"I must dress and put on my face," she said, swinging her legs out of bed and winking at her granddaughters.

"So, you girls run along and have fun. Olivia will be back this afternoon."

They both heard the joy and wonder in their grandmother's voice when she spoke the name that had not been spoken for so, so long.

It was not the time to ask about Theo, but surely, the right opportunity would come soon.

That afternoon the opportunity came all too quickly, but not the way they had imagined.

They were outside running in the maze with Max and Biscuit. A light snow had fallen overnight, leaving a fresh whiteness to the landscape. As the dogs chased them through the hedge maze, they heard their grandmother call and wound their way out, running across the snowy yard to the conservatory door. As Silver opened the door, they were met by a blast of warm, humid air. It was almost shocking during the winter, coming into what felt like a rain forest from the snow and frigid temperatures. They knew instantly something was wrong from the expression on her face.

Theo. It had to be.

"I had a call from Headmaster Green a short while ago. He told me Theodore is missing. When he went to bring him breakfast yesterday morning he was gone and was nowhere to be found. He immediately contacted the Dark Harbor police, but they have not been able to find Theodore. Headmaster Green told me he found a length of rope tied to Theodore's bed and the third-floor window was raised. Obviously, Theodore left The Pine School by climbing down a rope. And that is not all." She paused while looking at the doorway to her room.

"Come in, Nicolas."

Nicolas walked into the conservatory with Noir on his shoulder. They both looked smug. Alexandra and Jaclyn glanced at each other quickly. This was definitely not good.

"Tell Alexandra and Jaclyn what you told me, Nicolas."

"I told Grand-Mère I heard the door to the third floor being opened and footsteps going up the night before last. I also told her that from my room I have heard le monte-plats go to the third floor and back down. Today, I heard it ce matin et au déjeuner."

"Thank you, Nicolas. That will be all. And Nicolas, this will be the last time Noir is loose. Do I make myself clear?"

Nicolas looked disappointed, annoyed, and angry all at once.

Noir was clearly angry. It seemed as though Nicolas was going to say something but reconsidered and left in silence.

"Come and sit with me, Alexandra and Jaclyn."

Alexandra's mind was racing. How could they prevent Theo from being sent back? What were the right words—in French or English—that would make her grandmother understand it was like sentencing Theo to prison to live at The Pine School? How would you say that in French, sentenced to prison, solitary confinement?

As they sat down, Taco flew into the conservatory to his perch. He was studying everyone, and Alexandra was certain he understood this was serious business.

"My dears, I understand you are concerned for Theodore, but he is not our family, and Headmaster Green wants him to board. From what he said, and he was quite agitated on the phone, Theodore is the only boarder this year, so the income is important to the school. This is what his aunt and uncle had wanted. As you know, I am paying for these costs and I am happy to do so, but he must live at the school. However, I have decided he may come and visit occasionally. So, please retrieve Theodore from the attic and bring him to the conservatory so that we may be introduced. Tell him not to be afraid. I am sure he is a very nice young man. And I am sorry, truly sorry, he is an orphan."

Alexandra swallowed hard and fought back the tears, but they slipped down her cheeks. This was cruel and unfair and had to be stopped, but how? How??

Just at that moment, Olivia appeared in the doorway. To Alexandra, she looked like an angel who had arrived in a moment of need.

"Hello! I was told all the ladies were in the conservatory . . . but am I interrupting something?"

Her broad smile faded as she scanned their faces.

"Hello, my dearest Olivia! Come and give me a hug. We are

discussing something. Perhaps we should ask your thoughts as you know the person we are talking about. Come and sit."

Alexandra felt relief flood through her. Olivia hugged her mother and then sat next to her, listening intently as Silver Chadwick repeated all that had transpired. Periodically she looked at Alexandra and Jaclyn with interest, at times struggling not to smile. After the story was told, Olivia sat in silence for a few moments, then got up and walked over to the glass wall of the conservatory and stood looking out at the vast backyard of Chadwick Manor. The soft splash of water from the fountains was the only sound. It felt like the stress that had filled the room was beginning to subside. Olivia began speaking while still looking outside with her back to them.

"I know Theo. He is a wonderful student and young man. He has had a very rough year finding out about his parents and the lack of funds. I also know that no young person should have to live alone. Theo must have people around him who care. I am certain I can convince Headmaster Green he should live here with Alexandra and her cousins. Mother, this is something within your power to do. It will make a huge difference in this young person's life. I hope you will agree with me . . . Theo should live here."

Olivia turned around and faced her mother as she spoke the last words. Her green eyes looked gray, like a winter sky, and were deeply serious.

Both girls studied their grandmother's face. She was looking intently at her daughter, her new daughter, and seemed almost to be in a trance, lost in thought and far away. Then she came back to the present and nodding her head said, "Yes, Olivia, you are right."

THEO GETS SETTLED

"Yes, Olivia, you are right."

They were the best words *ever*.

Everything happened quickly as soon as they were spoken. Alexandra and Jaclyn practically flew to the stairs but stopped suddenly, smiled at each other, and then raced back to the kitchen. They quickly told Evelyn, who said she was glad it was sooner rather than later, then Alexandra grabbed a piece of paper and pencil and they scrambled into the dumbwaiter and pressed 3. As the small elevator began to make its ascent, Alexandra wrote in large print, "WELCOME HOME THEO!" The tiny compartment still smelled of tuna fish salad, which Evelyn had obviously sent him for lunch. They were grinning so hard it hurt.

The bell rang, the door opened and there was Theo looking perplexed and a little scared. He had just returned his lunch dishes, having now had three incredible meals in a row. Slowly, he walked toward them, almost as though he didn't want to, reluctant to read whatever was written on the piece of paper. Pushing up his glasses, he stood there looking like he could not believe what he was reading, shaking his head. Alexandra and Jaclyn jumped out of the dumbwaiter and in seconds they were all hugging and laughing. An ending that had seemed all but impossible just a short time ago had come true. Then they breathlessly recounted everything. Mostly that their aunt had come to his rescue. Theo listened, took off his glasses, and wiped his eyes.

In an instant, they were running down the stairs from the third floor with a clatter of footsteps—silent steps no longer necessary.

Alexandra realized Nicolas must have heard them as they sailed by his door. He had lost. They had won. For a fleeting moment, she felt sorry for him. All he had was Noir, no other friends. They rounded the hallway corner with Theo in the lead. He ran directly into Alexandra's room, around her bed and to the corner. With a huge grin, he grabbed on to the brass pole and was downstairs in a blink, followed by Alexandra and Jaclyn.

First stop was the kitchen where Evelyn was washing dishes with bubbles up to her elbows.

"Nice to finally meet you, Theo. Sorry I did not send any notes. 'Twill be jolly to have another Brit at Chadwick . . . and if a growin' lad were to want a midnight snack, no one would be the wiser," she said with a wink and a big smile.

Theo swallowed hard and thanked her, then looked around the large kitchen at the gleaming copper pots, the oak cabinets and long marble counters, the fireplace and round oak table. Spying the dumbwaiter, he walked over and looked through the tiny porthole, shaking his head, grinning.

Then they were through the swinging door and running down the back hall. Alexandra and Jaclyn were in the lead, heading toward their grandmother's rooms and the conservatory, but Theo suddenly slowed and then stopped. He was looking at the stained-glass windows, walking slowly, studying each scene. Theo loved to draw and had a strong interest in art. When the books had begun appearing in Classroom #6, he always wanted to read any books about art. Upon reaching the double doors leading to their grandmother's rooms, he stopped again and adjusted his glasses, looking back in wonder and amazement. The grand hallway resembled the sanctuary of an ancient cathedral, its beauty and serenity powerful and captivating, and Theo had obviously fallen under its spell. After a few moments, Jaclyn gently took his hand

and led him into the pink rooms infused with the fragrance of roses. The door in the wall was open and they could see Olivia and their grandmother sitting in the Adirondack chairs talking. Alexandra went through first, followed by Jaclyn, and then Theo. Theo once again paused to look before stepping into the conservatory.

It was like entering a tropical garden, with green lush plants everywhere from floor to ceiling. Roses were blooming on trellises and the sound of water slipping over tiered fountains filled the room. Taco was still sitting on his perch and when Theo appeared in the doorway, he excitedly opened his wings twice to greet him. Theo pushed up his glasses, grinning, and gave him a quick salute.

"Grand Mama, this is Theo, Theodore Arthur Eddington," Alexandra said, smiling proudly at Theo as she introduced him by his full proper name. From the first time he had written his full name on a note, she thought it sounded so impressive and *so* British.

Then she continued.

"Theo, this is my grandmother, Silver Chadwick."

Theo's cheeks became noticeably red as he walked across the conservatory and extended his hand to the petite figure.

"It is very nice to meet you, Mrs. Chadwick. And, um, thank you for inviting me to stay here for the school year. Thank you. Thank you, so very much."

She shook his hand and looked into his face, approvingly.

"It is very nice to meet you, at last, Theodore. And please call me Miss Silver. I know you have been a good friend of Alexandra's at The Pine School. She has spoken of you more often than you could know. I understand my two granddaughters have settled you into an attic room. However, you are more than welcome to move to a room on the second floor, whatever is your preference. I think it can get quite chilly on the third floor."

"I will be fine, thank you. The girls found a space heater that works brilliantly. There was hardly any heat at The Pine School for boarders, so this is quite lovely, thank you."

Silver Chadwick was nodding, smiling and taking him in. Alexandra could tell her grandmother liked him. How could anyone not? Then Olivia gave him a quick hug.

"Theo, I am so glad you will be living here and not to worry about Headmaster Green. I will speak with him and he *will* understand."

There was a noticeable emphasis on the word "will." She paused and then continued.

"And Theo, we have just had a very special family reunion. It is a most unusual story . . . I'm sure Alexandra and Jaclyn will tell you more, but best to keep mum at school."

Theo nodded, smiled, and looked around at everyone and then looked back at his teacher.

"Thank you, Miss White . . . for everything."

What no one could have known was that one black bird had flown into Silver's rooms, and hidden from view, secretly listened through the open door to all that was said, and then flew back to his second-floor roost.

* ◆ *

They were headed to Theo's attic room and approaching Nicolas's room when the door suddenly flung open. Nicolas walked through his doorway with Noir on his shoulder and quickly stepped into the hall in front of them. In that moment, Alexandra noticed Theo was almost as tall as Nicolas. He was just much thinner.

"I understand you are moving in here, as a boarder."

Nicolas's eyes were dark and unfriendly.

"That is not true, Nicolas. Grand-Mère invited Theo to stay here as our friend. He is not a boarder."

Jaclyn glared at her brother and then gave another glare to Noir, who was leaning toward Theo as though he was about to interrogate him, too.

"If he is staying here and he is not family, he is a boarder. He should have to pay back, rembourser, Grand-Mère."

Theo had taken one large step backward, as this was a most unexpected sight. Nicolas was dressed in black and sitting on one shoulder was a very large black bird whose black beady eyes were drilling into his own. Theo knew Jaclyn had a brother and had seen him from a distance at school; however, he had no idea Nicolas had a bird for a pet, much less one so scary looking.

"Um, I was invited, by Mrs. Chadwick to . . . live here. Just for the school year. I . . . I have no funds . . . I have no parents."

Theo's voice was quiet but steady, and his gaze did not leave Nicolas's as he spoke.

Nicolas seemed unprepared for this, for what was obviously the truth. He dropped his eyes for a brief moment, and then looked back at Theo as though he accepted what he had heard and was no longer challenging him. He turned, walked into his room, and shut the door.

THE MOOSE'S CLOSET,
SOME TIGERS . . . AND A WOLF

The next weeks were an adjustment for everyone at Chadwick Manor.

There was a new person living with them, waking up each day and having breakfast, then riding to school with Blackie, Max, and the girls, and a very sullen Nicolas, who would sit alone in the rumble seat. Three happy students would pass by Headmaster Green, who would smile weakly and say hello, looking like it was a huge struggle to smile (as though what he really wanted to do was grab each of them with his gnarled hands, but some greater force prevented him from doing so), and then run up the stairs to Classroom #6. Their teacher would send little smiles and winks their way throughout the day, but very discreetly, so no other students would see. Occasionally, Alexandra and Jaclyn would find notes included with graded papers as they filed out of class at the end of the day: "See you for dinner tonight! XO Aunt O." Or, "Bringing some treats from Weston's this weekend! XO Aunt O." Or, "I'll beat you all at Monopoly this weekend! XO Aunt O." Or (this was the most frequent note), "Study hard, no special treatment for relatives of the teacher! XO Aunt O."

Afternoons were spent having hot chocolate in the kitchen and then doing their homework. Theo offered to help Alexandra with her least favorite subject. She had always hated math, but he seemed to be able to explain it in a way that she understood, and she actually began to enjoy doing her math homework. Dinner was wonderful—everyone gathered around the kitchen table, Taco happily eating his fruit and vegetables. There was more conversation and laughter than Alexandra could believe, except from one person who would eat quickly and leave, never saying a word.

The first weekend after Thanksgiving they had gone into Dark Harbor because Olivia decided Theo needed some new clothes. Blackie drove with all three of them riding in the rumble seat. It was very cold, but they dressed warmly and it was great fun as they rode the winding coast road, looking at the frosty ocean and seeing the village below, nestled between the harbor and tall pines. As they approached, Theo whistled softly, his eyes dancing. He had never been into Dark Harbor, and his head swiveled as he tried to take everything in. Alexandra had told Theo about the sailboat and pointed to the *Windswept* bobbing in the harbor. Theo immediately asked if they could go for a sail one day and Alexandra said of course, but not until spring.

They parked and headed to The Moose's Closet, where Olivia was waiting for them.

Theo was speechless as he walked along the main street, looking at the shops, crammed full of marvelous things. All the shops and streetlights were now dressed for Christmas with balsam wreaths, red ribbons, and green garlands. Alexandra smiled, knowing they would be going to the closing night of The Claw & Tail for Christmas Eve dinner. Theo and Jaclyn would see the huge Christmas tree at the end of the wharf lit up with thousands of colored lights, and white luminary bags with flickering votive candles lining the main street. Christmas was a time Alexandra looked forward to every year, but as she had grown, she also realized it marked the end of the hustle and bustle of Dark Harbor. She knew that after Christmas Eve, the shop lights would be snuffed out like candles, one by one, and for the rest of the winter the little village would hibernate like a sleepy bear.

Above the door to The Moose's Closet there was a large moose head mounted on a wooden plaque. He was wearing a Santa's cap with a string of illuminated Christmas lights draped between his two massive antlers. He had large brown eyes with long, thick eyelashes and he seemed to be looking at each person who entered the shop. Alexandra had grown up seeing him so never thought twice about it, but Theo was quite shocked as he gazed into the very real, almost alive, brown eyes. Alexandra whispered to him the eyes were made from glass—she had asked a long time ago.

However, Theo did not seem convinced and very quickly ducked under the moose's head and into the shop.

Olivia was, among many other talents and attributes, very organized and efficient. So in no time, Theo was escorted to a dressing room with the moose's face painted on the wooden door, and piles of sweaters, trousers, and shirts were passed over the top to try on. Both girls gave Theo more advice than he needed, and Olivia told him to choose whatever he liked and not to look at the price tags because it would be taken care of. In the end, a small pile of clothes was rung up. Theo insisted he did not need very much; he said he had done just fine with a few things at The Pine School. The carefully chosen clothes were two sweaters (red and hunter green), three white shirts and two pairs of black slacks for school, two pairs of brown corduroy trousers, and flannel pajamas with matching bathrobe and slippers. (Nicolas had extra jackets, gloves, and boots, which his grandmother said could be given to Theo. Hearing this, Nicolas had shrugged. He rarely went outside, and if he did, he always wore the black wool cape he had arrived wearing.) The purchases were soon folded and placed in a large handled shopping bag. The moose's face, wearing the Santa's cap with the string of lights between the antlers, was on both sides of the bag. The moose was smiling, and he had very large teeth. "Merry Moosemas" was printed next to the moose's mouth. It was quite funny and they all laughed.

Next, Theo went into The Book Nook by himself, as the girls and Olivia headed to the Quill & Parchment. Olivia had suggested Theo look at the art section, and with a smile, swiftly put some folded bills in his coat pocket while propelling him to the front of the shop. Just before he opened the door of The Book Nook, Alexandra whispered not to be shocked by the strange woman behind the counter. Theo's eyes had sparked with interest, but he seemed not the least bit concerned as he ventured through the door. He was gone a while, finally emerging with one book he had wanted about architecture, carefully chosen from the Art & Design section of the bookstore. Upon meeting up, he rolled his eyes and whispered to Alexandra that the old woman was "a bit dodgy." Then they all went into Moo Bar for the special Christmas Tree Snow Cone, an icy mixture of shaved green, red, and white colored ice, which became a delicious syrup once it melted a little and could be slurped. It tasted like peppermint, vanilla, and red-hot cinnamon candy all swirled together.

Moo Bar was a most unusual dairy bar. The walls were painted fire-engine red with colorful murals of black and white cows dancing, reading, sailing a sailboat, jumping over a large moon, playing musical instruments, sleeping in beds, sitting at a picnic table wearing large bibs and eating lobster, even licking ice cream cones. *And*, seated on various spinning stools that bordered the large rectangular marble-topped bar (the soda fountain was in the middle) were life-size cows. Just sitting there, usually wearing some kind of funny hat, their front hooves resting on the counter. They were very authentic looking, made from fake black and white fur, with glass eyes and thick black eyelashes. Their long swishy tails hung down behind the stools. In the summer they wore very large sunglasses and red baseball caps worn backward that read, "Moo Bar Farm Team." At Christmas, they all wore Santa hats with colorful scarves tied around their necks—and they were joined by one full-size moose, also seated on a red leather stool, wearing a Santa's hat with ornaments hanging from his antlers. Everyone wanted to sit next to a cow or the moose; those stools were always taken first. As luck would have it, one of the coveted stools opened up and Theo found himself eating his Christmas snow cone while sitting next to—a moose.

The last stop was Weston's Market. They each filled a brown bag with penny candy and introduced Theo to Mr. Weston. Mr. Weston clapped him on the back and shook his hand, saying to Alexandra with a wink that if more people kept arriving at Chadwick Manor they would run out of rooms. Alexandra watched Theo as he picked out his candy. He was thoughtful and deliberate and had selected maybe ten pieces when he folded the bag and walked toward the counter. Alexandra followed him, grinning, and then led him back to the penny candy, telling him only full bags were allowed.

They rode back to Chadwick Manor in silence. They were too busy eating candy.

◆

Neither Alexandra nor Jaclyn had forgotten about the calendar or the letter. In spite of everything that had happened with Aunt Olivia and Theo, they had never stopped thinking about December 23rd . . . which was now approaching with the speed of a very fast train.

They had noticed Nicolas was nervous and on edge. He never spoke unless he was spoken to, and he seemed very distracted. His bedroom light was on unusually late at night. It was obvious he was reading or studying about a subject of great interest.

They were about to find out what.

Their grandmother had bank business in Boston, something about a trustees' meeting, whatever that was, and would be gone all day the next Saturday. They would be leaving early in the morning. Blackie was driving and Evelyn was going with them, so it meant they would be on their own until evening. However, they could call Aunt Olivia if they *needed anything*, as their grandmother said repeatedly, seeming to need to reassure herself more than them, Alexandra thought.

The prospect of being alone with no grown-ups around was exciting.

Alexandra, Jaclyn, and Theo planned to make a pancake breakfast with lots of bacon on Saturday morning. Alexandra had been helping with the Saturday pancake breakfasts for a while and knew how to light the burners. Nevertheless, Evelyn was always nervous whenever Alexandra was cooking, and fluttered around close by. It was a huge stove with six large gas burners, and to light one of the burners required a match and turning on the gas. One night before the Boston trip, Evelyn asked Alexandra and Theo to show her how to light, adjust, and then turn off the burners. Smiling after they each went through the steps successfully, she told them to be *very careful*, and then, with one eyebrow raised and a most serious expression, she explained how to operate the nearby fire extinguisher; in her words, "better to be safe than sorry."

They had stayed up late talking and playing Monopoly on Friday night and were sleeping soundly Saturday morning when events began unfolding, all too quickly.

Theo had fallen asleep on the rug in Alexandra's room, and he was sound asleep under a down comforter. Jaclyn was in bed with Alexandra. Biscuit was almost hidden in the fluffy comforter that puffed up around his little body at the foot of the bed, and Taco was snoring softly. The game of Monopoly was on the rug, next to Theo, where they ended before going to bed. Theo was winning, as usual. He had bought all the railroads and the electric and water companies as soon as he landed on them, telling Alexandra and Jaclyn utilities and transportation were better "investments" (whatever that meant) than Boardwalk or Park Place. He also had the most cash on hand. Not withstanding the higher cost, Alexandra always wanted to buy the luxury properties because of their fancy addresses, which were so much more impressive sounding than an old railroad. "I own Park Place" certainly sounded better than "I own B&O Railroad."

"Wake up, réveillez-vous, tout le monde, vite, vite!!"

Nicolas was standing next to the bed shaking them. Noir was on his shoulder.

Three heads bobbed up. In seconds, three bodies were sitting straight up. Theo and Jaclyn were looking for their glasses and Alexandra was so shocked she could not speak. What was Nicolas doing in her room so early? What was going on? It seemed like a dream, it was so bizarre. Then there was an ear-piercing screech. Taco had awakened and the shock of seeing Noir only a few feet away in his room was just too startling. Nicolas yelled for Theo to help him as he began pushing a large, heavy wooden trunk that was at the foot of her bed toward the bedroom door. Why? Why was he barricading them *in her bedroom?*

"*Vite*, Theo, aide-moi! *Vite*!!!"

It was a command. Nicolas's voice was deep and urgent, and his dark brown eyes were wild looking.

Theo jumped up and began helping Nicolas push the trunk. There was no time to ask why. Theo just knew he had to do what Nicolas said. The trunk was filled with her mother's things—stuffed animals and dolls, school papers, photos, and favorite books. Alexandra had handled each item so many times she was sure she had memorized the contents. They were grunting and pushing and finally it was against the door. Nicolas looked frantically around the room and then spied the nightstand closest to the door. He quickly removed the lamp and Theo helped him lift it on top of the trunk. Just as the nightstand was placed on the trunk, they all heard it.

A thundering roar shook the floor. It seemed to come from where the brass pole dropped off on the first floor.

Noir flew to the opening in the floor and looked down.

"Tigre. Nous sommes en danger."

It was perfect French. The tone was controlled, factual.

Alexandra felt like she was frozen. Fear was coursing through her entire body. She felt it from her head to her toes. She stared at Nicolas.

"What have you done, Nicolas? *What?*" she asked in a hoarse whisper.

Nicolas did not answer. He walked quickly to the pole and knelt down. Theo followed. Biscuit had gotten himself completely under the covers and Taco had blown up—his feathers looked like they were standing on end, all puffed up, and his wings were spread wide as though he was in flight. His beak was opening and closing, but nothing was coming out.

Alexandra slowly crept off the bed toward the pole. She had never felt fear like this in her life. Jaclyn sat frozen on the bed, clutching a bed pillow. Then it came again, another roar, followed by another. Alexandra felt her knees go weak and she felt Theo's hand grab hold of her arm to steady her. Kneeling near the edge of the hole, she breathed in, almost too afraid to look, and then looked down. She was looking into the most amazing emerald-green eyes *of a tiger*. The enormous and powerful front paws with raptor-like claws were only a short distance from where they were kneeling. The tiger was standing on its hind legs, its front paws braced by the brass pole. She could see everything so vividly it seemed like she was looking through a magnifying glass . . . the long white whiskers, the razor-sharp white incisors, and the very large pink tongue as it panted heavily. The tiger's face, deep burnt-orange fur with symmetrical black markings framed by a thick white beard, looked like it had been painted it was so perfect.

Suddenly, another tiger appeared in view and looked up at them. They were a matched pair. Alexandra realized in that instant what had happened.

"*Nicolas, what did you do*?? You made the statues come to life! How? You must have cast a spell?!"

Silently, she realized the obvious. It had worked. Nicolas would be getting powers on his fifteenth birthday. This was the proof. She felt like she might faint, but Theo gripped her arm more tightly.

"Oui. Je suis désolé. I am sorry."

His voice was just a whisper as he looked at Alexandra. She could see in his eyes he was afraid, but she was not sure he really was sorry.

"*What is the antidote*? What is the way to undo it? You must have studied this, too? *Nicolas*??"

She was searching his eyes for the answer she hoped to hear.

"Non. Je ne sais pas."

Jaclyn crept off the bed, gingerly kneeling between Alexandra and

Theo while holding onto their arms, and then peered down, gasping loudly at the sight.

The tiger that had been standing dropped down and both of them were looking up. They slowly began circling the pole. Alexandra was reminded of a story about two tigers chasing each other so fast in a circle they became melted butter, but that was a story and this was *real*. Then they moved out of sight. Jaclyn squeezed Alexandra's arm hard and every head turned at the same moment to the barricaded door. Would it hold when they found their way up the stairs, as surely they would?

Alexandra knew the only person who could help them was in Dark Harbor. But how to tell her? The telephone was in the kitchen and they could not leave the room. She quickly went to Taco, lifted him onto her shoulder and walked to the large bank of windows above the window seat. She rubbed his ears and stroked him.

"Taco, you must fly to Dark Harbor and tell Aunt Olivia what has happened. Tell her she must come *right away*. I know you can do this, Taco. Her apartment is right over Weston's Market, so just follow the coast road into town and then read the signs to find Weston's Market. Go to the top of the stairs on the outside of the building and rap your beak loudly on the window. If she doesn't hear you, you must screech as loud as you can so she does hear you. Tell her the tiger statues have *become real* and we need her *right away. Hurry, Taco!*"

Taco nodded solemnly as Alexandra opened the far window. She felt his powerful feet grip her shoulder as he pushed off. They had all come to the window. Jaclyn climbed up on the window seat holding Biscuit. Nicolas was standing with Noir on his shoulder. Theo stood next to Alexandra. They all watched as the bright blue wingspan caught one of the sun's morning rays as it pierced through the cloud cover, and then he was out of sight.

They stood in silence looking at the empty gray winter sky when, suddenly, down below near the driveway, Alexandra saw something that made her gasp. She was looking at a wolf and he was looking back at her. His fur was drab brown, mangy looking. His eyes were yellowish brown and outlined in black, just like Max's eyes. He began walking slowly toward the maple tree and he was staring up at her as though he knew her.

Jaclyn saw him at the same time and then the others crowded around the window. As he got closer, Alexandra could see a very familiar brown leather collar with tags hanging off the front. Max's collar. She whirled around at Nicolas.

"*What have you done*?? Is that our Max? He has on Max's collar—I can see it! *Did your spell make him a wolf*??"

Nicolas was looking at the wolf with as much surprise on his face as anyone else, and he shook his head in disbelief.

"The spell was to make inanimate objects come alive. That is why I chose the tigers. It is called transfiguration, but I never thought it would work . . . and it should not have affected a live animal. Noir and your parrot are fine."

Nicolas did not look at her as he answered. He was staring at the wolf and the wolf was still staring back at them.

Before Alexandra could respond, there was a heavy swipe of nails on the bedroom door. The tigers were outside the door, panting loudly. Then one growled. They must have heard them talking, or as Alexandra realized with a shiver, smelled them. Instinctively, she jumped up on the window seat but, of course, she knew that would not help—at all—if they got through the door. She was looking at a very large limb of the maple tree that came close to her window. It looked like it would support them if they could reach it and climb on. Maybe they could get out that way if Olivia did not come in time.

"They are both outside the door right now, so what if we quickly go down the pole to the back hall and then run to the garage?" Theo whispered urgently as he was walking toward the pole.

Alexandra thought quickly. It would take too much time for them all to get down the pole. The tigers would hear the first person coming down and would be down the stairs in two leaps and . . . well, she didn't need to think any further than that.

"No, Theo—there won't be enough time for all of us to get down."

Theo nodded. He knew she was right.

"Je vais voler et distraire les deux tigres."

It was the cool, monotone voice.

They all looked at Noir, who was sitting calmly on Nicolas's shoulder.

"What did he say?" Alexandra looked at Nicolas.

"He said he would fly and distract them both."

They all considered this. Maybe it would work. Then there was another nail swipe at the door. This time more weight was applied, and the door moved slightly in the frame. Then there was one long roar. Panic swept the room.

"Oui, Noir. Avance! Lead the tigers up to the third floor and into the attic as far as you can, then dive at them and distract them for as long as you can. We will go down the pole and out to the garage as Theo said."

Nicolas's instructions were clear and detailed, but the fear in his voice could not be disguised.

Noir flew to the opening, looked back at Nicolas quickly, and then was gone. They waited, knowing it would take just seconds before he flew to the front of the foyer and up the staircase to the bedroom. The loud caws started immediately and got louder as Noir approached the bedroom door. Then the cawing was going in the direction of the second-floor hallway and third floor. Nicolas peered through the keyhole in the door. The tigers were not in sight. It was perfectly quiet. Then he went to the opening in the floor and looked down. Nothing was in view. Nevertheless, how could they be certain the tigers had followed Noir? It was the question everyone was silently pondering when Taco flew back through the open window and landed on top of his cage.

Alexandra ran to him. His feathers were ruffled and cold and he was shivering. All of a sudden, she remembered it was winter and he had flown in very cold temperatures. It made her stomach turn. How could she not have thought of this? She had put him in danger to save them. Quickly, she brought him to the bed and covered him with the down comforter. All you could see was his small painted face.

"Taco found Olivia. Olivia coming. *Hurry,* Taco said. *Hurry, Olivia! Two tigers loose!*"

His voice was noticably weaker than usual; however, there was an unmistakable inflection of having successfully accomplished his mission.

In what seemed like seconds, they heard her car on the stone driveway and ran back to the window. Olivia parked, quickly opened the car door, and stepped out. She was wearing the magnificent cape and looked up at them with a serious expression. Then she saw the wolf. He was sitting under the maple tree, studying her. Very slowly, she walked toward him and then stopped, about fifteen feet away.

"Come to me, Max. Come to Olivia."

Alexandra heard the familiar, hypnotic voice.

The wolf seemed to think for a moment, but then decided to move toward her and approached her slowly. What they all noticed was his tail was wagging, just like a dog's. As he got close to her, she told him to sit and he did. Then she put her hand on his head and in that instant, the familiar brown and white border collie appeared where the wolf had been. Max licked her hand, and Olivia swiftly led him by the collar to the safety of the garage, then turned back toward the house.

"Stay in the bedroom. No matter what, do not leave Alexandra's room!" she called up to them and then opened the side door of Chadwick Manor.

What happened next is only known to Olivia and Noir. He had led the tigers to the third floor and was flying around, diving and darting to keep their attention, when she had appeared.

Moments later, she was outside Alexandra's door. They watched in awe as the nightstand lifted off the trunk and returned to its place next to the bed. Then the trunk slid back to the foot of her bed and the bedroom door opened. Olivia walked into the room with Noir on her hand and held him out to Nicolas. He placed the black bird on his shoulder, affectionately stroking him. Then, without speaking, they all rushed to the balcony and looked down into the foyer. The two tigers were back on their pedestals, sitting regally, the porcelain statuesque sentinels they had always been.

In a hushed and serious voice, Olivia said she wanted to speak with Nicolas privately. They walked slowly toward his bedroom, three figures in black, and the door closed behind them. Alexandra wondered what she was telling him, probably that he had to stop any attempt at magic. What would happen at midnight on December 23rd? Just the thought made her shiver.

When the travelers returned from Boston and questions were asked about their day, they were all believably nonchalant. Everything was fine. The pancakes turned out perfectly. There was no need to call Aunt Olivia. They had gone sledding and played in the snow with Max. However, when Taco sneezed later that night, Silver Chadwick had raised an eyebrow and looked intently at Alexandra, who shrugged her shoulders and said he must have slept in a draft . . . just another typical day at Chadwick Manor.

Later, as Alexandra drifted to sleep, the events of the morning replayed in her mind. It was at that moment she realized something for the first time—the importance of both birds. The outcome, and possibly their lives, had required the efforts of both birds. Taco *and* Noir.

SKATING BY MOONLIGHT

There was another large estate directly across from Chadwick Manor. It was called Devonshire. The Duke and Duchess of Devonshire, England, lived there, at least some of the time. Alexandra's grandmother told her they were like elegant migratory birds (Siberian cranes and greater flamingos were mentioned), dependably arriving at Devonshire and in residence every December. It was true. They *always* visited at Christmas, and Alexandra *always* looked forward to seeing them. First, they were unusual looking and second, they were *royalty*. (When she was very young, she had asked if they could please bring the King and Queen of England with them one Christmas. However, that request had never been met.) Third, they had two unusual dogs.

The Duke and Duchess were both exceptionally tall and quite thin. They almost looked like they could be on stilts, like the tall people at the circus. The Duchess had a large round face that had always looked almost flat to Alexandra. Her nose was tiny, and her heavily lidded green eyes were set widely apart on her face and always looked half closed. She had long, thick silver hair that was quite beautiful and looked like the hair of a much younger woman. The Duke also had a round face, but he had very large ears that stuck out from his head and a prominent nose. Bushy white eyebrows framed large blue eyes. His thick white hair was always combed straight back and almost touched his shoulders. For some reason, their faces reminded Alexandra of the Man in the Moon hanging in the Chadwick kitchen. When she was little, it had been hard to learn what to call them. Her grandmother told her they were to be addressed as either Sir John and Lady Isabel *or* Duke and Duchess, but depending on what she had never understood. So she used both titles, Sir Duke and Lady Duchess, which they seemed to like.

Their dogs were Harlequin Great Danes. They looked like Dalmatians but were much, much bigger with large pointed ears. Her first memory of them was looking up at their huge dappled heads and square jaws, towering over her; however, she never remembered being afraid of them. Their names were Beatrix and Bentley. They each wore a red leather collar with a large silver plate that had their name engraved on it. Alexandra always thought they looked like they belonged together—that the dogs matched their owners.

The Duke and Duchess were both as old as her grandmother, and they had known her mother from when she was a baby. Her mother had grown up skating on their large frozen pond every winter. It was the winter scene painted on her bedroom wall, and the skaters in the mural were very recognizable—Blackie and Evelyn, the Duke and Duchess, her grandmother and grandfather, and her mother when she was a young girl—all skating under the light of a full moon. Every year, the week before Christmas, there came the invitation to skate under the moonlit night sky, now a Christmas tradition for Alexandra, just as it had been for her mother.

One night at dinner, her grandmother told the others about the invitation. It was always a formal invitation on heavy cardstock with a red satin ribbon woven around it inviting the "Residents of Chadwick Manor to a Moonlit Christmas Skating Party with the Residents of Devonshire." There was always an asterisk after the words "Residents of Chadwick Manor" and at the bottom of the invitation it read, "* including any and all pets."

"But Grand-Mère, I have never been ice skating and neither has Nicolas," Jaclyn said, looking both excited and concerned.

"I have never been ice skating either, Mrs. Chadwick."

"Theodore, my dear boy, as I have said, please call me Miss Silver. It makes me feel very old to be called Mrs. Chadwick."

She was very old so this made everyone laugh. Theo turned a little pink and nodded.

"Blackie is going to get skates for all of you and will take you for some practice sessions this week. He is an expert teacher, as Alexandra will tell you. After you get the feel of it and with practice, it is not difficult. Skating is like riding a bicycle. Once you learn, you can do it forever."

Theo grinned. "Brilliant!"

"Grand-Mère, I would prefer not to go."

She turned and looked at her grandson as though she had expected this.

"Well, Nicolas, this time I will have to say your attendance is required. Nécessaire. It is our family tradition and has been for as long as I can remember—and that is a long time. Besides, I think you will enjoy it. Their granddaughter is visiting from England. She is your age, and even her name is most similar to your own. It is Nicole."

She smiled at her grandson, who did not attempt to disguise his frown, and then he lowered his eyes.

"Nicolas, elle parle français couramment."

He looked up for the briefest moment. It was clear he was surprised to hear Nicole spoke fluent French. Then he asked to be excused, and he left. Alexandra had heard about their granddaughter for years and asked many times if she could visit, but they always told her Nicole had to be with her parents for the holidays. So this would be interesting, to finally meet her. Alexandra wondered if she would be very, very tall. Maybe she would tower over Nicolas. The thought made her smile. That would be funny to see.

* ◆ *

There were three practice sessions after school. They had about an hour before the sun went down. Blackie brought their skates when he picked them up at The Pine School, along with some snacks from Evelyn, and they headed straight to the pond. The gates leading into Devonshire were tall and wide with a large shiny gold *D* in the center where the gates met. While there had to be an explanation, Blackie would just smile mysteriously as the gates slowly opened each time they pulled in.

Like Chadwick Manor, the grounds of Devonshire were unusually beautiful. There were groves of trees and manicured lawns with expansive flowerbeds in the spring and summer. Devonshire was built to look like a European castle, constructed from limestone blocks with turrets on both corners and a sweeping circular drive leading to a large and elegant portico. In the middle of the circular drive was an expanse of grass with a single, tall pine tree in the center. At Christmas, the tree was decorated with red and green lights with a shimmering star at the very top. The double front doors looked like a castle entrance. Each door was twelve feet high and six feet wide with giant iron hinges. Everything in Devonshire, from the doors to the furniture, was exceedingly large—and perfectly proportioned to the people (and dogs) who lived there.

It was the final practice session before the skating party. Blackie parked at the end of the gravel drive on the left side of the property. In the distance, a long walk from where the driveway ended, the land gradually sloped down to a large pond, now frozen solid. Jaclyn and Alexandra scrambled out of the car and ran through the snowy field while the others walked behind, heading for the shallow valley and the sheet of black ice.

There were some wooden benches at one end of the pond near a large stone fire pit. Alexandra had her skates on and laced up in no time. Then she helped Jaclyn and Theo, making sure their laces were tied tight. Both took tentative steps onto the slippery surface. They had made some progress; however, this was just their third time on the ice and learning how to skate takes a lot of practice. Jaclyn had a fairly easy time because she was short and low to the ground (and because she had no fear). Whenever she fell, she would get right back up, grinning. Her glasses fogged up quickly from the very cold air, as did Theo's, and they both had to keep wiping them with their scarves. Theo was having more difficulty and fell many times—he really needed Alexandra or Blackie to steady him. Blackie would call out, "Give it some welly, Theo!" which apparently meant to try harder in British. Theo always grinned and gave a thumbs-up. Not surprisingly, Theo was a very good sport and never seemed to mind all the falls.

Nicolas sat on the bench more than he skated, but when he had gone out on the ice for the first time, everyone had been astonished. It really looked like he had been skating all his life. His blade strokes were strong and smooth and he leaned into turns with his hands folded behind his back, most unusual for a beginner. Alexandra was a very good skater, she had been on skates from the time she could walk, but she was not as good as Nicolas. After the first practice, she had asked Jaclyn about it. Jaclyn was completely mystified. She said they had never gone skating in France, not once.

* ◆ *

At last, it was the night of the skating party.

The invitation was for five o'clock, but Silver Chadwick asked if she could come earlier for a special reason. She told Alexandra she wanted to introduce Olivia quietly before the party, because she knew how shocked they would be. So around four o'clock, Silver and her daughter walked across the street and through the gates of Devonshire. Olivia was wearing a red wool cape, red wool plaid slacks with a matching plaid scarf, and white fur earmuffs and mittens. The laces of her white skates were tied together, and the skates were draped across one shoulder. Silver Chadwick was wearing an ivory wool cape with matching slacks and a brown mink hat and hand muff. Her grandmother's skates were ice-blue leather (her favorite color other than pink), neatly tied together and hanging over one petite shoulder. As Alexandra watched them walk across the street from her bedroom window, the feeling it gave her was not describable.

At five o'clock sharp, the black touring car drove the short distance to Devonshire. As they drove, Theo whispered excitedly to Alexandra something about "knees up," and she looked back at him with a complete blank. He whispered, grinning, "It's a British expression for a party!" She smiled, thinking about how different Theo was in such a short time—for the first time she could ever remember, he was happy. It was dark now and they had just passed through the gates of Devonshire. Ahead of them, the red and green lights and glittering star shimmered on the tall evergreen tree. Thick pine garlands entwined with red and green lights wrapped around the portico roof and columns. They slowly made their way around the circular drive and parked under the elegant stone portico. Blackie helped Evelyn out of the car first. Max hopped out next, wearing his Christmas reindeer ears and a red bow tie that twinkled with tiny multicolored lights from a well-concealed battery pack. Alexandra told him he looked like he should be leading Santa's sleigh, and his wolf face seemed to smile back in response. Jaclyn, Alexandra, Theo, and Nicolas, all dressed warmly, climbed out next with skates in hand. Taco never attended the skating party, mostly because of the frigid cold, but also because he had heard Alexandra's description of the *giant* dogs, so he was happy to stay at home in the toasty kitchen munching on pineapple. Noir was disinterested and was *locked* in his cage, Nicolas told Alexandra before they left Chadwick, just as she was about to ask. She had realized, with some trepidation, that once they left for the skating party, the only residents of Chadwick would be two birds and one very small dog. (Biscuit was just too tiny to be outside; he would freeze to death in the cold.) So it was a relief to know Noir would not be able to leave Nicolas's room.

The massive castle doors slowly opened.

The Duke waved them in toward the Duchess, who was standing between the two Harlequin Great Danes, both sitting perfectly still. The Duchess was wearing a long red velvet skirt and jacket, all trimmed in white fur. She looked seven feet tall. The two dogs were wearing green and red elf hats with bells dangling from each point of fabric, tied with red ribbon under their large square jaws. The Duke was wearing a red wool jacket encrusted with medals and ribbons on one side, and from the other shoulder, a blue satin sash hung diagonally across the front, pinned with even more medals of all shapes and sizes. There were impressive gold epaulets on each shoulder of the jacket, and his hunter-green slacks were sharply pressed. Both the Duke and Duchess were wearing red velvet Santa caps trimmed with luxurious white fur.

Jaclyn could not help but giggle and Theo was grinning from ear to ear. He whispered to Alexandra, "Blimey, this takes the biscuit!" Only Nicolas was expressionless.

"Well, come in, darlings! Merry Christmas! Let us meet all the new residents of Chadwick Manor!"

The Duchess's voice was melodic and lilting.

There was so much talking and laughing that no one conversation could be heard above another. Everyone was introduced, and Beatrix and Bentley both slobbered over all the guests. When the dogs first approached her, Jaclyn had grabbed Alexandra for dear life—they were like lanky horses, galumphing around everyone, but completely lovable. Max knew them well and they greeted him with special woofs.

Inside the enormous room—it was like the great room of a castle with very tall ceilings and heavy wood beams—sat Olivia and Silver, looking almost lost in giant embroidered chairs. The chairs faced a fireplace larger than Chadwick's, ablaze with huge logs. Hanging above the fireplace was a large, elaborate coat of arms with carvings of horses, lions, and swords surrounding an elegant letter *D* in burnished gold that glimmered in the firelight. On either side of the fireplace were life-size knights in armor holding shields and tall spears with large axe blades. Alexandra remembered being afraid of them when she was very little, thinking there might be real people inside and they could come to life at any moment. In the midst of all the greetings, she had found a moment to ask her aunt how the introductions had gone. Olivia whispered back they were in total shock when they first saw her, but overjoyed at the same time and could not believe the amazing story.

"Nicole, come down and meet everyone, tout de suite!"

The Duchess was calling up a circular stone staircase, which led to a turret at one end of the long front hall. Moments later Nicole appeared, and Alexandra immediately saw the striking resemblance to her grandmother, the Duchess. Nicole had long, thick blonde hair and a round face with wide-set green eyes, and she was tall and thin, but probably no taller than Nicolas. The Duchess introduced her to Alexandra first. Smiling, she approached Alexandra with her hand extended. She was wearing a navy-blue turtleneck sweater and Black Watch tartan kilt with navy-blue leggings.

"Alexandra, lovely, I have wanted to meet you for so much longer than a fortnight! At last!" she said, as she shook Alexandra's hand.

There was no hint of a French accent, but the British accent was unmistakable. Alexandra reminded herself to ask Theo later what a fortnight was.

Nicole was then introduced to everyone else. As she met Nicolas, Alexandra thought she saw the slightest bit of interest in his eyes, but there was no hint of a smile, and she wondered if his handshake was as cold as she remembered.

Mimicking the fanfare of a horn with his hand to his mouth, the Duke announced it was time for the Christmas skating party to begin. The large doors opened, and out they all went into the cold Maine night. As they rounded the corner of Devonshire, Alexandra knew what would be there, but had kept it a secret—two sleighs: one large black sleigh with red leather upholstery, pulled by a dark brown stallion named Chestnut, and a smaller red sleigh with white leather upholstery, pulled by a tan-colored pony named Napoleon. Theo was walking next to Alexandra. He whistled low and said, "Brilliant," under his breath, shaking his head in amazement.

The grown-ups, followed by Nicolas (who had obviously decided he belonged with them), climbed into the larger sleigh while the others clambered into the smaller one. Beatrix and Bentley jumped into the large sleigh and sat on the floor of the sleigh between all the feet. Their black and white dappled heads were on the same level as the people. Max bounded into the small sleigh and jumped up next to Blackie, who was driving it. The Duke was driving the large sleigh. Blankets were pulled over laps and with a snap of the reins, they were off, bells jingling from the harnesses of both the horse and pony. The sleighs swept over the snow with speed that had everyone laughing and gasping. Alexandra could feel the familiar power of the small sturdy pony, her beloved Napoleon. In the past, Evelyn had ridden in the smaller sleigh with her, just the two of them, with Blackie in the front. Tonight the little sleigh was full. It seemed more like a dream than reality as they flew across the snowy fields.

Looking at the back of Napoleon's wheat-colored shaggy mane, Alexandra could see his head was held high. She knew he was happiest when he was with people. From the time she could sit on a saddle, Blackie had ridden Chestnut and would hold a lead attached to Napoleon while they went around and around the circular drive of Devonshire. The little pony seemed to know he was carrying a very young rider, so he always walked very, very slowly. This was the routine until she was five years old and wanted to take the reins herself. She could still remember telling Blackie, "I can do it myself." His eyes had looked into hers with serious consideration, and then he had nodded his head and handed her the reins, saying, "S'pose you can, lassie, s'pose you can."

As they approached the frozen pond, a huge bonfire was blazing high into the night sky. Then the sleighs came to a stop. Alexandra, Jaclyn, Nicole, and Theo hopped out and ran to the benches near the fire, pulling on their skates in no time, and then they were out on the black ice where the bright moonlight and bonfire cast just enough light to see. The three dogs were off exploring the entire area, staying away from the ice, running in the snow through the pines. The dogs' hats had been taken off, but Max's bow tie could be seen glowing in the dark, seemingly suspended in midair as the night enveloped his brown and white silhouette.

Soon the grown-ups were on the ice. Silver and Olivia skated by in what seemed like effortless glides. On the ice at night, they almost could have been mistaken for sisters. Silver appeared youthful and agile with smooth blade strokes and quick stops. Blackie hooked arms with Evelyn, who needed support and preferred a slower pace near the edge. The Duke and Duchess crisscrossed their arms as they always did, and in perfect unison, glided around the perimeter with speed and grace, the Duchess's long red skirt billowing behind her. They were both wearing heavy red wool capes and earmuffs under the Santa caps because the night was very cold. Nicolas sat on the bench longer than anyone else. Only with the urging of his grandmother did he finally take to the ice. He skated apart from everyone, never speaking, his black cape sweeping behind him. Alexandra noticed Nicole watching him as he gained speed, hands clasped behind his back, his long, smooth blade strokes cutting into the ice as he expertly crossed one skate in front of the other. Nicole was also a very proficient skater, but she was happy to assist Theo, who seemed to enjoy the help. In a very short time, Jaclyn had become a little speed demon and was now careening around the ice "like a professional hockey player," Blackie said. Their laughter and conversation echoed into the night and were carried away by the wind.

In a while, Blackie brought thermoses and cookie tins from the sleighs and they all gathered on the benches around the fire to have hot chocolate and Christmas cookies. Looking at everyone, their faces brightly lit by the blazing fire, it again felt like a dream to Alexandra.

She had sat at this bonfire for so many years, the only child. Now Jaclyn and Theo were sitting next to her. Then her gaze fell on Nicolas, and it felt like a dark cloud had drifted across the sun. He was sitting by himself, looking into the blackness, not talking or eating. Alexandra wondered, again, why he was so different, why he always wanted to be alone. Why he always looked serious and sad. She noticed that her grandmother was also studying him, and found herself wishing very hard that somehow she could help him.

After warming up, they all returned to the ice, finally heading back to the sleighs when their feet were completely numb. The dogs had given up earlier and were lying on blankets draped over the sleigh seats. Once they were back at Devonshire, Alexandra noticed Nicolas helping the Duke unhook the large stallion from the sleigh and then lead him into the stable. Nicolas looked very at ease, as though he was used to handling a large horse, and needed no instructions from the Duke.

Alexandra looked back at Napoleon. She was standing in front of him and reached out with one mitten to rub his long nose. His large brown eyes were looking at her *most* expectantly, and she suddenly remembered. Hunting around the bottom of the picnic basket, she found the bag of fresh carrots and gave it to Jaclyn. Fresh carrots were a long-standing—and very much expected—reward. The small pony raised his head a couple of times in anticipation. Watching Jaclyn feed him the carrots, Alexandra realized she had fallen in love with Napoleon. It was all over her face.

"Thank you!" and "Good night!" and "Merry Christmas!" filled the night air followed by "Joyeux Noël, Nicolas et Jaclyn!" Nicole's voice floated through the cold air as they climbed into the car and then headed the very short distance home.

There was only one person who had seen the raven fly overhead as they headed to the frozen pond, then land on a thick pine branch, watching everything from a high, windy perch.

And only one had seen the raven discreetly follow the sleighs back to Devonshire, soaring high above on the cold night wind, his black wings disappearing into the black night sky.

CHRISTMAS PREPARATIONS

The night of the skating party Alexandra had not thought about Nicolas's impending fifteenth birthday. Otherwise, it was on her mind nearly all of the time, as it was on Jaclyn's—they did not have to talk about it. They would just give each other a look and instantly know they were thinking the same thing: *OH NO*. That was about it, in a nutshell. However, it was also true so much was happening the week before Christmas, including shopping, wrapping gifts, and decorating the huge tree now in place in the living room, at times they did forget. School was officially out and as they filed out the last day Olivia had whispered, "This is my first Christmas with my *real* family. I can't wait!"

The Christmas boxes had been brought from the garage—miles of strings of white lights and hundreds of ornaments. Blackie always put the lights on the tree while no one was watching, except Max. It was his rule. He could sometimes be heard muttering, and occasionally was heard to say quite loudly and with obvious exasperation, "Well, Max, 'tis a dog's dinner!" and Evelyn would roll her eyes. With a very flushed face, he would finally announce he was finished, and ask them all to come into the living room as he plugged in the "fairy lights." Alexandra would never forget one year when only half of the tree lit up. Shaking his head in disbelief, he said they had worked perfectly when tested just moments before.

The ornaments were silver, white, and every shade of blue to match the blue décor in the living room. Evelyn, Alexandra, and Taco were the ornament brigade. Before the decorating commenced, Blackie always placed an angel at the top of the tree. Dressed in white lace with gossamer wings, with a wreath encircling her head and carrying two lit candles, the angel had been given to Alexandra's mother when she was a little girl. Blackie would always pause at the top of the very tall ladder, studying the angel for a few moments before making his way down, and then the brigade would get to work. Taco had a very important job, which he took most seriously. He would hang the ornaments at the highest parts of the tree, taking each ornament to the well-chosen branch, hanging it carefully and then flying back to the floor. He would pace back and forth and look at it from all angles, even flying to other vantage points, like the fireplace mantel. Sometimes he would make a change or if it was placed to his satisfaction would announce, "Perfect!" The ornament he would hang last, right below the angel, was a small blue and gold macaw parrot, which was very realistic looking (except for the glitter).

This year the lights seemed to go on the tree like a charm. They all lit at the appropriate moment, much to Blackie's obvious relief. Jaclyn and Theo did most of the ornament hanging on the lower branches. Theo had never seen such a huge tree, having only had a tabletop tree in his aunt and uncle's small apartment in London. He told them it came with the lights and little plastic ornaments, so they just pulled it out of a box and plugged it in. Jaclyn said their tree was real, but half the size of the one in the Chadwick living room, and she decorated it each year with Chantal. She told them neither her father nor her brother ever helped with decorating. So it was not a surprise when Nicolas never came to help them, even though his grandmother asked him. They all sank into the down feather couches and watched as Taco made his final ornament adjustments, the finishing touches. Jaclyn had to stifle a giggle more than once—he was so serious and very particular. At last, when the blue and gold macaw ornament was placed to his satisfaction, Theo said, "Smashing good job, Taco!" and began to clap. Everyone joined in. Taco's white cheeks turned pale pink and with a dramatic flair, he swept one long wing in front and took a bow.

* ◆ *

One afternoon they went to Dark Harbor with Blackie to Christmas shop. They were each given the same amount of money to buy "bits and bobs," as their grandmother had said, using one of Evelyn's expressions that meant "little things" or "odds and ends." They scattered and went in different directions, looking for small treasures they could afford to buy. Alexandra and Jaclyn had made lists.

Alexandra's list looked like this:

> Grand Mama — Rose scented soaps—Sweet Blooms
> Blackie—Pipe tobacco—Weston's Market
> Evelyn—Hand lotion gardenia scent—Sweet Blooms
> Jaclyn—Purple feather pen and writing paper—Quill
> & Parchment and if enough $, full bag of penny
> candy from Weston's
> Theo—Drawing book and pencils—Book Nook—
> and candy?
> Nicolas—?????
> Aunt Olivia—look around for ideas
> Taco—Cage accessories and toys—Weston's—
> and toys for Max

Of course, they all kept running into each other in the small village, and then one (or more) would have to leave the shop so as not to spoil any surprises. The last stop for Alexandra was The Book Nook. She would get Theo's gift here, which meant everyone was crossed off her list except Aunt Olivia. Nothing she had seen thus far seemed right for her aunt.

The Book Nook was very . . . odd.

As Alexandra pushed open the door, the distinctive smell of very dry paper met her nostrils. She remembered being afraid of the woman behind the counter until just a few years ago when she began to venture in alone. However, even now it took courage. Miss Ima wore thick, square, black-framed glasses and had frizzy white hair, which usually had some sort of bizarre hair clip oddly placed. She wore very strange clothing, unusual colors with nothing ever matching. Whenever Alexandra saw her, Miss Ima was always wearing the same outfit—multiple sweaters, one on top of the other, all different colors; the largest sweater was first, and then a medium size and then a small one that barely fit, along with a long skirt with many flouncy layers. Each layer was a different color and fabric, checked, striped, or floral. Her fingers were thin and knobby, but her long fingernails were actually very attractive and always painted bright red. (The truth was Miss Ima did not have to dress up very much for Halloween parade night. She just put on a witch's hat and painted her face and hands green.) Miss Ima always stroked each book with her red fingernails as the books were placed on the counter, remarking in a hoarse, sandpapery voice, "*Excellent selection.*" She said this to *every* customer. Alexandra had always wondered who she was and where she lived. But no one, not even her grandmother, seemed to know anything about Miss Ima. No one even knew her last name.

There was a staircase in The Book Nook that led to the second floor. It, too, was very odd. The staircase was actually a series of separate staircases, each with a landing, and zigged and zagged in a way that made no sense because the building was narrow and small. In other words, it took a long time to get to the second floor when it should have taken seconds. Once you finally got to the second floor, the bookshelves were so close together that sometimes you had to go sideways down the aisles. Alexandra did not like going up there. It was too claustrophobic and dimly lit, and it took way too long to get there. It had been relief to know Theo's gift would be on the first floor. Subjects A-K were on the first floor and L-Z on the second.

"Hi, Miss Ima."

"Hello, Alexandra. And what are we looking for today?"

Alexandra did not like it when anyone said "we" instead of "you" and Miss Ima always did.

"Just a drawing book and some pencils."

"That would be under 'Art,' right over there," she said, pointing with one long, crooked, red-tipped finger.

Alexandra began walking toward the Art section.

"I think your cousin, a young man with a French accent, is upstairs. He was looking for a very rare book, *Levitation, Incantations and Transfiguration*. Very lucky for him we had one copy left. He went upstairs to get it, but he has been up there for some time. Maybe you want to go and check on him, *sweetie*."

There was nothing sweet about the way she said *sweetie*.

Alexandra wondered how Miss Ima would know Nicolas was her cousin, and then she shivered as she looked up at the ceiling. He was preparing for his fifteenth birthday, which was just days away. Levitation, that meant floating in air, and made her think of her grandmother, who seemed to float as she walked. Incantations . . . that was spells. She thought of her aunt. And she now knew the meaning of transfiguration, *all too well*. Her stomach twisted and her hands felt clammy. There was no way she was going up to the second floor. It was like a cave up there, dark and scary, but perfect for Nicolas, who reminded her of a reclusive bat. As these thoughts swirled in her mind, she shuddered wondering what December 23rd would bring. Then, remembering what she had come in for, she went straight to the Art section.

She quickly found a drawing book with pencils and headed back to the counter. As she set it down, her eyes fell on a slim book next to the register, *Daily Diary of Reflections*. On the cover was an image of a face in a reflecting pool. It was the face of a young woman with chin-length black hair and green eyes.

The old woman traced the face with one red fingernail and said in her creepy voice, "This is perfect for Olivia."

It was so startling that all Alexandra could do was stare into her magnified eyes. As she looked at Miss Ima very closely for the first time, she realized she had no eyelashes, just red-rimmed, sunken eyes that were staring back at her so intensely it felt like they would burn right through her body. Alexandra wanted to run out of the shop but fought against it with all the strength she could muster.

"Well, yes . . . I will take both. What do I owe?" She tried hard to keep it steady, but her voice was shaking.

"*Excellent selections.* Let me see, my sweet," she said, slowly pushing down the keys on the register with her red-tipped fingernails.

"That will be four dollars and fifty cents."

In seconds, the exact amount was placed on the counter, the purchases collected, and Alexandra was out the door.

They all met up at Weston's Market, as was the plan. Both Theo and Jaclyn looked as pleased as punch, each holding many different bags. Nicolas arrived last, looking sullen, holding one shopping bag identical to one she was holding. On the bag it said, "The Book Nook ~ A Place to Travel Through Time." Underneath the words, there was a sketch of an hourglass with sand running through it, and the hourglass was sitting on a stack of books. Alexandra wondered if he had bought the levitation book. It had to be expensive. And she wondered if he had bought gifts for anyone else, but it didn't appear so.

They each bought some carefully selected pieces of candy, even Nicolas, with the few pennies they had left. Alexandra watched what he picked out, finding it interesting he wanted any candy after his dismissive comments at Halloween. He chose black licorice and fireballs. He had looked up at her as he was picking out what he wanted, sensing he was being watched, but with no real expression.

As they made their way to the car, Alexandra was thinking about what Miss Ima had said. How could she possibly know anything about Aunt Olivia or their relationship? Or that Nicolas was her cousin? It made no sense at all.

When they got back home, Alexandra showed them the "wrapping closet," as Evelyn called it. The "closet" was actually the size of a small room and well organized with all kinds of wrapping paper, gift bags, colored ribbons, tissue paper, tags, tape, scissors, etc. for every holiday and occasion. Theo said he was not good at wrapping and had only wrapped a few things in his life. Nicolas looked completely disinterested and went straight upstairs. At that moment, Alexandra was certain he had not bought anything for anyone else, just for himself. The others chose paper and ribbons and headed to their own rooms.

As Alexandra spread out the gifts on her bed, Taco immediately flew from his cage to look everything over. One at a time, he guessed whom each gift was for—all correct, which pleased him. He did have to study the compass a little longer than anything else. Then, nodding with certainty, he said, "Nicolas." The compass had seemed right to her as soon as she saw it at The Moose's Closet in a bin labeled, "For Those Hard to Buy For." What would happen on December 23rd? Fleetingly, she had imagined the compass needle spinning and spinning and then stopping as midnight struck. However, it actually was a practical gift for anyone living in Maine . . . maybe it would help Nicolas find his way somewhere or back again.

Taco was looking at her with his head tilted to one side, then looked at the gifts and then back at her. He did not have to say anything.

"I haven't finished shopping yet, Taco. And you can't see what I bought you! It has to be a surprise!"

Alexandra smiled and stroked his head. Still hidden at the bottom of one bag were some new toys and a small mirror for his cage from Weston's Market. He was always using her mirror.

The next day was December 23rd.

AN UNEXPECTED VISITOR,
SOME POKER FACES,
AND MIDNIGHT STRIKES

December 23rd was gray and blustery.

Winter snow squalls were coming in from the ocean. Outside Chadwick Manor, it was all swirls of white snow and bitterly cold, but inside it was warm and cheerful. There were fires in the kitchen, living room, and library fireplaces during the day and night. A few nights, Blackie built fires in Jaclyn's bedroom fireplace, or as she called it, her petite cheminée. Alexandra slept in Jaclyn's room with Taco on those nights, all of them mesmerized by the beauty of the flames, then falling into a deep sleep from the warmth of the blazing logs. The Christmas tree was lit continuously, and packages had begun appearing under the tree. When they looked at the tree in the morning, five new stockings had suddenly appeared, hanging from the large mantel. Every other Christmas there had only been three, for Alexandra, Taco, and Max. Hanging next to their stockings were the others, for Jaclyn, Biscuit, Theo, Nicolas, and Noir. The new stockings had obviously been handmade by Evelyn, made from the same red velvet fabric and trimmed in thick white fur around the top with the name embroidered in silver rope. Theo was grinning and admiring the stocking with his name on it.

"My stockin' was one of me own socks. This is the bee's knees!"

Theo had heard Evelyn use the British expression for something fabulous and had started using it himself.

"Well, Theo, I hope you don't find just a lump of coal in your stocking on Christmas morning. Depends on whether you've been un vilain garçon ou un gentil garçon?" Jaclyn asked with a twinkle in her eye.

"Vilain garçon, of course!"

They all laughed.

"What do you think Noir and Nicolas will find in theirs?" Theo asked Jaclyn, his eyes mischievous and questioning.

"Morceau de charbon."

Jaclyn's tone of voice and expression were now completely serious.

They all looked at one another but said nothing.

✳ ✦ ✳

Alexandra and Jaclyn had not told Theo anything about the letter possibly arriving on December 23rd. Nor had they told him about Mercy Disbrow being their ancestor or the magical powers carried down for generations in their family. For reasons they did not understand, Theo had not talked about time travel, the tigers, and the other magical things he had seen. He seemed to accept everything—that Olivia had certain powers and Nicolas might have them as well, that two birds possessed human intelligence and speech—and asked nothing about what he had witnessed. In spite of this, they decided it was best not to tell him, as even they did not know what to expect. So although Theo knew it was Nicolas's fifteenth birthday, he had no idea what might happen at the stroke of midnight.

When her grandmother had given her the Christmas shopping money, Alexandra asked about Nicolas's birthday and offered to buy some birthday presents for him. She realized people with birthdays close to Christmas might not have separate parties or gifts, and she always thought this was unfair. However, her grandmother had smiled rather mysteriously and said, "It is taken care of, my dear. Nicolas will have a very nice birthday party . . ."

It was late in the afternoon and already dark outside when Taco suddenly awoke from his nap and screeched. Alexandra, Theo, and Jaclyn were playing cards on the bed and nearly jumped off because his shriek was so loud and unexpected.

"What is it, Taco?"

Alexandra went to his cage and tried to take him out, but it was clear he was not going to leave.

"Philippe."

Taco's eyes were dark and his feathers were beginning to ruffle and stand up. A moment later, there was a loud and powerful knock on the front doors of Chadwick. They all leapt up and went to the banister overlooking the foyer. Evelyn had come running from the kitchen, looked up at them and told them to go back in the bedroom, but no one moved. As she grimaced at them and was about to open the door, a voice came from beneath the staircases.

"Evelyn, please let me answer the door. I know who it is."

It was their grandmother's voice, calm and commanding.

Evelyn stopped and turned back toward the kitchen, glancing up at them again, this time with a very worried look on her face. Silver Chadwick seemed to float over the black and white tiles and was at the door quickly and silently. She opened the front door and in stepped a tall figure wearing a navy-blue cape. Then the hood was pulled back, revealing a middle-aged man with straight brown hair that came to his chin. He looked like Nicolas, only older—the same pale face and the identical dark brown eyes.

"Philippe."

She whispered his name.

"Oui, c'est moi."

Silver reached out and gripped both his arms with her hands. There was no hug or kiss, just that. After a moment, she turned and looked up at them. Jaclyn was already running down the stairs to greet her father. Upon reaching him, he lifted her up as if she were a feather and kissed her cheek.

"Papa, Papa! Quelle bonne surprise!"

"Oui, mon petit lapin."

He set her down gently and stood looking at her, nodding, a faint smile on his face. However, Alexandra thought he looked more sad than happy, and she wondered why he was here, why he had come. Then the answer was obvious.

Nicolas appeared at the center banister with Noir, who swooped down with a loud caw and landed on Philippe's shoulder. Philippe reached up, stroking the black bird affectionately while speaking to him in French as Nicolas ran down the stairs, taking two steps at a time. His father hugged him tightly for what seemed like a long time and then put his hand on the back of Nicolas's head, whispering something in his son's ear.

Then Philippe looked up at Alexandra and Theo, and said something in French to his mother. Her answer was also in French and included their names. She beckoned them to come down. They walked down the stairs, and then Alexandra found herself standing in front of Philippe, shaking his hand. His hand was cold, like Nicolas's, but his handshake was stronger. He was obviously a powerful man, tall and very muscular. Alexandra noticed he seemed to study her intently, as though he was observing or appraising an object of interest, and after a moment, nodded seriously. Then he shook Theo's hand and with that, Silver Chadwick suggested they all go into the living room.

Evelyn scurried into the living room behind them, taking Philippe's cape and greeting him quietly. Her face was noticeably flushed, and she hurried out of the room only to quickly return with crackers and cheese spread, some olives, and pretzels on a large silver tray. Then she returned with a tray of ginger ale for everyone. Noir continued to sit on Philippe's shoulder. Nicolas was sitting on a blue velvet ottoman pulled up close to his father's chair. Jaclyn sat next to Alexandra on a nearby loveseat and Silver and Theo sat in chairs.

They all sipped their drinks and ate some snacks in silence. It actually felt very peculiar. It felt like a complete stranger, not family, was suddenly in their living room. No one could think of what to say. Silver sat facing her son, and although her face was hard to read, Alexandra thought she looked more worried than happy. The awkward silence was like an invisible, unwelcome guest in the room and became increasingly uncomfortable, and then Silver cleared her throat.

"Philippe is not as proficient in English as are his children, so I will tell you he came as a surprise for Nicolas's fifteenth birthday, which I alone knew. I kept it a secret so his visit would be a surprise for both Jaclyn and Nicolas, who I know have missed their father. And it is most wonderful to see my son after too many years to count."

Silver paused and smiled at Philippe. The expression was so familiar to Alexandra, a smile that was somehow sad. Alexandra turned and looked at Jaclyn, knowing she was thinking the same thing. He had come a great distance because this was a very important birthday.

"So we will have a real family party tonight. However, if you children will please excuse us, I need to speak privately with Philippe. We will see you in the dining room at six o'clock sharp. Take some cheese and crackers with you to tide over."

Nicolas stood up.

"Grand-Mère, I want to stay. Avec Noir. I have missed him beaucoup . . . il est mon père."

His last words were like a gauntlet had been thrown, as though he was daring her to challenge his right to remain with his father.

Silver Chadwick looked deeply into her grandson's dark brown eyes, and after a moment, nodded that he could stay. Jaclyn did not seem to mind or want to stay and left with Alexandra and Theo. As they were leaving the room, they all heard the name "Olivia" and knew she was telling Philippe he had a stepsister.

A little before six o'clock, Olivia arrived through the side door and walked down the hallway and into the kitchen. Everyone had gathered there, so when she pushed open the swinging door, there were many faces looking at her, including one she did not recognize.

"Olivia, darling, this is Philippe, my son and your stepbrother. He came to surprise Nicolas on his fifteenth birthday. I know this is a bit shocking, but that is how surprises often are, as we all have come to know recently."

At that moment, Alexandra realized her grandmother had not told Olivia about the surprise visit ahead of time. Olivia's eyes darkened, changing to slate gray as she slowly put out her hand. Philippe stepped forward and shook her hand quickly, nodding his head once. They were both looking at each other. Neither had spoken.

It almost seemed as though they were communicating in silence. Their eyes seemed locked on to each other, and it was a more intense and prolonged stare than Alexandra had ever seen. The silence was, again, very uncomfortable. As though on cue, Evelyn announced in a high-pitched voice (that was not normal), it was time for dinner and shooed them out of the kitchen and into the dining room. Philippe sat where Olivia had been for Thanksgiving, and Olivia sat where Blackie normally did. He was nursing a cold and staying in bed so he would be better for Christmas. He did not even know Philippe had arrived. Alexandra wondered how he would have reacted had he been well.

The dinner was far quieter than usual. There was very little conversation. Nicolas and his father spoke quietly in French, with Jaclyn joining in here and there. Silver tried to make conversation about the weather in France, and where had he been traveling on business (very exotic-sounding places like Tangiers and Belize). Olivia did not say a word and looked very serious.

Taco stayed in his cage upstairs, not wanting to see Philippe, and Noir had quickly usurped his dining room perch. Alexandra could see he was clearly gloating and gave him the meanest look she could, but it did not even faze him. The whole thing did not feel right to Alexandra; it felt "crooked" as Evelyn would say. As dinner ended, Evelyn announced birthday cake would be served in the living room at eight o'clock.

Never before had Alexandra felt such doom and gloom on someone's birthday.

* ◆ *

After dinner, Silver Chadwick suggested a penny poker game around the kitchen table before cake. This was a Christmas tradition at Chadwick and one Alexandra always looked forward to because Blackie and Taco made it so much fun. This suggestion caught most everyone's interest, including, for the first time ever, Nicolas and Noir. Nicolas looked surprised when he heard penny poker mentioned, and Noir had actually cawed twice with excitement. Alexandra quickly ran up the stairs to her room.

"Taco, it's penny poker night! You have to play! You are so good at poker, Taco! Philippe is not playing . . . he's tired from his long trip and lying down for a while. And after the card game we're going to have birthday cake for Nicolas in the living room, and you love birthdays, Taco!"

It was all Taco had to hear.

"Taco, card shark, full house, two pairs. Taco ready!"

He was clearly happy and hopped onto her shoulder.

"Taco, I have to tell you who is playing . . . Noir."

She was rubbing his neck and ears at the same time, trying to calm him.

Taco turned his head to look at her directly. It was a look of utter disbelief. He began shaking his head "no," then flew back into the cage and promptly put his head under one wing. He would not even look at her.

"Well, it's your choice, Taco."

She walked to the brass pole and swung her leg around.

"But you could beat him."

And down she went.

They were crowded around the large oak table—Theo, Alexandra, Jaclyn, Nicolas, Noir, and Olivia. Evelyn and Silver declined, saying it was a young people's night.

Nicolas volunteered to be the dealer. Everyone nodded in agreement. It was the first time he had played any games with them. He picked up the deck of cards and began shuffling. The cards seemed to fly out of his hand and shuffle themselves, just above the table. It happened so fast no one could really tell if he was holding the cards. Then, in a blink of an eye, he dealt five cards to each player around the table. Alexandra and Jaclyn looked at each other. No one shuffled cards like Nicolas. Just as they were all picking up their cards, the kitchen door swung open, propelled by a blue and gold macaw who landed on the table and squeezed in between Alexandra and Theo.

"Budge up, Taco in for the money."

Taco looked up at Theo, expecting a reaction, and there was. Theo grinned and laughed, and then stroked his long blue feathers. ("Budge up" was one of his British expressions, which meant to make room for someone else.)

Everyone looked pleased and surprised to see Taco, except Nicolas and Noir. They were cool and calm as always. However, Alexandra noticed Noir's beady eyes had sparked with interest when Taco flew into the room. Although ravens have a natural poker face, it was clear he was relishing the game ahead. Nicolas swept up all the cards and dealt again.

Alexandra felt like some kind of a major breakthrough had happened. Here were two birds at the same table and only a short time ago it seemed like they wanted to kill each other. Tonight they were going to have a civil game of cards. Then she felt her stomach flip. This was a day that had already brought unexpected twists and turns— and the night ahead loomed.

What would midnight bring?

Theo had never played poker before but quickly learned the rules and with beginner's luck began winning the penny pots in the center of the table. It was actually quite funny, because both birds began to look unhappy, pacing short distances on the table, glaring at Theo. (And became obvious to everyone Taco and Noir were both rather sore losers.) Then things started to go Noir's way, and he began to win, one hand after the next. Taco became increasingly agitated, his eyes never leaving Noir. With the skill of a professional poker player, Taco began to mount his comeback. It was interesting to watch how they played. Both birds stood on the table with their dealt cards laid out in front of them face down. Each would pick up a card with one foot (with great dexterity), look at it, and then move the cards around by memory, pushing any discarded cards away with their beak and signaling with a nod to the dealer they wanted new cards. Alexandra noticed how Noir was eyeing the shiny pennies in the pot, and only played his dull copper pennies, keeping the shiniest ones closest to him.

It was not long before Taco matched Noir in winnings.

Right about this time, Evelyn announced the game had to stop because it was time for birthday cake. This was as good an ending as there could be, Alexandra thought with great relief. A draw. They were equals.

"I think Noir and Taco should have a one-off. They can play a final hand to determine the winner and winner takes the whole pot."

Theo looked around as though he expected everyone to agree.

Alexandra scowled at him, but before she could say anything Nicolas spoke.

"Oui, mort subite. Sudden death."

His words hung in the air. It felt like a cold wind swept through the warm kitchen. Alexandra shivered. *Sudden death*. It sounded so . . . ominous. Alexandra looked at Taco. He was nodding his head "yes." She looked at Noir, who was perfectly still. Then he nodded once.

Everyone other than Olivia stood up and cleared the table for the two birds, who paced back and forth on their respective sides, continually eyeing one another. Olivia dealt the cards for neutrality— Theo decided this as the self-appointed referee. She began to shuffle the cards, and everyone immediately noticed the similarity to Nicolas.

They shuffled cards *exactly* the same way. Alexandra and Jaclyn looked at each other in shock, thinking the same thing. Another ominous sign and midnight was drawing closer.

Alexandra stood behind Taco and Nicolas stood behind Noir. Back and forth it went, each bird requesting new cards, discarding unwanted ones. Finally, the end came when Noir looked intensely at Taco and using his formidable black beak with a dramatic flourish, turned over one card at a time, revealing what he assumed was the winning hand. It was a straight flush, all spades in consecutive order, from five through nine. The winning hand. Everyone knew it. All eyes swiveled to Taco. Alexandra felt sick. He was such a proud macaw and was about to lose to a raven. She stroked his feathers to comfort him.

Then, very, very slowly, Taco turned over each one of his cards with his large curved beak. First, an ace of hearts, then king, then queen, then jack, and then the ten, all hearts. A royal flush. The highest winning hand in poker. Alexandra could not believe her eyes and apparently neither could Noir. He flew to the cards as if a closer inspection might prove them fake. He took his time looking closely at each card with his black beady eyes. Then he flew to Nicolas's shoulder. It was deathly quiet. The only sound was the crackling of the fire.

"Le perroquet a gagné par la chance."

The tone was cold, without emotion.

Taco understood the implication of the raven's words—he had won by chance or luck—but it did not diminish his feeling of triumph. He led everyone out of the kitchen like the Pied Piper and headed to the living room, plumped up with victory. However, the feeling diminished quickly. Philippe was sitting on one of the couches. Taco landed on his perch a distance away and cast sidelong glances at him, but Philippe ignored him. Evelyn brought in a large cake with fifteen candles lit and everyone sang "Happy Birthday." Of course, neither Nicolas nor Noir looked happy—at all. Taco momentarily forgot about Philippe and sang along, off-key, but with great enthusiasm. Nicolas blew out all the candles and then swiftly opened the gifts his grandmother had chosen, one from each person. A cool "merci" accompanied each gift as it was opened, "Merci, Alexandra. Merci, Theo," etc. As the cake was being served, Nicolas announced he did not eat cake, thanked them all again, and left with Noir and his gifts. Philippe quickly followed his son into the back hallway.

Everyone ate the cake in silence and then drifted away to go to bed. But not all were going to sleep.

It was late that night. Eleven bells had tolled from the grandfather clock and then one, so it was eleven thirty. There was a closet full of cleaning supplies across the hall from Nicolas's room, and the door was cracked open slightly.

Sconces dimly lit the hallway, and everyone was asleep except Alexandra and Jaclyn, who were sitting silently in the closet amidst the mops and pails waiting for midnight. Of course, Nicolas and Noir were also wide awake.

Light was coming from under Nicolas's bedroom door, but no voices were heard. The silence and anticipation made it nerve wracking and scary. When Olivia left, she whispered to them, "Don't be afraid, whatever happens is meant to be."

However, that advice was impossible to accept and had not made them feel any better. They had to live with Nicolas—and Noir. Olivia had said good-bye to Philippe last. She nodded once, shook his hand, and left. They had never even spoken to one another—very odd for a brother and sister meeting for the first time.

The deep chiming toll of twelve bells began.

No letter had been seen from the time they snuck into the closet at around eleven o'clock. One, two, three bells, the deep rich chimes kept ringing, echoing through the foyer and up the stairs. The hallway was empty. At the tenth bell, they heard a sound like a strong wind rushing up the marble staircase. Then they saw it, flying low across the hall to Nicolas's room. Just as the twelfth bell rang, a letter went right under his door with a swooshing sound.

They sat in silence.

Alexandra put her arm around Jaclyn. She was thinking about Mercy Disbrow and all the generations that had come and gone since 1692. Once again, the magical powers had been passed to a new generation, but this time a terrible mistake had been made.

As she was pulling Jaclyn up to leave the closet, they heard footsteps running up the marble stairs and quickly crouched down again. Through the crack, they saw Philippe stride across the hall, open Nicolas's door, and then shut it behind him. They could hear them talking in hushed voices. Before Alexandra could stop her, Jaclyn suddenly opened the closet door, tiptoed across the hall and stood listening right outside Nicolas's bedroom door. Alexandra motioned frantically for her to come back as she braced to hear the raven's caw. However, Jaclyn shook her head and put her finger to her lips, and the black bird was silent. In another minute, she waved for Alexandra to follow her, and they ran on little cat feet back to Alexandra's room.

"Bonne chance, Alexandra! Nicolas est probatoire!" Jaclyn's voice was breathless with excitement.

"What do you mean?? He did not get his powers tonight??"

"No, he did not. Nicolas must wait and prove he is worthy. My father was very angry. He said this has never happened before—

probation. I know he came here tonight to be with Nicolas, to celebrate what he expected would happen."

This outcome had not been anticipated. Olivia had said if the letter came, he would have powers and if not, he would not. Now what would happen? How long would it be? And what would determine if he was worthy?

Alexandra knew she wanted to look up the word "probation." Maybe it would give them a clue.

One painted eye was open and watching them from under a blue feathered wing.

CHRISTMAS EVE

When they awoke the next morning, Alexandra and Jaclyn smiled at each other.

They had fallen asleep in Alexandra's bed. It was the day before Christmas: a day Alexandra looked forward to almost more than Christmas. As she had grown older, she realized anticipating something exciting was almost better than experiencing what you could not wait for. Because what you could not wait for, once it started to happen, ended all too quickly. However, most of all this morning she felt relief. Her worst nightmare had not happened, at least not yet. They bounded out of bed, put on bathrobes, and zipped down the brass pole. Taco was not in his cage. He had already gone to breakfast.

"Well, top of the morning to my two lassies! Pain perdu?"

They all laughed. Evelyn had begun to try to speak a few French words (mostly that had to do with food).

"Oui, Madame Evelyn, merci. French toast would be parfait!" Jaclyn replied, grinning.

Taco was busy slurping his fruit and looked up as they entered.

"Un jeu de cartes, mesdemoiselles?"

It was perfect French. Taco was still relishing his victory, inviting them to play cards again, and his eyes were dancing with happiness.

"Taco, how did you learn to speak French?!" Jaclyn asked, looking amazed.

Alexandra wanted to hear his answer. He had said only a few common French words when he had first spoken about Philippe.

"Taco a étudié le français dans la bibliothèque de Chadwick."

Again, it was perfect pronunciation and inflection.

"Formidable, Taco!" Jaclyn replied in amazement.

He went on to explain he had studied in the library when Nicolas and Noir were not there.

"Taco surprise de Noël pour Jaclyn."

Taco looked at Jaclyn with great affection. His Christmas gift to her was learning her language.

Jaclyn went over to his perch and rubbed his ears, grinning.

"Merci, Taco, merci beaucoup. De tous les perroquets, vous êtes le meilleur!"

Of course, Jaclyn only knew one parrot, but Taco was nonetheless delighted to hear she thought he was the very best. However, he was dismayed when he heard a French word that sounded more like "parakeet," not parrot, for the second time. Noir had used the same word at the end of the poker game. A South American macaw was obviously not a parakeet, and he made a mental note to look this up.

The kitchen door suddenly swung open and in came their grandmother, dressed in a long hunter-green velvet skirt and matching cashmere sweater. Fastened to one side of her sweater and glittering in the morning sunlight was a pin she wore each Christmas—a Christmas tree made with diamonds and rubies that sparkled even in the dark.

"Jaclyn, my darling, I found a note from Philippe under my door this morning. Your father has left. He departed early this morning. He wrote that he had to return to France due to urgent business, and to give you and Nicolas his love and Joyeux Noël. I hope this is not too very sad for you, Jaclyn. I know you would have wanted him to stay."

Jaclyn looked down quickly, then looked up into her grandmother's eyes and put a brave smile on her face.

"No, Grand-Mère, it is fine. I know my father is very busy. That is why we came here to live, and I know it will be a wonderful Noël . . . I did not expect him to be here. I'm glad for Nicolas he came for his birthday . . . Nicolas is very close to him and I know he has missed him."

"Jaclyn, my dear, you are a very good sister to Nicolas, which I am not sure he entirely deserves. I went to tell him as soon as I found the note, but he said he already knew. His father told him last night he would not be staying. We spoke through his door . . . I could hear the deep sadness in his voice."

Silver drew in her breath with her brow furrowed. She appeared to be grappling with her grandson's seemingly perpetual unhappiness, and then she continued.

"Hopefully, as the day goes on, his spirits will improve. We are going to Christmas Eve dinner tonight at The Claw & Tail. Maybe that will cheer him up and of course, tomorrow is Christmas."

She turned and went out through the swinging door.

Alexandra and Jaclyn both knew Nicolas's sadness was not just because his father had left.

After breakfast and before going upstairs, the girls went to the library. On the reading table was the very large dictionary. Alexandra turned the pages to *p* and then *pr*, running her finger down the words until she found it.

She read aloud, "Probation: A critical examination and evaluation. An individual is subjected to a period of testing and trial."

They looked at each other. Nicolas would have to be tested before he would be given any powers. And he would have to pass.

They hurried out of the library and upstairs, as there was a most important note to write. Alexandra got out the paper and pen and began to write. She read aloud as she wrote, sentence by sentence, with Jaclyn nodding in agreement. Jaclyn really liked the explanation of detective work, exclaiming, "Parfait!" Whenever Jaclyn said that word, as she often did, it always made Alexandra think about a delicious dessert Evelyn made with chocolate or butterscotch pudding and whipped cream.

The note read:

> Dear Aunt Olivia,
>
> Nicolas did receive a letter at midnight. We saw it arrive from a distance, but through some detective work we would rather not talk about, we found out he is on probation. We looked up this word and he will have to pass an examination and go through a period of testing and trial and will not have his powers until he proves he is worthy. You are a teacher, so maybe you will give him this test.
>
> So for now, we are very relieved.
>
> Can't wait to see you tonight at The Claw & Tail!
> Love, your nieces,
> Alexandra & Jaclyn
> P.S. Just a reminder that you promised you would sleep over tonight, so don't forget your suitcase. We always have coffee cake and open presents in our pajamas and bathrobes on Christmas morning.

Alexandra folded the note, sat with it in her lap, and looked at Taco. He was looking at her from the top of his cage. After a moment, he flew to the bed and picked up the note in his beak.

"Taco, I have something for you. It's a Christmas present from Evelyn. I asked her if I could give it to you early and she said that I could."

Alexandra placed a small gift bag on the bed and gently took the note from his beak. Taco knew how to open presents with ease. Using his beak, he untied the ribbon around the handles and lifted out some red tissue paper. Then he put his head deep into the bag and pulled out a small bundle wrapped in tissue that was at the bottom. The tissue paper was peeled away in seconds, revealing the tiniest pair of red earmuffs and a miniature red and green striped scarf, about two inches wide and maybe a foot long. Alexandra gently placed the earmuffs on his head, asking if they felt all right. He nodded. Then she wrapped the scarf around his neck a number of times and tied it. Taco immediately flew to the floor in front of the armoire mirror, walking back and forth many times, looking at himself from every angle. He did look dashing. (And he seemed to know it.)

"Airmail delivery! Airmail delivery to Aunt Olivia!"

Alexandra and Jaclyn burst into laughter. He did not realize how funny he could be and looked a little insulted by their laughter. Nevertheless, he quickly flew back to the bed, grabbed the note in his beak, and flew to the window seat. Alexandra ran to the window and opened it.

"Hurry back, Taco. I will have the hot-water bottle ready for you this time!"

He gave them a small wave with one long wing, and then was through the window heading to Dark Harbor.

In about ten minutes, he returned. They were sitting on the window seat and saw him round the tall pines. The scarf was trailing behind with the red earmuffs still in place. He zoomed through the window straight to the bed and dove under the comforter. When his head appeared from under the edge of the comforter, they could see he had a piece of paper in his beak. Alexandra retrieved it as she put the pink rubber hot-water bottle next to him. He was cold, but not shivering this time, and quickly looked content, snuggled next to the warm bottle. She opened the note and saw the distinctive, elegant handwriting, now so familiar.

> *To my dear sweet nieces,*
>
> *I have packed my pajamas, slippers, bathrobe, and tooth-brush. I cannot wait for my first sleepover at Chadwick Manor on Christmas Eve! It will be hard to go to sleep tonight!*
>
> *Very interesting news about Nicolas. We will have to wait and see.*
>
> *See you at The C&T at 6:00 p.m.!*
>
> *XOXO*
> *Aunt O.*
>
> *P.S. Taco is an excellent airmail deliverer! On time and no matter the weather, very impressive. Loved his winter attire!*

The evening approached, with Silver reminding everyone to dress properly as The Claw & Tail was a "white-tablecloth restaurant." Alexandra and Jaclyn were thrilled to find new holiday outfits when they opened their armoires. There was a note pinned to each one:

"Merry Christmas, Alexandra ~ Love, Grand Mama" and "Joyeux Noël, Jaclyn ~ Love, Grand-Mère." Alexandra's outfit was a long red tartan plaid skirt and red sweater. Jaclyn's was the same, only in green. They got dressed together in Alexandra's room, twirling around in front of the mirror and admiring their long skirts. When they were ready, they walked slowly down the sweeping staircase, feeling quite grown-up.

Nicolas and Theo were already standing in the foyer. Both were wearing dark green blazers, navy slacks, and crisp white shirts with navy-blue ties. It was shocking to see Nicolas in something other than black, and both girls kept staring at him. As they got closer, they could see Nicolas's tie had small evergreen trees on it and Theo's tie had small green wreaths. They were both wearing new penny loafers. Theo had put shiny pennies in each loafer. Nicolas had not. Theo was grinning from ear to ear. Nicolas was not.

"Like my new Christmas dinner jacket, ladies?"

They all laughed except Nicolas. Theo looked so different from just a month ago. His red hair was no longer wild and dull looking, but neatly combed and shiny. On his nose were new tortoiseshell glasses. A few weeks earlier Blackie had taken him to Kennebunkport (a bigger town than Dark Harbor, but not by much), where there was an eye doctor. The doctor had pronounced Theo needed new glasses. Theo decided the wire-rimmed glasses were too young looking and after careful consideration, chose tortoiseshell frames. The new glasses did make him look more grown-up and very studious, which led Alexandra and Jaclyn to calling him "Professor" for fun, but he actually seemed to like it.

Nicolas stood in silence with an unhappy expression. It was clear he was uncomfortable in the new clothes. Like Theo, he too looked handsome, but in a dark, mysterious way. However, Alexandra knew it was not what he was wearing that was causing such an unhappy look—it was what had *not* happened the night before.

Suddenly, there was a light knock at the front door. They all looked at each other in surprise, and then Nicolas walked to the door and opened it. There stood Nicole. In an instant, Alexandra realized she and Jaclyn did not even come close to what they were looking at. Nicole was wearing a luxurious ice-blue velvet cape with an elegant hood trimmed in matching satin ribbon. As she lifted back the hood, Alexandra could see an unusual braided headband made from the same ice-blue velvet in her hair—and she was wearing makeup: silvery blue eye shadow, velvety black mascara, glossy pink lipstick, and her cheeks were the color of soft peach. Her eyes looked more blue than green, matching her outfit. With a beautiful smile, she was asking if she could come in. It was obvious the whole effect had not been lost on Nicolas or Theo, as neither seemed able to respond.

"Why, of course, come in, my dear Nicole! You look simply gorgeous. Naturellement, ma couleur préférée!"

Her grandmother had appeared, soundlessly moving across the black and white tiles. She was wearing a magnificent silver cape and matching long dress, with a white fur hat and muff. Alexandra had never seen the outfit before, and it occurred to her the cape and dress were a perfect match for her name. Once again, she marveled at her grandmother's elegance, and looking at Nicole, she realized Nicole had the same, almost regal appearance. Then she remembered—Nicole was the granddaughter of a Duke and Duchess, and she wondered if Nicole had some type of royal title, not mentioned when they were introduced.

"I invited Nicole to come with us to The Claw & Tail this evening. Her grandparents said they could live without her as long as she was back before midnight when they have a glass of champagne. A

Christmas tradition at Devonshire, one I think we shall begin at Chadwick tonight!"

Alexandra had never had champagne. That would be interesting.

As Nicole stepped into the foyer she immediately stopped, obviously surprised to see the two life-size tigers staring at her with gleaming emerald eyes. Silver rested her hand on one of the tiger statues, assuring her they only *looked* real, and then escorted Nicole through the foyer and down the back hallway. Nicolas followed, and the others trailed farther behind, silently exchanging amused looks.

The black touring car was idling in the driveway. Blackie was much improved, and very glad because he did not want to miss his last lobster dinner of the season. Evelyn was sitting in the front seat with him. Everyone else climbed in for the short ride to Dark Harbor. The interior was warm and inviting, the heater turned up high. The long touring car had room for a second bench seat, which Blackie had installed to accommodate all the passengers. Jaclyn, Alexandra, and Nicole were on one seat and facing them on the other seat were Silver, Nicolas, and Theo. As it ended up, Nicolas was sitting directly across from Nicole.

Going down the drive, Nicole began to speak in French to Nicolas, something about faire du patin à glace and cadeaux de Noël. Alexandra noticed he responded with only "non" or "oui," and glanced at her once or twice, mostly staring out into the dark night.

Theo was talking to Blackie about wanting to go skating again, "to give it another welly!" Blackie laughed and said, "Jolly good, Theo!" Then Evelyn was talking to Blackie about the lobster dinner, and Jaclyn was asking Theo if he liked lobster (he answered that he had never had a posh dinner in his life), and Alexandra was once again thinking how different her life was this Christmas. For as long as she could remember, it had been just the four of them riding to The Claw & Tail on

Christmas Eve. Tonight, as they headed down the winding coast road, there were four more in the car with one more person waiting at the restaurant. Alexandra could not help but smile, and then she realized her grandmother was looking at her. She was smiling, too.

They arrived minutes later. Blackie drew the car right up to the awning-covered entrance. Olivia was waiting outside, waving as she saw them approach. She was wearing a gorgeous green velvet cape with white fur trim and white furry mittens.

The Claw & Tail was an elegant restaurant.

A man dressed in a fancy black suit (complete with tails and black bow tie) stood inside the front door with a white linen napkin folded over one arm. The outfit he was wearing was identical to what the lobster was wearing on the sign above the restaurant. His black hair, neatly parted in the center and slicked down, was quite dapper look-ing. A handlebar moustache swept out over his cheeks, sleekly curled up on each end. Alexandra knew from her grandmother he had been at The Claw & Tail "forever," and had known her mother since she was a baby. His name was Pierre and he spoke with a heavy French accent. Her grandmother always spoke to him in French, and she had told Alexandra in an approving voice (many times) that he was a "true Parisian," whatever that meant. Pierre escorted them to a round table at the far end of the restaurant, overlooking the harbor, right in front of a bay window. A large wreath was hanging on the inside of the window, lit with tiny white lights and decorated with an enormous red velvet bow. Evergreen boughs trimmed the windows, and the wonder-ful scent of pine was in the air. At one end of the dining room, a stone fireplace was ablaze with a crackling fire and standing next to the fire-place was a tall and heavily decorated Christmas tree. As they followed Pierre, Alexandra quickly detoured and took Jaclyn to see the tree. The ornaments on the tree were related to the sea—shiny red lobsters with wreaths as neckpieces, starfish encrusted with gemstones, colorful fish coated with glitter, lobster traps covered with sparkling netting, brightly painted lobster buoys, and too many more to be described, each one unique. At the top of the tree was a large pearl nautilus shell. Jaclyn's eyes were full of delight as she gazed at all the elegant sea creature ornaments.

"Fancy that! A nautilus shell for the tree topper!"

Theo had appeared and was admiring the tree.

"Do you ladies know that a nautilus shell, if cut in half, reveals tiny chambers built by its occupant, a rather unfortunate-looking squid-like creature that builds larger and larger chambers as it grows, one after the next, in a perfect logarithmic spiral? It is a *mathematically perfect* equiangular spiral as defined by Descartes in 1638. The nautilus is only found in the Indo-Pacific oceans, and nautiloid fossil remains prove that in the early Paleozoic era, the shell, if uncoiled, would have been up to *nine meters*."

He pushed his glasses up on his nose, a habit Alexandra had seen him do for as long as she could remember, still staring at the opalescent pearl shell in awe.

"Merci, Professeur Eddington, très intéressant. Exactly when was the early Paleozoic period, Professeur?"

Jaclyn gave him a most serious look, and then burst into laughter, as did Alexandra.

"That would be 540 million years ago, give or take a few years, Mademoiselle."

Theo bowed slightly to Jaclyn, grinning, and then led them to their table.

Alexandra wondered how Theo could possibly know so much about a seashell, and why he liked math so much. As they walked to the table, she was trying hard to remember the conversion from meters to feet, surprising herself when she did. Stretched out, she calculated, the shell would be up to thirty feet long. It was unbelievable, but for that matter, she thought it was hard to believe dinosaurs once roamed the earth or that modern-day *birds* were their descendants.

At each place setting, intricately folded red and green cloth napkins looked like miniature Christmas trees. A basket of dwarf red poinsettias was in the center of the table, surrounded by crystal votive candles. There were place cards for everyone (which Alexandra knew had been arranged by her grandmother), and Nicolas and Nicole were seated next to one another. It was quickly apparent that while Nicole was most pleased with the seating arrangement, Nicolas was not. He looked ill at ease, shifting in his seat and looking down, not wanting to talk.

Ice water was poured and the drink and dinner orders taken and soon, large trays were being placed on folding tables next to them. Covered serving dishes were set down on the table, each filled with different vegetables, along with baskets of hot popovers (these were Alexandra's favorite). All the grown-ups ordered lobster and all the children chose turkey with creamy mashed potatoes and gravy, except Nicolas, who also ordered lobster like the grown-ups. Theo was in heaven with the food, as he always seemed to be. The years of having so little to eat were fading away, and he had begun to grow bigger in the short time he had been living with them. Throughout dinner, Theo was happy and talkative, as was everyone at the table. Everyone except Nicolas. Nicole tried to engage him in conversation a number of times, but he hardly responded and rarely looked at her or anyone else. Slowly, the dinners were consumed and then dessert was served . . . a thick, rich brownie with vanilla ice cream and hot fudge, topped with whipped cream and a cherry. It was the dessert spécialité of The Claw & Tail.

Quite stuffed, they said, "Merry Christmas!" to Pierre, who responded with "Joyeux Noël, Chadwick famille!" and walked out into the cold night air. Alexandra led the way to the large wharf and toward the Christmas tree at the far end. It was a giant evergreen covered with colored lights. The lights reflected in the icy harbor water like brilliant gemstones scattered across a black surface. Some of the sailboats anchored in the harbor were outlined in colored lights. Alexandra hooked arms with Blackie, and as they walked, she asked him if they could light the *Windswept* next year. He raised one eyebrow and was obviously thinking . . . lights, for some reason Alexandra did not understand, were very challenging. However, he answered, "Yes, lassie, we will." Nicolas had gone to a far corner of the wharf by himself and was staring out into the black harbor. Alexandra saw Nicole looking at him, but she left him alone. As they were leaving the wharf, Blackie asked if anyone wanted to join him for a spin around the harbor in a small, motorized skiff. Theo had immediately jumped at the invitation, Nicolas declined as did Nicole, and Alexandra knew she wanted to take Jaclyn to see the shops, so just Blackie and Theo headed out into the icy harbor. Silver, Evelyn, and Olivia said they would wait in the car.

Alexandra always felt bittersweet after Christmas Eve dinner. She knew Dark Harbor would not be the same again until spring. During the frigid winter months most of the shops closed. The village became hushed and insulated by all the snow and felt almost desolate, so few people ventured out.

On Christmas Eve, Alexandra liked to walk the main street, looking into the warmly lit and decorated shops one last time. She and Jaclyn ran toward town, their breath forming white clouds in the frosty air, and they hurried down the snow-covered sidewalk. Both sides of the small main street were lined with luminaries, white paper bags holding candles, which cast a festive glow in the snow. Alexandra quickly led Jaclyn to the far end of town, explaining she liked to start at Moo Bar first.

They looked in each shop window.

Moo Bar was filled with people eating ice cream, along with some cows and one moose. As they approached The Moose's Closet, they could see the brightly lit colored bulbs draped between the moose's antlers, and his Santa's cap covered with a dusting of snow. Very strangely, as they got closer, it appeared as if frosty swirls of breath were coming from the moose's large nostrils. Alexandra had never seen this before, and the moose had always been above the shop door. They looked at each other in astonishment, and then Alexandra said there was a lot of frost in the night air, so maybe it just *looked* like he was breathing. She remembered Theo's reaction to the moose and thought it was probably a good thing he was not with them. As they passed underneath the large head, they stopped for a moment. Swirls of frosty air were coming from the end of his long nose—*in regular intervals.*

Awestruck looks were exchanged.

The Moose's Closet was jammed with shoppers taking advantage of the end-of-season sales—who were probably so focused on find-ing last-minute presents no one noticed the glimmer in the large brown eyes or the moose's breath as they stepped through the shop door.

Next, they came to Sweet Blooms. The shop window always reminded Alexandra of looking through an Easter egg at a springtime scene. Fresh cut flowers and flowering plants in clay pots filled the window with bursts of color, and tucked between the flowers were wooden crates piled high with scented soaps and lotions. Crystal bot-tles of perfume tied to red and green satin ribbons hung suspended from the ceiling, appearing to float above the flowers like glass butter-flies. Boxes of chocolates wrapped in the shape of angels with silver and gold gossamer wings were scattered everywhere. As they stood looking at the beautiful spring-like scene through the frosted glass, the shop door opened and as the shoppers emerged, a heavy *rose* fragrance escaped into the frigid air.

Then they came to the Quill & Parchment. They glanced in and then stopped, peering through the fogged-up window. Nicolas was standing at the counter next to a stack of items being rung up at the register. They stepped out of his sight and continued to watch. There were many people milling around inside the shop, and as they watched, they both saw a shimmering ice-blue cape sweep by the front door and then disappear in the crowded shop. Nicole was with him. They looked at each other in complete surprise. He had not even talked to her at dinner. And the other amazing discovery . . . Nicolas was going to give Christmas presents.

They walked along in silence.

Alexandra was thinking about Nicolas. Less than twenty-four hours ago he found out he might not get the powers he so obviously, desperately wanted. Tonight he was buying presents. Maybe something was changing for the better. The letter said he had to prove himself worthy.

In silence, they continued walking . . . past The Book Nook (Alexandra did not even glance in) and Chadwick Bank & Trust, open late for those who needed shopping money. Then they crossed the street, walked by the tiny post office and on to Weston's Market where they went in to wish Mr. Weston a "Merry Christmas." As she pushed open the door and the wonderful aroma of Weston's Market enveloped them, the thought occurred to Alexandra she could be blindfolded in fifty years and would still know it was Weston's Market. Mr. Weston gave them each a wrapped Christmas chocolate, two more for the boys, and a couple pieces of red licorice for Blackie. They said their good-byes and "Merry Christmas!" and then were running down the snowy street and back to the car waiting for them outside The Claw & Tail. Nicolas, Nicole, and Theo were already in the car. Alexandra and Jaclyn noticed the rumble seat was open, and the "passengers" were various shopping bags.

Olivia followed them home in her red sports car, having reassured Alexandra during dinner she *was* spending the night. She would stay in one of the second-floor bedrooms Evelyn had opened and readied for her. When they got back to Chadwick, everyone gathered in the living room and Evelyn sat down at the grand piano. As she began to play Christmas carols, she led the way singing. Taco flew into the living room soon after the music began and was quickly singing along. He knew all the words to the carols.

They were singing "Deck the Halls" when Alexandra noticed Nicolas had disappeared, as had her grandmother. She felt somewhat alarmed and kept watching the large archway leading into the back hall. In a short while, they both reappeared. Her grandmother had her arm through Nicolas's arm. It was the first time Alexandra had ever seen this and it was almost shocking. Nicolas had changed his clothes, again wearing his black slacks and black turtleneck, and was carrying Noir in his cage. He led his grandmother to a chair and sat near her on an ottoman, placing Noir's cage at his feet. He did not sing, but he actually did not look quite as miserable as he had earlier in the evening. Having changed his clothes and having Noir by his side probably helped lift his spirits, Alexandra thought.

Everyone admired the beautiful tree and all the stockings, with Silver expressing her appreciation to Blackie and Evelyn for all their efforts, and there was a round of applause for Evelyn after singing the last carol. Sometime during the evening, two introductions were made. Nicole was enchanted upon meeting Taco, who bowed when they were introduced, having heard for so long the Duke and Duchess were royalty. However, she had to ask Nicolas to be introduced to Noir, which was very brief, and he was obviously not impressed—at all. He appeared to study her, quite coolly, and from the look in his eyes did not arrive at a favorable opinion. Soon the grandfather clock chimed eleven bells, then one for the half hour, and Nicole put on her cape and said her good-byes. Blackie was getting ready to drive her the short distance home when Nicolas spoke for the first time all evening.

"Nicole, voulez-vous que je marche avec vous jusqu'à votre maison?"

All eyes were on Nicole.

"Oui, merci, Nicolas."

She was obviously surprised and quite pleased that Nicolas had offered to walk her home.

Nicolas put on his cape and they left through double doors that opened directly into the foyer from the living room. Everyone watched from the living room window as they walked together across the snow-covered front lawn of Chadwick toward Devonshire under the light of a full moon.

Alexandra wondered if they were talking, and if so, what about. It was almost midnight. This time last night, she and Jaclyn were nervously awaiting the letter. No one could have guessed that one day later Nicolas would be walking Nicole home, at his own invitation.

Blackie and Evelyn went to get the champagne, which was to become a new Christmas Eve tradition at Chadwick Manor, and they had just brought the bottles and glasses into the living room when they all saw Nicolas reappear in the moonlight. He was walking back across the front lawn of Chadwick—he had not lingered at Devonshire. With a smile and a twinkle in his eye, Blackie took the two bottles outside. They watched through the window as he explained to Nicolas how to pop the champagne corks. Each bottle was then expertly opened, with loud pops as the corks flew off, the vapor forming misty swirls in the cold night air. They came back inside and Blackie poured everyone a small glass of champagne. Alexandra was studying Nicolas. For the first time ever, his eyes looked *almost* happy.

Silver raised her glass as the deep chiming bells in the grandfather clock tolled twelve times, as did everyone.

"Merry Christmas, Joyeux Noël, all my dears."

They all drank a sip. The bubbles felt amazing going down Alexandra's throat and it tasted delicious. She smiled at Theo and he smiled back. Then he raised his glass again *to her*.

Alexandra knew she was looking at the best friend she would ever have.

As the last drops of champagne disappeared, Blackie brought out a large, antique book from a chest of drawers, giving it to Silver. Everyone gathered around her chair and then, as she had done every Christmas Eve, she began reading "The Night Before Christmas." Every other Christmas Alexandra had been the only child listening, but not this night. Her grandmother's silver dress shimmered in the soft lights of the tree, and the voice Alexandra loved so much filled the room. As she looked at Nicolas and Jaclyn, Alexandra wondered if this was a poem known in France. There was laughter when one line was smoothly changed, "Not a creature was stirring, not even a mouse . . . or a macaw . . . or a raven . . ." Silver paused, smiling at Nicolas and Alexandra and then at Noir and Taco. Noir was expressionless in his cage, but Taco raised his wings in response, clearly enjoying the recognition. Nicolas did not smile, but his expression had noticeably softened; it was in his eyes.

With the poem finished, the book was closed for another year, and they all went straight to bed—except for Nicolas. Alexandra noticed when he detoured on the way to the staircase and quickly ducked into the wrapping closet. She felt like Christmas had worked some of its magic on Nicolas after all. He had even walked Nicole home.

As visions of sugarplums danced in her head, Alexandra was sound asleep as soon as she laid her head on the pillow.

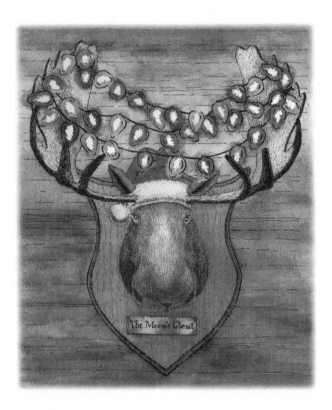

The Moose's Closet

CHRISTMAS DAY AND THE KEY

The first thing Alexandra remembered every Christmas morning was waking up and pushing one foot around her bed until she felt the heavy weight of the filled stocking.

Awake, and having found the familiar heaviness with her foot, Alexandra quickly sat up and excitedly pulled the stocking toward her. As she began looking in the stocking, she suddenly thought of Jaclyn and jumped out of bed running toward her room. Just as Alexandra approached the bedroom door, Jaclyn emerged from her room with sleepy eyes, holding her stocking and grinning. Then they heard the door to the third floor open and out came Theo in his new flannel bathrobe (or "dressing gown" as he called it, which always made them laugh) holding his filled stocking. His hair was a bit wild looking, and he was grinning as he said, "Cheerio, ladies!" There was no sound from Nicolas's room, so they went to Alexandra's room, and were soon sprawled under the canopy looking at their stocking gifts. Taco was wide awake and admiring his stocking, which was hanging on the outside of his cage. After a few minutes, he climbed around the outside, grabbed the stocking, and flew to the bed with the others.

There was every little thing imaginable in Alexandra and Jaclyn's stockings—from gum to socks to new playing cards to barrettes to small bottles of lotion and perfume. Theo's stocking held candy, socks, a comb and brush set, a new eyeglass case, and something called after-shave lotion, which he opened, smelled, and pronounced, "Brilliant!" They each found an orange and a silver dollar at the bottom of their stockings.

Taco dumped his stocking onto the bed with a kind of exuberant parrot squeal. There were small bags of palm nuts and walnuts in shells (special treats), a section of birch tree branch for his cage for chewing (parrots naturally like to chew and it's important for their beaks), ropes to knot, and little puzzles with sliding pieces secured within frames (the puzzle pieces could be easily pushed around with his beak). However, he seemed most pleased with the tiniest English-French dictionary. Holding it in one foot, he flipped the pages with the other, quickly finding the page he was looking for.

"Parrot est perroquet? Parrot not parakeet."

He looked at Jaclyn, rather insulted, thinking the French word sounded more like "parakeet" than "parrot."

"Look up parakeet, Taco. Parakeet est perruche. Parrot est perroquet. Il y a une grande différence entre les deux!"

Jaclyn grinned at him and he looked *most* relieved.

They could hear voices downstairs, so once all the treasures had been inspected they hopped on the brass pole (including Taco, who wrapped his wings around it) and headed to the kitchen.

Taco was the first through the door, loudly proclaiming, "Joyeux Noël!"

The smell of coffee and bacon greeted them. Blackie and Evelyn were already at the table having coffee with Silver and Olivia. Everyone was wearing bathrobes and slippers. It was always a funny sight to Alexandra as everyone was properly dressed early every day except for Christmas morning. To see Blackie and Evelyn in their bathrobes always made her smile. Then her gaze fell on her aunt, for the first time waking up at Chadwick and having breakfast with them. Olivia was wearing a white robe with red satin trim to match her red slippers. She looked more like Snow White than ever, Alexandra thought . . . she was even wearing a red ribbon tied in a bow in her hair.

Most of all, it felt like she belonged with them and had finally come *home*.

There was a large coffee cake in the center of the table, along with assorted fruit, muffins, a large platter of crisp bacon and scrambled eggs, and pitchers of orange juice, milk, and coffee. Soon they were all eating something delicious, when suddenly the kitchen door swung open and in came Nicolas and Noir. Noir was in his cage. Nicolas was wearing a black bathrobe, but he had not dressed as Alexandra thought he would. Without speaking, he sat down and began eating some coffee cake.

"What did you get in your stocking, Nicolas?"

Jaclyn was obviously very curious.

"Many useful things. Très pratique."

"Like what?"

"Socks, a new toothbrush, nail clippers, a small flashlight, some candy, and other things."

"Did you get an orange and a silver dollar?"

"Oui."

"And what did Noir get in his stocking?"

"Treats and games. New coins and some shiny brass objects. You can see them right there in his cage next to the Halloween ring."

Jaclyn frowned at the memory, peering into his cage.

"Taco got the tiniest English-to-French dictionary you've ever seen, très petit. It was the perfect stocking gift because he is learning French. *He is teaching himself.* It was his Christmas surprise for me."

Jaclyn looked at him with pride and affection. Taco was enjoying the compliments.

"Je désire avoir le petit déjeuner dans ma chambre."

It was Noir's impeccable French, in his typical cold, flat tone.

"Taco, what did Noir just say?" Nicolas suddenly asked, his dark brown eyes looking intently at Taco. It was a test.

"I want to have breakfast in my bedroom."

The translation was said quickly, without hesitation, and he resumed eating his watermelon and grapes.

"Du pain grillé avec de la confiture et du bacon et des oeufs. Le service de chambre, s'il vous plaît."

Again, the cool monotone voice.

Everyone looked at Taco, who kept eating. After finishing a slice of watermelon, he looked up directly at Nicolas.

"Some toast with jam and some bacon and eggs. Room service, please."

It was most impressive and Taco knew it.

"Well, blimey, Noir, dearie, there is no room service at Chadwick Manor for birds, ravens or parrots. Am I right, Taco?"

Evelyn could not help from weighing in.

"That would be *correct*. C'est exact. No room service for birds."

Taco was clearly enjoying himself as an expert on house rules and showing off his newly acquired language skills. He was looking at Noir quite coolly and shaking his head "no."

The kitchen erupted in laughter. Alexandra was watching Nicolas and she could see the faint edges of a smile. It was funny—no room service for birds. However, it was obvious he was taking a moment to think about everything. Alexandra wondered if he would just leave as he normally did when he or Noir did not get what they wanted. He did not. Instead, he got up, made some toast with jam, and carefully cut it up in small pieces, and then he took some bits of egg and bacon from the platter, putting it all in Noir's cage. Everyone watched in silence. Next, he picked up the cage, walked over to the dumbwaiter, opened the door, put in the raven's cage, and pressed 2. They could all see Noir's eyes widen with surprise as the door closed. The hum of the motor began and up he went.

"Noir will have breakfast in our room, as requested."

Nicolas might as well have said "checkmate." There was a hint of a smile on his face. Then he was out through the swinging door and up the stairs to meet the dumbwaiter as it arrived on the second floor.

*

They all went to the living room after finishing breakfast. Even more presents had arrived overnight. The two stockings for Max and Biscuit were still hanging from the mantel. They were lumpy and obviously filled, and both dogs were lying below the stockings wagging their tails. Theo got them down and gave them to Alexandra and Jaclyn, and the girls sat with the dogs at their feet and began pulling out the stocking gifts.

Max had a package of rawhide sticks and a gray squirrel squeaky toy. At the bottom of the stocking was a large soup bone almost too big for his mouth. Before giving him the bone, Alexandra asked him to sit, shake, and then roll over both ways. Then he was off, prancing around the room so everyone could admire his prized possession before he settled down to the serious business of chewing. Biscuit was playing with two very small squeaky toys, a frog and a mouse, but they were dropped cold as soon as a fancy bag of "Weston's Market Delectably Delicious Dog Cookies" was pulled out of his stocking. Before opening the bag, Jaclyn made him perform his two tricks. One was to play dead, lying flat as a flounder and not moving (except for his eyes, which would shift to the cookie bag and then to Jaclyn and then back to the bag). The other trick was to stand on his little hind legs and paw the air until he could no longer keep his balance. He was in heaven as she gave him four cookies, one at a time, each a different flavor.

Alexandra, Jaclyn, and Theo read the tags and parceled out the gifts to each person. Soon there were piles of presents at each person's feet. They made a pile for Nicolas, who had not yet reappeared.

"The tradition we have had in the past was for each person to open one gift and then to the next, and so on, until the last package was opened. However, if we did that today, my dears, we might be here until the evening. So everyone may open their gifts as they would like."

Silver looked at everyone and nodded. The unwrapping began.

There were oohs and aahs, thank-yous, and lots of low whistles from Theo, along with any number of "brilliants," as the fancy packages were unwrapped. It was impossible to keep track of what everyone was opening, but Olivia said they could look at each other's gifts later in the day. Nicolas soon returned with Noir, who looked quite smug having had his "room service" breakfast after all. He set the cage down and began opening his gifts. They all received clothing and practical things, like new snow boots, winter hats, and gloves.

Olivia gave both girls woolen hats she had hand knit in random-width stripes using every color of yarn imaginable. The hats went all the way down their backs, ending with large tassels attached to the pointed ends. Alexandra and Jaclyn immediately put them on their heads and never took them off as they continued to open gifts. There were identical gifts from their grandmother—lighted makeup mirrors and a tiny trunk filled with eye shadows, lipsticks, and powders with a note that read, "For special occasions only, not for school. Please observe this rule." Alexandra remembered how Nicole had looked the night before and what she had been thinking. Why did it sometimes seem her grandmother could read her mind? The girls received flannel pajamas from Evelyn and fluffy slippers from Blackie. Somehow, Max and Biscuit had managed to do some shopping and picked out matching silver bracelets for Alexandra and Jaclyn. Their names were engraved on one side of a small silver heart with "Love, Max" and "Love, Biscuit" on the other.

Theo did not stop grinning. Olivia gave him a slide rule that he was thrilled with (but that made Alexandra almost nauseous just looking at it), and she gave Theo and Nicolas hand-knit scarves in the same wild striped patterns as the girls' hats. When Theo opened his, he had whooped and put it around his neck, and just like the girls, he did not take it off. (Nicolas thanked his aunt politely, folded the scarf, and put it back in the box as he had done with all his gifts.) Theo loved the drawing book Alexandra gave him and the set of paints from Jaclyn. A book about famous artists from Blackie and Evelyn was a clear favorite, as was a book about European architecture from Miss Silver.

Nicolas was very methodical and serious as he opened each gift.

As he opened the compass, Alexandra watched him. He gently pulled it out of the leather case. The compass was encased in thick, lustrous silver. The needle bobbed in different positions as the compass was moved, hovering over a black and white compass rose. The needle and all the compass settings, N, S, E, and W, were shiny red. Noir was craning to see it with transparent envy.

"In case you ever take a walk with Noir and get lost, it would help you find your way back home," Alexandra said, feeling she should explain its usefulness.

"Oui, yes, but ravens have a keen sense of direction. They can always find their way home. But if I go alone, I will take this. Merci, Alexandra."

"That one is from me. You could open it."

Nicolas pointed to a small square package wrapped in plain white paper with dark green ribbon. Not very Christmas looking, but it was a very neat wrapping job and the ribbon was tied perfectly in a crisp bow.

She picked it up. The tag read, "To Alexandra, From Nicolas." It was heavier than she expected for a small box. She untied the ribbon, unwrapped the paper, and lifted up the top of the box. When the tissue paper was pulled away, she could see it was a snow globe. Carefully, she lifted it out of the box and could not believe what she was looking at. Inside the globe was a miniature red sailboat with white sails and very familiar nautical lettering on the main sail, "JYS 12." Painted on the stern in very small gold lettering was "*Windswept.*" The name had also been painted in the tiniest letters along the bow of the boat.

"Agite, shake it."

She shook the globe. Snowflakes swirled around the sailboat, and to her complete astonishment, she could now see there were tiny colored Christmas lights outlining the mast and both the large and small sails. They lit up when she shook it. She felt her throat tighten and tears come into her eyes. So many thoughts swirled through her mind like the tiny snowflakes floating in the globe. How did he get the name *Windswept* on the tiny sailboat and how could he have known she had just asked Blackie about lighting the *Windswept* next Christmas? Nicolas was watching her and seemed to know she was adrift in a sea of questions.

"There is a wood carver in Dark Harbor on a small fishing wharf just outside of town. He is a lobsterman in the summer, but in the winter he carves wooden boats. I told him what I wanted and pointed out the *Windswept* in the harbor. I saw the lights on the sailboats one night when I walked to the bluff overlooking the harbor. He went to Boston to have it made into a snow globe and to add the lights. There is a small battery for the lights underneath."

Alexandra was speechless. It was the most he had ever spoken to her since the day in the library. When did he go into Dark Harbor by himself and find the wood carver, or go out at night to look at the harbor? He had put so much thought into this gift, yet he seemed so selfish and only concerned about himself and Noir. Jaclyn and Theo came closer to look at it. Their expressions mirrored hers. They, too, were completely amazed. As she sat holding the globe, she looked at Olivia and her grandmother, who were both looking at Nicolas. For the first time, she could see in their eyes something she had not seen before. It was approval.

"Nicolas, thank you. Merci, merci beaucoup. I love it."

He nodded, and his brown eyes were different; they were not as dark and cold.

Then, like the snowflakes settling to the bottom of the globe, she realized something with great clarity. He had thought of this gift well before December 23rd.

Before he found out he would have to prove himself worthy.

◆

The rest of the presents were opened, the paper and ribbons picked up, and slowly, everyone drifted away from the living room, going to their bedrooms to relax and get dressed. They would have Christmas dinner at five o'clock as always, but Evelyn said there would be something different this year that would be a surprise. Alexandra fleetingly wondered what it was, but her thoughts were elsewhere. The snow globe was the only gift she brought upstairs to her room. She put it on the nightstand, between the photograph of her parents and her father's pipe, and could not wait to see it at night when the room was dark. Taco was also intrigued and hopped on her bed to examine it more closely.

She finished dressing and was lying on her bed, thinking. Her aunt had loved the daily diary and from what was said, the other gifts she had picked out were good choices, too. *It was the best Christmas ever*, she thought as she looked again at the snow globe. It was an exact replica of the *Windswept*, only miniature.

Taco was back in his cage busily arranging his stocking gifts and other toys Alexandra had given him for Christmas, placing the mirror exactly where he could see his face from his perch, and wedging the thick tree branch securely where he could chew it easily. After looking everything over, and seeming to be most satisfied, he hopped down in one corner of his cage and then flew back to the bed. In his large curved beak was a tissue-wrapped bundle that he dropped next to her.

"Merry Christmas, princess."

His painted eyes were filled with love.

"Whatever is this, Taco?! When did you go shopping? On one of your airmail deliveries to Dark Harbor?!"

Alexandra laughed at the thought of Taco flying into The Moose's Closet to do a little Christmas shopping while the other customers watched in shock. She reached out to stroke his head and then picked up the mysterious little package. He had obviously wrapped it himself. The red tissue paper had some beak tears and the Scotch tape was messy but did the job. The package was small and rectangular, maybe four inches long. She slowly tore away the tape and unwound many layers of tissue. Inside was a very elaborate gold key with a small gold tag attached to it.

On the tag was an engraved message, "To the bearer of this key, a place to travel there shall be, of sun and sand and sea."

She stared at the key and reread the tag again. The key was polished gold, with fancy embossed scrollwork, most unusual looking. It looked nothing like Evelyn's keys. There were wavy prongs of different lengths at the end that would fit in a keyhole. The one at the very end was a cone-shaped spiral, which for some reason reminded her of a seashell. She looked questioningly at Taco, then at the key, and then back at Taco.

Taco flew from the bed to the floor and landed in front of the beach scene mural covering one entire wall. A realistically proportioned white picket fence ran along the entire length of the mural following the ups and downs of sand dunes dotted with sea grasses, blue hydrangeas, and sea lavender. In the center of the fence was a gate. The perspective was as though you were standing at the gate, looking down on the beach from a sand dune.

On the beach were sunbathers, colorful umbrellas, beach blankets, and people swimming in the ocean and sailboats on the horizon. More sailboats were in slips at a long dock, and a couple of lifeguards were sitting in tall white chairs along the beach. There was a small shed with a sign, "The Snack Shack," and people lined up in front of the large open window to buy food. The mural continued to the left all the way to the window seat and to the right until it reached a bedroom window. It then continued around the corner of the room to the wall next to the bedroom door. Painted in the section of wall to the left of the door was one side of a weathered beach cottage. The front of the cottage was facing the ocean and not visible. There were two windows with red shutters on the side of the cottage, and in the left window a black cat with yellow eyes was sitting on the inside sill. A weather vane rose from the peak of the roof, a sailboat with the four points of the compass. Above the two windows was a decorative banner painted red, and in gold lettering it read, "Chadwick Cottage."

Long ago, Alexandra had asked her grandmother if they had a cottage at the beach, but her grandmother had frowned and said no, it was just the artist's idea. Having grown up looking at it, Alexandra knew every detail of the mural.

Taco was walking back and forth in front of the painted gate.

Then, with his powerful wings, he elevated himself, suspended in midair in front of the gate. Using his beak, he began chipping away at the paint in one spot. In a few seconds, he stopped and flew back to the bed. They were both looking at what was now exposed—a gold keyhole on one of the slats of the painted gate. Alexandra could not move. She swallowed hard, and then looked at the key in her hand and reread the tag again.

"Taco, if I put the key in that keyhole . . . what happens?"

She felt her voice drop to a hushed whisper as she said the last two words.

"To the beach . . . go to the beach . . ." came the whispered reply.

Alexandra felt like it was all a dream. This could not be possible. Or could it? There were magical powers in her family. She slowly turned and looked at Taco.

"Taco, are you telling me that I can use this key to go to the beach painted on the mural? How can that possibly be true?! Did my mother use this key when she was growing up? Does Grand Mama know? Taco, you must tell me everything!"

The blue and gold macaw nodded his head.

"Elisabeth used key. No one else. Taco keeps secret," he answered, tipping his head to one side and looking at her very intensely. He had obviously not gotten over the matter of secret keeping.

Alexandra sat holding the key, running one finger over the embossed scrollwork and then over the cone-shaped end, silently thinking about what she had just heard.

"How do I get back once I'm there? Do I put the key back in the real gate? How long can I go for? What if someone comes looking for me? What if I cannot get back for some reason? *Taco, this is too incredible.* I can go through a painted gate to a *real* beach . . . do I have to wear a bathing suit?!"

Alexandra began to laugh and shake her head. It was all too much—unbelievable, exciting—even scary.

Suddenly, there was a quick tap on her door. It swung open and in came Jaclyn, beaming. Alexandra quickly pushed the key under her bed pillows and tried to look normal. She knew instantly she was not ready to tell anyone, even Jaclyn, about the key.

As she looked at her cousin, she could see Jaclyn had tried out her makeup kit. Alexandra grinned. Jaclyn was going to need some practice.

Before Jaclyn could say anything and because Alexandra wanted to think about something else having felt so overwhelmed, she jumped on the brass pole and ran to the living room for her mirror and makeup. She was back upstairs in seconds, but just as she was setting up the mirror, Evelyn called them to come for dinner.

The delicious aroma of rib roast had been wafting up into her bedroom from the kitchen all afternoon. The makeup would have to wait, as would the key, now buried under downy bed pillows. They hopped on the brass pole with Taco following them.

Evelyn was waiting at the base of the pole, looking flushed and smiling.

"The surprise is your grandmother wanted to have Christmas dinner 'al fresco,' so, on to the conservatory, lassies. I will be right there."

The girls ran the length of the hallway. Taco was flying ahead of them. He was first through the double doors and into their grandmother's rooms, then into the conservatory. When they arrived at the conservatory doorway a moment later, both girls stopped and looked around in wonderment. They were looking at a magical Christmas forest scene. Night had fallen and inky blackness surrounded the glass walls and ceiling. The conservatory was entirely lit by candlelight.

A long glass table was in the center of the room, with everyone else already seated. Two crystal candelabras with red candles anchored each end of the long table. Crystal vases holding red and white roses with sprigs of holly ran down the center of the table, intermingled with votive candles. Scattered around the slate floor between the plants and fountains were luminaries holding flickering candles. A tall evergreen tree covered with white lights was in one corner, and large red poinsettias were nestled in the greenery. This had never happened before; they had never dined in the conservatory. Alexandra realized this was what "al fresco" had to mean—dining outdoors, or almost outdoors.

Then they looked up. High above the table, all the way to the peak and filling the entire length of the glass roof, were thousands and thousands of sparkling white snowflakes. The snowflakes were all different sizes and intricate designs, some very large, others very small, and they were *suspended* in midair. Taco was on his perch surveying the room with great interest. Noir was in his cage on the floor, his eyes fixated on the glittering snowflakes high above.

Everyone was now seated, and eyes met filled with wonder at the scene around them. Alexandra looked at her grandmother. The

Christmas tree pin on her red sweater was sparkling so brilliantly in the dark that it looked like tiny fireworks. Her cheeks reminded Alexandra of pink roses, and she looked so happy as her gaze swept slowly around the table, lingering on each face. Then she folded her hands, bowed her head and said a blessing.

That night Alexandra fell asleep looking at the small sailboat adrift in snowflakes, illuminated by tiny colored lights, holding the key in her hand.

COMPASS SETTINGS
AND THROUGH THE GATE

For Alexandra, Theo, and Jaclyn, the rest of Christmas vacation was spent sledding, skating, playing in the snow, and going inside for hot chocolate to warm up, and then back outside again. Repeated many, many times. Nicolas still preferred to be by himself, but occasionally looked at them from his bedroom window. They would always wave to come and join them, but he never did. It had snowed a lot so there was always something to do outside. They built a big snow fort over a couple of days. Theo designed the floor plan (he had been reading his new book about architecture). There was a tiny bedroom for each of them and a miniature living room with snow benches to sit on. He even sculpted a life-size snow macaw for the top of the snow house. It looked exactly like Taco, who was watching from the conservatory with great interest, and he flapped his wings with excitement when he saw himself placed on the roof.

They made families of snowmen and snow girls or, as Jaclyn said, "bonshommes de neige et filles de neige." Evelyn had plenty of carrots for the noses and Blackie found charcoal pieces for their eyes. He even found some old top hats stashed away from the high society parties their grandfather Thaddeus used to attend in England. He also donated some of his own bow ties and a couple of corncob pipes. Jaclyn wanted to dress up the filles de neige and asked her grandmother if she had some old things they could use. She was soon diving into a box filled with dressy scarves, ornate necklaces, a couple of tiaras, and even some old makeup used to paint their charcoal eyes blue or green and pink blush for their snowy cheeks. (However, when she tried to put lipstick on snow, it did not work. Evelyn suggested cherries, which worked perfectly for their red lips.)

Max was outside with them all the time. He *loved* the snow, chasing snowballs, rolling in the drifts, and playing hide and seek in the snowy maze. Even at the end of a long day, when their feet and faces were frozen, he was reluctant to come indoors. His fur was so thick that he never seemed to get cold. They also went on more sleigh rides with Napoleon. Blackie showed Theo how to handle the reins and reviewed what needed to be done upon returning to the stable, and then they were allowed to go by themselves.

Alexandra noticed her grandmother was more accepting of her doing things on her own now that Theo and Jaclyn were with her. The truth was she had wanted to do things independently at a very young age. Alexandra could still remember her grandmother calling her "intrepid" after hearing she wanted to ride Napoleon at age five all by herself. She had not understood what intrepid meant until she was old enough to look it up. When she read the definition was "fear-lessness and endurance, traits needed by explorers," she had been surprised . . . and proud.

One afternoon Alexandra, Theo, and Jaclyn were lounging around the library trying to decide what to do. They were finding it harder to come up with new ideas over the long Christmas break when Nicolas walked through the door without Noir.

"Are you going to take Napoleon out today?"

"Pourquoi?" Jaclyn looked at her brother with surprise.

"I thought I might go along."

The three of them looked at one another and then Alexandra answered.

"We can go if you want to."

"I do . . . and I thought we could ask Nicole."

They all looked at each other again trying not to grin. They had not seen Nicole since Christmas Eve. She had gone to New York City to see other relatives right after Christmas. It was just the night before their grandmother had told them Nicole was returning to Devonshire and would be going back to boarding school in England in two days.

"Why don't you go over and ask her if she wants to meet us at two o'clock at the stable? We can bring some thermoses of hot chocolate and we can skate," Alexandra said, smiling at Nicolas.

"Oui, I will go and ask her."

Nicolas was not smiling, but his eyes had a happier look, the same as Christmas Eve when he had returned from walking Nicole home. He turned and left.

"Il est amoureux d'elle. He is in love with her," Jaclyn said in an overly dramatic voice as she stood up holding one hand to her forehead as though she was swooning, then fell backward on the couch in a faint.

They all laughed, and then Theo pushed his glasses up and seemed to be thinking.

"I can see why . . . she is smashing."

Theo's tone of voice was very matter of fact, but his cheeks were slightly pink.

Alexandra felt a twinge. Why, she was not sure. She wondered if Nicolas were not here if Theo would have asked her. Probably.

At two o'clock, they met at the Devonshire stable. Nicole was wearing ivory ski pants and a matching hooded jacket with thick chocolate brown fur around the edge of the hood. Her boots looked like Eskimo boots, made from the same chocolate brown fur. Alexandra looked at her own mismatched jacket, hat, and boots and had to admit, Nicole did look like she stepped from the pages of a magazine, or as Theo had said, smashing. She seemed happy to see all of them again, but it was obvious she was most happy to see Nicolas. Nicolas asked Theo if he could drive the sleigh (which Theo was obviously less than pleased about), but he reluctantly agreed. As Alexandra watched Nicolas take the reins, she realized he was naturally good at anything he tried. He handled the sleigh and the little pony just like Blackie, as though he had done it for years. They soon arrived at the frozen pond and put on their skates.

They skated for about an hour, stopping only to have the hot chocolate. Nicolas was more talkative and made some conversation. He skated around by himself but would come back and stand with all of them as they talked about Christmas, the gifts they had received, and Nicole's trip to New York City. She told them about Rockefeller Center—the large ice rink, the restaurant overlooking the rink, and the tallest Christmas tree on earth (but she actually was not sure if this was true). She stayed at a very fancy hotel called "The Plaza" with her relatives, all royalty, but not the King and Queen (Alexandra asked specifically), and she went shopping on Park Avenue—very fancy shops, she said. As Nicole was talking,

Alexandra noticed how obviously interested Nicolas was, and he always stood next to her.

Unseen by all but one, a lone raven had followed them. For most of the time, he sat in the highest branches, well hidden by thick pine branches. Then, tiring of the inactivity, he flew to a steep, snow-covered hill behind the frozen pond. Had anyone been watching they would have been astonished at the sight. With wings clamped to his side and feet tucked in, Noir slid all the way down to the bottom. Unlike people who have to trudge back up the hill after the fun, he flew quickly back to the top of the hill and repeated his run many times. Few have witnessed ravens at play, but they do. As serious and somber a bird as Noir was, he would occasionally do something for the pure exhilaration of having fun. It was yet another sign of his unusual intelligence.

As the skies began to darken, they returned to Devonshire. Jaclyn fed Napoleon his carrots as soon as they got back to the stable. From the first time she met him, it was love at first sight. Jaclyn adored Napoleon and he seemed to feel the same way. He would raise his head up and down and stomp with one hoof when she called his name. Alexandra had felt little pangs of jealousy at first, but realized she had had him all to herself for years and soon accepted the special pony would now be shared. Theo and Jaclyn got him bedded down with hay in his cozy stable and then they all said good-bye to Nicole as they headed home to Chadwick. However, it was noticed when Nicolas hung back saying something in French to Nicole. She answered in French. It was too faint to hear, so whatever was said was known only to them.

One lone raven flew above them, blending in with the dark sky.

The next morning, Alexandra and Jaclyn were having breakfast in the kitchen with their grandmother and telling her all about Nicole's trip to New York City. Evelyn had already sent Theo a breakfast tray on the dumbwaiter. He had asked her the night before if a person could request room service for breakfast. She told them her answer was, "As long as the person does not have feathers."

Silver listened with interest, and after the girls finished telling her all the details, she told them she would take them to New York City, perhaps during the next Christmas holiday. At that moment and before they could even respond, Nicolas came striding through the swinging door. He was dressed in a warm jacket (not his usual cape), *and* he was wearing the new scarf from his aunt and new snow boots. He walked quickly to the counter, wrapped two muffins in napkins and stuffed them in his jacket pockets, turned, and was heading to the door when their grandmother spoke.

"Nicolas. Where are you going so early?"

"For a walk."

"With who? You took two muffins."

He stopped and then slowly turned around. His pale skin had the faintest touch of pink on his cheeks.

"Avec Nicole. We are going to walk around the Devonshire property. Actually, I am going to try out the gift Alexandra gave me," he said, pulling the compass out of his pants pocket.

"I have determined the compass settings for Chadwick and Devonshire, so I will be able to find our way back from any place."

Alexandra realized this was what they had spoken about the day before.

Silver Chadwick did not smile, but her eyes were smiling.

"Be careful, my dear. There are black bears in Maine, and they are partial to muffins."

Nicolas was not expecting this and all of a sudden, he grinned. It was such a surprise, even shocking, to see him smile. Alexandra could not believe how different he looked. He was handsome when he smiled.

✳ ✦ ✳

Theo was busy reading his new books and Jaclyn wanted to organize her armoire with her new clothes, and this left Alexandra alone in her room with Taco. She told Taco about Nicolas and Nicole going for a walk with the compass. His eyes had sparked with interest. He asked if Noir was going with them, but Alexandra said she didn't think so, that was why he was taking the compass. She flopped on her bed and began thinking about Noir.

Nicolas had said ravens could always find their way home. What couldn't a raven do? A couple of days after Nicolas had told her so much about ravens she had gone into the library and found a book open on the table. The book was titled *Birds of the World*, and was open to a chapter about ravens. She knew Nicolas left it there for her to see—and it confirmed all he had told her. Ravens were considered the most intelligent of all birds, something she would never, ever tell Taco. (She had shut the book and put it back on a shelf after reading, for fear he would see it.) There was a lot of information about ravens, but one part she had not been able to forget. The words had replayed in her mind, "*Ravens possess unusually large brains, proportionate to the size of chimps'. They are on the same level as non-human primates when it comes to tool-related cognitive abilities.*"

It was hard to believe. Noir was more like a flying monkey than a bird, and he was not to be underestimated. Ever.

As she was lost in these thoughts, Taco suddenly flew to her and landed on her chest, maybe sensing she was thinking about another bird. She found herself looking into two painted eyes—and what was hanging from a curved beak. *The key.* They had decided the safest and best place to hide the key was in his cage, under the salt lick, where no one would ever look, and where, he told her, he had always kept it hidden.

She stared at the exotic key, then back into eyes that were only inches from her own, and she slowly reached for the key.

"Shall I go, right now, for just a minute, and then come right back? To see if it still works?"

She felt her heart start to pound as she examined the heavily embossed gold key she was now holding, and then looked back at Taco.

He nodded once and then flew to the top of his cage. As she got up from the bed, she suddenly realized she was still in her pajamas and bathrobe.

"Do I have to change into summer clothes? A bathing suit or shorts?"

Taco shook his head "no."

"Is there a keyhole on the real gate that I put the key into when I want to come back?"

Taco nodded.

"Taco, are you sure, absolutely, one hundred percent, sure of it? What if there is no keyhole and I can never get back home? I cannot go if there is *any* chance of not getting back, Taco."

Suddenly he flew to her, quickly taking the key out of her hand, and then, suspended by his wings in front of the mural, he was turning the key in the keyhole of the painted gate. At that moment, to her complete amazement, the painted gate became *real*. With the key clamped securely in his beak, he hopped on the top of the gate as it swung into pitch-black darkness. In a split second, the gate swung back to the wall, and she was again looking at a painted gate in the mural. She was frozen. It felt like she couldn't breathe. All of a sudden, the gate was real again and came swinging into the room with Taco riding on top, still holding the key in his beak. He hopped down to the floor, the gate swung silently closed, and poof—there was the mural again.

Taco flew to her shoulder and then dropped the key into her hand.

"Nice day at Cape Cod beach. Sunny, eighty-five degrees. Perfect for macaws."

Alexandra was surprised to find out the beach was on Cape Cod; he had not mentioned this before. She reached up to stroke him, smiling at his weather report, and feeling a little more relaxed. After a moment, Taco flew to the bed and she walked over to the painted gate. Taking a deep breath, she put the key in the keyhole, and turned it. She felt the key turn and click in the lock, and as she pulled the key out of the keyhole, the real gate materialized and swung open.

She stepped into the blackness and closed her eyes.

The first thing she felt was warm sand under her bare feet. Then she opened her eyes. She was standing near the top of a sand dune, looking at the gate in the middle of a long white picket fence. She could see a heavily embossed keyhole on the gate that resembled the key and wondered if she needed to use the key to get onto the beach. As she stood wondering what to do, the gate slowly opened. Taking a deep breath, she walked through. She was now looking at a beach scene that was *identical* to the mural in her room. It was amazing, incredible, but in that second, she suddenly remembered and whirled around, her heart racing. The gate was now closed. *Glinting in the sun, she saw the keyhole.* Relief flooded through her body—the way home. She was holding the key so tightly that her hand hurt. As she loosened her grip, she noticed for the first time what she was wearing—blue shorts and a plaid shirt she did not recognize. Her hair was in two braids, with blue ribbons tied on the ends. She breathed in the salt air and stood staring at the scene below her. It was all *real*. People were laughing, walking, and swimming. She heard the lifeguard whistle and the seagulls cawing overhead, and felt the warm sun on her face. There was a line of people at The Snack Shack, and the delicious aroma of hamburgers cooking on charcoal wafted on the sea breeze.

A long dock extended out from the beach with moored sailboats, just like the mural. Then she looked to her right and sucked in her breath. It was real. Weathered wooden shingles, the color of driftwood, covered the exterior. A rustic staircase led from the beach to the front door. Red and white striped awnings hung over the two windows facing the ocean. Hanging above the two side windows was a red sign with gold lettering that said "Chadwick Cottage," and a coppery green sailboat weather vane rose from the peak of the roof—identical to the mural. As she was studying the cottage, a black cat jumped up in the left window and sat staring at her with yellow eyes. *The same cat that had stared at her from the same window in the mural for years and years.*

She stood like a statue, trying to understand what was all so amazing and overwhelming. She had traveled through a mural to a real place. The cottage had her family's name on it. Why? Who was living there? To whom did the black cat belong? Her mother had used the same key when she was her age. How could her grandmother not know about it? Or did she? There were only questions, and she felt certain, secrets that had been kept.

Alexandra knew Taco was waiting for her, so she slowly turned back toward the gate, her eyes never leaving the cottage. The black cat was still staring at her as she reluctantly put the key in the keyhole and turned it. A real gate opened into her bedroom. As she stepped into the room, the gate swung shut behind her. She was back in her pajamas with no braids in her hair, looking at Taco, who was waiting expectantly for her on the bed.

She went over and sat down next to him, putting her arm around him, and together they stared in silence at the mural. Then her eyes fell to the floor in front of the painted gate.

There was sand on the floor of her bedroom.

BACK TO SCHOOL
AND A GET-WELL SURPRISE

All too quickly, the winter vacation was over.

With groans, they were once again up early each day, eating breakfast when it was still dark and bitterly cold outside, then piling into the car with Blackie and Max and heading to The Pine School and listening to the raspy, droning voice of Headmaster Green. A week before school started, Nicolas had been invited by the Duke and Duchess to see Nicole off from the airport in Boston. He had accepted. It was obvious, as their grandmother had said in an approving voice, that he was smitten. Whatever it was, Nicolas was noticeably different. Friendlier and more talkative, he began seeking out Theo, even spending time in Theo's room talking with him and looking at the books Theo had received for Christmas. It was soon known to everyone that he was writing to Nicole, as envelopes addressed to her were placed on the silver tray for pickup, and one letter had already arrived from England. It seemed Nicolas wanted to get home from school as fast as possible every day just to check the mail.

What was also clear was that Noir was *not* following in his master's footsteps.

Quite to the contrary, he was noticeably more cranky and demanding. One day he did something he had never done before. Evelyn told them the story, breathlessly, not missing a single detail, when they returned from school. She was busy making corn muffins for dinner and had propped open the kitchen door as she sometimes did. Blackie was sitting at the table having his morning cup of tea, when suddenly Noir flew into the kitchen just above his head. The oddest part, she said, was that he had a purple bandana clamped in his beak. Evelyn told them she immediately recognized it as the one Jaclyn had worn for Halloween. "In a blink of me eye," she said, "Noir landed next to the plate of warm muffins, spread out the bandana like 'twas a picnic, and pushed one of the muffins onto it. Then, neater than a sailor's knot, he tied up the four corners and flew right out of the kitchen, carrying it like 'twas his baby, in his beak." She said he never looked at her, that he was "all business."

When Alexandra heard the story, she immediately thought of what she had read about ravens and what Nicolas had told her. Noir had made his own tool. He had figured out how to take the whole muffin, and with far more serious implications, he had also escaped from his locked cage and Nicolas's room, and taken the bandana from Jaclyn's room. Upon hearing what happened, Nicolas had frowned and quickly climbed the staircase to his room. Alexandra, Theo, and Jaclyn slowly ate their snacks in silence with the image of what happened vivid in their minds.

Alexandra felt a chill go through her. What would Noir steal next when no one was looking?

As she pondered what had happened, she thought of the key. It was safely hidden under Taco's salt lick, which she now felt certain was the best place for it to be, considering what Noir had done and his well-known fixation with shiny objects. She had not told Jaclyn or Theo about the key and had not used it again during Christmas vacation, but she had asked Taco if they could go with her through the gate. He had not answered right away, obviously needing time to think about it. Then he told her he didn't know, because her mother had never taken anyone with her. So that was something else to ponder.

◆

It was strange at first seeing Olivia in front of the class, as their teacher, after the long vacation and having seen so much of her as their very own aunt. Another secret, but it really was not hard to keep. The truth was Olivia treated them as she did any other student. It was just once in a while there would be a quick wink or a note tucked in with graded papers handed out at the end of the day. Everyone in Classroom #6, in fact in the whole school, had quickly learned about Theo moving into Chadwick Manor. He had been the only boarder, but after Thanksgiving was seen arriving and leaving with Alexandra and her cousins. All the students were happy for him, except for Katherine Briggs, who still seemed to enjoy it when others were miserable. She told Theo he really should not have accepted the invitation to live there, that he was, after all, an orphan and *orphans were always boarders*. However, before he could respond, Jaclyn had overheard and said, "Pardon moi, Katherine, orphans and mean girls can be boarders. You should apply to take Theo's place."

Jaclyn had smiled smugly and then returned to her seat.

* ◆ *

The days and weeks began to pass with the routine that school required . . . homework, studying, tests, repeat. But one day things were suddenly not routine at all. It began with a cough.

"Jaclyn, my dear, it looks like you have a rash on your face, and I don't like the sound of that cough. Have you been taking the vitamins Evelyn puts out with breakfast?"

Silver Chadwick was studying her granddaughter and looking at her plate. They had all finished dinner, except Jaclyn, who had hardly touched her food.

"Oui, Grand-Mère, c'est délicieux," she replied softly.

Her green eyes looked tired and watery behind the thick glasses, not their normal sparkle, and her face did appear to be blotchy and very pink.

"Let me feel your forehead, my dear," Silver said, gently placing her hand on Jaclyn's forehead.

"Hmm, very warm. Evelyn, please get the thermometer and come to my room. Jaclyn, come with me."

She took her granddaughter's hand, and they left the kitchen.

They were down the hall and into Silver's bedroom in no time, shutting the doors behind them. Alexandra and Theo sat on the carpet outside the double doors. Nicolas walked slowly up and down the hallway. Alexandra was watching him and could see the concern in his eyes.

"Le médicament. We must call the doctor, tout de suite."

His voice was urgent and serious and he was looking at Alexandra.

"We have a doctor in Kennebunkport. His name is Dr. Brenton. That's his first name, what I have called him since I was little. I have only seen him for my check-ups—I have never been sick."

Both Theo and Nicolas looked at her in disbelief.

"It's true. You can ask Blackie or Evelyn. Evelyn always told me it's because of the vitamins, you know, in the blue bottle on the kitchen table each morning . . . that taste different every day."

She looked at them expecting that would explain it. Instead, they looked unconvinced.

"Alexandra, vitamins cannot keep anyone from being sick. You must have been sick before. No one is healthy all the time, no one. You just don't remember," Theo said, pushing up his tortoiseshell glasses.

Before she could answer, the double doors opened and Evelyn all but flew out down the hall, heading to the kitchen. They ran after her and listened just outside the door.

"So sorry to trouble you, Doctor, but Mrs. Chadwick would like you to come to Chadwick Manor straight away. 'Tis her granddaughter, a young lassie visiting from France. She's hotter than an oven in the summer, poor dear. Her temperature is one hundred and four degrees, and she has a bit of a rash on her face and a cough. Yes, thank you. Come to the side door near the driveway. Godspeed."

They quickly jumped away from the swinging door when Evelyn came back through, very flushed, her neat bun now wispy. She had to have seen them as she passed by, but never looked at any of them as she flew back down the hall.

In about twenty minutes, the doctor arrived. He nodded seriously to Alexandra as he rushed by, then was whisked into her grandmother's rooms by Evelyn.

They waited and waited. It seemed like forever. He finally emerged, holding his black bag with the stethoscope still around his neck. His expression was deeply serious, and he was speaking to both Evelyn and Silver in a low voice as they slowly made their way down the hall. They could hear him say good night, and he told them to call if anything *worsened,* and then he left.

Silver approached them looking very worried.

"Jaclyn has scarlet fever. She will need complete rest and medicine. And no visitors . . . it is highly contagious, so you must not go in her room until her fever breaks, and that could take a few days. Blackie is going to take her upstairs, and Evelyn will help her to bed. Do you all understand? Do I have your word you will do as I say?"

As they all nodded, Blackie came through the doors holding her little body in his strong arms. As they swept by, she waved weakly and tried to smile. Her face now looked quite red. Evelyn followed right behind, and they were upstairs quickly.

"Grand-Mère, how did Jaclyn get this red fever?"

"It is not known, Nicolas. However, she is very sick, and we must now be careful none of you becomes infected. Children are more susceptible than adults to scarlet fever, so do not worry about us. Now, off to your beds. You have school tomorrow."

It had taken a long time for Alexandra to fall asleep. For the first time in a long time, she had the familiar nightmare, the wind and rain beating down, her screams carried away by the storm swirling around her.

* ◆ *

Olivia was shocked to hear the news and had driven to Chadwick as soon as school ended the next day. She had gone into Jaclyn's room with her mother and they had stayed awhile, but Jaclyn was sleeping and had not wakened. Olivia's face was filled with worry. It was hard to believe that one day Jaclyn was perfectly fine and the next day she was very sick. Evelyn checked on her constantly, even through the night, and the doctor returned during the day to see her. No change. She still had a high temperature and needed fluids and cold cloths on her head, but she was having a very hard time swallowing anything because her throat was so sore. All she seemed to want to do was sleep.

The days passed and Jaclyn did not seem to be improving. She would drift in and out of sleep, and when she was awake, she would try to talk in a hoarse whisper, but she did not always make sense. Alexandra heard her grandmother talking with the doctor about delirium, which she had to look up, but then wished she had not. It meant you were crazy, out of your mind. Alexandra did not tell Nicolas or Theo. It was too upsetting. It had to pass. Biscuit was on Jaclyn's bed all the time, and Taco insisted his cage be put in her room to help Evelyn with the night duty. As much as Alexandra did not want him to leave her room, she realized he wanted to be with Jaclyn. One night, as she was passing by Jaclyn's room on her way up to Theo's room, she heard his voice . . . Taco was talking to Jaclyn in French. It sounded like he was reading her a story. Tears filled her eyes. He loved Jaclyn as much as she did.

On the fourth day, her temperature was coming down, but still not fast enough. Alexandra overheard the doctor tell her grandmother he was worried about something that sounded like "roommatic" fever. Alexandra did not even want to look this word up, but wondered if it had something to do with her bedroom. Maybe Jaclyn needed to be moved to a different room. Maybe there were germs in the air, and then she started to panic thinking about Taco in the room with Jaclyn each night. Taco had told her parrots never get human diseases, but she asked Nicolas for confirmation because he was an expert on birds. Thankfully, Taco was right.

On the sixth day, Alexandra could no longer stand it. She had not seen Jaclyn once in six whole days. Riding to and from school and being in class without her had not felt right at all. Alexandra decided that even if she got scarlet fever, it was a price she was willing to pay. It was Taco's watch when she opened the door and crept in. He raised his wings in alarm, but she whispered to him it was all right and to be quiet. She had tied a bandana around her nose and mouth, which seemed the right thing to do, and crept over to the bed. Jaclyn looked even smaller lying in bed and was very pale, but there was no red rash on her face. She had a facecloth on her forehead, and Alexandra gently took it off to cool in the basin of water on her nightstand. The room was dimly lit by one small lamp. As she was wringing out the facecloth, she heard her name.

"Alexandra?"

It was very weak but clear.

"Yes, Jaclyn. It's me, Alexandra. I'm here. Don't mind this silly bandana . . . it's just in case. Are you better? I am so glad to hear your voice! I have missed you so much, everyone has!"

She could see that Jaclyn's eyes had opened a little.

Jaclyn smiled weakly and then slowly reached for Alexandra's arm. Her hand was still very warm.

"You must do something for me. I know it will make me better. I know it . . ." Her voice was fading, so Alexandra leaned in toward her face.

"Anything, I will do anything, just tell me."

"Bring Napoleon to me. Right here in my room, you must bring him to me."

Alexandra could not believe what she heard and felt a wave of panic rush through her. Delirium. Jaclyn must now have roommatic fever. Alexandra turned and looked at Taco, expecting him to look as frantic as she was—this was such a terrible development. Instead, he looked very calm and nodded his head "*yes.*"

Later, she could not understand why she did it. But without another word, she left the room, went downstairs, put on her winter jacket, scarf, boots, and gloves, took a flashlight and two carrots from the kitchen, and quietly let herself out the front doors, leaving them unlocked. Thankfully, Evelyn had not been anywhere around.

She ran across the snow-covered lawn and across the road to the gates of Devonshire, which suddenly loomed as an obstacle. As she walked closer, the gates silently opened, and she said a silent "thank you" in return.

Devonshire was entirely dark. She ran to the stable where Chestnut was blinking at her in the flashlight and then on to the next stall, where it appeared Napoleon was expecting her. He was pawing at the ground, his eyes bright and alert. She attached his harness and lead, and then he was leading her out of the stable, which had never happened before. He was moving fast, almost at a trot, and she had to run to keep up with him. The gate had remained open and Napoleon headed straight for Chadwick. He had never been outside Devonshire before, so Alexandra had no idea how he knew where he was going. But he did.

In no time, they were at the large front doors of Chadwick. She opened them a crack and with no one in sight, she opened them wide and he went right in, as though walking through the front doors of a home was something he did every day. His hooves made a loud clip-clop on the black and white marble floor. He stopped, his large gentle brown eyes taking everything in—the two sweeping stairwells, the pair of tigers that did not even make him blink—and then he walked to the staircase on the right. Pausing for a moment, his eyes scanning the steep staircase, he seemed to be assessing the situation.

Then, as if it was the most natural thing for a pony to do, he started climbing up the marble stairs. He was careful as he placed each hoof, but with obvious confidence, he slowly began to make his way up. His hooves made loud clopping noises on the stairs, and each time Alexandra winced, expecting someone to appear and become hysterical. Thankfully, no one did, not even Nicolas, whose bedroom was right next to Jaclyn's. When Napoleon reached the second floor, he threw his head back and shook it as though he had just won a race. Next, he quickly surveyed the hallway and then, as if he had been there before, headed straight to Jaclyn's door and pushed it open. In another second, he was standing next to Jaclyn's bed, looking down at her, his large brown eyes filled with concern. The whole thing did not feel real to Alexandra, and she wondered for a moment if it was a dream. Here was a pony standing in Jaclyn's bedroom, having just climbed up a marble staircase. She shook her head. It was unbelievable.

Napoleon pawed the rug and whinnied, and Jaclyn's eyes opened a tiny bit. Then he nuzzled her face with his nose and her eyes opened all the way, big pools of green. A broad grin followed. Slowly, she lifted herself up on one elbow and hugged his furry face with her other arm and then laid her head on his long nose.

"Napoleon, I missed you so much! Je t'aime!"

Jaclyn's voice was noticeably stronger than it was just a short time ago.

"Alexandra, I will never forget this. I had to see Napoleon! I knew it would make me feel better, and I do! I feel so much better already!"

Smiling at her cousin in amazement and some disbelief, Alexandra suddenly remembered the carrots. She reached into her pocket and handed them to her cousin, and Jaclyn fed each one to Napoleon, who looked blissfully happy. Alexandra looked over at Taco. He was nodding his head with great approval. It was as if the sickness had been vanquished and everything returned to normal, all because of a visit by one very special pony (who happened to be able to climb stairs as well as a person).

Then they heard the grandfather clock chime ten bells, and Taco said Evelyn would be coming up at 10:30 p.m. *sharp*. Napoleon seemed to understand it was time to go and nuzzled Jaclyn's face one last time. Alexandra led him out of the bedroom, and they were quickly at the top of the stairs.

Which was when things screeched to a halt.

Apparently, ponies can climb up stairs but are deathly afraid of going down. Napoleon would not budge, and even shook his head *"no."* Alexandra quickly ran down to the kitchen and back up with a carrot and put it in front of his nose, slowly backing down the stairs, hoping he would want it enough to follow her. He did not. She could hear the ticking of the grandfather clock and knew precious minutes were going by. Just as she was madly trying to think of what else she could do, Theo suddenly rounded the corner from the second-floor hallway.

"Blimey, Alexandra, what is Napoleon doing here—how did he get up here? *Can he bloody fly?*"

His eyes were enormous behind his glasses, and he whistled low and then started to laugh.

"Oh, Theo, you have to help me, it's really not funny! I have to get him down the stairs, but he won't move, not even for a carrot! He climbed up so easily, but he will not go down. Jaclyn begged me to bring him to her room—she said he would make her better, and I think he did—it was amazing—but right now, I have to get him down the stairs and outside as quickly as possible! Evelyn's going to be climbing up these stairs any minute! Think of something, Theo!"

Theo pushed his glasses up and was now clearly studying the predicament.

"We'll get this sorted. Well, it might be it's too frightening for him to look down, as opposed to looking up. We could try covering his eyes and then leading him very carefully. You could place his front hooves on the stairs and I'll do the same with the back, and so on. Might be a bodge job, but if it works, that's all that matters. Take your scarf off and give it to me."

Alexandra handed him her scarf.

"What's a bodge job?"

"Quick and dirty, on the cheap, but gets it done."

"As long as we get him down and out the front doors quickly, a bodge job will be just fine, but we have to hurry!"

Theo carefully placed the scarf over Napoleon's eyes and tied it behind his neck, in two big knots. Surprisingly, the little pony did not seem to mind and actually appeared to relax once the scarf was over his eyes. When she reached for one front leg, he did not resist as she placed it on a step, and then the same with the other front leg, then again and again until Theo could place each of his back legs on the stairs. Very, very slowly Napoleon began to descend the marble stairs. They both talked to him in soothing tones, telling him he was the bravest pony ever and he would soon be down.

When the last hoof was on the foyer floor, it felt like they had accomplished the most difficult job imaginable and against all odds. Alexandra had taken her jacket off early on, feeling the sweat on her forehead, and could now see the tiny beads all over Theo's face. She quickly threw her jacket back on while Theo untied the scarf, and then she opened the front doors and hurriedly led Napoleon outside. As the doors were closing behind them, she heard the half-hour chime. It was 10:30 p.m. Then she heard Theo, "Cheerio, Evelyn," and Evelyn's voice, "Why are you mucking about at this hour, Theo?" Then Theo, "Fancied one of your lovely desserts, Evelyn, on my way to the kitchen." She could hear Evelyn laugh and then, "Best to filch a cream puff, only one left."

Alexandra walked slowly across the snow, letting Napoleon lead the way home, which he did, but not with the same energy as earlier. Her body felt weak with relief. As she closed the stable gate, she hugged the brave little pony and told him she was certain Jaclyn would now get better.

He nuzzled her face and nodded his head, *"yes."*

As Alexandra walked home, she looked up at the stars and thought about the tiny diamond star on her necklace and Olivia's.

Stars can guide you home.

To the people you love the most.

CHAPTER FORTY-FOUR

TRAVELS TO CHATHAM

Jaclyn recovered completely and in a few days was back in school. Everyone was so relieved, and the doctor had been very surprised. He was about to put her in the hospital, certain she had roommatic fever, when she suddenly recovered.

"Astonishing," he had told Silver, "not medically explainable." Listening to this recounted at dinner by her grandmother had challenged Alexandra and Theo to keep straight faces, but they did.

If Nicolas knew what happened, he never said a word.

* ◆ *

One Saturday morning, Alexandra woke up earlier than usual for a weekend. She got out of bed and sat on the floor looking at the beach mural.

"Good day for the beach."

Taco was awake and looked at her questioningly, having made the suggestion. Then he dug under the salt lick and flew to her bed with the key in his beak, dropping the key on the bed when he landed.

"I think I will go . . . but how long can I go for? Should I take a watch, Taco? I don't want Jaclyn or Theo looking for me and not find me anywhere."

She looked at her parrot, who was obviously thinking.

"No time lost, no time lost here."

Alexandra had to think about this, what he meant.

"Do you mean no time passes here when I am gone? That I come back to the exact same time it was when I went through the gate?" she asked, astonished at what she had just heard.

"C'est exact."

"What about the time there? Is real time passing at the beach?"

Taco nodded.

"Is it the same time of day at the beach as here? Seven o'clock in the morning is early for the beach?" she asked, looking at Taco intently.

These questions were important. Did he know all the answers?

Taco put his head down and began walking back and forth on her rumpled bedcovers. He did not answer right away; it was obvious he was thinking.

"Taco not sure," he answered, shaking his head as if quite puzzled.

"Hmm, well, I will just have to try and find out. Maybe there is a clock somewhere. I'm going to bring my watch anyway to see what happens—it will be like an experiment."

She smiled to herself. Theo would be impressed she had thought to bring the watch with her.

However, what Taco had confirmed was the most amazing of all. Time stopped in Dark Harbor once she went through the gate. It did not seem possible, but just a short time ago she would never have believed she could pass through a painted scene into a real one. She would stay longer this time so she would be able to find out if time really did stop.

Thinking about all of this reminded her of something Olivia had said in school just recently about scientists—sometimes they had to suspend their normal beliefs in order to discover new things. They were studying cell structure, and Theo had passed her a note. She remembered what it said. He had written just two words, "Darwin. Einstein."

Today she felt like a scientist and decided she would have to wait and see what happened.

She found her watch in the nightstand and put it on. It read 7:10, Dark Harbor time. Then she picked up the key from the bed, walked to the mural, put the key in the lock, and turned it. She felt the lock click open. The real gate materialized and swung open.

Alexandra stepped into the blackness.

She was standing in the exact same place as the first time, but she was wearing different clothes—a bathing suit with a cover-up—and, most surprisingly, there was a beach bag next to her feet on the sand dune. Her hair was pulled back into a ponytail, and she was wearing sunglasses. In her right hand was the key. She picked up the beach bag, and as she walked toward the gate, it slowly opened, just like the last time. As soon as she stepped through, she immediately turned to look at the gate closing behind her and saw the shiny gold keyhole. Relief again—the way home. Then she turned to look at Chadwick Cottage. There was no sign of anyone. Suddenly, the black cat with yellow eyes appeared in the same window and sat staring at her, again. She shook her head in amazement and then turned her gaze to the beach.

It was another perfect day, and the beach was filled with people.

She walked down the dune and found a spot that was not close to anyone else, farthest from the water, reached in the beach bag and pulled out a small quilt and sat down. Then she began looking at other things in the bag. There was a bottle of suntan lotion, a beach towel, a small bag of cookies (she opened it and could smell the molasses— her favorite), a small zipped coin purse with $2.50 in quarters, and at the bottom of the bag, a book. She pulled it out and read the title, *The Salem Witch Trials*, and then set it down with everything else on the quilt. It was obvious everything in the bag had been chosen *for her*. She looked around at the people closest to her; no one was looking in her direction. Then she looked back at the fence and gate, relieved nothing had changed. Realizing she was hungry, she reached for the cookies. She bit into one. It tasted exactly like the molasses cookies Evelyn made and she quickly ate the other three.

Then she looked at her watch for the first time. It read 7:20 and the second hand was moving. She figured about ten minutes had passed, so her watch was keeping track of Dark Harbor time as though it had not stopped. She thought about this and concluded it would be very helpful to know how long she was gone, even though when she returned to Dark Harbor the time would still be 7:10. She smiled as she thought of Theo. He would approve of her scientific method. Then, still hungry, she grabbed the key and the coin purse, got up, and headed toward The Snack Shack.

There was a small line of grown-ups and children ahead of her, and she tried to see around them for the menu. She was craning her neck when she saw a large round clock hanging on the back of The Snack Shack. It was a little before noon. So another mystery was solved— time at the beach was obviously not the same as Dark Harbor time.

As she waited her turn, she wondered what all these people would think if she told them how she got to their beach. She smiled just thinking about the reaction. Her mouth watered as she thought about a charcoaled hamburger and wondered if she had enough money. As the tall man in front of her moved, she saw the menu. At the top of the menu she read, "The Snack Shack ~ Best on the Cape ~ Chatham Beach." It sounded familiar to her, Chatham, but she didn't know why, maybe because it sounded a little like Chadwick. Her parents had sailed to somewhere on Cape Cod, she never knew where. She was thinking about this when she realized someone was speaking to her.

"Can I help you, missy?"

"Oh, yes. I would like a hamburger and lemonade. But could you tell me how much that is first?"

She was looking into the smiling face of an older man who was wearing a starched white cap, a white shirt, and a blue apron embroidered with the same slogan, "The Snack Shack ~ Best on the Cape."

"Of course, missy, $2.50."

For some reason, he reminded her of Blackie, except his face was thinner and tanned. Looking into his face, she realized his eyes looked similar; they were twinkling and the same color blue. And when he said "missy" it reminded her of "lassie."

"That will be fine, thank you."

She reached in the coin purse and pulled out all the quarters, placing them on the counter.

"Will do, missy. If you just wait over to the side, we'll call your number. Here it is. You want ketchup?"

"Yes, please."

"One burger with sauce, Ima!" he said loudly, calling back to someone facing the grill.

Alexandra felt like an electric shock ran through her . . . Ima. What was the chance that was the name of the cook? It was an unusual name. She swallowed hard and felt her heart beating faster. Alexandra could only see her back, but she could see the woman's hair—white and very frizzy. She was wearing the same starched white cap as the man, and then she saw it—a purple and green hair clip oddly placed to one side of the cap. Alexandra felt like her legs were going to collapse. Why was she here? She must be some kind of a witch after all . . . but good or bad?

For the first time, she felt scared. She was all alone and could only get home through the gate with the key she was clutching in one hand. There was no one here who knew her or could help her. *No one.* She wanted Blackie or Aunt Olivia or her grandmother to appear at that exact moment. She felt like a scared, lost child. Then she heard the distinctive voice.

"Number 15, that is you, *sweetie.*"

The familiar hoarse voice and the term of endearment that was not.

Alexandra was looking down, trying to decide if she should just run back to the gate as fast as she could or look at her. Slowly, she looked up. She was looking into the face of Miss Ima from The Book Nook, but there were no crazy clothes, just a white shirt with a blue apron.

"Come and get your delicious charbroiled hamburger, *my sweet.*" The voice was gravelly, yet hypnotic and reminded Alexandra of the evil queen offering the apple to Snow White.

Alexandra felt like she was under a spell and walked forward slowly. She could see the brilliant, red-polished fingernails caressing the sides of the tray. Then she was looking into red-rimmed eyes behind thick square black glasses.

"*An excellent selection, sweetie.*"

The same words.

As Alexandra reached for the tray, the key suddenly fell out of her sweaty hand onto the tray. In a split second, Miss Ima was holding it and examining it. Alexandra felt light-headed and thought she was going to faint.

"My, what an unusual key, and what does this unlock, *sweetie?*"

Alexandra felt something surge through her body like another electric shock. In a split second, she grabbed the key out of Miss Ima's hand, spun around, and ran as fast as she could toward the quilt. As she was running, she decided she did not want to spend even one second putting everything back in the beach bag. She ran as fast as she could up the dune, shoved the key in the lock, and turned it.

She was back in her room.

Taco was on the bed waiting for her, exactly where he was when she left. She was again wearing her nightgown and immediately collapsed on her bed. She was breathing heavily and her whole body felt hot. She looked at her watch. The minute and second hands were moving backward and in the blink of an eye, her watch read 7:10.

She lay there a few minutes without saying a word to Taco, who was looking at her with concern and puzzlement. Then she told him who was behind the counter of The Snack Shack.

"Miss Ima, Book Nook?"

Taco was in deep thought, pacing up and down on the comforter. He was shaking his head, his opalescent patch deeply furrowed.

"You have never heard of her, from Grand Mama or my mother, or anyone? She has frizzy white hair and thick black glasses that are square-shaped, and she wears crazy clothes. All Grand Mama ever told me is that Miss Ima has owned The Book Nook forever. But why would she know about Aunt Olivia? She said Olivia's name when I was looking for a Christmas gift at The Book Nook, and I had not said one word about her. And why was Miss Ima at The Snack Shack today serving me a hamburger?!"

Taco kept walking back and forth shaking his head, but not speaking.

"Taco, you must know something. Think!!"

Taco stopped suddenly. He had remembered something.

"Olivia had baby nurse in England. Taco saw through window. Square black glasses, white frizzy hair. Taco never heard name."

He was looking at her questioningly, but Alexandra did not answer. She was lost in thought.

That had to be it. But why had she come to Dark Harbor so many years ago, and why had she appeared at The Snack Shack today?

There were still so many unanswered questions; however, some had been answered. One, time did stand still in Dark Harbor once the key was turned. And two, Miss Ima was somehow connected to her family.

* ◆ *

Theo and Jaclyn were lying on her bed the next afternoon.

"It's too cold for me to go outside today, Grand-Mère said. What can we do, Theo? Do you have any ideas?" Jaclyn asked.

Theo was lying on his stomach facing the beach scene, propped on his elbows with his hands on his cheeks.

"Lovely day for the beach. Fancy that, ladies?"

He was grinning.

"Brilliant, Theo, easy-peasy, as you would say. Let's go!" Jaclyn teased him back.

Theo and Jaclyn started to laugh.

"Would . . . would you like to go to that beach?" Alexandra asked.

Taco was sitting on top of his cage and began opening and closing his wings in alarm. She gave him a stern look.

Theo and Jaclyn turned and stared at her.

"Alexandra, I have never known you to be either daft or dim, or are you just being cheeky?" Theo grinned at her.

She walked over to Taco's cage, reached in, and pulled the key out from under the salt lick, whispering to him that it would be fine, not to worry, and then held it up for them to see.

"I'll read this tag," and she did.

"We can go through the painted gate to that beach, it's called Chatham Beach. It's on Cape Cod. I have already been—twice. We use this key and when it turns in the keyhole, the painted gate becomes real. You have to step into darkness, but it really isn't scary and in a split second, you are standing right there . . . on a real beach." She pointed to the spot on the mural in front of the gate.

"And then we use the key to come back through the gate to my room. We come back to the exact time we left, so we will never be missed here."

Theo and Jaclyn were mute, transfixed, staring at the key.

"It was my mother's. She used it, but no one else has. Taco kept it safe all these years, and gave it to me for Christmas. He's not sure if you both can go, but let's try. Ready?"

Smiling, she gestured for them to get up. If Miss Ima was still behind the counter at The Snack Shack, she would tell them before they saw her.

"Bloody amazing. Ready, Jaclyn?!"

Theo was trying to pull Jaclyn off the bed, but she looked afraid, not excited.

"I think . . . I think I will wait here with Taco. You two go. Maybe I'll go next time. But don't you have to change your clothes?"

Jaclyn was looking at Alexandra and Theo, both dressed in heavy wool sweaters and corduroys.

"No, the clothes change magically, and the second time there was a beach bag waiting for me, filled with everything I needed," Alexandra answered.

Alexandra smiled at Jaclyn and told her they would be back in the blink of an eye. Then she told Theo to put his arm through hers, inserted the key in the keyhole, and turned it. The real gate materialized and swung open into blackness. They stepped in together and disappeared.

A second later, the gate swung open into the room. Alexandra and Theo stepped out of the blackness into the room, wearing their winter clothes. Theo was beaming. His normally pale skin was flushed with color, and he was shaking his head in complete disbelief.

"*Bloody incredible*!! *Takes the biscuit*!! Jaclyn, we arrived right there, at the top of the dune, and we both had on beach togs and there was a tote right by the gate. Inside was a small purse with some shillings, towels, and suntan lotion. There was a note attached to the lotion that said, 'Theo, be sure to use this.' Blimey, I could not believe it! We walked the beach, then popped by The Snack Shack and had the most delicious strawberry milkshakes this nice gent made for us. And Chadwick Cottage looks exactly like the mural and blimey, if the same black cat wasn't in the window and . . . it was all . . . *real*."

Theo looked like the cat that had swallowed many mice, not just one.

"Next time, Jaclyn, you're coming too," Alexandra said, smiling at her cousin. She felt happy and much more relaxed. Miss Ima had been nowhere in sight.

What no one had seen was one black beady eye peering through the bedroom door keyhole.

SUSPICIONS AND
A SHOCKING DISCOVERY

I t was the deepest, darkest time of the Maine winter, January and February.

The wind howled around Chadwick Manor, sweeping in from the ocean with strong blustery gusts, often carrying more snow. The snow was piled in deep drifts around the conservatory. Huge heaters blasted warm air into the glass room, and large humidifiers provided the moisture needed by the plants. Inside the conservatory, it was like being in a tropical rainforest surrounded by arctic tundra. Often Alexandra, Theo, and Jaclyn did their homework in the conservatory, snug and comfortable in the cushioned Adirondack chairs, their books piled on the wide arms, periodically gazing out at the frozen world.

Schoolwork, like the weather, was the most intense now, too.

Mr. Gingerroot had given Nicolas more work for extra credit. Nicolas told them his teacher said he needed "plus de défi," more challenge, which he seemed to be quite proud of. He actually seemed to enjoy the extra schoolwork, but this was not surprising to any of them. It was also true Nicolas was happier than he had ever been, reading letters from Nicole or writing to her, and occasionally making conversation. If he was still worried about what *the letter* had said, it was well hidden.

Jaclyn, Theo, and Alexandra were under less pressure, being in their sixth year, but Olivia was also adding more homework assignments to help them get through the "winter doldrums," she said. (Alexandra actually thought the extra work made the doldrums worse.) Like Mr. Gingerroot with Nicolas, Olivia also decided to give Theo extra-credit work and told him she thought he might belong in the seventh or eighth year. One day she gave Theo some tests to take, and he sat by himself in a corner of the classroom for most of the day. Theo told Alexandra and Jaclyn that Olivia wanted to move him to Mr. Gingerroot's class as a result of the tests, but he had refused, telling her he did not want to compete with Nicolas, or have such an ugly teacher, which he said made her laugh. Olivia had reluctantly agreed to let him stay in Classroom #6, as long as he would do work that was more challenging.

Alexandra admired Theo. He liked being a student and was curious about everything, but he never seemed to take it as deadly serious as Nicolas did, and he was never boastful about his very good grades.

During these dark and bitterly cold winter days, they often took quick trips to the beach. Jaclyn joined them after the first trip and quickly became comfortable as a "barrière voyageur," or gate traveler, as she called it. (The first time she went, and every trip thereafter, they had locked arms in a row, with Jaclyn between Alexandra and Theo, where she said she felt safest.) So it was proven the key holder could definitely bring guests. On weekends, they would sometimes spend five or six hours at the beach, coming back at the same time they left, but therefore needing to go to bed much earlier than usual. This caused some raised eyebrows by Evelyn when they yawned at the dinner table and were not very hungry, having eaten too much at The Snack Shack. Nicolas was also suspicious and began raising the obvious questions at dinner.

"Theo, I have noticed you seem to be a bit pink in the face . . . it looks like you are sunburned, but of course, that is not possible?" or "Why are you three so tired tonight? You did nothing all day but play cards?" or "You have hardly eaten your dinner, Jaclyn, aren't you hungry?" Each time, they were able to sidestep with excuses and without raising any real concern. Jaclyn would glare at her brother, but he seemed to enjoy taking jabs. They all wondered if he somehow knew, yet could not see how that was possible because they always returned within seconds of leaving—and Taco was always standing guard in Alexandra's room.

It was all becoming almost routine. . . . Go to the beach, eat at The Snack Shack (there was always sufficient money in the same zippered coin purse for all of them to get whatever they wanted), go for a swim or read a book. (They would each find a book in the bag with their name on it, and it would be in the bag each visit until it was finished, and then replaced by another book. Theo had the most new books because he was the fastest reader.)

The nice man at The Snack Shack began to know them by name.

His name was Brownie, which took them all by surprise because it sounded so much like Blackie. There was something familiar about his face; Alexandra had noticed it from the moment she first saw him. She realized it was his blue eyes—they looked identical to Blackie's eyes. And like Blackie, he always seemed cheerful. Brownie asked them if they were vacationing or if they had moved to Chatham. They had moved from Maine, answered Alexandra, who was the spokesperson. A few times, he said he hoped to meet their parents. She said they both worked all the time, which was met with a skeptical look. When he assumed they were brother and sisters, but was puzzled by Theo's accent, Alexandra explained she and Jaclyn were sisters, and Theo was their cousin visiting from England. (Theo's British accent could not be disguised, but Jaclyn's French accent was not noticeable unless she was speaking French.)

The interesting thing was Miss Ima had disappeared, to Alexandra's great relief. She never returned to The Snack Shack after the one time Alexandra had come alone. The new cook was an older man named Mike, and he made *delicious* charbroiled hamburgers. It was a relief Miss Ima was gone but also a mystery. Why had she been there one time? Alexandra never told Jaclyn or Theo—as long as she was gone, that was all that mattered.

During the week, they usually stayed only an hour or so because they had to study, but on weekends, they sometimes stayed as long as five or six hours. The "time" aspect of their travels was something they learned to adapt to; however, it was not normal in any sense of what time is known to be. They always arrived during the day at Chatham. (Theo wondered what would happen if they left at night from Dark Harbor, but Alexandra was too afraid and decided only daytime trips would be allowed.) Interestingly, it was never the same time of day there, or even slightly predictable. For example, when they left Dark Harbor at 4:00 p.m. one day it was noon at Chatham Beach. Another day when they left at 3:00 p.m., it was 10:00 a.m. at the beach. One Saturday they left at 10:00 a.m., but it was already 4:00 p.m. at the beach. Alexandra always wore her watch so they would know how long they had been gone, or what Theo began calling "DH Elapsed Time." He said it gave them a necessary frame of reference, because how long they stayed and the time of day they left Dark Harbor did have an effect upon them. It was difficult getting used to this part—they knew they would never be missed at home, yet the longer they stayed, the harder it was to return to Dark Harbor time because the time that passed at the beach was real time to them. So if they left at 9:00 a.m. on a Saturday and stayed five hours, it felt like it was 2:00 p.m. when they returned, not 9:00 a.m. The time differential was the worst when they stayed the longest, and the early evening yawns were hard to stifle.

Another aspect that initially interested Theo was the calendar. He noticed when they started going it was the third week of June on the calendar at The Snack Shack. For a while, he kept track of the dates, but they were not going every day and he soon lost interest. It really didn't matter at all what day of the week or month it was in Chatham.

They always kept to themselves and did not make conversation with other children, but occasionally others would try to make conversation with them. Sometimes it did feel awkward or like they were being unfriendly. One boy accused Theo of being a "snobby Brit," to which Jaclyn responded with hands on her hips, "Some Americans are snobby, too."

Their beach outfits often made them laugh. Each time they gate traveled, they were wearing different clothes and the girls' hair was styled differently, usually in braids or ponytails with ribbons. Not the latest fashions, like The Moose's Closet, but they did fit right in with everyone else on the beach. Theo's bright madras plaid swim trunks were not his "cup of tea," he said, but all the other boys were wearing the same thing, so at least he did not stand out. The girls always had on a one-piece bathing suit with a little skirt and decorative flower, or pleats with a bow, and matching beach cover-ups, hats, and sandals. Alexandra was reminded of her grandmother more than once. She would have approved—everything was coordinated. Theo loved to tease them about their "swimming costumes," explaining this was the British word for bathing suits. "Here is Mademoiselle Jaclyn, a vision in purple in her swimming costume, or are you a real sugarplum?" or, "Miss Alexandra St. Germaine has arrived on Chatham Beach, directly from the fashion houses of France, so posh in peach!" He was merciless, but they would end up in fits of laughter from his unique fashion reviews.

It was on their third or fourth visit when Alexandra decided to walk up close to Chadwick Cottage. She approached from the side and the black cat was sitting in the left window, his normal spot, but as she got closer, he hopped down from the sill and was out of sight. She could not see in the windows, they were too high, and she did not want to climb up the front steps, so she walked around the cottage and then back to the others. There was no sign of anyone, just the cat. She wondered who fed the cat and who lived there, but on all their trips, she never saw anyone inside the cottage, only the black cat.

One Saturday started out the same as any other.

They were through the gate, quickly on the beach, and then into the ocean for a swim. None were very good swimmers, but Alexandra was the best of the three. Blackie had given her lessons over the years in the frigid summer waters of Dark Harbor, but Alexandra never wanted to practice for long because the water was numbingly cold. The ocean water at Chatham Beach was usually about seventy degrees, the sign said, and it was cold at first, but much more bearable than Dark Harbor. They read, talked, swam, and then (as always) got hungry. This particular day Theo said he would get their lunches, hot dogs with French fries (Jaclyn *loved* them, especially the name) and lemonade. He grabbed the coin purse and headed to The Snack Shack. It seemed he was gone longer than usual, but finally returned, balancing everything on one tray. He passed out the food and the girls began to eat right away. However, Theo sat looking out to the ocean, not eating, and then pushed up his glasses, his brow furrowed.

"I was waiting for the order and happened to look at the calendar on the back wall. Today is July 8th."

Jaclyn and Alexandra nodded, not very interested. They had known it was June and then July from the same calendar, having seen it so many times when ordering food. It was the kind of calendar with a very large, bold number for the day of the month. The month was printed in small letters above the date. At the end of each day, the calendar page was torn off revealing the next date. They had never paid much attention. What date it was did not matter to them.

"Umm . . . well, I could see the year. I hadn't noticed it before. It's in very small print below the date."

CHAPTER FORTY-FIVE

His voice was very serious, as was his expression.

"Well, what is so choquant, shocking, Professeur Eddington? Did you find out we are in the Paleozoic era?" Jaclyn started to giggle.

"Uh, no, I did not. But I did find out we are eleven years earlier here than in Dark Harbor . . . once we go through the gate."

They stared at Theo as if he had just said the sky was falling. There was silence for a few minutes, and then Alexandra heard herself speaking, but it really felt as though someone else was talking.

"What . . . what are you saying, Theo? That we time travel when we go through the gate?"

Her voice was a whisper, and she felt lightheaded.

"Yes, that is what I am saying. I asked Brownie if I could see a newspaper to check something, and he showed me today's *Chatham News* . . . we are back in time exactly eleven years."

TIME TRAVEL REDUX

They sat staring at each other, not hungry anymore. Alexandra's mind was spinning . . . their clothes and hairstyles were a little different, but it had never even occurred to her they were not in the same year. Nothing else was obvious or would have been a clue on Chatham Beach. The cars in the parking lot all looked similar to the ones in Dark Harbor, and she knew Blackie's car was not common; she had never seen another one like it. The bicycles were the same, the beach toys . . . and then, like a fog was lifting, she gasped and put her hand to her mouth.

"What is it, Alexandra, what's the matter?"

Jaclyn's face was full of concern.

"My . . . parents . . ."

She felt as if she was in a trance, staring out to the ocean, her voice just a faint whisper.

"They died on July 20th . . . *eleven years ago* . . . somewhere off Cape Cod . . ."

Theo was slowly shaking his head in disbelief. Jaclyn was staring at Alexandra with her mouth open.

"Today is July 8th. . . . They haven't died . . . yet." Theo's voice was also a whisper as he stared into Alexandra's shocked face.

They looked at each other in silence, too stunned to speak. Alexandra did not remember much after that. They had left soon after, but she did remember staring at Chadwick Cottage and the black cat sitting in the window before stepping through the gate . . . and feeling as though it held a secret she absolutely needed to know.

For some reason Alexandra did not fully understand herself, she did not want to tell Olivia about the key or the gate—or what they had just discovered—at least not yet. However, she did want to ask her something and passed her a note at the start of class on Monday. As she read it, Alexandra saw her aunt's eyes widen, and she looked back at her niece with a puzzled expression. On their way out in the afternoon, Alexandra received a reply that she opened on the way home and then passed to Theo and Jaclyn to read. Nicolas already had his nose in a book and never noticed.

> *Dearest Alexandra,*
>
> *I am not sure why you are asking, but I will answer. No, I can no longer time travel to a particular date. My challenge, as I told you, was to save Mercy Disbrow from the gallows, and to accomplish that I was given the ability to travel through time. Although I do have other powers, time travel is not one of them.*
>
> *I am wondering why you have asked, but I assume you will tell me when and if you want to.*
>
> *All my love,*
> *Aunt O.*

Both Theo and Jaclyn nodded solemnly. So that was answered. Olivia could not help if needed. It was now critical to find out something else. Alexandra knew whatever she learned could make the difference between life and death. Blackie pulled into the driveway at Chadwick and everyone piled out, but Alexandra hung back.

"Blackie, I have a question . . . that I think you must know the answer to."

Alexandra was looking into his kind blue eyes, and there was such a strong resemblance to Brownie's eyes, it gave her goose bumps.

"Well, lassie, I'll certainly try, but 'tis about your family, you best talk to your grandmother."

He looked quite serious.

"It is and isn't . . . but it's not about anything, you know . . . magical. It's an easy question. Where did my parents sail to on Cape Cod? What town? You must know, Blackie?"

He relaxed and nodded his head.

"'Tis an easy question. They sailed to Chatham. The Chadwicks had a cottage there for years, right on the beach, where your parents stayed, and they moored the *Windswept* at the dock next to Chatham Beach. Your grandmother sold the cottage . . . after the accident."

Alexandra felt tears in her eyes and she hugged him as hard as she could. He hugged her back, but looked puzzled by her reaction.

"Thank you, Blackie . . . I've always wanted to know that, thank you," she said, and ran straight to her room.

Chadwick Cottage belonged to her family.

✳ ◆ ✳

Jaclyn and Theo were waiting for her, their faces filled with anticipation and trepidation. As she told them what Blackie had confirmed, they all looked at the mural and the painted beach cottage.

"We have to go every day, just to check the calendar. I'm not sure if there is an equivalency . . . it is very mathematically complex. I'll go to The Book Nook and see if I can get any books about time travel. The more we know, the better."

Theo's voice was serious, as was his expression. He was pacing the floor, looking at the mural. Alexandra was sitting on her bed with Jaclyn and Taco, who looked utterly confused.

"I'll ask Blackie to take me to Dark Harbor right now, and you girls go to The Snack Shack and check the calendar."

It was agreed.

Alexandra told Theo he could charge the books to her grand-mother's account (which she had occasionally been allowed to do), then grabbed the key from under the salt lick, and she and Jaclyn were gone through the gate. Theo jumped on the pole and went out the side door, looking for Blackie. He walked to the garage, expecting to find him puttering around like he usually was, but Blackie was nowhere in sight. Then he climbed the stairs to the carriage house and looked through the window in the door. Blackie was sound asleep on the couch. Theo hesitated, thinking about what to do. He slowly went back down the stairs and was shocked to see Max sitting in the front passenger seat of the car. He wasn't there just a moment ago. How had Max gotten into the car, he wondered? The doors were closed. Theo opened the driver's side door to let him out, when quicker than a blink of an eye, Max pawed the key in the ignition and the black touring car rumbled to life. Theo jumped back while staring at Max, who seemed to be saying, *get in*, or at least that was what Theo felt looking into the intelligent amber eyes. After a second, he slid into the driver's seat.

"Blimey, Max, I have never driven anything but a bicycle!"

In the next second, the human-like paw moved the gearshift in the center console to REVERSE, and Max stared at Theo's right leg. The gas pedal was below his right foot and Theo put pressure on it, and the long car began going in reverse. They went backwards pretty quickly and up on the snow-covered lawn a bit, missing the huge maple tree, but not by much, and then Theo hit the brake and they stopped with a lurch. Max shifted into DRIVE and looked at him as if saying, *of course you can do this*, and Theo applied pressure to the gas pedal—this time much more slowly as he turned the wheel, and then they were very slowly heading out the long driveway.

What happened on the ride to and from Dark Harbor is known only to Max and Theo.

About an hour later, the long car pulled back into the driveway and stopped in front of the garage. Max pushed the gearshift into PARK, and with a quick move of his paw, turned the engine off. It was almost dark. Max had turned on the headlights on their return trip, and with another paw stroke, quickly extinguished the lights. In the shopping bag were three books about time travel. Theo thought it was a very odd coincidence the slogan for The Book Nook was, "A Place to Travel Through Time." When he had set the books on the counter, the bizarre old woman had looked at them with great affection, running her long red fingernails over them, telling him in her sandpapery voice they were the *most excellent selections*.

However, strangest of all was when he first pushed open the shop door.

Miss Ima had immediately told him to go upstairs and look under *T* for time travel, but he had not said one word. Too shocked to question her, he followed one long red fingernail pointing to a grimy door in the back of the shop. As he got closer, he could read what it said on the door, but just barely: "Second Floor. Proceed at Your Own Risk." He shivered. He had never been to the second floor of The Book Nook. He breathed in deeply, pushed up his glasses, opened the door, and began climbing the stairs. They zigged and zagged in a way that seemed architecturally impossible to Theo. He was certain the dimensions would not fit in the narrow two-story building, and it took far too long to get there. At one point, he felt panic sweep through him—he would never get to the second floor, or be able to get back to the first, and would be lost in a maze of staircases forever. Finally, he reached a platform and pushed open another grimy door. Once inside, he had never felt more claustrophobic in his life. He had to walk sideways, up and down the narrowest book aisles. It was very dimly lit and altogether creepy, but he finally found the *T* section. There were three books about time travel theories lined up on the bookshelf, so he quickly grabbed all three and made his way, all too slowly, back down the zigzag stairs.

Theo was never so glad to get out of anywhere . . . except the third floor of The Pine School.

The car parked, Theo got out holding the shopping bag, and Max hopped out behind him. Then they climbed up the stairs and peered through the window in the door (Max jumped up and looked through, his front paws braced on the door). Blackie was still sound asleep. Max almost seemed to smile at Theo and they went back down the stairs to the driveway.

"Well, mate, fancy that . . . I just drove to town and back. You are brilliant, Max! Our secret . . . bloody fun . . . hope we can go again sometime . . . all I need is some practice!"

Max barked once and jumped up, and with his front paws on Theo's chest, licked his face. Theo was sure it was a "yes, we will go again." As he looked into the brown eyes flecked with gold and lined with what looked like black eyeliner, Theo really felt he was looking into human eyes.

Seconds later, he was walking into Alexandra's room.

"July 11th!"

Jaclyn announced the date with great relief in her voice as he walked through the door. She was looking intently at Theo, as was Alexandra.

Theo sat down on the bed. Saturday was July 8th at Chatham Beach.

Today was Monday, so it should be July 10th, if following a normal calendar sequence. It was a day faster. Theo realized this was going to be very difficult, and would take time to try to figure out how to be there on July 20th—before the storm. He also knew it was time they might not have, and quickly pulled the books out of the bag and put them on the bed. Both girls studied them, as did Taco, who still looked very confused.

The titles were: *Superstring Theory* (there was a drawing of a ball of string on the book cover along with a clock face and six separate pieces of string, both open and closed), *Through a Black Hole ~The Event Horizon* (image of a large black tunnel with swirling tornado-like vortex), and *Bending Time ~Down a Wormhole* (sketch of a bent piece of steel with an inchworm going down one side heading toward a dark tunnel).

Each book was thick, and just paging through one of the books, it was obvious they were filled with complicated mathematical formulas written in Greek letters and symbols (Theo explained that was how physicists wrote), and strange-sounding scientific terms that were not even pronounceable. The enormity and complexity of what they were dealing with became apparent to Alexandra . . . she knew it would be impossible for Theo to figure it all out, even if he was very smart.

"Theo, I think we just have to go through the gate every day, before school, after school, and even at night, maybe even the middle of the night. We can take shifts and Taco will wake one of us to go—that's the only way. You can't possibly figure this out in the little time we have. I know you are very smart, Theo, but we cannot risk that you might be . . . wrong."

Theo turned a little pink at the compliment and then sighed deeply.

"You're right, Alexandra. We need to keep going as often as possible to check the date and see if there is a pattern. In the meantime, I'll read as fast as I can. You never know what might be helpful," and he scooped up the books and headed for his room.

As he left, he offered to go through the gate after dinner. Alexandra agreed. They did not all have to go, and this would be the first night trip.

It was eight o'clock that night when Alexandra handed Theo the key.

"Don't let the key out of your hand, Theo."

He nodded and put the key in the keyhole and tried to turn it. It would not turn. He tried again with more pressure. Then the other direction. Nothing. It was just a painted gate. Jaclyn was sitting on the bed, her green eyes wide. Taco was watching intently from the top of his cage, and then he flew to Theo's shoulder.

"Taco open."

Theo placed the key in his beak and watched as Taco suspended himself in the air with his large wings, inserted the key in the hole, and then turned it. The real gate materialized and opened into blackness. Taco flew to Theo's shoulder with the key securely clamped in his beak, and Theo stepped through and they disappeared. At that moment, Alexandra realized the key would *only* work if she or Taco used it. Interesting.

They were back in a second. Taco was looking most important as he rode on the gate as it swung into the room, the key dangling from his beak.

"It is now July 13th and . . . it was daytime."

Theo's voice was grave.

Time was speeding up. In the afternoon, it was July 11th, but about five hours later, it was July 13th.

A TERRIBLE TIME

I t was very hard, almost impossible, to concentrate on school or anything else.

From the moment Theo had said "July 13th" and they understood the date could change in a matter of hours, it was like a wild ride. Every day Alexandra went alone through the gate. She felt Taco should not appear on the beach and check the calendar at The Snack Shack—he would draw too much attention. She went first thing in the morning and twice each night, once after dinner, and again right before bed around 10:00 p.m. (it was always daytime at Chatham, never night). Over time, they had been very relieved to determine there was never any date change between 10:00 p.m. and early in the morning, so at least she did not have to go during the middle of the night. During the week, she went through the gate right after school and always with great trepidation, fearful the date had changed while she was at school. On weekends Alexandra was going to Chatham Beach constantly.

Taco repeatedly offered to go and seemed offended she would not let him. He kept telling her he would remember the date—that he could do it, just like airmail delivery, "Always dependable, on time, never late," he would tell her. She tried to explain without hurting his feelings that it would be too suspicious for a macaw parrot to swoop in on a beach in Cape Cod and check the calendar with everyone watching. And she told him she *knew* he would not forget the date, but he didn't seem to believe her.

What was happening at Chatham Beach was beyond strange.

The date held at July 13th for a few days and then changed to July 15th, skipping the 14th. Then, for the next two weeks straight, the date did not change on The Snack Shack calendar—it was July 15th every day. Theo told her to peek at Brownie's newspaper, just to make sure. It was the same newspaper day after day, with the same headline and date, July 15th, and the same people were sitting on the same blankets. In other words, time was standing still at Chatham Beach.

Theo was madly reading about time travel and so immersed in books that he hardly talked to them. He would mutter about wormholes and exotic matter, the theory of relativity and the space-time continuum, superstring theory and M-theory, gravitons and negative energy density, but nothing he said made any sense to Alexandra or Jaclyn. He told them it was terribly complicated, entirely based on physics, which he had just begun studying, and that scientists, called astrophysicists or cosmologists, had been working on theories of time travel for years, but it was all theory—very little had been proven as scientific fact. There was, however, one indisputable fact: time seemed to be stuck on July 15th at Chatham Beach. If counting by a normal calendar there were five more days until July 20th, but there was nothing normal about the passage of time once through the gate. When would that date occur? Tomorrow or in a month or a year? There seemed to be no way of knowing. It was like living in a constant state of panic and none of them slept very well.

Alexandra wanted to live in the cottage, as it appeared to be empty. They discussed it, and all agreed she could go without being missed at Chadwick, or school, because she always came back to the exact time she left. But there were so many unknowns. Would she be safe? They wouldn't be able to contact her to know if she was. What if she couldn't get into the cottage? Where would she live? What about food—she would run out of money quickly. "What if it took a year or more?" Jaclyn asked, her eyes filled with fear. However, nothing Theo or Jaclyn said changed her mind. She told them she had to go and could use the key to get back anytime she needed to. Theo and Jaclyn realized nothing they could say would stop her.

One cold, gray afternoon Alexandra told them she was ready to go. The date was still holding at July 15th after a month. She told them she felt all of a sudden time could speed up and she would miss July 20th. That it was her *intuition*. She had packed her own bag this time, not sure if it would gate travel, but she hoped it would. Alexandra knew it might be a long wait. She showed them what she packed: pajamas, toothbrush and toothpaste, hairbrush, summer clothes, a raincoat, sneakers and socks, a flashlight, a notebook and pen to make notes or keep a diary if her stay went on for a while, and twenty-five one-dollar bills she had saved over time. Lastly, wrapped very carefully in the bottom of the bag, was the photograph of her parents on their wedding day. Jaclyn started to cry when she saw the photo.

Alexandra went to get the key and say good-bye to Taco when he suddenly began squawking, flapping his wings, and vigorously shaking his head "no."

"Cannot go, cannot go through gate and stay. Must return before midnight Dark Harbor time or *never come back*."

Taco was boring into her eyes with his own and standing on top of the salt lick, defending the key. He looked so fierce that Alexandra was reminded of the time he flew to the banister when Noir first arrived. In that moment, as confused as she was by what he said, she also knew with absolute certainty he would not give her the key. Alexandra went back to her bed and sat down, her eyes filling with tears.

Theo interrogated Taco because what he was saying made no sense at first. They knew time stood still in Dark Harbor, so how could it ever cross midnight? After a lot of questioning, Theo concluded Taco was telling the truth. It was, like everything to do with time, very complicated. Taco told them even though time stopped in Dark

Harbor and resumed when they returned, they could not be in Chatham when midnight would have normally struck in Dark Harbor, or they would never be able to return. He told them a *master clock* kept running, as though time had not stopped, each time they went through the gate. *It was the grandfather clock in the Chadwick Manor living room*: the clock kept track of the time as though they had not left Dark Harbor, but as soon as they were back through the gate, the time on the clock would adjust itself back to when they had left. Alexandra realized this was exactly what her watch was doing. Taco said he had not told them before because he never thought they would be in Chatham at the exact moment the grandfather clock would strike midnight in Dark Harbor. And he told them he was always very nervous about the ten o'clock trip before bed, until Alexandra was safely back through the gate.

What Taco said made some sense to Theo. The books he was reading about time travel contained many strange and complex theories. Apparently, the direction of time travel was very critical. Some theories concluded that time travel to the past was either impossible (those traveling back in time would not live long in this dimension—their bodies would begin to disintregate and vaporize); or, that it was possible but could result in the "grandfather paradox," which would essentially require the existence of multiple versions of the future in parallel universes. Most theories seemed to conclude that time travel to the future would be possible, but there was not any consensus on how it might impact the time traveler's aging process. Theo had decided not to share any of this with Alexandra—it was all theory, not proven fact, and would just worry her.

This was a lot to try to comprehend, and silence soon settled on them like a cloud, each lost in thought, thinking about the implications of what they had just learned.

In silence, Jaclyn helped Alexandra unpack her bag, hugely relieved her cousin was not going.

The days were passing; however, the date in Chatham was not changing.

Theo began wondering if something had gone wrong on what he now referred to with great authority as the "space-time continuum." He started mumbling about wrinkles and strings being crossed and used crazy-sounding words like "quarks." (And *most* bizarrely, he said quarks came in different flavors and colors: up, down, strange, charm, top, bottom and red, green, and blue.) Alexandra was going through the gate every day at the appointed times, but nothing was changing. It began to feel very strange, as if she was stuck in a movie scene that was being replayed over and over again. She would normally quickly peek at the calendar between cracks in the wood siding, hiding so Brownie didn't see her, and then leave, already knowing it was the same day when she spotted the same people on the same blankets as she walked toward The Snack Shack.

One day she decided she had to ask some questions.

"Hi, Brownie, do you know who lives in that beach cottage, right over there? I always see a black cat in the window, but never see any people."

"Well, hello, Alexandra! Haven't seen you in a while, or Theo, or Jaclyn! Bet you're trying another beach. Well, that's okay! I know you'll be back! Chatham Beach is the best. Oh, that cottage? That cottage is owned by a very wealthy family, the Chadwicks. In fact, they're from Maine like you are, a place called Dark Harbor. Ever heard of it?"

She shook her head no, just wanting him to keep talking.

"Well, if you go into most any town in New England you'll see that name on a bank. Anyway, let's see, what day is it today?" he said, turning to look at the calendar.

Alexandra almost blurted out the date before he turned. He had no idea how the date of July 15th was burned into her mind—or July 20th.

"July 15th, well, right about now a young couple in a sailboat are leaving Dark Harbor headed to Chatham, and when they arrive they'll stay at that cottage. Elisabeth and Graham, just the nicest folks. Her mother, Silver Chadwick, owns the cottage—and all the banks," Brownie said, winking at her when he said "all the banks."

She felt glued to the spot and unable to speak.

"Yup, the nicest young couple. Heard they have a baby girl. She's staying home, too young for a long boat trip. Funny thing, I just remembered her name is the same as yours, Alexandra," he said, smiling at her. Then he continued.

"I expect them sometime in the next couple of days . . . you never know exactly with the Atlantic weather. I'm the caretaker of the cottage and their cat. His name is Samuel Adams. Graham is a headmaster of a private school, and when he's not sailing he has his nose in a book . . . loves American history . . ." Brownie's blue eyes were twinkling.

Alexandra felt like she could collapse any minute.

"Here you go, Miss Alexandra, a glass of lemonade, on the house. Now I'm back to work!" he said, and he helped the next customer in line.

◆

The next day after school Alexandra ran upstairs to make her quick trip through the gate, but she froze at the doorway of her bedroom.

There were blue and yellow feathers all over her comforter—and blood. A lot of blood.

Her screams echoed throughout Chadwick Manor.

BANISHED

Alexandra flew to the pole. Then it seemed like she was flying down the hall toward her grandmother's rooms. It felt like her feet did not touch the ground. Theo and Jaclyn were right behind her, running from the kitchen, where they were when they heard her scream. She was almost to the double doors when they opened. Her grandmother stepped out and then closed them behind her.

"Alexandra, come with me. Jaclyn and Theo, I will speak with you next. Wait outside the library door."

Alexandra felt the strong grip of her grandmother's arm around her waist and was so grateful because it felt like she was about to collapse.

Silver led her down the hallway and into the living room—it almost felt like they were gliding, not walking—then into the library to one of the peach velvet couches. Alexandra felt herself sink into the soft cushions. Her grandmother began stroking her hair, and as she breathed in the rose perfume, she began to sob. This was just like the time in the garden, only now she was going to hear her beloved Taco was dead, not her parents.

"Alexandra, my dear, listen to me. He is not dead. Taco is not dead. He has been wounded very badly and has lost a lot of blood. I am going to be honest with you, my dear. It is possible he may not live. I hope and pray that he will, and I will do everything *in my power* to save him."

Through her sobs, she heard the inflection, *"in my power."* She could save him. She had to. It felt like a knife was in her side. Sharp. It was hard to breathe.

"He is sleeping now and will continue to need to sleep, probably for many days. The veterinarian, our wonderful Dr. Burke, who takes such good care of Taco, Max, and Biscuit, came as soon as I found him. He needed to stitch the wounds and gave Taco antibiotic shots and vitamin injections. Dr. Burke will check on him every day or anytime I call. Taco will be in my room while he recuperates. I put him in your hanging baby cradle, and he fits perfectly, my dear, even his long feathers fit. He is snug and warm. Alexandra, I truly believe he will recover."

She handed Alexandra a handkerchief infused with the fragrance of roses. Slowly, Alexandra wiped her eyes and nose. Her grandmother was still stroking her hair, which was very calming, and Alexandra began to feel like she could control her tears.

"Now, my dear, there are two things I must tell you. As you have probably guessed, Taco was attacked by Noir. I do not know why. Noir will not talk to me or even to Nicolas. He is locked, actually heavily padlocked, in his cage and I have the only key. He will not escape again. Alexandra, look at me. This you must honor. I, alone, will deal with Noir. You are to stay away from him. Do not blame Nicolas. He was at school and had no idea this would happen. He is devastated, Alexandra. He knows what it is to love a pet with all your heart, just as you do, and in some ways this is harder on him. I am certain he feels deeply responsible, mortified, his pet would do such a terrible thing."

She paused, breathed in deeply, and then continued.

"The second is that you may not see Taco. No one will see him until I say it is all right. I do not know when that will be. You will have to trust me, Alexandra. I will tell you every day how he is doing. I will be honest. If, for any reason, I do not think Taco will live I will tell you, and of course, you may be with him."

Alexandra cuddled against her grandmother, not wanting to leave her warmth and strength. She could feel both, as always. Slowly, she felt her tears subside, her breathing became more regular, and she prayed.

Let him live. Let Taco live, please.

When Alexandra left the library, Jaclyn and Theo were waiting. They were sitting in chairs right near the library door and got up and hugged her in silence, their faces full of worry. Silver beckoned them into the library.

Alexandra had not felt this pain since the day in the garden so many years ago. She climbed the stairs very, very slowly. As she walked into her room she saw the comforter had been replaced with another. Everything was clean. There was not a feather or a drop of blood to be seen. Then she walked over to Taco's beautiful brass cage with all the toys hung just where he wanted them, the mirror positioned perfectly, and the tears came again in a flood. She was sobbing on her bed when she heard a familiar voice and her bedroom door opened.

"Alexandra, I knew you were terribly distraught. I felt it, so I came right away. Evelyn just told me Taco has been badly injured."

Olivia sat down on her bed and quickly scooped her up, hugging her tightly.

"My darling, you must have courage. There is not a single person who can help Taco more than your grandmother, my mother. She is the most powerful *of all.*"

Olivia looked at her with great seriousness, and reached for Alexandra's hands, holding them in her own.

"You must be strong and patient. I know you can be both."

Alexandra loved looking at her aunt's face because she knew it was her mother's. She breathed in deeply, and nodded her head "yes." She would be strong. For Taco. He would be for her. And now she knew what she had always felt but not understood, from the time she was little, was true. Her grandmother was special.

"I am going to talk with her now. Be strong, Alexandra."

She stood and blew a kiss as she left the room.

In a few minutes, there was a soft knock on the door. Theo and Jaclyn came in, climbing gently on her bed. No one spoke for a long time. Later on, Evelyn brought up a tray of soup and sandwiches. They ate a little, mostly in silence. That night Theo brought his blankets and pillow and slept on the rug, and Jaclyn slept with her. Alexandra had not even once thought about Chatham.

* ◆ *

The nightmare returned. Alexandra slept poorly, tossing and turning all night, and she woke up feeling exhausted and panicky. Suddenly remembering, she jumped out of bed, ran to Taco's cage, and picked up the salt lick. She stood frozen, staring at the empty space. *No key.* Theo and Jaclyn had both wakened and were standing next to her. No one spoke. Alexandra inspected every inch of the large cage. Then her eyes scanned the room and she was quickly searching under the rug and the bed, in her nightstands and armoire, under the window seat cushions, everywhere. But the key was not anywhere. She sat on the edge of her bed.

"Noir has it. That is what he came for, and Taco fought to protect it—with his life."

It had not occurred to her until this moment. She thought it was pent-up rage, jealousy, or just plain evil, his attack on Taco. Now it was obvious. Noir somehow knew about the key. And he loved shiny objects. She threw on her bathrobe and headed for the door, but Theo was faster and stood at the door, facing her.

"Alexandra, wait. You can't accuse Noir of nicking the key. He will just deny it. We have to think about this very carefully. We have to outsmart him if there is any chance of getting it back."

Alexandra scowled at him, but she knew Theo was right. She wanted to strangle the black bird with her own hands and force him to tell her where it was. She would punish him for what he had done with stale bread and water for months or years and take away every shiny object he had ever squirreled away—and never, ever, let him out of the cage again. Double, triple padlocked. She paced her room, as she had seen Taco do so many times. Think, think, think hard. How? How could they find the key as quickly as possible?

Today might be the day the date would change to the 20th. Just the thought of it made her sick and panic-filled.

"Let me talk with Nicolas. I'm not family and even though we're not mates, I think he likes me. Let's see what he knows, what I can find out. I'll have a good look at Noir's cage and what's in it. I'll go right now."

Theo pushed up his glasses and left.

There was not a lot to report back.

Nicolas did not say much except that he had no idea what key Theo was talking about and asked what it was for. Theo told him that it had been Alexandra's parents' key and was a keepsake. It was all he could think of quickly. Nicolas told Theo to look in Noir's cage, which he did, even though Noir was glaring at him the entire time. He said he could see the Halloween ring and some of the brass trinkets from Christmas, but no key. Then Theo said what Alexandra had realized—Noir could have hidden the key anywhere in Chadwick.

Shaking his head, he said, "Noir is like the Artful Dodger, pickin' pockets and hidin' the loot."

He told Alexandra the padlock on Noir's cage was massive, like the locks he had seen at the Tower of London, and there was no way he could break out of his cage. Alexandra wasn't convinced. She had not forgotten about his tool-making abilities.

All very grim.

The key was missing. And time was passing.

* ◆ *

Unbeknownst to Alexandra, Silver Chadwick made numerous visits to see Nicolas and Noir over the next few days. She brought the raven food and would unlock the cage, place the food inside, freshen his water, and lock the padlock again. Then she would sit in a chair and talk to Noir about what he had done and why, about how terrible it was and how Taco could die, and she told him it would be very hard for anyone to ever trust him again. Surely he must be deeply sorry and re-gret his actions. Speaking fluent French, Noir understood every word but he never responded with a single "oui" or "non," not one word. His only response was a dark glare.

Each visit, Silver expected he would finally apologize. He did not.

After three days, Silver told Nicolas what she had decided to do. Nicolas turned away with a sharp sob and pulled the curtains around his bed. Through the velvet curtain came a desperate, anguished whisper.

"Je vais mourir sans Noir."

Silver Chadwick left his room with the cage.

Minutes later, they were at the edge of the backyard, overlooking the cliffs and the immense Atlantic Ocean, the black water roiling with frothy white tops, lonely and forbidding on a cold, gray late afternoon.

The winds were blowing strongly and her long dress was whipping around her. Silver took out a key from her pocket, opened the padlock, and then the cage door.

"Noir, you are now banished, never to return here again. If you do, you will die. You are banished to the *back of beyond*."

Her voice was carried on the swirling winds over the ocean. A powerful and absolute command, much stronger than the petite frame would have suggested was possible. One arm was outstretched, pointing out to the vast ocean.

The raven stared at her and then lowered his head. He stepped from the cage and paused a moment with his head still down. Then his massive wings slowly opened and soon he was in flight. However, he was not headed toward the ocean. He banked sharply and flew back toward Chadwick.

Nicolas was standing in his window, one hand pressed against the glass as though he was trying to reach through it. His face was white and stricken. Noir flew in a large loop toward the house, then close by the window. As he passed Nicolas, he slowly tipped his black wings toward him and then the other way. His final salute. His final good-bye.

With one long, melancholy caw echoing in the winds, he flew back toward the ocean, dipping low near one large bush, and then straight out over the dark, forbidding sea, a glint of gold hanging from his beak.

Soon the tiny black speck disappeared from sight on the vast horizon of sea and sky.

Noir was gone to the *back of beyond.*

DARKNESS FALLS OVER CHADWICK

From the moment Noir was banished, Nicolas changed.

Everything that happened after December 23rd that had seemed so positive simply vanished. He never left his room, locking himself in. Food was left by Evelyn on a tray outside his door for each meal, but little was ever eaten. Letters from Nicole that were slipped under his door were pushed back out into the hallway, unopened, and no letters were written to her. And he refused to go to school.

Silver Chadwick had assembled everyone in the library the same evening she watched the black bird fly out over the ocean. She told them about her many visits, and her request for an apology that never came, and her decision. Jaclyn had gasped and tears spilled down her cheeks as she realized what this would do to her brother. Alexandra had been shocked as well, and wrestled with two feelings. One, that it was justice for a terrible crime, and two, that Nicolas could not bear the separation—it would somehow destroy him. Theo also seemed very conflicted and looked terribly concerned. Evelyn kept wringing her handkerchief and shaking her head, very red faced, saying, "Poor lad." Blackie sat very still, looking the most serious Alexandra could remember, and said nothing.

It was a shock to all of them—that this had actually been done.

Alexandra had wanted to kill the black bird herself, but realized even if she had the chance, she couldn't have. It was almost as though her grandmother had killed Noir. And where was he banished *to*? But no one dared ask.

The daily reports about Taco were less than encouraging. On some days, the veterinarian would come twice, rushing down the hallway and into Silver's rooms, leaving with a serious look on his face.

Dr. Burke had told Silver privately the wounds could prove fatal to Taco. He told her the beak of a raven was as sharp and deadly as a bowie knife, used to tear apart the bodies of dead prey in the wild, and that Taco's beak had been no match in their battle. He explained the power of a macaw's curved beak was in its pressure to break seeds and nutshells, their natural food in the wild, helped also by their tongue, which actually had a bone in it. With sad eyes cast down upon the frail macaw, he said nature had given each bird what it needed to best survive, but in the case of the raven, it was a deadly weapon.

Evelyn seemed to be a bundle of nerves, going between the kitchen and Silver's rooms and preparing food trays for Nicolas. The rides to school were somber. It felt strange to all of them that Nicolas was not riding with them, and Alexandra realized she missed him. He was not going to school and was not at any meal, and even though he had never been very conversational, he had been physically there. And now he wasn't. Jaclyn was deeply affected and not herself at all. She hardly talked anymore and began going to her room more than Alexandra's. Theo buried himself in his books on the third floor and Alexandra spent endless hours lying on her bed, holding her father's pipe, looking at the snow globe and her parents' photograph, then at Taco's empty cage, and then, with a sadness that filled her entire body, at the mural. There was no hope of saving her parents. She was certain July 20th had come and gone at Chatham Beach.

It felt like all she wanted to do was cry.

However, more than anything else, each day she waited anxiously for her grandmother's report, which came right after school. Her words were always carefully chosen, and there was every attempt to be positive, but Alexandra knew the truth underlying the words. Taco was not improving.

These were very dark times at Chadwick Manor.

UPS AND DOWNS . . . AND A MURDER

Nicolas was never seen or heard from.

It felt like a ghost was living with them. They realized he had to come out of his room when they were at school or late at night when no one would see him. Jaclyn often knocked on his door, asking to see him, and when he did not answer, she would speak softly to him in French. The response was always silence from the other side of the door, which was always locked. She also wrote notes to him that she slipped under his door. At least her notes were not pushed back into the hallway, but she told Alexandra she somehow knew he was not reading them.

Dinnertime was very hard. Everyone sat around the kitchen table and sometimes Olivia would come for dinner, but other than some forced conversation, they ate in silence. Taco was not on his perch and Nicolas's place was empty. No one ever seemed very hungry. Soon they would leave, each to his or her own room.

Schoolwork was almost a relief, something to focus on. Mr. Gingerroot sent home study packets for Nicolas, which were placed outside his bedroom door each afternoon. The paperwork always disappeared by morning, but no completed work was ever put outside to be returned to school. Olivia tried to talk to him a number of times outside his door, but he refused to answer her.

One afternoon, Alexandra was waiting outside her grandmother's doors as she always did right after school, and for the first time she heard her name being called to come in. Every other day she had waited for her grandmother to come out and talk to her, never being invited in. She felt her heart race with hope and anticipation, but this was quickly dashed with stomach-clenching fear, as she suddenly realized perhaps Taco was much worse. Very slowly and with considerable apprehension, she opened the doors and walked into her grandmother's bedroom. The hanging baby cradle was right next to the bed where her grandmother was sitting with one hand on the cradle, gently rocking it.

"Come in, my dear, come and see your Taco. He is much better today . . . at last."

Alexandra could not believe it—*much better today*. She crept closer to the cradle and peered in. He was lying on his back. His long blue and yellow wings were folded along his sides, his eyes were open just a little, and his head was resting on a very small pillow. Quilts decorated with tiny blue and gold macaws were tucked along the sides of the cradle. His body was very thin, and there was a large bandage across his chest and a smaller one above one eye. She could see that most of his yellow chest feathers had been shaved off.

"Taco, it's me, Alexandra," she whispered, leaning over the cradle.

"I am so glad to see you at last. It has been a long time, and I have missed you so much. More than you will ever know . . . Grand Mama has taken such good care of you!"

She smiled at him and then at her grandmother, tears spilling from her eyes.

Taco's eyes had widened as she was speaking and she could tell he knew her. Then she saw him swallow and try to talk.

"Taco miss princess . . ." It was faint, just a hoarse whisper, but she heard each word.

"Oh, Taco, this is so wonderful! You know me and you're *talking!*"

Through her tears, Alexandra grinned at her grandmother, who looked equally happy.

As she looked back at Taco, her gaze fell on the blue vitamin bottle sitting on the nightstand with a dropper next to it. So they were very special vitamins after all, for children . . . and birds. She wondered what flavors Taco had been given, hopefully watermelon and pineapple.

"Taco sleep now."

His eyes closed and he was softly snoring in seconds.

Alexandra went to her grandmother's bed. As she sat next to her on the bed, the memories of doing this so many times when she was little flooded back. She remembered climbing into bed with her grandmother every weekend morning and how huge the bed seemed then (not anymore), and how safe and happy she had felt snuggling next to her (that would never change). Then she felt her grandmother's small but strong arm wrap around her.

"Taco will live, my dearest."

In the next few days, Theo and Jaclyn were allowed to visit a couple of times. From then on, they all could visit regularly. Taco's speech was improving quickly, his appetite had returned, and he was eating—but he was still very weak and spent most of the time lying in the cradle. Dr. Burke had prescribed watermelon, oranges, bananas, and grapes and they all took turns feeding him chunks of fruit, and administered water (and vitamins) with the dropper. One day, Taco asked Jaclyn to bring him the English-to-French pocket dictionary, and he asked Alexandra for the small mirror. They had debated about the mirror, thinking it would be too shocking for him, but finally decided he would have to see the bandages and lack of feathers at some point. When Alexandra first held it up, he had screeched in shock, but slowly he came back to it, calmed down, and began carefully looking at himself. During his next checkup, he asked Dr. Burke when the bandages would come off and was told in another week, and with a big smile, the veterinarian said he could go back to Alexandra's room once the stitches were out.

In the meantime, Taco was to do what Dr. Burke called "flight therapy," because his wings had lost almost all their strength in the time he had been confined to the cradle. All three took turns helping with this and each day he became visibly stronger. When the flight therapy began, he was placed on the perch in the conservatory, told to fly to the cradle, not too far, and back and forth as many times as he could. The first time he was only able to fly one way and had collapsed back in the cradle. The next day, he managed to fly back to the perch and then Theo carried him back to the cradle. However, each day there was real progress. After a week, he was flying the length of the back hallway a couple of times each day and began sitting on his perch for longer periods. To Jaclyn's delight, he also began to speak in French now and then, one day asking her for "un bol de la pastèque" (having consulted his dictionary for the French word for watermelon).

The week ended with a good report from Dr. Burke, who watched Taco fly the length of the long hallway twice, smiling with approval, and congratulating the three young "flight therapists" who had assisted in his care. Then he carefully removed the bandages. That part was not easy to watch. Both Alexandra and Jaclyn had to look away, but not Theo. He wanted to watch everything, including when the stitches were removed.

Taco had winced and said "ouch" a couple of times but was otherwise quite brave during the entire procedure. The scar that was left was very long, almost the entire length of his chest, an ugly reddish color, and nearly all his gorgeous yellow feathers were gone. It looked like he would have a scarred eyebrow as well—a swath of blue and opalescent feathers had been shaved above his right eye. As soon as all the stitches were out, Taco had flown to the large mirror in Silver's powder room to look at himself from all angles. The shock and skepticism immediately reflected on his face were greatly alleviated when Dr. Burke reassured him all his feathers would eventually grow back and the scars would not be visible once the feathers had regrown.

As the doctor left, he gently rubbed Taco's ears and said, "Taco, you will be as good as new." As Taco grimaced at his image in the mirror, he kept repeating "good as new." Saying these words definitely helped him adjust to what he was looking at.

Everyone was feeling better with this positive turn of events—even Jaclyn was obviously cheerier. When it was time for Taco to return to the second floor, they decided to celebrate and have a parade. It had been Theo's idea the night before. He said everyone needed a bit of a "knees up." Alexandra asked her grandmother if it was all right because Nicolas would hear them. Silver had thought for a moment and then said it was time for Nicolas to move on, and Taco's recovery was a happy occasion, so it was fine. The party planning commenced. They blew up balloons and Jaclyn made a sign that said, "Hip, Hip, Hurray for Taco!" Everyone wore a birthday hat, including Blackie, Evelyn, Silver, and Olivia. Evelyn played the harmonica and suggested "Yankee Doodle Dandy," which they all agreed would be a good song. (Jaclyn especially liked it because of the pony part.)

Alexandra dressed Max as a Red Cross nurse, complete with a nurse's cap, red cape, and fake stethoscope that had been hers when she was little.

When they all walked into Silver's rooms on the day of the move, it was a total surprise. Taco was obviously delighted, bobbing his head and dancing back and forth on his perch. He loved the Halloween parade and was thrilled when Alexandra told him they were having a parade *in his honor.* Alexandra gently placed his own tiny birthday hat on his head, with the elastic under his chin. He rode on Alexandra's shoulder as they made their way down the hallway and up the stairs, all the while singing along (he knew all the words to "Yankee Doodle Dandy"). The sound was a bit deafening in her ear and off-key as usual, but Alexandra loved every minute of the short trip. And Jaclyn beamed at Theo and Alexandra as they walked up the stairs singing the refrain, "riding on a pony."

Most of all, Alexandra loved seeing Taco hop in his cage, back in their room, looking everything over with approval and contentment.

The noise and commotion had to have been heard by Nicolas, but he never opened his door or made a sound. It was silent behind his door.

Deathly quiet.

✳ ◆ ✳

The days went by with Taco improving each day. His feathers were starting to grow back, and he was eating well and gaining back the weight he had lost while he was recovering. Alexandra still had some things to tell him but waited a few more days. The time seemed right one afternoon when they were alone together in their bedroom.

"Taco, I have to tell you about what happened after you were . . . injured." She had thought a lot about the right word to use and decided "injured" was better than "attacked."

Taco looked at her with interest, but also wariness, saying nothing.

"First, Noir is not here anymore. He is not in Nicolas's room. Grand Mama tried to make him realize he had done something terrible, but he never would admit it or apologize. So she banished him—we don't know where to—but he is gone . . . forever."

Taco looked shocked and lowered his head.

"And the second is I know why Noir attacked you. You were protecting the key with your life . . . and you almost died defending it."

It was hard to even say these words. Taco continued to hang his head and did not look at her.

"But Noir did take it and no one knows where it is. Theo looked in his cage, but it wasn't there. Nicolas didn't know anything about the key—Theo just said it was something I had saved that belonged to my parents and it was missing—and before we could try to talk to Noir about it, he was banished. Grand Mama does not even know about the key, much less that he stole it."

Alexandra paused, looking at the mural, and then continued.

"The key is gone, Taco, and we will probably never find it. It could be anywhere. So I never got back to Chatham on July 20th to try to save my parents."

The deep sadness in her voice resonated with the last words.

Taco was moving things around in his cage, having first shoved the salt lick aside, staring at the empty spot where the key had been. It was obvious he assumed the key had not been taken—that he had defended it. He became more frantic when he realized it wasn't there . . . flying first to the window seat and pushing all the pillows to the floor, lifting the seat cushions with his beak, then flying to the top of the canopy, then to the nightstand, then back to the top of his cage, his eyes frantically scanning the room.

"It's all right, Taco. I have accepted it. You're probably not supposed to change history," but then she thought of Mercy Disbrow, "at least most of the time . . . and I have Aunt Olivia. Having her is like having my own mother."

Taco was now shaking his head and he looked angry and upset, which was not good for his recovery. Dr. Burke had said he should not become agitated.

"Key important. Can't be lost. Taco find."

Taco spent the next week flying throughout Chadwick Manor, looking in every hiding place he could think of. He told Alexandra he was certain he could find the key because he was a bird and would know the types of hiding places another bird would use. Evelyn said he did look in some difficult spots no person could easily get to that were very high up—the tops of paintings, above window moldings and valances. He practically turned the house inside out, which Evelyn did not appreciate at all. Pillows were pushed to the floor, seat cushions removed, edges of rugs picked up, cabinets and drawers opened. It was an amazingly thorough search, but no key was found. He wanted to get into Nicolas's room most of all, and asked if he could open the locked door late one night, but Alexandra told him that would not be right and Nicolas would just make him leave.

It was also true that aside from the missing key and Nicolas's self-imposed exile, life at Chadwick Manor was improving. Taco's recovery had boosted everyone's spirits and he looked more like himself with every passing day. His butterscotch chest feathers were growing back, and the scar above his eye could hardly be seen. Just having Taco flying around Chadwick and at meals made things seem more normal for everyone.

Yet Nicolas's absence still hung like a dark cloud over Chadwick.

Then, one afternoon, a black cloud actually appeared.

Alexandra was reading her American history book on her bed after school. She was reading about John Adams, his presidency, and his son John Quincy Adams, who also became president, and his cousin Samuel Adams, an American statesman and Governor of Massachusetts. Her mind drifted. Samuel Adams was also the name of her father's cat. As she thought of this, she turned and looked at the mural. There he was, the black silhouette sitting in the window of Chadwick Cottage, a painted image. But she had seen him in real life—or whatever dimension it was when they had gone through the gate. She sighed deeply, feeling the now familiar weight of heavy sadness which seemed to have settled permanently within her body. Her gaze then fell on the shiny keyhole. She would never go through the gate again . . . and her parents would never be saved from their watery graves. Then she found herself thinking about the trip to Salem, Massachusetts, in the year 1692, about a hundred years earlier than when John Adams lived, and how they had saved Mercy Disbrow, and by doing so—incredibly—had actually saved themselves. She was still looking at the mural as all these thoughts were swirling in her head when she came out of her daydreams, remembering there were more chapters to read for a test the next day. It was as her gaze shifted from the mural back to her history book that she saw them. Taco was napping in his cage. His back was to the window.

There were hundreds of black birds sitting in the huge maple tree on the barren branches, all facing her. Every branch was filled with large black birds, so densely packed the tree appeared to be solid black.

They were motionless and staring at her through the large window.

She had never been more afraid in her life, not even when the tigers were roaming the halls. Frozen with fear, her heart pounding, she tried to focus her thoughts on what to do. Staring back into hundreds of pairs of black beady eyes, all of a sudden she remembered the day in the library with Nicolas, what he had said as he left the room. Did she know a flock of crows was called "*a murder*"? That was what she was looking at . . . a murder. Only they actually wanted to commit murder. Noir had sent them to kill Taco. "Crows are cousins of ravens," she could hear Nicolas's hypnotic voice in her head.

She knew she had to get Taco out of their sight and reach. Very, very slowly she crept off the bed as quietly as she could and tiptoed to Taco's cage.

"Taco, wake up, wake up! You need to wake up, right now!"

Her voice was an urgent whisper, shaking a little, her eyes glued to the window. They were watching her every move, and seemed to become more alert, shifting slightly on the branches.

Taco's eyes sleepily blinked open and he stepped on her outstretched hand. She quickly brought him close to her body, turned her back to the window, and was out of the room in a second. She ran to the dumbwaiter across from Nicolas's room and pressed the button. The motor started, and slowly (much too slowly) the small elevator made its way to the second floor. The door finally opened and Taco began flapping his wings and looking at her like *what are you thinking?*

"Taco, you must do exactly as I say. *You must.* Punch the button for 3. It will take you to the third floor and the door will open. Get out and go straight to Theo's room. Tell him I sent you and you must stay with him until I come for you. Be sure to tell him to pull down the blind on his window *right away*. Taco, you must remember all of this! Now, quickly, push number *3*!"

Taco looked disgruntled and annoyed, as though this was unnecessary drama and he wanted her to please explain what it was all about, but he nodded, seeming to know from her tone there would be no explanation. He pushed the button with his curved beak. The door slowly shut and he was out of sight and going up.

Alexandra ran back to her room. *They were gone*. She ran to the window and looked. There was not a single crow left on the tree. Had she imagined it? Was this a nightmare or real? She actually did not know. Without thinking anymore, she ran to the pole and was running down the hallway when she saw a black cloud in the clear glass borders of the stained-glass windows. *Black birds flying*. They were moving quickly toward the conservatory. She burst through the double doors and found her grandmother seated in a chair reading a book, in front of a window that looked out to the back of Chadwick. Then she saw the black mass fly by the window and disappear from sight.

"Grand Mama, *they have come for Taco, hundreds of crows*! They just flew by your window—Noir must have sent them—they are cousins, ravens and crows—Nicolas told me. He said they're called a murder when they all fly together. *And I know they are here to murder Taco, I know it*!!"

Alexandra was breathless and scared to death as the words tumbled out. Her grandmother had folded her book but appeared very calm and did not speak or look out the window.

"I was studying and all of a sudden I looked up—and there they were—*hundreds, maybe thousands*, of black birds sitting on the tree outside my window. *Staring at me and Taco*! I took Taco to the dumbwaiter—he never saw them, thank goodness—and sent him up to Theo, where I know he'll be safe. *They must be right outside now, near the conservatory*. Oh, Grand Mama, you have to protect Taco!!"

As her grandmother rose from her chair, a single crow landed on the windowsill. Alexandra gasped and pointed to the window. He was a very large bird, almost the size of Noir, but did not have the distinctive throat ruffle of a raven. Her grandmother slowly turned around. The bird looked at her with an intense, intimidating glare and then flew away.

Silver walked to her closet and emerged wearing her velvet cape with her broom in one hand. However, unlike on Halloween, the broom was now pulsing with vivid colors, purple, orange, red, teal, and shimmering with tiny sparkles. It looked *alive*, Alexandra thought.

"My dearest Alexandra. I do not think it will come as a shock to you that I do have certain powers. Blackie told you the truth. I did not. I did not tell you the truth because I wanted to protect your innocence for as long as I could. We will talk more about this another time. Now I must be left alone. Please go and get Jaclyn and then go to Theo's room. Nicolas will be fine in his room. Stay there until I come for you. Keep the blinds drawn and do not look outside—*you must not*. Do I have your word?"

"Yes, yes, Grand Mama, I promise. Please be careful!"

"Go now, Alexandra."

It was a command.

Silver pulled the hood up over her head and Alexandra could see the lining was silver, not red like Olivia's. There were tiny ice-blue crystals encircling the edge of the hood, now illuminated and shimmering like the broom. Alexandra went to her grandmother, quickly hugged her, and then ran out of the room.

With her broom in one hand, Silver opened the door that led to the conservatory.

Black birds covered the entire glass roof. Motionless, they all faced the conservatory door, their black eyes intense and glaring.

The afternoon sun was going down quickly.

Silver Chadwick stepped into the darkened conservatory and closed the door behind her.

THE RETURN

No one witnessed what happened after the door to the conservatory was closed.

The next day there was a thick swath of black feathers scattered on the snow leading from the conservatory to the ocean cliff, and the feeling of being threatened by something ominous had completely disappeared. Silver Chadwick looked and seemed entirely herself, as though nothing had happened. No one spoke about it and Taco never knew how close he had come to "a murder."

Nevertheless, he did not hesitate to complain (repeatedly) about how he had been awakened from his nap and abruptly forced into the "small box with no windows" as he called it. And he clearly did not appreciate Alexandra's lack of explanation.

There was still no sign of Nicolas. They knew he was eating at least a little, but that was about it. Alexandra tried to have a number of conversations with her grandmother about him, but she always said the same things. He would get over it in time, time heals all wounds, and in time he would rejoin his family. The word "time" seemed to haunt Alexandra—time travel, time to get over something, time speeding up or slowing down, or standing still. Time, time, time. She began not to like the word at all.

She also talked to her aunt and sent her notes. Nicolas had missed almost two months of school, which concerned Olivia, but she said he would catch up easily because he was so smart—that he just needed *time*. Olivia tried to be reassuring, but both Alexandra and Jaclyn were deeply worried. How much time would it take? And Alexandra wondered, *what if time runs out and something terrible happens?*

Then one night Alexandra saw him. It was almost midnight and she was reading in bed, immersed in a story about witches. She had not brushed her teeth, sleepily got out of bed, and was headed toward the hallway and to the bathroom when she saw him returning from the bathroom. She quickly stepped back into the shadows so he would not see her. The hallway sconces were dimly lit, but she was close enough to see him. He was wearing his black bathrobe.

It actually looked like a skeleton was wearing the bathrobe, not a person. His face was emaciated and whiter than a sheet. The bathrobe hung on him like he was just bones. Her hand was over her mouth as she stared in shock and horror.

She knew what she was looking at.

Someone who was dying.

* ◆ *

The next day she told her grandmother exactly what she had seen, what Nicolas looked like. Her grandmother's face immediately reflected deep concern. She told Alexandra she would speak to Evelyn about how much he was actually eating, but Alexandra felt panicky. It might already be too late. He could die any day. She decided she could not tell Jaclyn or Theo, it would be too hard, especially for Jaclyn. However, she knew with absolute certainty she wanted her aunt to know and passed a note to her on the way out of school.

That afternoon Olivia drove to Chadwick and came to Alexandra's room.

"I am going to see him. He will let me in."

It was the same voice that had addressed the Chief Judge and told Max to come to her. Hypnotic and controlled. She walked out of Alexandra's room toward Nicolas's room.

Alexandra listened from her bedroom door. She heard the light tapping and then she heard her aunt's voice, but she could not hear what she was saying. In a few seconds, she heard the door unlock, open, and then shut again. Olivia was in Nicolas's room.

Alexandra felt nervous but also hugely relieved. Her aunt would know what to do.

In a few minutes, Olivia returned, her face reflecting deep worry.

"He is very, very weak. He is not well at all. I am going to see my mother right now. It is as though he has no will to live."

She quickly hugged Alexandra and left.

Alexandra waited. She paced the floor, sat on her bed and then on the window seat, then paced the floor again, back and forth, feeling very afraid and desperate. She was certain they were almost out of time . . . that Nicolas would die very soon. Looking at Taco, she knew he was also concerned about Nicolas, even though it was his bird who had caused so much pain and suffering. He flew to her shoulder and together they waited.

In about half an hour, Olivia returned and closed the door. It looked like she had been crying; her eyes were red and teary, which made Alexandra's stomach twist. She sat down on the window seat next to Alexandra.

"Your grandmother will try everything she can think of to make him better. But even so, it may not work. Nicolas was bound to Noir in a way that is hard to understand. When he was banished, Nicolas began to . . ."

Olivia's voice was just a whisper and then trailed off.

"Die."

Alexandra finished her sentence with a whisper.

Olivia nodded.

"We have to bring Noir home."

Alexandra could not really believe what she was saying, and Taco immediately flew from her shoulder to the top of his cage with his back to her.

"That is not possible, Alexandra. Noir was banished to the *back of beyond*. It is a place no one can return from . . . and live."

Her aunt's voice was hushed and gravely serious.

Alexandra stared at her. She had heard the same mysterious words from Nicolas. What had he said exactly? She tried hard to remember. Then it came to her.

"Nicolas told me. He said he thought Noir could fly there, to the *back of beyond*. He never said where it was, and I did not ask him. If Noir can fly there, he must be able to return. Nicolas told me ravens can always find their way home. If he cannot, Grand Mama must have the power to bring him home—you told me she is the most powerful of all—and where is the *back of beyond?*"

Suddenly Alexandra felt stronger, like this was something that could be solved. Instead of crying and feeling like there was no hope, they had to *do something*.

Even if it meant bringing back the terrible black bird.

Olivia just looked at her with great sadness.

"There is no possibility of ever getting Noir back, Alexandra. Even if he tried to return on his own, he would die trying. The *back of beyond* is a place I have only heard of . . . I do not know where it is or how to get there. However, I do know it is impossible to return from and live."

Olivia stood, leaned over to kiss Alexandra on the forehead, and then walked to the door. She looked back as she was leaving.

"I know your grandmother will do everything she can to save Nicolas. She loves him. He is her grandson, but whether he will live is . . . unknown."

The letter took a while to write. She went through many sheets of paper trying to find the right words.

Dear Nicolas,

I am writing because I'm very worried about you. Everyone is. Most of all, your sister, Jaclyn, who loves you very much.

I am so sorry about what happened. I know you had nothing to do with it. Noir attacked Taco all by himself. Grand Mama told me how upset you were when you found out. I didn't know she was going to banish Noir. I thought he would just be locked in his cage with a huge lock he could never open. I never thought Noir would be sent away.

Taco is getting better every day. Dr. Burke said he would be as good as new.

Please try to understand why Grand Mama did what she did. And please try to think about all the people here who love you and your father. He would be so upset about all of this.

You probably don't miss Mr. Gingerroot, but he asks about you all the time. You are his very best student. I am sure of that.

I love the snow globe you gave me and look at it every night. So far, the batteries still work.

I hope I will see you very soon.

Love,
Your cousin Alexandra

She found an envelope, wrote his name on it and hers in the upper left corner, put the letter inside and sealed it, then slid the envelope under his door.

And waited.

◆

Like the notes from Jaclyn, her letter was not pushed back under the door into the hall as Nicole's letters had been. (There were fewer and fewer of those. He never wrote back to her.) Alexandra wondered if he had read it or just threw it in some drawer, unread. She hoped he would be curious enough to read it; she had put her name on the envelope so he would know it was from her.

Days passed. Nothing changed, just the food trays being put out in the hallway, hardly touched. Alexandra was consumed with worry. Neither Jaclyn nor Theo had seen him, so they did not know how bad it was.

The burden of worrying about someone seriously ill and being powerless to help was taking its toll on Alexandra.

Late one afternoon, she was suddenly overcome with fear that something terrible was going to happen at any moment. She threw on her coat, walked to the gazebo, and sat looking at the ocean. Why did she feel certain Noir had flown over these cliffs and out to sea? She had not seen what happened when he was banished, but somehow she knew. The horizon was vast, and the sea and sky seemed endless, never meeting. The *back of beyond* was out there, somewhere. She searched the empty gray sky, now wishing more than anything else that one lone raven would reappear. After a while, she got up and walked to the rope swing. She sat on the sturdy wood bench she had watched Blackie make for her many years ago, pushed off, and began swinging higher and higher. The swing was near the cliff. If you pumped hard enough and went high enough, you could see the waves crashing on the huge rocks far below. She had been afraid to swing to the highest point when she was little, but as she got older she had gone higher and higher. Now she loved the feeling as she approached the highest and farthest point in the arc, suspended for a mere second in midair. It felt like she was flying.

Gradually, she let the swing slowly come to a rest, not pumping anymore, finally got off, and began walking back to Chadwick. It was getting dark and the wind was picking up. As she walked, she looked up at Nicolas's room. There were no lights on and the sail curtain was pulled across the window. Tears came into her eyes as she thought of his thin body lying in darkness, not wanting to live, and her stomach twisted with fear once again.

She had almost reached the house when something caught her eye. There was a row of evergreen bushes along the back of the house. It looked like there was something lying on the snowy ground, partially under one bush, directly below Nicolas's window. Her heart started to pound—she could see something *black* against the white snow. She started running, tears falling down her face. She dropped to her knees, frantically pushing apart the branches while crying out.

The body was withered and thin, the black feathers dull and ragged. There, in the thick black beak, was the key. *Her key.* One eye opened in a small slit. There was a very slight nod of the head, and the key dropped on the snow. The eye closed.

The black body shuddered and then was completely still.

SAVING LIVES

Alexandra shoved the key in her coat pocket and quickly took off her scarf. She carefully picked up his gaunt body, gently wrapped him in the scarf, and holding him close to her chest, she ran through the conservatory into her grandmother's rooms. Her grandmother was sitting in her chair reading.

"*Grand Mama, I have Noir*! I found him in the bushes outside Nicolas's window, just now! You have to help him . . . *you must save him . . . Nicolas will only get better if Noir does . . . Grand Mama, please, you must save Noir!*" Her voice was breathless and urgent and tears were still falling from her face as she gently opened the scarf with trembling hands.

Her grandmother walked over to the bed.

Lying on the pink comforter was the emaciated body of a once powerful raven, near death or already dead. He was not moving at all. It looked like he was not breathing.

"Alexandra, I think he is gone . . . it is impossible to return from the *back of beyond*. That he made it here alive is nothing less than a miracle. However, Noir cannot survive. No matter what I do, I cannot help him, my dear."

Silver was looking at the lifeless body with great sympathy, but her voice was resigned.

Alexandra had never felt so certain her grandmother was wrong. She could and must help Noir because Nicolas's life depended on it. At that moment, Alexandra felt a strength and determination flood into her that were so powerful she was no longer crying.

"I know you love Nicolas as much as Jaclyn and me. You would never give up trying to save Jaclyn or me. I know you wouldn't. Grand

Mama, you must do everything you can to save him. *We must save Noir to save Nicolas.* They have some kind of bond . . . one cannot live without the other . . . you know this is true. *Please, I beg you, Grand Mama!*"

Her grandmother's eyes were filled with tears as she gently put one hand on Alexandra's face. Then she reached down and lightly placed her hand on the thin, battered body, studying Noir intently.

"Get the cradle out of the closet, then fill a hot-water bottle and bring the vitamin bottle from the kitchen. I will try, Alexandra, but the odds are very much against Noir. Hurry, my dear. There is little time left."

Alexandra flew to the closet and wheeled out the cradle, watching as her grandmother laid Noir gently on the quilts decorated with tiny macaws. She thought fleetingly, *that will need to be changed,* as she ran out of the rooms and toward the kitchen.

✱ ◆ ✱

Jaclyn and Theo were wide-eyed when Alexandra told them what had happened, but she decided not to tell them about the key, at least not right away. They both wanted to see Noir. Alexandra had not been hopeful; however, to her great surprise her grandmother not only agreed, she said they could all help with his care, unlike her rules with Taco.

Together they tiptoed in and stood staring at the very sick raven, shocked by his appearance. He was breathing, but his breaths were very shallow. He was lying perfectly still with his eyes closed. Silver gently lifted him up, wrapped him in a small blanket, and took him to her chair. She slowly opened his beak, and while stroking his throat, gave him the liquid vitamins with the dropper. He swallowed, but just barely. Then she laid him back in the cradle next to the hot-water bottle and gently placed the blanket over him. She beckoned them to follow her into the conservatory.

Silver sat in one chair and they sat around her on the slate floor.

"Theo, I will ask you to help with the medicine and feedings. I will show you how to administer the medications and food."

Theo nodded seriously, but was obviously very pleased to be asked.

"Alexandra and Jaclyn, I will ask you both to be responsible for keeping him company and talking to him. Jaclyn, you must speak to Noir only in French."

"Oui, Grand-Mère."

"As I told Alexandra, even with the best care, Noir may not live. So you must understand this is a very real possibility . . . perhaps even likely. I will take care of him while you are at school, but afternoons and evenings and weekends he will be in your care. Do not fail in your responsibilities."

She looked at each of them with great seriousness and then continued.

"And Nicolas is not to be told. Do not send him any notes about this. He cannot be told until I am certain Noir will live."

Silver led them back to her room and showed Theo the medicine bottles on her nightstand, each one filled with a different colored liquid. She said she would tell him which medicines and the amounts to be administered each day. There were also large black bottles with antique gold lettering that read "Liquid Protein Raven Food" that he would need to administer. She showed Theo how to measure the right amount in the dropper and explained he would need to hold the raven's beak open and stroke his throat to help him swallow, just as she had done with the vitamins. Theo was totally focused. It seemed he was memorizing every word.

Later that evening, Theo gave Noir his medicine for the first time.

He measured very carefully, pushing up his glasses, rechecking the dropper several times before giving it to Noir. He had wrapped Noir in a small blanket and held him like a baby. As she watched him, Alexandra realized Theo was completely confident. He really looked like a very young doctor, and she decided at that moment he had to be a doctor or veterinarian, not an architect. Noir took two full droppers of medicine and swallowed with Theo rubbing his throat. Then he took one full dropper of raven food. Theo whispered to him, "Jolly good show, Noir, jolly good show."

The first night they all slept on the thick pink rug in Silver's bedroom, covered with down comforters. Theo asked to stay because he wanted to watch his patient the first night. Silver had nodded with approval. Noir was obviously breathing better and had swallowed four droppers of medicine and two of liquid raven food by the time they went to sleep. Silver told them the liquid protein food was the flavor of corn muffins.

It was the one time they had all smiled.

* ◆ *

Days passed and Noir began to show small signs he was improving. His eyes would open briefly a couple of times during the day, and when the food was administered he seemed to want more, so Theo began to gradually increase the number of droppers of food. And he learned how to give Noir vitamin injections, which Silver decided were also necessary. He would carefully wrap Noir in a towel, then sit holding him on the bed or chair and insert the needle under one wing. Noir never even winced. It was obvious to Alexandra that Noir was comfortable being handled by Theo, and she realized her grandmother had known this was best for Noir's recovery from the beginning. Theo was replacing Nicolas for the moment.

After about a week, Noir opened his eyes for longer periods. He had been very wary and uncertain of his surroundings at first and was especially frightened when he first saw Silver. However, she told them she had spoken with him privately, and ever since their conversation, he was obviously at ease and comfortable around her. In a few more days, he began to stand up for short periods in the cradle. (Alexandra had changed the macaw quilts to plain bedding when he was first put in the cradle.) Then one day he flew from the cradle to the bed. A very short distance, but it was tremendous progress. His black feathers began looking less straggly, and he did not look as thin.

It began to feel like Noir would live.

His recovery was having another effect. They all noticed more food was being eaten from the trays left in the hallway. One day Evelyn told them she found a note asking for bigger portions. She was thrilled, loading the trays with food from then on, and most was eaten. Another day, a letter was found on the food tray, addressed to Nicole at the English boarding school. Evelyn presented it to the postman with a very big smile on her face.

Nicolas did not know anything about Noir, so they all knew he must not have understood why he was feeling better. Piles of completed schoolwork began appearing outside his door from what had been placed there over months. Every day Jaclyn would pick it up in the morning and turn it in to Mr. Gingerroot, who would give her more homework to take home. Nicolas made up his schoolwork in no time. Mr. Gingerroot told Jaclyn to tell her brother that he was already ahead of the rest of the class—again—and to please return to school as soon as possible! Jaclyn wrote this in a note with the pile of new homework.

Nor did Taco know that Noir had returned to Chadwick Manor

and was being nursed back to health. Alexandra did not know how or when or what she was going to tell him, but she had shown Taco the key right away. He had been so happy, dancing around on the window seat and then tucking it safely back under the salt lick. However, the happiness was short-lived and had quickly turned serious when he asked (with a most piercing stare) where she *found* the key. It was like an inquisition and clear what he was thinking. He had done the most thorough search possible and had not found it. So how could she? Alexandra decided to stick to the truth as much as possible and told him she found it near the bushes running along the back of the house. He thought about this for a few minutes, mulling it over, and then slowly nodded. It had not occurred to him that Noir might have hidden the key outside.

Alexandra actually dreaded using the key again. She had a terrible feeling in the pit of her stomach. It would be August or September, or worst of all, July 20th right after her parents had sailed out of sight. She kept procrastinating and even though Taco repeatedly brought the key to her, she said "no" each time. He seemed very perplexed and would shake his head and mutter about time travel and wormholes, repeating what he had heard Theo say, but clearly did not understand any of it.

The days and weeks passed and Alexandra tried not to think about the key. She still had not told Jaclyn or Theo about it. Her focus was on Noir's progress more than anything else. As Noir was getting healthier and stronger by the day, Nicolas was also eating more and letters began going to England again. It seemed like the black shadow cast over Chadwick Manor was beginning to lift.

All because one raven had returned from the *back of beyond.*

And lived.

THE REUNION

It was a time of great expectation.

As each day passed, Noir was getting stronger, his black feathers now shiny and thick, and the purple and green opalescent hues once again vibrant. He was flying from the conservatory to the cradle, back and forth, many times a day with no trouble. Alexandra told Taco the heaters were not working well and until they were fixed, he could not go in the conservatory. It was the first time this had ever happened, and he seemed a little suspicious but had accepted the restriction. (The doors to her grandmother's rooms were always kept shut.) The medicine was being reduced each day, and Noir was slowly reintroduced to real food. He was conversing a little with Jaclyn, mostly listening to her talk about school or what homework she had, but occasionally he would respond in the familiar monotone voice . . . and his French was parfait.

They all felt the time was drawing closer to tell Nicolas, who had still not emerged from his room. In the weeks Noir was regaining his health, Alexandra was certain Nicolas was as well. He was eating huge platters of food; even snacks that Evelyn left late at night vanished with only crumbs left in the morning.

One day an envelope appeared in the hallway outside of his bedroom door addressed to "Jaclyn, Alexandra, & Theo." Evelyn found it and brought it to Alexandra, who had immediately gone for the others. They were all sitting on Alexandra's bed staring at it.

"Open it, Alexandra, vite, rapidement!!"

Jaclyn was staring at the envelope with excitement.

Theo nodded, as did Taco, who was sitting on Theo's shoulder.

Alexandra felt her hands tremble as she ripped open the envelope. She pulled out one piece of paper and read it aloud.

> To my sister, my cousin, and my friend,
>
> I am sorry to have worried you. I became very sick when Noir left. I did not want to live without him. I still miss him terribly and will always, but for reasons I do not understand, I am now feeling better, stronger. I do not know why because my heart is still broken, and I do not think it will ever heal.
>
> I will be going to school tomorrow and will see you at breakfast. Please tell Evelyn I will not need any more trays of food.
>
> Nicolas
>
> Postscript
> Alexandra, I am truly glad Taco recovered and will be as good as new.
>
> Second Postscript
> I am also glad the batteries still work.

Alexandra immediately told Evelyn, "No more trays," and Nicolas would be coming to breakfast the next morning, to which she replied, "Lovely, just lovely," beaming. Then she brought the letter to her grandmother, whose eyes brightened as she read it.

"When?"

Alexandra knew her grandmother would know what she was asking—when would Noir and Nicolas be reunited—but she dared not ask the full question as she really suspected Noir understood English, even if he only spoke French. He was watching her from the perch, his black eyes questioning, focused on the letter.

"Soon, very soon, my dear. I will make the arrangements."

That night no one slept very well. What would he look like? It had been over two months. Alexandra felt certain he had to look better than the night she had seen him. He had been eating well for almost three weeks. Yet there was still a feeling of apprehensiveness. To Alexandra it felt like guarded anticipation, both wanting to see him and afraid to see him.

They were all in the kitchen earlier than usual the next morning. Evelyn, Blackie, Theo, Jaclyn, Alexandra, and Silver. Olivia had come too, having heard the news from her mother the night before. Taco was the only one eating, happily slurping his watermelon. Everyone else was anxiously watching the swinging door. Evelyn was fussing with muffins, pancakes, and bacon, pouring coffee, and nervously chattering about the importance of breakfast when the door silently swung open.

Nicolas walked in and nodded, looking first at his grandmother and then at the others. He was very pale and noticeably thinner, but he did not look like the skeleton Alexandra had seen. It was his eyes, though, that were most different. For the first time, there was a light in them, something warmer than had ever been there before, and the color was more amber, not the dark, stormy brown she remembered.

Jaclyn, Theo, and Alexandra exchanged relieved looks.

"Bonjour, tout le monde, and Evelyn, merci, thank you, for all the food you brought to me for many months. Merci beaucoup."

Nicolas looked directly at Evelyn, and his eyes reflected the gratitude that was in his voice. Then he sat down at the empty seat and began filling his plate with food.

Nicolas had also returned from the *back of beyond*.

Everything began to feel more normal again. Breakfast, dinner, the rides to school, all felt right now that Nicolas was back with them. He seemed to be friendlier, often riding with them and not always by himself in the rumble seat, or occasionally having a snack with them in the kitchen after school. Sometimes he went up to see Theo in his room. Jaclyn was so happy and relieved that she would often just stare at her brother and smile.

Mr. Gingerroot had been beside himself with happiness. His unattractive face looked even more so when he smiled (just like Headmaster Green's), and the day his best student returned to school, the smile never left his face. Apparently as an expression of his gratitude, he gave Nicolas piles of homework each night, but Nicolas never complained and actually seemed to like it. Once again, Nicolas seemed anxious to get home to check the mail, and often there was mail from England.

It was about two weeks later when Silver decided the time was right to have the reunion. However, before it could take place, Alexandra had to tell Taco about Noir. The hard part. The very, very hard part. A few days before the planned reunion, Alexandra decided the time had come.

"Taco, come sit with me."

Alexandra was sitting on the window seat. The late afternoon sky still had traces of pink. The days were getting longer; it was not getting dark quite as early. Spring was finally coming, very slowly, to Maine.

He flew from his cage, and she picked him up, and lay down on the window seat. His painted face was only inches away from hers. She loved looking at the amazing details of his face, the distinct demarcation between the blue and yellow feathers, the white cheek patches with fine, decorative black lines framing each eye, the bib of dark feathers under his chin, and the gorgeous green opalescent patch on his forehead. She could not even see where the stitches had been above one eye; new feathers now covered the eyebrow scar. His chest, too, was once again thick with brilliant butterscotch-yellow feathers, completely concealing the long scar. Most of all, she loved looking into his eyes, they were so expressive and intelligent.

"Taco, I have to tell you something. You have to try and stay calm," she said, stroking his feathers.

He immediately looked concerned and tilted his head to one side. She could feel his body stiffen.

"You know Noir was banished by Grand Mama after he attacked you because he never apologized for what he had done. She sent him to some place called the *back of beyond* . . . you remember Aunt Olivia telling me Noir could never return from there—and live."

Alexandra paused to let Taco absorb what she had said. His painted eyes were glued to hers. He was staring at her with an intensity she could not remember seeing before.

"A few weeks ago I found Noir outside . . . he was almost dead. He was lying under the bushes in the back, under Nicolas's window, and he had the key in his beak. He had taken it with him when he was banished. Remember, I told you I found the key outside? That was true. I didn't tell you about Noir because I was not sure he would live . . . no one is supposed to be able to return from the *back of beyond* and live, and I knew you would not want him to come back here, after what he did . . ."

Taco's eyes were serious. He was listening intently to every word.

"You know when Noir left, Nicolas changed. He stopped eating and never came out of his room. I saw him late one night . . . he looked like a skeleton. He was dying, Taco. So when I found Noir, I brought him to Grand Mama and asked her to do whatever she could to save him."

Taco was frozen like a statue. It did not look like he was even breathing. She was reminded of the macaw ice sculpture Theo had made. He might as well have turned to ice.

"I hope you understand, Taco. I really believe Nicolas would have died if Noir had not lived."

Taco suddenly moved like a statue coming to life and flew to his cage. He sat on his perch with his back to Alexandra.

"Taco, if it had been us, I hope Nicolas would have saved you."

She got up and slowly walked to the cage and around to the far side to look him in the face. His head was hanging down.

"Taco, look at me."

He slowly looked up, and she could see tiny tears on his face.

"Taco not want Noir to die."

She reached in and offered her hand. He slowly stepped on and she held him close again, kissing his head. Once again, his kindness and selflessness overwhelmed her. Noir had tried to kill him, but he did not want Noir to die. She walked around the room, gently stroking his feathers, tears silently running down her face.

"I know, Taco, I know you wouldn't have wanted that, despite what he did to you. And he did not die . . . Grand Mama and Theo saved him. Noir has been living in Grand Mama's rooms and the conservatory for the last few weeks. The heater was never broken—I'm sorry

I had to lie to you. Nicolas does not know about Noir, but he has been getting better every day because Noir lived. There's going to be a wonderful reunion very soon . . ."

After a few moments, Taco flew to the window seat and stared out the window. Looking at him, Alexandra was reminded of the terrible sight of the tree filled with crows, which thankfully he had not seen. That would have made it all but impossible for him to ever accept Noir again.

Then he turned around and faced her, his head slightly tilted to one side.

"Noir nice to Taco?"

As he was looking at her, she could see both hope and doubt in his eyes.

"Taco, I am sure it will be different now. Noir did some terrible things, attacking you and stealing what was not his, but he realized his mistakes. He returned the key, and he was willing to pay for that with his life."

* ◆ *

It was nighttime.

Colorful paper lanterns were strung from the conservatory roof. A cake decorated with "Welcome Home Noir" was on the center of the table with candles lit. Next to the cake, on a small plate, was an extra-large corn muffin. Taco was sitting on his perch and everyone was seated around the long glass table.

Theo slowly led Nicolas into the conservatory. A bandana was tied behind his head, covering his eyes. Noir was sitting on a perch in Silver's bedroom. As they walked by, his black eyes never left Nicolas and he opened his wings to their full expanse. It was a silent greeting, not heard or seen, to the person he loved more than life itself.

Theo guided Nicolas to the center seat in front of the cake, sat him down, and then sat down next to him.

"Je ne comprends pas. What is going on?"

Silver beckoned to Noir, who flew the short distance from the perch and landed in her lap. She stroked him lightly.

"Nicolas, my dear, we have a wonderful surprise for you."

She nodded to Noir, who flew to Nicolas and landed on his shoulder.

Nicolas was perfectly still. He was breathing deeply. Then one hand, visibly trembling, very slowly reached up and gently touched the familiar body. He pulled down the bandana and looked into the eyes he never thought he would see again.

BIRDS OF A FEATHER AND TIME STANDS STILL (OR DOES IT?)

The days and weeks after the reunion were the best times at Chadwick Manor.

Life not only returned to what it had been, but it was better, so much better. Nicolas gained weight by the day and was more talkative than ever before. The reunion with Noir had made his recovery accelerate rapidly. His eyes were now warm amber brown, no longer dark and unfriendly, and he would occasionally smile for no apparent reason. It was like watching someone come back to life from the dead, and everyone felt it. Noir was reintroduced to the household gradually. At first, Nicolas kept Noir in his cage and Noir did not appear to mind at all. After a while, he began taking Noir to the library or into the kitchen on his shoulder. However, the real breakthrough came one afternoon when Nicolas knocked on Alexandra's door.

"Alexandra, it is Nicolas. May I come in?"

Alexandra was studying on her bed and Taco was napping in his cage.

"Oui, entrez, Nicolas."

Alexandra was trying to speak a little French, in baby steps, as she said. Taco had immediately assumed the job of French tutor (and was very good at it).

Nicolas opened the door. As he did, Taco woke up.

"Actually, I came to speak to Taco. Would that be all right?"

Alexandra nodded. Taco was now fully awake and obviously curious. Nicolas walked over to his cage.

"Taco, I want to ask you something. I will understand if you do not agree. Would it be all right with you if Noir flies freely inside Chadwick and has his own perches in the kitchen and the conservatory? Noir and I will respect whatever you decide."

Alexandra was watching Taco's face the entire time Nicolas was speaking. He had listened calmly, not displaying any alarm or fear. He was studying Nicolas and clearly considering everything.

"Oui," Taco replied softly with a gentle nod of his head.

"Merci, Taco, merci beaucoup. Tu es très gentil."

As Nicolas turned to leave, the gratefulness was transparent in his eyes.

"Merci, Alexandra. Pour votre confiance en Noir."

Alexandra knew he was saying something about confidence or trust and she felt certain it was true. Noir had changed.

❋

Blackie immediately got to work making the new perches.

The perch for the kitchen needed a tray attachment like Taco's, and the one for the conservatory was a simple perch, just for observing or napping. They were both ready in a few days and set up with great fanfare. The first meal was breakfast. Noir had quickly flown from Nicolas's shoulder to his perch, his black eyes gleaming. On his tray sat one corn muffin, compliments of Evelyn. The two perches were on opposite sides of the kitchen table. Both birds settled in easily for their first breakfast together. That afternoon after school, they had all gone to the conservatory and watched as Noir flew to his new perch and Taco to his, one in each corner. They all, including Nicolas, decided to do their homework in the conservatory. Between the books and notes, the birds were being observed. It was peaceful and calm. Noir was looking outside with interest, flying to many different vantage points, landing on small trees and shrubs, eventually returning to his perch.

Taco also enjoyed the view and then fell asleep, snoring. There were smiles all around. Dinner that evening was just like breakfast. Both birds enjoyed their meals, and once or twice Noir was asked something by Jaclyn in French. He responded with just a few words, monotone as always, his French parfait. Alexandra and Jaclyn smiled at each other. This was like a dream come true. It was a happy family, at last.

✦

"I have something to tell you both."

Alexandra was looking at Theo and Jaclyn, who were lying on the rug in her room playing cards.

"There has been so much going on that I decided to wait to tell you this. Taco . . ."

She nodded to Taco and he pushed aside the salt lick. At the same time, both Jaclyn and Theo gasped loudly, their eyes wide with surprise, as they watched the blue macaw fly to the rug and drop the key. They sat in silence just looking at it. Theo whistled softly, then reached for it and held the key in his hand, shaking his head.

"Noir took it with him when Grand Mama banished him. He brought it back. It was in his beak when I found him. He risked his life to bring it back."

Both Jaclyn and Theo were silent. It was a lot to absorb.

"Have you . . . used it? Is it . . . is it too late?" Jaclyn asked, her voice just a whisper.

"No. I have not. I could not. I just know it's too late. I feel it. I will never go back."

They all sat in silence, looking at the key in Theo's hand.

"Blimey, Alexandra, you can't know if it's too late! Time was standing still for weeks—it may still be the same date! *We have to find out!*"

"Theo, that was months ago. I have accepted it. You are not supposed to change history. I know we did with Mercy, but that was because of Aunt Olivia. It would not happen again."

She thought of Noir and could hear his monotone voice speaking the one English word, "nevermore." *Nevermore* would she go through the gate.

Theo reluctantly gave the key back to Taco, who looked like a person whose shoulders had slumped with crushing disappointment. Sad and dejected, he flew back to his cage and tucked it under the salt lick.

✦

It was the next Saturday.

Olivia had invited Jaclyn and Alexandra to come to her apartment for afternoon tea with Silver and Evelyn. It was a "Ladies' Tea," she said, hoping the boys would understand. They did. Tea was definitely not interesting. So on this afternoon Nicolas and Theo were home alone.

Nicolas was in the library reading about the Wangchuk Dynasty, a hereditary monarchy in the country of Bhutan, located in the Himalayas. He was deeply engrossed in reading about the first King of Bhutan, who had adopted, as the unique symbol of his authority, a crown surmounted by a replica of the head of a raven. It became known as the *Raven Crown*. The king's father, who was known as the Black Regent, had worn the raven affixed to the top of his helmet into battle, often winning against formidable opponents. Thereafter, the raven became the guardian deity of Bhutan.

Noir was sitting on his shoulder. Before turning each page, Nicolas would give him a quick look and Noir would nod, his black eyes gleaming with interest.

Theo was reading in his room, but after a while, he went down to the second floor and into Alexandra's room.

"Taco, cheerio, wake up!'

Taco blinked and woke from his nap.

"What do you say? Shall two chaps take a quick trip to the beach?"

Taco sat straight up and his eyes sparked with interest. He quickly pushed the salt lick aside, grabbed the key in his beak, and flew to the keyhole. Theo walked over to the gate and then Taco turned the key. The white gate materialized and swung open into darkness. Taco hopped onto Theo's shoulder as Theo stepped into the blackness.

In what seemed like one second, the gate swung open with Taco riding on it, and then Theo stepped back into the room. Taco flew to his cage as the gate silently swung shut, once again becoming part of the painted mural.

Theo was grinning and tossing the key in the air.

It was July 18th.

ANTICIPATION

After dinner Theo, Jaclyn, and Alexandra were walking down the back hallway. Nicolas and Noir had gone to their room to do more reading about the history of Bhutan. Alexandra wondered how it could possibly be that interesting. Who had ever heard of Bhutan?

Tea with Olivia had been delicious. There were different spiced teas, some with orange and cinnamon, and others that had exotic names like jasmine and chamomile and chai, each in its own pretty china teapot, along with heavy cream and sugar cubes that could be dropped in the teacup with tiny tongs. Jaclyn and Alexandra sampled each one, but noticed their grandmother and Evelyn only drank something called Earl Grey tea, which sounded so bland and boring it reminded Alexandra of The Pine School.

Olivia served all kinds of buttery tea cookies and chocolates with the tea, and the girls had eaten far too much. Evelyn only had two "biscuits," as she called them, and had given them disapproving looks as they piled their small plates high with treats.

"So, ladies, you must have eaten too many crumpets this afternoon. Evelyn was obviously not happy. You did not polish your plates at dinner!"

Theo was grinning and rubbing Taco's ears. The blue and gold macaw was happily perched on Theo's shoulder.

"Everything was so delicious, Theo, sorry you missed it," Jaclyn said, looking at him with pity.

"Well, you both missed something, too. Taco and I had a jolly good time. Didn't we, chap? Taco had some fresh fruit, and I had one of Brownie's delicious strawberry milkshakes. Beach was smashing—

eighty-five degrees and sunny. And, let's see, what was the date, Taco?"

"July 18th! July 18th!"

Taco was bobbing his head up and down with excitement.

Alexandra stopped and stared at Theo and then Taco, back and forth.

"Did you go there *today*?"

Theo nodded and grinned.

"*Are you sure*—July 20th has not come yet?!"

Theo grinned and produced the key from his pocket. "Shall we go now, ladies?"

They had run to her room as fast as they could, but it was a quick trip to Chatham Beach. Theo knew as soon as they got there that it was still July 18th. After returning, they sat on Alexandra's bed talking about what might happen next on Chatham Beach—and what they should do on *the day* to stop Alexandra's parents from sailing out of the harbor. Assuming luck would be with them, and they would get there in time. However, there were so many unknowns, it was hard to make any plans.

For Alexandra, the anticipation that came roaring back when she heard the date was like a huge pit in her stomach. Again, it felt like she was stuck in some other time and space dimension, and life at Chadwick was once again less real, less important—and life through the gate was once again all that mattered. She wondered if it would be weeks or months, she could not let herself think years, before the calendar moved or how fast it would go.

And what if she missed July 20th?

BIRDS FLY OVER THE RAINBOW (OR THROUGH A GATE)

Taco always wanted to be helpful. That was just the kind of bird he was.

On Sunday night when the weekend was over, he told Alexandra he would go through the gate to check the calendar during the day while she was at school. There had been no change in the calendar on Sunday—it was still July 18th at Chatham Beach.

Taco had rifled through his box of Halloween costumes and found his miniature Boston Red Sox baseball cap, sunglasses that wrapped around his face and covered both eyes, and a tiny, striped beach towel. He told her he could go in disguise so no one would notice him—he would fit right in at the beach. With amazing dexterity, using one foot and bending down, he draped the towel around his neck, put on the tiny sunglasses (held in place with a small eyeglass cord pulled snugly at the back of his head), and then with a flourish, put on the baseball cap backwards.

Alexandra had a hard time not laughing and kept having to look away. The memory of the Halloween when they had agreed on the beach costume also made her grin. She looked back at him, smiling. He really thought no one would notice a macaw parrot dressed like a teenager on a Cape Cod beach. However, the more she thought about it, the more it seemed the right thing to do, and she decided he might as well go. He really wanted to help, and as long as he took great care of the key, it should be okay. She could not stay home from school and someone should go during the day. There could be no way to predict when the date would change, and they could not take any chance the 20th would be missed.

BIRDS FLY OVER THE RAINBOW
(OR THROUGH A GATE)

Every day Alexandra raced upstairs after school to hear Taco's report. Time was holding at July 18th. He had explained his routine—each time he went, he would fly around to one side of The Snack Shack and peek through a split in the wood building where he could see the calendar. He had seemed puzzled (and a bit offended) when he told her people pointed and stared at him, some even laughed, but he said he ignored them and flew back to the gate as soon as he checked the calendar. He also told her about the gray and white birds that were very noisy, and with a look of *complete* disdain and disapproval, told her he saw them eating food from people's blankets while they were swimming.

Before school, after school, and before bed, Alexandra went through the gate. On weekends, she and Taco would take turns. The weeks went by, but just like before, the date was not changing. Again, Alexandra felt nervous and panicky. She was completely distracted at school, which was reflected in some low test scores and very disapproving looks from Olivia. Alexandra was concerned about not raising any suspicions. For reasons even she did not understand, she did not want Olivia to know about the gate and the key. It just felt like the plan could be jeopardized or she could be stopped before she could try to save them. Olivia had told her she could no longer time travel, so what would she think about this?

Then one day there was a startling development.

Alexandra ran up to her room after school, but Taco was not there. She quickly went down the pole and checked in the kitchen and then the conservatory. She did not find him anywhere, nor did she see Noir. She ran back up the stairs with an increasing sense of dread and a feeling something was very wrong, and went straight to Taco's cage.

The key was gone.

So Taco was still there and would return any moment. A relief, but at the same time she was worried—he was always waiting for her after school with the report. Today he was not. With fear flooding through her, she realized she could never get there to help him . . . what if it was July 20th and he had tried and failed to save her parents? What if something had happened to him in the storm? Why had he not already returned? Something had to have gone terribly wrong. As she sat down on her bed feeling sick with worry, there was a knock on her door.

"Alexandra, it's Nicolas, may I come in?"

"Yes, come in."

As he came through the door, she knew immediately from his face something was not right. He looked as worried as she felt.

"Noir is missing. I cannot find him anywhere in Chadwick. I walked outside and called him. He did not come as he always does when I call him."

Alexandra had heard the call in the last few months since Noir had returned. Nicolas would go outside with Noir and let him fly free, and then call him. It was a very good mimic of Noir's caw, one long followed by three short.

She stared at her cousin. This was not good at all. Both birds were missing, as was the key. She had not even answered Nicolas when suddenly the gate swung open into the room. Noir and Taco were riding on the top of it. Taco had the key in his beak and was dressed in his beach outfit.

Nicolas was frozen in complete amazement. Taco looked scared to death when he saw Nicolas in the room, and flew to his cage with his back to them. Noir casually flew to Nicolas's shoulder, cool and calm.

"On va à la plage? Il fait beau aujourd'hui. La nourriture a l'air délicieuse."

The tone of voice was monotone and factual, as always.

Alexandra could not speak. There was too much to comprehend. Taco had taken Noir without telling her, and now Nicolas knew about the gate and the key. And why had it taken so long for them to return?

Nicolas turned to Alexandra with the look of utter amazement still on his face. Noir was relaxed, almost bored looking.

"I . . . I don't know what to say. What you have just seen is—or was—a secret. Not even Olivia or Grand Mama knows. The key used to belong to my mother. Taco gave it to me this Christmas . . ." Her voice was hushed and shaky.

Nicolas came over and sat down on the bed next to her.

"Alexandra, I will not tell anyone. You can trust me. You can trust Noir. We will not tell, but you did not mention Theo or Jaclyn? Do they know?"

She looked down, nodded, and then looked up again. Looking into his eyes, she knew it was all right. He would keep this secret. She actually felt relieved. Since he had changed, it had crossed her mind he could be trusted, that he could be told.

But she never thought it would happen like this.

She got up and walked to Taco's cage. He moved to the farthest point from her on his perch. As she moved around the cage, trying to look him in the face, he kept switching himself on the perch so he would not face her. He was still in his beach outfit and she could not help but smile. He was too adorable, and she knew how sorry he was. That was obvious.

"Taco, look at me. It's all right. You heard Nicolas. He will not tell anyone. You trusted Noir enough to take him, so he will keep this secret, too. It's okay, Taco, look at me. Please, Taco."

He slowly turned to face her as she reached in and gently took off his sunglasses. His head was lowered, and his eyes were downcast.

CHAPTER FIFTY-SIX

Then he looked up, straight into her eyes.

"Today July 19th. July 19th."

Nicolas's eyes were wide with astonishment as she told him everything. Taco was sitting on her shoulder and Noir was on Nicolas's. She and Nicolas were sitting with their legs folded, facing each other on her bed. As she spoke, she knew he had not known anything about the key, the gate, or their travels. He had been suspicious of their behavior at meals, but he had not known why they appeared tired or not hungry. And as she told him about her parents and the importance of July 20th, she knew from his expression that he understood the seriousness of what she was trying to do, and she saw him look over to the snow globe more than once.

"Alexandra, it is now one day before July 20th—so you will have to go through the gate constamment! What if the date changes while you are at school? You cannot miss this date!"

"I know—it's all I can think about, Nicolas. I wanted to go and just stay in the cottage, but Taco told me I have to return every day before the clock strikes midnight in Dark Harbor or I can never come back. It's so nerve wracking. I'm so scared I will miss it, or even worse, try to stop them, and fail . . ."

Her voice trailed off as she stared at the painted scene.

Nicolas nodded with grave seriousness.

"Une difficulté sérieuse."

It was the monotone voice, but the tone had changed. The words were spoken softly, thoughtfully.

She looked into the black eyes that were usually expressionless, like a poker face. This time she saw something she had never seen before. It was concern . . . for her.

Theo and Jaclyn were both relieved when Alexandra told them what happened. They felt the same way she had—Nicolas should not be left out. They all felt certain he had changed, and the more who could help, the better.

Everyone knew the stakes could not be higher.

The plan was set, and each person and bird knew what they had to do and when.

Taco and Noir would take the night shifts as well as during the day when they were at school. Because the birds would be going so often, Alexandra told Taco that Noir should fly to The Snack Shack to check the calendar and he should stay near the gate with the key. She knew from his expression he did not like this, but she explained ravens and crows were commonly seen on beaches, not macaw parrots—and they needed to be careful not to draw attention to themselves because it could jeopardize their plan. He had reluctantly agreed.

What also had to be planned was what Noir would say to Taco once the calendar changed to July 20th. Noir immediately said, "Aujourd'hui est le 20 juillet," to which Taco replied, clearly a bit insulted, that he already knew this from his French studies.

But the trickiest part of all was what to do if the date changed while they were at school. It was Noir who suggested the plan (in French, with Nicolas interpreting), and they all agreed it was very good. Noir would fly to The Pine School, making one long caw and three short caws while circling around the school. He would do this twice. That would be the signal they all had to leave school at once.

Nicolas knew Mr. Gingerroot would let him do anything he asked, so he would ask to take the attendance or something else to the Headmaster's Office. Alexandra and Jaclyn would ask to go to the bathroom, and then a few minutes later, Theo would. They knew Olivia might be suspicious, but they figured she would let them. Then they would all meet at the downstairs stairwell, and when the hall-way was clear, slip out through the front doors, run back to Chadwick as fast as possible, and get up to Alexandra's room without being seen. They all knew there were many potential obstacles. Would the hallway at school be clear? Even going into Chadwick without being seen was going to be difficult. They just had to hope that some-how it would all work out.

When they were not in school, Alexandra would take one other person with her, rotating between Theo, Jaclyn, and Nicolas. Every-one agreed it was necessary to go through the gate every hour—*but always skipping midnight*. Even though the calendar had never changed during the middle of the night before, no one wanted to take any chances this time. It was going to be exhausting to keep this up for very long, and they all hoped the 20th would come very soon. Most of all Alexandra.

Thus began the vigil for July 20th.

Day and night, every hour except midnight, two people or two birds were going through the gate.

THE SANDS OF TIME
AND THE SANDMAN

Taco knew there was an hourglass in the library at Chadwick and had managed to get his beak through part of the wooden frame and brought it to Alexandra's room. He told Alexandra it had belonged to Thaddeus Chadwick, and was on his desk in England for years. When the hourglass was tipped over, sand would filter through the tiny center, and once all the sand had fallen to the bottom, an hour had passed.

"Why do you need this, Taco? You always know exactly what time it is," Alexandra asked, her voice reflecting her puzzlement.

"Just in case, just in case. Taco go to beach, come back, turn it over, then go again when empty."

He looked very pleased with himself. He had figured out a backup system to be sure he never missed going on time. So every hour during the birds' watch, the hourglass was turned over, "just in case."

It was Monday afternoon, and a week had already passed. They were all getting more and more tired, especially the birds. When she got home from school, Taco reported it was still July 19th. Soon it would be 5:00 p.m. and Alexandra would be going with Jaclyn, at 6:00 p.m. with Nicolas, at 7:00 p.m. with Theo, and then the same rotation again for 8:00, 9:00, and 10:00 p.m. Then Taco and Noir would take over.

"Taco take nap," he said yawning, and immediately fell sound asleep, snoring loudly.

Taco and Noir had already been up all night and much of the day. During the week, the birds could only sleep from around 4:00 p.m. until 10:00 p.m., and both had to be wakened for dinner. Evelyn had begun to be a little suspicious when both birds did not eat as much as usual and were obviously very sleepy, often falling asleep on their perches during dinner.

Alexandra looked at her beloved Taco. He was so good, so loyal. She knew he would do anything to help her; he had already flipped the hourglass over so she would be reminded of her 5:00 p.m. trip. She watched as the tiny stream of sand slipped through the hourglass and wondered how many grains of sand it would take until the calendar finally said July 20th . . . and how exhausted they would be when the day finally came . . . and whether the past—and the future—could be changed.

That evening was uneventful. Each rotation was done on time and still there was no change. Alexandra was tired and ready for bed. She and Theo had returned at 10:00 p.m. and it was "time for the changing of the guard, just like Buckingham Palace!" Theo said to Taco, who looked quite puzzled. Theo then explained about the men dressed in red jackets wearing very tall black bearskin hats who guarded Buckingham Palace, the "Queen's Guard," who could never even blink an eye while on duty. Taco looked like he did not believe it.

"You are Princess Alexandra's guard, Taco. Now carry on, chap, and don't blink!"

Theo and Alexandra laughed and smiled at each other. Birds, not palace guards, were now in charge. As Theo headed off to his room, Noir swooped in and landed on top of Taco's cage to await their 11:00 p.m. rounds. As she drifted to sleep, Alexandra remembered something from a conversation long ago. Nicolas had told her common ravens guarded the Tower of London, and the birds could never leave the grounds or the monarchy would fall. Alexandra was now certain having Noir with them would bring good luck, not bad, and his strength and intelligence were necessary and important. She even felt that without him they could fail.

Soon she was sound asleep.

She was in a very deep sleep when her room echoed with one long caw, three short, and then a familiar voice.

"Wake up, princess, wake up! Can't be late!"

"Go away, Taco. Go away. It's not time for school. Go away. I'm so tired . . ." Her voice was groggy and thick.

"20 juillet! July 20th!! Wake up, princess!"

Alexandra felt something walking on her through the covers and then it was as if a lightning bolt went through her body. She sat straight up and turned on the light. Taco was on her bed, pacing back and forth on the bedcovers. Noir was sitting on top of Taco's cage, very calm, as always. She reached for her watch—it was 1:05 a.m. Dark Harbor time.

"Noir, va chercher Nicolas et Theo. Dépêche-toi! Taco, get Jaclyn, hurry!"

Alexandra had just learned how to say "go and get" and "hurry up" in French. Both birds flew out of the room. In seconds, they were all standing in her room in their pajamas, rubbing the sleep from their eyes.

"Taco, it's already past midnight, so we have almost twenty-four hours before we have to be back—is that right?"

Alexandra was surprised by the steadiness of her voice and how clear her mind was.

Taco nodded his head "yes" as she strapped on her watch and checked the time again, 1:08 a.m. She reached for her necklace, realizing she felt calmer than she had expected to, and then looked at each person, her gaze serious and determined. Then she looked at the birds, suddenly thinking to ask some other questions.

"Did either of you notice the time at Chatham Beach—and was it raining?" Alexandra asked, looking intently at both birds.

Both Taco and Noir shook their heads "no." They did not know the time of day, but at least the storm had not begun. That was hopeful news. However, Alexandra realized there was no way of knowing whether her parents had already left the marina.

They were all now wide awake, and they were all wondering the same thing. What time of day was it and would they be too late? Jaclyn quickly hugged Alexandra and Theo gave her a wink and a quick smile, then pushed up his glasses while looking at the mural. Nicolas, saying nothing, guided Alexandra to stand next to him, then positioned Jaclyn and Theo to stand behind them. Noir was on his shoulder. Alexandra took a deep breath.

"Let's go." Her voice did not waver.

Taco flew to the keyhole, inserted the key, and turned it. Just as the gate materialized, Alexandra felt Nicolas reach for her hand. His grip was strong and *warm*. She looked at him as the gate opened into blackness. He was looking straight ahead and did not look at her, but he did not have to. Strength and courage seemed to flow from his hand into hers, giving her confidence they would succeed. And there was something else. Looking down at his hand holding hers, Alexandra could feel that he genuinely cared about her.

Then they all stepped into darkness and disappeared. The gate slowly swung back into place, once again a painted image.

The bedroom was quiet.

On a small nightstand next to the bed, a pipe, snow globe, and black and white photo waited in silent vigil.

JULY 20TH ~ A LONG DAY'S JOURNEY

Alexandra felt the steady, humid wind first and then she opened her eyes.

Nicolas and Theo were wearing plaid swim trunks and navy-blue T-shirts that said, "Chatham Beach" in red letters. She and Jaclyn were wearing white shorts and checked gingham cotton blouses tied at the waist. Her blouse was red and white and Jaclyn's was powder blue and white. A canvas tote bag was at their feet, stuffed with beach towels. Alexandra instinctively reached up and held the familiar round disc in her fingers as her gaze swept down to the dock where the moored boats were bobbing up and down in the wind. No sailboats were coming or going and no one was on the dock. The gate opened and they walked through.

"Noir, quelle heure est-il, vite!"

Nicolas's voice was urgent. Noir nodded, flew to The Snack Shack, and returned quickly.

"Il est midi."

"It is noon. When do you think they left, Alexandra?"

Alexandra felt relief flood through her. They were not too late.

"I don't know, except that it was the afternoon. I assume they left early, before there was any sign of a storm, so it could be any time now . . ."

As she answered, her eyes were again searching, scouring, the long dock and the boats tucked in their slips. From this distance and the low profile of the boats, it was difficult to see the color of the boat hulls as her eyes swept the dock looking for any glimpse of the red *Windswept*. However, it was clear the dock was empty and no one was on the deck of any boat. Then she looked over at the cottage. The black cat with yellow eyes was sitting in the left window staring at her, as always. Suddenly she felt overwhelmed by the enormity of it all and the challenges ahead. She was at Chatham Beach on the exact day her parents had sailed. Would they actually be able to stop them? If they did succeed, she would be meeting her own parents for the first time. They would look just like the wedding photo, but they would not know her. And they would not believe what she would tell them.

"Alexandra, let's go to the cottage. Maybe they're inside. Let's have a look."

Theo was staring at the cottage. Alexandra nodded, feeling like she might start crying at any moment, and then looked at Taco. He was still perched on the gate with the key in his beak. She realized in that moment she had to be totally focused and fought back the tears.

"Taco, I'll take the key. It will be in my pocket where it will be safe," she said as she walked toward him.

Taco looked doubtful and cocked his head to one side as if asking her to reconsider, but her expression and extended hand made it clear she would not. Reluctantly, he dropped the key in her hand. She slipped it into her shorts pocket and then put Taco on her shoulder. Theo grabbed the tote and they all began walking toward the cottage.

The sailboat weather vane on the cottage roof was turning in the wind. Looking at it gave Alexandra a chill. The sky had no hint of darkness—yet. The sun was still shining through the wispy clouds, but the wind was picking up. As they got closer to the cottage, the black cat jumped down from the sill and was out of sight. Then someone walked by the same window. They all saw a figure, briefly, in the shadows. It was unmistakable—someone was inside this time, not just the mysterious black cat. Alexandra felt her heart beating faster and her hands became clammy and sweaty.

"Noir, vole à la fenêtre."

Nicolas pointed to the window. Noir flew from his shoulder, landed on the sill and peered in from one corner, then flew back to Nicolas.

"Il est Brownie."

The front door of the cottage opened and down the steps came Brownie, whistling. He saw them right away.

"Well, if it isn't my old friends, finally returning to the best beach on Cape Cod!"

He was smiling as he looked at the boys' T-shirts, and then his eyes settled on Taco.

"Now I understand. The macaw is yours, Alexandra! He's been coming by The Snack Shack without you, lookin' for some grub. Sorry to spill the beans, old chap! Quite the talk of Chatham Beach! No one has ever seen a macaw parrot here before, much less dressed for the beach. You must have dressed him up, Alexandra! Very clever! Gave everyone a good laugh!"

Taco's cheeks turned pink and he put his head under his wing. Alexandra reached up to stroke his feathers.

"And who is this fellow?"

He was looking at Nicolas and Noir. No one knew if he meant the person or the bird, then his eyes settled on Noir. Before anyone could answer, he nodded his head again.

"I recognize this bird. He's been hanging around, too. He's a very big crow, the biggest I've ever seen. Your pet, young man?"

"Actually, he is a raven and he is my pet. I raised him from a baby. He was abandoned."

Brownie nodded, studying the black-eyed bird.

"They are very intelligent, I have heard?"

"Yes, they are."

Nicolas smiled, reached up, and stroked Noir, who was obviously enjoying the attention and the compliment. Taco peeked out from under his wing and glared at Brownie.

"Brownie, did the couple who stay in this cottage arrive on their sailboat from Maine? You told me about them."

Alexandra could not wait any longer to ask and was trying to see if anyone else was inside.

"Yes, missy, they arrived safe and sound late yesterday afternoon. Just fixin' their kitchen faucet, a bit rusty after no use for so long. Nicest young folks. Showed me photos of their baby girl, *Alexandra*, cute as a button," and he winked at Alexandra, who was just staring at him.

"I told Graham this morning the weather looked a bit dicey for sailing today, but they love to sail. Hopefully they'll stay close to shore . . ."

Brownie looked out over the ocean and shook his head. His brow was furrowed.

"Yep, looks to me like a storm is brewin'. Let's see . . . they should be leaving about now," he said as his gaze swept over toward the dock.

"There she is—the *Windswept*'s just pullin' out of the slip."

Then he gave them a small wave good-bye and sauntered off toward The Snack Shack.

It felt like she was flying.

She was sure her feet were not touching the ground. Across the sand, down the long dock, crying, waving, and yelling to *stop! stop! stop!* Her voice was carried away by the wind. When she reached the end of the dock, even though the sailboat was steadily moving out to sea, she could read the familiar gold lettering of *Windswept* on the stern. And she could see them both—*her father* holding the tiller, standing with his back to her, looking ahead, and *her mother* sitting on a bench seat, who waved once, thinking a young girl was waving them off, not close enough to see the tears streaming down her face or to hear the cries to stop. The growing distance between them and the sound of the wind, seagulls cawing, and the small outboard motor drowned out her cries.

As the *Windswept* headed out of the marina to open sea, the lone figure waving frantically at the end of the dock grew smaller and smaller.

The ocean water was shockingly cold.

She swallowed some water when she jumped in and was coughing, trying to catch her breath while swimming in the choppy waves. Alexandra was not a strong swimmer, and it quickly felt like her legs were weighted down. Instead of propelling her forward, it felt like they were dragging her down. She could not see the sailboat anymore but kept trying to move forward, pushing herself through the cold water, her mind spinning with chaotic thoughts—to swim harder, to keep trying no matter what.

Then something changed.

Without any conscious thought, she realized she was no longer swimming. It felt like she was drifting. The currents were gently moving her body and a calmness, almost a serenity, came over her. She would not save her parents. This time history would not be changed. She felt her body weaken and then sink, legs first. In the last moments, she understood she was going to die with them, on the same day they did, and this was meant to be. Deep peacefulness. The coldness fading away. She was entering another realm.

Suddenly the serenity was ripped apart.

A shocking feeling of force, of tremendous strength being exerted on her body, and struggling, pushing, trying to resist. Roughly awakened from a deep, luxurious sleep, not wanting it to end. Yet somehow, she knew any resistance was futile. She was far too weak and whatever was wrapped around her was far too strong, lifting her straight up, pulling her through the water, and then with a sensation of being lifted—pushed from below and pulled from above—she felt her body leave the water and she was lying on a hard surface. Pressure on her chest over and over, and salt water rushing out of her mouth, choking, coughing, gasping for air. Muted voices, her body shivering and shaking. Wrapped in something warm, lifted, and laid down on something soft. The coldness disappearing and warmth slowly spreading through her body. Someone was stroking her head and she heard her own voice saying, "Grand Mama, Grand Mama."

Her eyes opened.

Her vision was cloudy and blurry. She could not see who was sitting right next to her, and she blinked trying to focus. Slowly, the cloudiness lifted and the face came into focus. Green eyes, black hair, tiny freckles across the nose. She reached up to feel if this face she had only dreamed of seeing was real.

Her hand felt warm skin.

"You scared us so much! Your friend jumped in when he saw you were having trouble, and we came back to help him. Here he is. Come, Nicolas, let her see you. She does not know us at all."

The same voice as Olivia. Suddenly Nicolas was sitting next to her, a towel wrapped around him, his hair and clothes soaked. He was smiling. A smile she had never seen before. It was the most brilliant smile she had ever seen in her entire life, on the face of someone who for the longest time never smiled at all. His eyes were sparkling like brown gemstones. She thought of the skeleton he was not long ago, near death. Now he seemed like a beacon of light, of life.

"Alexandra, it's me, Nicolas. You will be fine, thank goodness! These good people helped us, Elisabeth and Graham St. Germaine."

Then he leaned closer to give her a quick hug and whispered, "You saved them, Alexandra, votre mère et père."

She looked up and saw them both looking down at her. *Her mother and father.* Under the blankets, she slowly reached up and found the small round disc. Her necklace had not been seen or was not noticed in the frenzy. She stared at them. Her father had sandy blonde hair, straight like hers, and kind brown eyes. He was tan, young, and handsome, just like the photos she had seen. Her mother looked exactly like Olivia, only younger. They both looked concerned, but very relieved.

Then she heard her father speak for the first time.

"We have a baby daughter named Alexandra! Now that's a coincidence! Someday we'll tell her we rescued a girl with the same name. So, Alexandra, we're tied up in the slip, and we're going to take you and Nicolas back to our cottage. It's right on the beach. We'll get some hot chicken soup into you both and make sure you're all right. Then you can call your parents . . . have to say, I think the rescue happened at the right time. The wind has really picked up, not the best day for a sail. Brownie was right . . ."

Then he headed up the cabin steps, followed by her mother.

Alexandra thought his voice was like melted butterscotch, warm and wonderful. The wind was blowing harder now, and they were being jostled, even in the slip. It felt so good to be under warm blankets in the small cozy cabin that was so amazingly familiar. As she looked around at the red and white curtains and red pillows, she felt a lightness fill her body. It felt like she was floating in a cocoon of happiness.

Nicolas sat on the bunk opposite hers. They did not have to speak; they just looked at each other. There were no words to express what had just happened. After a while, he reached for her hand, gently pulling her up and she made her way up the cabin stairs to the deck. As she stepped onto the deck, Graham reached for her hand to steady her. She looked down at his warm, tan hand wrapped around hers . . . her father's hand. The tiller was straight ahead and she walked a few steps closer to it. There were the initials she had run her fingers over so many times, "G, E & A." As she turned to follow her father off the boat, she let one finger trail lightly over the carved letters. The initials of three people, *alive and together again.*

High above them, sitting on the top of the mast was a raven, the strong wind ruffling his black iridescent feathers. As they made their way slowly down the dock, one long raven caw followed by three short caws was carried by the winds. Then it repeated.

It was July 20th.

And a miracle had happened.

JULY 20TH ~ INTO THE NIGHT

As they walked down the dock toward the cottage, Alexandra could see the beach had emptied out and The Snack Shack was boarded up. The sky was darkening and large raindrops were falling. Both she and Nicolas scanned the beach looking for the others. There was no sign of Theo, Jaclyn, or Taco. They shared a concerned look and kept watching the deserted dunes near the gate.

Noir flew ahead and landed on the back side of the cottage roof, out of sight. With some relief, Alexandra thought that was probably where they were hiding. They made their way across the beach and up the front stairs, and then they were standing inside the cottage she had looked at for so long.

All the walls were pine paneled and there was a large stone fireplace at one end of the room. On the mantel was a model sailboat that looked like the *Windswept*, and on either side of the fireplace were built-in bookshelves crammed with books from ceiling to floor. The room had the distinct smell of a recent fire, and there was another familiar smell—pipe tobacco. There were comfortable-looking chairs and sofas in red, white, and blue fabrics and pillows with nautical designs. On a large blue and white braided rug lay the black cat with yellow eyes, who was clearly studying them. The cat stretched, got up, and slowly walked to them, first rubbing up against Nicolas's leg and then Alexandra's. It felt so strange—the painted cat, now real, rubbing up against her legs.

"My, that's unusual! I've never seen Sam do that before. He is never friendly to people he doesn't know. His full name is actually Samuel Adams, but we call him Sam."

Graham was watching the black cat, clearly surprised and puzzled.

"Well, now, let's get some clothes for you both. They'll be a bit large but at least dry!"

Graham went into a back room and emerged with sweatpants and sweatshirts that he put in the bathroom. Alexandra changed first and then Nicolas. Dry, warm clothes felt wonderful, and they stood for a moment smiling at each other, then looked around the cozy living room.

"Nicolas and Alexandra, come into the kitchen . . . I'm going to heat up some soup, and you can call your parents. I am sure they are worried sick about you both!"

Hearing her own mother's voice calling to them, Alexandra felt like she was dreaming. As they walked toward the kitchen, she wondered if the room would be empty and she would suddenly wake up. They walked into the kitchen. Her mother was real, standing next to the stove, smiling at them. She pointed to the wall phone, reached for a pot, and began opening some cans of soup.

Her father was sitting at a square pine table in the center of the room, smoking his pipe and turning the dial to find a weather report on the small portable radio in his lap. A serious voice was saying something about a severe summer storm with hurricane-force winds. Alexandra sat down at the table, staring first at her father, trying to see every detail of his face, and then at her mother as she stood at the stove. She was identical to Olivia, just younger.

Nicolas immediately went to the back door, looking through the glass panes, saying something about the bad weather. He was searching for any sign of two people and two birds when he saw them. They were huddled in a small woodshed off to the left side of the cottage, which at least offered some protection from the storm until they could be introduced. As he was looking at them, Nicolas wondered how this was all going to be explained—it was stranger than any fiction and beyond comprehension.

Theo had seen him and waved. Nicolas gave him a quick and discreet thumbs-up. Grinning, Theo returned the same signal. Theo and Jaclyn were wrapped in beach towels and Taco and Noir were nestled between logs at the top of a woodpile. Nicolas turned away from the door and gave Alexandra the same thumbs-up when neither Graham nor Elisabeth were looking.

"Alexandra, please call your parents now, before we lose power, which I think could happen if this storm keeps up. I'm sure they are desperately worried," Elisabeth said in an urgent voice, her expression now very serious.

Alexandra looked at Nicolas. It was time.

"I . . . I don't have to call them."

"Of course, you do, dear—they have to know you're all right. They may have already called the Chatham police. Now go ahead and call and then Nicolas."

"I don't have to call them because . . . because . . . they already know I am fine."

Elisabeth stopped stirring the soup and turned to look at her.

Graham stopped smoking his pipe and took it out of his mouth.

"How would they know that?"

Elisabeth's voice was just a whisper and her eyes were guarded, as though she was preparing for something. She looked quickly at Graham. Alexandra stood up, and then reached inside her sweatshirt and pulled out the necklace.

Elisabeth stared at her and then began walking slowly toward her as though she was in a trance, her eyes fixated on the necklace. She stopped, close to Alexandra, and then gently lifted the gold disc.

"Where . . . ? How . . . did you get this?"

Elisabeth's voice was barely audible as she held the small disc in her fingers. She looked into Alexandra's eyes, searching, wanting an answer, but Alexandra knew there was no recognition. Why would there be? She was twelve, not one.

"It was given to me by my grandmother, Silver Chadwick. I . . . I am your daughter."

Elisabeth covered her mouth. A sharp cry escaped as she was shaking her head in disbelief. Graham got up slowly, walked to Elisabeth, and put his arm around her, his eyes never leaving Alexandra. He was in shock and said nothing, staring at her. Alexandra felt the tears well up and spill over. She turned to Nicolas, suddenly so grateful he was with her and she did not have to do this alone.

"Let's go into the living room."

Nicolas's voice was strong and firm. He seemed to know they all needed someone else to take charge and walked to the stove, turned off the burner, and then led them into the living room.

Elisabeth and Graham sat close together on the sofa, his arm wrapped protectively around her. Alexandra and Nicolas sat across from them.

There was silence except for a clock ticking and the sound of the wind rattling the windows. Sam jumped up in Alexandra's lap and curled up. Alexandra began to stroke the cat and wondered how all of it would possibly be explained. There was too much to tell. To hear it all at once might make it impossible to accept. She was feeling overwhelmed and at a loss for words. Tears were running down her face when Nicolas began to speak.

"Maybe it would help if I explained . . ." he said, looking at Alexandra questioningly. She answered with a nod of her head.

"I am not her friend. I am her cousin. You have a stepbrother, Aunt Elisabeth, my father. His name is Philippe. He lives in France. My sister Jaclyn and I came from France to live at Chadwick Manor this year. This was when we found out we had a cousin . . ."

Alexandra stopped hearing his words. It was the tone of his voice. She was brought back to the day in the Chadwick library when he had told her about ravens. It was the same voice, soothing and calm, and somehow wise beyond his years. Nicolas was the only person who could tell this story without being overwhelmed with emotion, and she felt so deeply grateful. He was doing this because she could not. As she looked at him, not hearing what he was saying, she realized she loved Nicolas as much as she loved Jaclyn.

Slowly, like a distant voice coming closer, she began to hear his words again.

"Aunt Elisabeth, you have a twin sister. Your mother was told she died at birth. She did not. She was taken—kidnapped—by your mother's doctor and raised in England. Somehow, she came to Maine, to Dark Harbor, this year. She is Alexandra's and Jaclyn's teacher at The Pine School. Alexandra knew she looked identical to you from photos. And that is when Taco . . ."

"*Taco?!*"

Elisabeth seemed to come out of the trance when she heard his name, her voice reflecting shock and disbelief—-and recognition. It seemed as though she had heard nothing until she heard his name.

"Oui, yes, Taco, your macaw parrot. Taco knew you had a twin sister. Her name is Olivia, Olivia White."

Elisabeth's eyes were swimming in tears. Then she spoke, looking directly at Alexandra.

"I have a baby girl. Her name is Alexandra. She is one year old. She is in Dark Harbor right now where we left her when we sailed here just a few days ago . . . how could you possibly be my daughter?? It is not possible. None of this is possible. *This cannot be real . . .*"

Her voice was like cold steel, but her eyes reflected a wild desperation as she turned to look at Graham, wanting him to tell her, begging him to tell her that none of this was real.

"That is the hardest part of all to explain. We came back to save you. And we did. Or Alexandra did . . ."

There was a long pause before Nicolas spoke again.

"You both died in this storm eleven years ago."

Nicolas was watching them intently, as was Alexandra.

The wind was now whistling and howling. The windows were shuddering. It seemed like the cottage itself was groaning, shocked by the words just spoken inside the walls. Elisabeth and Graham looked like they, too, were in the grips of something as powerful and inescapable as the wind. They sat like two statues, not moving, frozen by words that were so truthfully spoken but impossible to comprehend.

"We traveled, actually we time traveled, through the gate in the bedroom mural—in your room, now Alexandra's—with the key. Do you remember the key, Aunt Elisabeth? The key that would open the gate and you could come here to Chatham Beach? Alexandra, get the key."

Alexandra put Sam down and went to the bathroom.

Then it seemed as if a ferocious screaming wind was ravaging the inside of Chadwick Cottage.

THE MIDNIGHT RIDE OF TACO REVERE

Just as Alexandra screamed, there was a high-pitched and demanding knocking sound coming from the back door, *toc-toc-toc*. Nicolas recognized it immediately, one of Noir's many vocalizations. Then there was a loud tapping on the glass. He did not know whether to go first to Alexandra or to the back door.

Nicolas had known instantly the reason for her scream and his mind was racing with all the implications. He sat frozen in indecision and then decided to go to the back door first. It was somehow easier. Noir was glaring at him through the window. He opened the door and in flew a very disgusted, wet raven.

"Il fait un temps affreux. Vous n'avez pas remarqué?"

Monotone. But his annoyance was unmistakable.

"Ah, Noir, je suis désolé. Entrez!"

Nicolas looked out to the woodshed and beckoned them to come.

Moments later, the kitchen was filled with two wet and disgruntled birds and two wet and bedraggled people. Jaclyn and Theo were soaked through, clutching wet beach towels and shivering. Their glasses were fogged up and specked with rain.

"Stay here. This is not going well. We have told them everything. Not surprisingly, it is too much of a shock to comprehend it all at once. So I think I will wait to introduce you. And there is something else, but I won't get into that right now."

Theo looked like he was about to insist they be told, so Nicolas decided on distraction.

"Make yourselves some tea? Sorry, no scones or crumpets, Theo. You can heat up the soup on the stove. I'll bring you some dry towels.

Wait here for me."

Nicolas went back to the living room. The two statues were still sitting exactly as he had left them.

"I'm going to start a fire, all right with you? We are going to need some warmth. It will be night soon."

Neither Elisabeth nor Graham answered or even seemed to notice as he set to work. Soon there was a nice blaze, which definitely helped. The fire seemed to bring some normalcy into what was a very abnormal situation. They were still staring into space as Nicolas left the room to find Alexandra, who was sitting on the edge of the bathtub gripping her wet shorts, also staring into space. She appeared to be in a trance, almost hypnotized.

"Alexandra, réveille-toi, écoute! I will dive in where you were swimming. I am taking Noir with me. I think that I will find it. Theo, Jaclyn, and Taco are in the kitchen. You need to be with them. Your parents are in shock. They probably have to sit for a while. Come on, let's go."

He took the shorts out of her hand, grabbed some towels, and gently led her to the kitchen. All eyes were on her as she walked in, seemingly still in a trance. Jaclyn ran to her and hugged her, not letting go. Taco flew to her shoulder, nuzzling her neck.

"Noir, vite!" Nicolas said urgently while tapping his shoulder.

Noir flew to his shoulder. In an instant, they were both out the back door.

The wind was now so strong that it was hard to walk and rain was coming in sideways stinging Nicolas's face. Noir's powerful feet were digging into his shoulder, but Nicolas did not notice. He held on to Noir's body with one hand, and slowly made his way toward the dock. Nicolas had to yell to be heard above the wind as he told Noir what had happened. Noir's normally placid expression changed. His black eyes were now intense with comprehension of the seriousness of their situation.

When they reached the end of the dock, Noir flew to a dock post, the wind and rain whipping around him, ruffling his feathers. He watched as Nicolas ripped off his sweatshirt and then dove into the thrashing waves. The water was cold, and it was black as pitch. Nicolas could not see anything, so he felt his way along the rocky bottom in the direction she had been swimming. He felt like a blind person desperately searching with his hands, his eyes unseeing, feeling only rocks and shells scattered across the sandy bottom. After many dives, he realized what he had known but could not admit. The key would never be found. In the last few hours, it was either buried by the currents or swept out to sea. He slowly climbed back on the dock and pulled his sweatshirt over his head, shivering and defeated. Noir was watching him intently.

Nicolas looked at his raven and knew the desperation he felt was reflected on his face.

Suddenly, Noir spread his powerful wings and he lifted off the post. He flew with apparent ease into the strong wind. As Nicolas watched in disbelief, Noir flew nearly straight up in the air, then turned and with great speed dove straight down into the ocean, his wings collapsing tight to the sides of his body seconds before he hit the water. Before Nicolas could even react, Noir surfaced and then lifted off and repeated the same dive. Again and again, the raven dove and surfaced. How could he dive into water and hold his breath? Nicolas had never read that any raven could do this. And how could he see anything in the black depths?

Nicolas sat on the dock, oblivious to the storm around him, mesmerized by Noir's power and determination, the saltwater sprays lashing his face now mixing with his own tears. The effort was beyond the realm of the possible, beyond the capability of any bird. But it would only end in defeat. Nicolas stood up and commanded him to stop, yelling his name.

He knew Noir had to be exhausted and the water was too cold for his small body. Noir ignored him and continued to climb and dive. Then, just as Nicolas was going to try to stop him, the raven surfaced from his last dive. This time there was a glint of gold hanging from his beak as he bobbed up and down on the white-capped waves, looking more seagull than raven.

Noir lifted off from the water and flew back to the dock post, his black opalescent feathers wet and glistening, the magical key snug in his powerful black beak. Nicolas walked to him and looked into the dark eyes he loved so much. Noir slowly nodded and then dropped the key into Nicolas's hand. Nicolas stared at what he was now holding, just moments before lost in the grips of the sea, never to be found. He tenderly reached up for his raven, held him close to his chest, and kissed his head, his tears falling on the black feathers like raindrops. Slowly, they made their way back to the cottage in the pelting rain, unaware of the weather.

All that mattered was they were going home.

Together.

When Nicolas climbed the stairs to the back door, he hung back for a moment, unseen by those inside. Graham and Elisabeth were in the kitchen. They looked human again, as though they had awakened from a deep sleep. They had their arms around Alexandra, who was standing between them, and Taco was perched on Elisabeth's shoulder. They were all in animated conversation, but as Nicolas opened the door, the room fell silent and the smiles vanished, replaced instantly by expectation and fear.

Nicolas walked in with Noir on his shoulder and stood by the door. He looked only at Alexandra as he gave the key to Noir. With the key now in the grip of the raven's formidable beak, Noir's black eyes locked onto Alexandra's, and he flew the short distance to her shoulder. The flight took seconds, but the actual distance represented was almost incomprehensible. It was a flight traversing space and time, free of all known earthly boundaries or limits.

Noir had delivered the key twice, both from places of no return.

Alexandra reached up and then held in her hand what was the key to life, to their future together. What had seemed impossible was no longer.

As they all gathered around to look at the key, Alexandra suddenly thought of something she had completely forgotten about. All that had mattered was recovering the key, but there was something else equally important. *Time. The time in Dark Harbor.* She immediately looked at her wrist. The watch was twisted so she could not see the face. As she turned it around, she knew what she would find.

The watch was filled with water, the hands frozen at the moment she jumped into the ocean. Theo was standing near her and moved closer to look at it. He whispered that he was certain twenty-four hours had not passed—they had not been gone that long. However, as their eyes met, the frightening truth was now understood. They did not know with absolute certainty what the time was in Dark Harbor. Or if the grandfather clock had already tolled twelve bells at midnight.

Theo suggested they all go to the living room. Even though there was a storm outside, the room felt safe and snug with the fire now blazing. Sam curled up on Jaclyn's lap, and as strange as it was, the birds and Sam Adams paid no attention to one another. Alexandra sat between her parents, who could not stop looking at her and hugging her. Taco was tucked between them, sitting on Alexandra's shoulder, with Elisabeth right next to him. He looked blissfully happy, gazing at Alexandra and then Elisabeth, back and forth.

Pushing up his glasses, Theo seemed to know it was now his time to take the lead. He was sitting near the fire, on the raised hearth, facing everyone.

"The space-time continuum is very complex . . . and not based on proven scientific fact. It is theory . . . and there are a lot of theories . . ."

He paused and looked around the room. Everyone, including two birds, was listening intently.

"I read about it when we were trying to learn about time travel. There may be phenomena called wormholes that link two separate places on the space-time continuum, something Einstein contemplated in his theory of relativity. Theoretically, wormholes allow space to be traversable, to travel great distances in space very quickly, and they permit time travel as well. There are three provable spatial dimensions—width, height, and length—also referred to as altitude, longitude, and latitude. The fourth dimension in Einstein's theory relies on the dimension of time, which is complicated and not well understood. We found out that time in Dark Harbor and time in Chatham were very different, not only in years, but in the passage of time, from hour to hour and day to day. Time here was often standing still. In other words, it was the same calendar date here even though days and even weeks had passed in Dark Harbor. Then time in Chatham would suddenly jump ahead, not just by hours but by days . . ."

Theo paused, looking at Alexandra, then continued.

"We knew we had to be here on July 20th—and *before* you sailed. So when Taco and Noir found out it was July 19th, we had rotations every hour, like the Queen's Guard at Buckingham Palace, right, Taco?" he asked, winking at Taco.

"And, well, the rest as they say . . . is history . . . or more correctly, altered history."

Theo smiled quickly at everyone, but then his expression became serious again. Once more, Alexandra was reminded of how smart Theo was, of how easily he could explain complicated things.

The lights in the cottage suddenly flickered on and off a couple of times and then went out. Graham jumped up, grabbed some matches, and began to light lamps with glass chimneys on the fireplace mantel and around the room. The room was now quite dark, cast in soft candlelight and the light of the fire. For a moment, Alexandra was reminded of Halloween. However, this time the darkness held a sense of foreboding, not excitement, and she wondered if it was a foretelling of what lay ahead.

"Not to worry. We have the trusty oil lamps sea captains used for hundreds of years. Power goes out all the time here. Go ahead, Theo."

Graham was obviously paying very close attention to what Theo was saying.

"From what I read, the most widely held theory is that you cannot stay in a different time and space dimension for very long before the physical body starts to deteriorate. But there is a growing consensus among astrophysicists this only happens if you travel back in time."

Theo paused and again looked directly at Alexandra.

"If you go forward in time, into the future, *theoretically* there is no impact—you should be able to stay indefinitely with no adverse effects. However, it's unknown how, or if, this would affect the aging process of anyone who time travels into the future . . ."

Everyone was trying to absorb what Theo was saying. Alexandra could not believe what she had just heard. It had not even occurred to her that her parents might not be able to live in a new dimension, going into the future, and all of this effort to save them might not actually save them . . . but Theo said it was only theory, and nothing was known with any certainty. Her stomach twisted.

"So Theo, if Elisabeth and I go through the gate and return to Dark Harbor, some eleven years into the future, we should be all right, but we cannot know for certain how it might affect our aging?

However, if you stayed here, back in time, that would not be the same?"

Graham's voice was now very serious and he was studying Theo intently.

"That's right. At least that is the current theory. After some unknown period of time, the human body would begin to die if the direction of time travel is to the past, back in time. It's all theory, but actually quite logical. And there's something else that is critically important. Taco told us we had to return from Chatham before the next midnight strikes in Dark Harbor . . . or we could never get back."

All eyes were now on Taco, who nodded with great seriousness.

"Alexandra's watch was set for Dark Harbor time, but it stopped working when she jumped off the dock. So the question now is, *has midnight struck in Dark Harbor?* My guess is no, but we won't know until we try to go through the gate. If midnight has passed, I assume the gate will not open and we . . . we will never get back."

He paused and looked solemnly around the room.

No one spoke. The clock was ticking and then struck seven bells. It was seven o'clock at night in Chatham. Alexandra wondered how many bells had chimed in Chadwick Manor. Closing her eyes, she could see the antique grandfather clock standing sentry in the living room. It had always been there, tolling the hours, day in and day out. The deep chimes had been a constant presence in her life and the sound had always been comforting. She desperately wanted to know the time, wishing that somehow she could see the face of the grandfather clock at this exact moment.

Then suddenly and instantaneously, it felt like she was transported back to Chadwick Manor.

She was in the living room, standing in front of the clock, looking up. The grandfather clock had grown much, much taller, and she was very, very small. The clock face was dark and menacing, the hands were spinning backward, then forward, then backward . . . faster and faster. Then the spinning stopped. Both hands were now straight up. The large brass pendulum was swinging back and forth, looking like the sharp, curved blade of a guillotine as the booming toll of twelve bells began. Each deafening gong was measured and unstoppable, and she knew it was a processional march to . . . death. Alexandra covered her ears, screaming.

Then as suddenly as it began, the nightmarish mirage ended. She was back in the cottage, shaken and very scared, wondering if this was a terrible omen, a forewarning of an unspeakable truth.

It could not have passed midnight in Dark Harbor. It could not. Then the memory of midnight on Nicolas's fifteenth birthday flashed through her mind. She had not wanted those bells to chime either, for fear of what would happen. As she looked over at Nicolas it seemed like another lifetime, so much had happened. So much had changed since that December night.

In a whispered voice, Theo said what they all now understood.

"If midnight has passed, it is very probable none of us who time traveled here, back in time, will live. I don't know how long we would have."

Elisabeth cried out and then covered her mouth. As tears came down her cheeks, she held Alexandra tightly. This possibility was so cruel and so impossible to comprehend, that she had been saved and reunited with her daughter only to watch her die.

Taco stepped onto Elisabeth's shoulder and nuzzled her neck, trying to comfort her, and then flew to the mantel, opening his wings to their full expanse. In the light of the oil lamps, he looked strong and commanding and reminded Alexandra of the night he met Noir, when he had flown to the upper banister.

"Taco, go. If gate opens, check time, come back . . ."

He did not finish.

Taco flew to Alexandra's lap and gently took the key out of her hand, looked deeply and lovingly into her eyes, then flew to the front door. In the light of the oil lamps, his blue feathers shimmered, both wings were spread wide, and the key was clasped tightly in his large hooked beak. He looked like an aircraft waiting for the signal to take off, staring at the front door that, once opened, would be his flight path to the gate.

Theo got up and opened the door into the wild night.

Taco lifted off and was gone.

Everyone was perfectly still. No one moved or spoke. The tension was nearly unbearable. They all knew Taco would be back very quickly, and the future and the lives of many hung in the balance.

Alexandra's eyes fell to the small table in front of the couch. There was the book. She reached for it. *Moby-Dick*. It was a very thick book. She saw the author's name, Herman Melville, and opened to the first chapter. "*Call me Ishmael.*" The very first sentence . . . what her father had written in the large book on the desk in the school library. She realized he was watching her.

"I saw what you wrote in the library book at school. You don't know this, but they closed the library when you did not come back. You took out the last book. I read what you wrote . . . that you would return it upon safe passage home," she whispered, looking into his warm brown eyes. He hugged her and kissed her head.

"Well, my darling daughter, I expect to have safe passage back to Dark Harbor because of you. Let me have it. I want to be sure it is returned to The Pine School library, which will once again be a library. I can promise you that," he said with a smile.

She smiled back weakly and handed him the book. He had not lost hope.

Suddenly there was a loud knocking at the front door. Nicolas sprang up, opened the door, and in flew a wet and wild-looking macaw. He dropped the key on the floor to make his report, picking it up again when he finished.

"Four minutes left, four minutes to midnight, Dark Harbor time!! *Hurry, hurry, follow Taco!*"

The next few minutes were a blur. Everyone running in the rain and wind following Taco to the gate. The sand was wet, which made it easier to run, but the strong wind and pelting rain made it impossible to see very well, and it was nighttime. They had to climb up a sand dune to get to the gate, but it really felt to Alexandra like she flew to the top. Taco landed on the gate, the key in his beak. Nicolas again took charge, yelling above the wind, his voice filled with urgency.

"Two by two! First Alexandra and Jaclyn, then Graham and Elisabeth, then Theo and me! Vite! Hurry!"

Everyone lined up in a second.

"Taco, ouvre la barrière! Everyone move forward quickly as soon as the gate opens! Do not wait! We must all get through before it closes!" Nicolas was shouting from his place behind them.

Alexandra looked back quickly and could see Nicolas holding Noir close to his chest and Theo standing next to them. Nicolas and Theo both looked so much older at that moment, like adults, Alexandra thought.

Her mother was holding Sam. Alexandra had not even seen her scoop him up and her father was standing right behind her, holding the book to his chest. Then he leaned forward quickly and whispered in her ear.

"No matter what happens, we love you, Alexandra. More than the moon and the stars."

She swallowed hard and felt tears flood her eyes as she watched

Taco put the key in the keyhole and turn it. The gate opened and she quickly stepped through. Instantly it was quiet and dark. Then she was standing in her bedroom and she swiveled, scanning the room.

In a split second, she had the same panic-filled, desperate feeling as when they were spinning and lifting from Salem. Only this time more than one person was missing.

Jaclyn, Taco, and her parents were in her room, all dripping wet. Sam looked wild-eyed. Taco's feathers were ruffled and wet, and he was sitting on top of his cage with the key in his beak. The gate had closed, again just a painting. She heard two bells chime from the grandfather clock and then the chimes stopped.

Midnight had just passed.

Alexandra ran to Taco, grabbed the key, and just as she was about to shove it in the keyhole, she felt a strong hand on her shoulder.

"No, Alexandra. You cannot go. They would not want you to. You cannot save them now, my darling . . ."

Her father gently took the key out of her hand, giving it back to Taco as she collapsed on the floor, sobbing.

Alexandra did not hear the door open, but she was overcome with the sensation something had changed and looked up through her tears. Her grandmother was standing in the doorway. She was wearing her cape and holding her broom. The colors of the bristles were lustrous and gleaming and the diamond crystals radiated light.

"My dearest, my dearest Elisabeth and Graham, welcome home. Welcome back, my darlings, back to Chadwick and to your family."

Silver floated to them and hugged each of them for what seemed like a long time. Then she turned to the crumpled figure on the floor.

"Come, my dearest Alexandra, come with me. Taco, come too."

She reached down and pulled her granddaughter up with ease, and Taco rode on Silver's shoulder. Alexandra felt a calmness and serenity envelop her and wondered if she was under a spell. They seemed to float down the stairs and then down the long hallway, through her grandmother's rooms and into the conservatory. She never felt her feet touch the ground. It felt like she was gliding.

They were in the conservatory.

Alexandra looked up and saw the moon and stars. It was a beautiful, calm night in Dark Harbor, so different from where she had just been. She was led to a chair and sat down. Her grandmother sat next to her. Taco was on her grandmother's shoulder, the magical key still in his beak. Bright moonlight was streaming into the conservatory and she could see her grandmother's brilliant blue eyes looking deeply into her own. The moonlight made the gold key shimmer with light refracting off the embossed scrollwork, and Taco's feathers appeared dusted with opalescence over luminous turquoise blue, his chest plumage a waterfall of golden feathers. It was so beautiful. She was looking at a mirage of blue and gold . . . and two faces she loved so much. Tears filled her eyes as her grandmother began to speak.

"My dearest child, you have been on a quest that required all you could give, all that you are, to save your parents. And you succeeded. You must understand it was equal parts magic and love that saved them. Tremendous courage and fortitude were required. These strengths come from love, my darling. They do not come from special powers or magic. If you did not have love in your heart, no amount of magic would have saved them . . . and no one, my dear Alexandra, other than you, could save them. Not Olivia, not me, no one but their own daughter."

She paused for a moment and then continued.

"I left the key for Taco to find many years ago. He figured it out from the inscription, as I knew he would, and he gave the key to Elisabeth when she was about your age. It was something I thought she would enjoy as an only child, in the cold Maine winters. She never told me about going, but of course, I knew she was. It was a sliver of magic I could give her, which I hoped she would like . . . and I am certain she did . . ."

Her voice trailed off for a moment.

"My dear, your mother does not have any powers. No letter arrived for her on her fifteenth birthday. So she experienced something quite magical going through the gate, but unlike her sister, she was not chosen."

Alexandra felt as though she was hearing what she already knew in her heart.

Most of all, that it was her destiny from the moment Taco had given her the key to save her parents and bring them back. However, she also knew that alone she would not have succeeded. Those who helped her, who she loved so much, were now gone. Tears ran down her face, and as if reading her mind, her grandmother continued.

"To save Nicolas, Noir, and Theo, you will now need magic more than love. I can help with this, Alexandra. Nevertheless, my dear, there is something you must understand—you must also know the risks. What will be required involves Taco. He will be put under extreme physical conditions that could prove fatal. You must both understand and accept this risk. This will be no different from Noir being sent to the *back of beyond* and daring to return. He could have died, which he knew . . ." She paused, and then turned to look at Taco, her eyes gravely serious.

"The key no longer works. The magic it held is spent."

She reached up and gently took the key from Taco's beak.

"There is only one way to time travel back to Chatham. Taco can fly there once and return. To do this, he will have to take a special potion that will make him grow very, very large. He will be large enough to carry you and then return with the others . . . however, this will tax his body to its limit."

Alexandra felt an exhaustion come over her, as though she had walked a hundred miles and was about to collapse. At the same time, it felt like she was suddenly in some strange, scary world where she did not belong. She felt like Alice or Dorothy and all that mattered was to find her way *home*. She closed her eyes. She wanted to go to sleep and wake up with Nicolas, Noir, and Theo back at Chadwick, *safe and sound*. No potions, no giant prehistoric bird who would live and then die . . . her beloved Taco.

She felt herself falling into a deep sleep.

"Alexandra, my dear, open your eyes."

She slowly opened her eyes. She was looking out of the conservatory to the backyard brightly illuminated by moonlight. Taco was growing larger and larger.

"*No, no*, stop this, Grand Mama, *stop this now*!!!"

Alexandra was screaming as she ran out the door toward Taco, who was growing huge before her eyes.

He kept growing and was soon enormous. Her grandmother was now standing beside her, holding her tightly.

"When you fell asleep, my dear, Taco flew to the cabinet, found the potion and drank it. I could not stop him. He is as determined to save them as you are, my dear. Now, go, climb on his wing, up close to his body, and hold on tightly. Nestle into his feathers . . . they are as warm as down feathers and will protect you from the cold. It will not take long and you will be there. I will be waiting for your return with Nicolas, Theo, and Noir. I have antidotes, which should help Taco survive. He survived Noir's attack and was very near death, as you know. Now go, my dear, quickly, there is not much time left to save them . . ."

"I want to go, too."

It was just a whisper in the stillness of the night.

Jaclyn was standing on the steps of the conservatory. Silver studied her with great seriousness and then nodded.

"You may, Jaclyn. Go around to Taco's other wing and do just as I told Alexandra. Vite, hurry."

Taco's eyes were now huge and still so expressive. They were soft, filled with love, and showed no sign of fear or stress. He blinked softly.

"Taco, time traveler, fly through time! Special air delivery!"

His voice echoed in the night air.

Alexandra could not believe his courage or his humor. This was nothing even close to delivering notes. This was his life or . . . his death.

Taco knelt down and spread his wings on the ground. Jaclyn and Alexandra each began to gingerly walk up the massive blue wings on either side, until the wing joined the body, and then lay down, holding the edge of the wing. Downy, soft feathers quickly enveloped them, and only their heads were visible. Alexandra could not believe the warmth of his feathers or that she was actually lying on one of his wings. Then Taco stood up and they were now a great distance from the ground.

Alexandra was high above her grandmother, looking down at the petite figure draped in her velvet cape. The ice-blue crystals around the hood of her cape were now shimmering and sparkling, just as they had when she banished the crows, and her voice drifted up to them.

"The hardest part for Taco will be as he takes off. It will require tremendous strength. His wings will be moving with great force, but by staying close to his body, the movement will be less noticeable as he lifts off and during the flight. Nicolas and Theo must also stay close to his body for the return trip. Taco will fly as level as possible and will glide more than fly on the wind currents. He knows he is carrying precious cargo and he will take very good care of you."

Silver Chadwick was standing under Taco's huge head and then began to slowly float up, holding the glistening broom in one hand, and was soon even with Taco's face and kissed his cheek.

Alexandra could see the pink blush come into his white cheeks in the moonlight. Silver reached out and stroked his cheek, looking intently into his face.

"Taco, you are the bravest of all macaws. Head out directly over the ocean for the best lift and then due south. Follow the brightest stars to the blackest part of the night sky, where there are no stars. It is a time tunnel. Fly into it, and when you emerge you will be at Chatham Beach eleven years ago on the night of July 20th . . . Alexandra and Jaclyn, if you have the courage, keep your eyes open as Taco lifts off over the cliff. It will be something you will never forget or experience again. Do not be afraid. It is just like the swing, Alexandra, only this time you will really be flying. Now up, up, and away, Taco!"

With that, she raised the broom and gently floated back down to the ground.

Taco slowly turned to face the dark Atlantic Ocean.

Alexandra did not feel afraid. She felt a calmness come over her and her eyes were wide open.

With a force that seemed to shake the earth, they moved forward, Taco's massive wings pumping with tremendous strength. In seconds, they had left the ground behind and were out beyond the cliffs and over the black Atlantic Ocean, banking gradually to the right. Looking back over her shoulder, Alexandra could still see the changing colors of her grandmother's broom. Then in a blink, Chadwick Manor faded from sight and they were flying past The Pine School and then Dark Harbor. She could feel the increasing power in his wings as they flew higher and higher, toward the brightest stars.

She felt warm and safe, closed her eyes, and laid her head against his body. The deep and powerful heartbeat echoed in her ear. It was the bravest heart of all.

The trip to Chatham seemed to take only minutes, but it was impossible to tell because there was no sense of time or space. Alexandra could feel Taco's tremendous strength as they climbed higher and higher and then his controlled restraint as they made a slow descent in a large and gradual spiral. It felt like they were floating and she had quickly opened her eyes but saw only blackness—there was not a single star. She realized they were descending through the time tunnel where there were no stars, as her grandmother had said. The entire trip had been silent except for the motion of Taco's wings and the sound of his heartbeat. Then, abruptly, there was noise as they were buffeted by turbulence and rain, but his feathers provided protection and she buried her head beneath them.

She could feel they were dropping in altitude, lower and lower, and she could feel Taco straining to keep as steady as possible. Suddenly, gently, they landed and came to a stop. Alexandra opened her eyes. She could see Chadwick Cottage straight ahead. There was a faint light from the oil lamps in the windows. The rain and wind were still strong.

Alexandra winced as she climbed out of her warm nest and was immediately pummeled by the storm. She scurried down the long wing to the sand, and as she ran around, Jaclyn hopped off the other wing. Together they ran toward the cottage.

"Taco, we'll be right back!!" Alexandra shouted as they were running.

His large head nodded as he tucked it under one massive wing.

"Jaclyn, whatever happens, we have to be strong!"

They were running as fast as they could and Alexandra looked over at her cousin, who looked back at her, nodding. Her little freckled face was strained and pale and her green eyes behind the thick glasses were full of fear. Alexandra felt her heart pounding. She was suddenly horribly afraid. What if they were too late? She got to the front steps first, ran up and tried to open the door, but it was locked. She pounded on the door, yelling their names and then peered through a window next to the door. There was a gauzy curtain over the window. As she looked carefully in the dim light, she saw them.

They were lying on the braided rug, not moving. It looked like they were sleeping, but with terrible fear in her heart, Alexandra knew it might not be sleep. She grabbed Jaclyn's hand and pulled her away from the door. Jaclyn had not seen them, and Alexandra knew she would go in first to find out whether they were alive.

"The back door, we can get in that way!"

They ran around to the back of the cottage. That door was open.

"Stay in the kitchen. I need to go in first. I will call you. Don't move, Jaclyn. Promise me."

"I promise," she whispered.

Jaclyn stood frozen in the kitchen as Alexandra ran into the living room.

Dropping to her knees next to them, she could see Nicolas and Theo were both breathing. Relief flooded through her. They were still alive. Noir was lying between them, and the image of his emaciated body lying in the snow flashed through her mind. Noir was also breathing, but with very shallow breaths, just as they were when he returned the key.

"Nicolas, Theo, Noir, wake up, wake up!! It's me, Alexandra! I came back for you with Jaclyn! *Wake up!*"

She gently shook Nicolas's arm and he began to stir. He weakly opened one eye.

"Je suis mort?"

His voice was so weak it could barely be heard.

"If you are asking if you're dead, no, you are not, at least not yet! Nicolas, we have to get out of here *right now*! You must get up!"

Then she tugged on Theo's arms as she watched Nicolas struggle to open both eyes and very weakly prop himself up on one arm.

"Jaclyn, come here! They're okay!" she yelled to her cousin.

"I . . . I don't think I can stand up . . ."

Nicolas had tried to get himself to a sitting position when he had to lie back down. It was obvious he had no strength. Then he saw Noir and gently stroked him. Noir opened his eyes, but they were just slits.

"Nicolas! Noir! Theo! It's Jaclyn. Wake up! Get up! Why are they so weak, Alexandra?!"

Jaclyn's face was filled with fear as she looked at them. Theo's eyes had blinked open and then shut again. He had not moved.

"It's the time . . . what Theo said . . . they have been in the past too long. This is not their normal dimension. Jaclyn, we have to get them out of here and back to Dark Harbor—this instant—they are dying!"

But saying the words—what they had to do—made Alexandra feel sick with panic. They could not get them outside and onto Taco's wings by themselves. Even working together it would be impossible to lift them. At that moment there was a pounding on the front door. Alexandra and Jaclyn looked at each other in shock. Who could this be? Then it was answered.

"Who's there? Elisabeth? Graham? It's Brownie!"

Alexandra and Jaclyn stared at each other in disbelief. This was their answer, their only hope. Alexandra flung open the door.

"Well, goodness gracious, why are you here, Alexandra? Where are

Graham and Elisabeth? I've been so worried about them . . . I hope they returned before the storm got bad . . ."

He was now looking rather quizzically at the two boys lying on the rug.

"Brownie, you have to help me—there's no time! Please trust me . . . we have to get Nicolas and Theo out of here *right now*—they're too weak to stand. Can you carry one and then the other outside? Graham and Elisabeth returned and they're safe, but they're not here. Please don't ask about what you will see—it's all too complicated to explain. Please, please help me, Brownie! *They will die if we don't move them quickly!*" Alexandra felt the words rushing out of her mouth, and her entire body felt coiled and wound tight, wanting to spring into action.

She looked desperately into the eyes that looked so much like Blackie's and without saying one word he quickly lifted Theo up over one shoulder. Alexandra could see Theo's eyes had opened and he seemed aware of what was happening. She led Brownie out the front door, down the steps, and looked into the dark where Taco had been, but he was not there. Her heart was racing and then she heard him call her.

"Over here, princess."

Taco was now on the other side of the cottage, hidden from view. Alexandra ran toward him, with Brownie following, the rain and wind still strong.

"Try not to be too shocked, Brownie! Taco, my parrot, is now much, much bigger. He will take us—fly us—home. Please just accept this. I can't explain—there's no time—please carry Theo up one wing until he is close to Taco's body and lay him down. *Hurry, please, and then get Nicolas!!*"

Brownie did exactly what Alexandra asked as though she asked him to put Theo to bed, as though it was entirely normal to be placing someone on the wing of a massive macaw parrot. Then he ran back for Nicolas, and was quickly outside and down the cottage steps with Nicolas over one shoulder. Jaclyn followed behind, holding Noir.

Brownie gently placed Nicolas on the other wing and hopped off. He never looked shocked or afraid. He just did what she asked, and then gave her a quick hug.

"Hope to see you all another time, lassie. Don't forget Chatham Beach! And good luck!"

He smiled at her as the rain whipped around them, and in that moment he looked so much like Blackie she could not believe it, and he had called her *lassie*. Then he disappeared around the corner of the cottage.

Nestled close together on one wing, Jaclyn had Noir under her chest and one arm wrapped tightly around her brother. Alexandra had one arm wrapped around Theo, on the other wing. They were all buried in the downy warmth of Taco's feathers. The boys were lying next to Taco's body and the girls were holding tightly to the edges of his wings with their other hands. Once again, Jaclyn and Alexandra felt the tremendous power required to lift off. This time the runway was Chatham Beach and the storm was still buffeting them, yet they rose in a gradual and controlled ascent.

In seconds they were airborne.

Alexandra could feel Taco straining to hold his body as level as possible during the climb and the gradual upward spiral through the black time tunnel, and her heart ached knowing how hard this was on his body. At the same time, she was filled with fear, terribly afraid of what would happen when they returned to Chadwick.

It was not long before they emerged from total darkness and were gliding on high wind currents under a full moon and a canopy of stars.

"Heading true north! To the future! Destination Dark Harbor!" Taco's voice was strong and confident, and filled with happiness.

RETURN TO CHADWICK

As they approached Chadwick Manor, Alexandra whispered to Theo to open his eyes.

Theo's eyes blinked open. Then he lifted his head weakly and slowly reached up to adjust his glasses. As she watched, the edges of his mouth became a broad grin. They were descending straight toward Chadwick over the black Atlantic Ocean. There were lights blazing throughout Chadwick, and the cliffs were straight ahead. The coastline was dark north of Chadwick, but as they were descending, Alexandra suddenly saw a very bright white light flash twice along the inky black coast—it appeared to be rotating. She wondered what it was and where it had come from, but her focus quickly returned to the landing. In the bright moonlight she could see the gazebo, the boxwood maze, and the large maple tree with the swing, coming closer and closer. In seconds, they were landing on the expansive backyard.

It was the softest, smoothest landing imaginable, and they had come to a full stop. Alexandra could see everyone gathered outside near the conservatory. Her grandmother, *her parents*, Blackie, Evelyn, and then Olivia stepped out from a shadow and put her arm around Elisabeth. It was the most unbelievably wonderful sight. Then her thoughts quickly returned to Theo, Nicolas, Noir—and Taco.

"Theo, how do you feel? Can you talk?"

Alexandra was looking at his profile; he was still staring straight ahead, grinning. They were both buried in downy soft blue macaw feathers up to their necks.

"That was bloody amazing. Absolutely bloody amazing."

His voice was very weak, but she knew he would live, as would

Nicolas. They had gotten there just in time. Even minutes later would have been too late.

"How are all my time travelers and Taco, my dearest?"

Silver Chadwick was standing where she had sent them off as Taco slowly crouched down, spreading his massive wings, making a gentle path to the ground.

"Nicolas and Theo, my dears. I know you feel terribly weak, but in a few minutes, you will be much stronger. Just rest where you are. You will both be fine in a short time. And Noir, who has Noir?"

"I do, Grand Mama. He is right here with me. I think he's feeling better already." Jaclyn's voice came from Taco's left wing.

A moment later Alexandra saw Noir fly to Silver and land on her shoulder. Silver looked at him tenderly.

"Noir, je suis fière de toi," she said as she stroked his feathers.

Noir already looked completely recovered, but it was obvious his eyes were glued to the far wing where Nicolas was. Everyone walked from the conservatory and gathered around Silver and Noir. Alexandra looked at each person's face, lingering over each one. Her family.

"Young lads, I'll give you a hand! Alexandra, come down and then I'll help Theo—give it some welly!"

Blackie was grinning at her as she carefully stood up.

Alexandra leaned over Theo and kissed Taco. Then she whispered, "*I love you, Taco.*" Her father's words came back to her and she added, "*More than the moon and the stars,*" as tears filled her eyes. Looking up to his face, she could vividly see the fine black feathers which made the beautiful design around his eyes. It was like looking through a magnifying glass at perfect pen strokes, and she thought only a master artist could have drawn such a magnificent face. He blinked softly, and then she heard his whispered voice, "*Safe and sound.*" Her heart was overwhelmed with love, and at the same time, with the deepest fear. He had risked his life for them, willingly, happily. Had saving them cost him his life? She could not bear the thought.

As tears slipped down her face, Alexandra slowly made her way down the long blue wing, and soon both her parents were hugging and kissing her, then Olivia and Evelyn. Blackie gave her a big hug and then made his way up the wing. He helped Theo stand up, put his arm around him, and together they made their way down the enormous blue wing. Her grandmother had been right—Theo already looked stronger as he stepped onto the ground—and the grin had not left his face.

Blackie was heading around to Taco's left wing, when all of a sudden Jaclyn and Nicolas appeared, their arms around each other. Alexandra could not remember them ever being arm in arm, and they both looked *so happy*. Noir immediately flew to Nicolas's shoulder and soon they were being welcomed and hugged.

"All my dearests, I must ask you to go inside now. I must tend to Taco right away. As you can see, he is beginning to diminish. Alexandra, stay with me."

Her broom was pulsing with color and shimmering with diamond sparkles as she gestured for everyone to leave. Reluctantly, they all made their way inside through the conservatory and then were out of sight. Taco was shrinking rapidly. Silver held Alexandra tightly around her waist as he grew smaller and smaller before their eyes.

"We have to wait until he has returned to normal size, Alexandra, just another minute or so, and then I will administer the time travel antidote. I know this is terribly hard for you, my dear. However, you must always remember, no matter what happens, this was Taco's choice. It was what he wanted to do, Alexandra."

Tears flooded her eyes and fell down her face as she watched the bravest and most courageous macaw, her beloved Taco, slowly shrink. His eyes were shut tightly, and his green opalescent patch was deeply furrowed. It looked like he was in great pain.

"Is this painful for him, Grand Mama? It looks like he is suffering . . . I feel so terrible . . . I want to help him!"

"I think he may be, my dear, but there is nothing we can do during this process. It is a bigger concern how he will look once he returns to normal size. During his flight to Chatham and back, exceptional strength was required, as you know. For energy, his body was first burning glucose, or sugar, but that was quickly depleted. Then he had to burn body fat for fuel, and when that was exhausted, protein was burned. On the return flight to Dark Harbor, Taco was in a race to get back to Chadwick before his body destroyed all of its muscle tissue. We will not know how badly it was depleted until he is back to his normal size."

She paused, looking sadly into her granddaughter's eyes.

"I have to warn you, Alexandra, Taco may be as near death as Noir was . . . and fighting as hard for his life."

Alexandra wept as her grandmother held her tightly. It felt like there was a knife in her heart. The pain of watching him suffer was beyond anything she had ever experienced. Taco's ever-changing body was blurry through her tears, but she kept watching as he became smaller and smaller, praying he would be alive and survive once he returned to normal. Praying so, so hard.

Finally, it ended.

Before them lying on the ground was a once magnificent macaw, now near death, his body emaciated and his feathers dull and ragged.

His eyes were closed.

A FLIGHT FOR LIFE

Silver gently picked up Taco and hurriedly carried him to her bedroom. Once again, Alexandra's baby cradle was positioned next to the bed. The tiny blue macaw bedding was back inside, and potions once again filled the nightstand. Silver carried him to her chair and patiently tried to administer the time travel antidote and some other potions. But Taco barely swallowed.

Her grandmother's words were true. Taco was as close to death as Noir had been. Silver laid him in the cradle and covered him with a small quilt. Then Alexandra climbed onto the bed. The last thing she remembered was lying next to her grandmother and falling into a deep sleep.

It actually felt like she slept for days.

When she awoke, the sun was shining into the room. She was in her nightgown in her grandmother's bed. Evelyn appeared almost instantly with a tray of breakfast food and the blue vitamin bottle.

"Here you are, my mouse, some . . ."

"Taco? How is Taco? Is he better?!"

Alexandra felt her heart start to race as she remembered everything and scrambled across the bed to the cradle. He was breathing and asleep. Her beloved Taco was still alive. Weak with relief, she very gently stroked his head, now so tiny and just a short time ago so massive. Tears welled up in her eyes as she looked at him. There had been so many tears, and she thought how strange it was people cried when they were desperately sad and when they were ecstatically happy. She knew she would give anything for her tears to be happy, for Taco to have miraculously recovered. Instead, it felt like her tears were falling into a sea of heartbreak.

"My mouse. Now sit back and eat some good food. If you're not healthy, you'll be of no help to your Taco. Your grandmother is in the conservatory, I'll tell her you are awake. Now get started, my mouse, and don't forget your vitamins . . ."

Evelyn scurried out the door and into the conservatory. Alexandra wiped the tears off her face and slowly climbed back across the bed, adjusted the pillow, and put the tray in front of her. It seemed like she had not eaten food in weeks. She could not even remember her last meal.

Her grandmother came into the room and sat on the bed next to her. She was dressed in a pale blue sweater and slacks. A silk scarf with swirls of peacock feathers was draped around her neck. The scarf was fastened with a peacock pin that sparkled with blue and aquamarine gemstones. She was holding a very large and fragrant pink rose and placed it under Alexandra's nose. Alexandra breathed in deeply. This was something her grandmother had done so many times while she was growing up. The fragrance of roses was something she would never, ever forget. It would always be a reminder of both the happiest and the saddest times, just like tears, she thought. Then her grandmother sighed deeply and looked at the cradle.

"My dear, Taco is unchanged. With coaxing, he has taken his medicines. I am giving him the highest-protein potions, but thus far, he is the same. He sleeps all the time, which he needs to do, so we will have to be patient. And we'll not lose hope. He is a fighter. You know that, my dear."

She stood up and kissed the top of her granddaughter's head.

"Once you have finished your breakfast, go upstairs to your room to change. Your parents are out and about on the property, as are the boys and Jaclyn . . . and your Aunt Olivia is coming soon. It is Saturday so you have the whole weekend before you have to think about school. Do not groan or roll your eyes, my dear."

The familiar sad smile had returned to her face.

School was the very last thing on Alexandra's mind.

* ◆ *

She had flown up the stairs and changed quickly. As she brushed her hair, she was studying the mural and the gate. She walked over to look very closely, running her fingers along the wall where the brass keyhole had been.

It was gone.

There was only paint. Even if the keyhole was still there underneath the paint, she knew the key would no longer work. Alexandra stood back and gazed sadly at the entire scene, realizing she could never go back. She would never see Brownie again, or have a delicious hamburger at The Snack Shack, or see Chadwick Cottage again. Looking at the cottage, her eyes widened with astonishment as she realized the black cat was *gone* from the mural. As if on cue, at the same moment, Sam Adams sauntered through her bedroom door and hopped up on her bed, staring at her with the same piercing yellow eyes that used to look at her from the mural. She smiled and shook her head. It was so amazing. It was incredible. She went over to him, rubbed his head, and could hear a deep purr. Then her eyes fell on the photo of her parents next to her bed, her father's pipe, and the snow globe of the *Windswept*. These things and her necklace had connected her to them. They were her most treasured possessions.

But now she had *them*.

Alexandra walked over to the pole and looked back at her room, her mother's room. The large brass cage was again empty, as it had been once before. She felt tears in her eyes and a hard lump form in her throat. Then, hooking her leg around the pole, with a swish she was gone.

She could not wait to see them, to see with her own eyes that they really were alive. She ran out the side door and stopped. There they were, laughing and talking, walking toward the cliff. *Alive*. Max was running around with Biscuit. Her mother had her arm around Jaclyn's shoulders, and her father was walking between Nicolas and Theo. Her father was pointing out to sea, and as he turned, he saw her. The sun was on his face. It was all she saw running toward him. Her father's face in the sunlight. Then she felt him lift her high in the air, just like the day he said good-bye, so many years ago. She had no memory of that moment. This she would always remember.

* ✦ *

Throughout the rest of the day, it was a vigil.

Everyone took turns sitting by the cradle, talking to Taco, stroking his head. He would take the potions, but it required patience and repeated attempts. He never opened his eyes for more than a second or two. Dr. Burke was called and came in the late afternoon. It was a grim prognosis. Taco had lost half of his body weight, which was going to make it very hard to recover. Between the carefully chosen words were long silences and in those silences, hope seemed to evaporate, and then like a fragile bubble bursting, disappear. Both Alexandra and Elisabeth left the room anguished and in tears. It was more than they could bear.

So they did not hear when Dr. Burke told Silver he thought the best hope for Taco was a very rare red berry which only grew at the highest altitudes in the Laurentian Mountains in Canada, just as the tree line ended and the rock and ice began. He told her hikers, facing starvation while awaiting rescue had survived for weeks in snow caves by eating these berries—that the berry was near perfect nutrition and because Taco's condition was comparable to starving hikers', he felt the berries would offer the best medicinal cure. Also, because parrots love fruit, he thought Taco might make an effort to eat them. What he did not say was how these berries could be obtained. They certainly were not at Weston's Market. He then closed his black bag, hugged Silver, gently patted Taco, and quietly left.

However, sitting on his perch in the conservatory was someone who did hear.

* ◆ *

Noir left in the early evening.

After dinner, when everyone gathered in the living room, he silently and quickly crept out. Alexandra had returned from sitting with Taco and was curled up next to her mother. Nicolas was showing the snow globe to Graham and Elisabeth. Olivia, Jaclyn, and Theo were talking quietly, as were Silver and Blackie. Evelyn was finishing the dishes in the kitchen. So no one noticed when Noir slipped out or heard him fly down the long hallway to Silver's rooms. In full flight, a raven's wings make a distinct sound, like the rustle of silk, but it was too faint to be heard.

He flew to the cradle and stood on its edge. Taco's eyes were closed. Noir studied him for a moment and then flew to the conservatory. Deftly, he pulled down on the door handle with his beak and flew through the opening. Once outside, he pushed the door shut and then flew to the highest point of the large maple tree near the cliff. It was another cloudless night with a full moon. The wind, always prevailing at the coastline, ruffled his black iridescent plumage and shaggy throat feathers. His dark eyes were bright, the intelligence unmistakable, his mission about to begin. He sat perfectly still, facing north, and for a moment the black silhouette of a powerful raven was captured in the orb of a yellow moon.

Then the finger-tipped black wings spread to their widest, almost four feet across, and he lifted off, heading out over the ocean, then turning due north. A dry, guttural *kraa, kraa, kraa* mixed with the ocean winds. Inside Chadwick Manor, Nicolas turned his head, listening to the distant sound, but then it stopped. He returned to the conversation, thinking it was just the wind.

Noir flew along the coastline of Maine for about fifty miles and then headed inland and northwest toward the Province of Quebec. He glided on high-altitude wind currents, which allowed him to preserve his energy and travel at very high speeds, much faster than had he used only his wings for propulsion. It took many hours but he was finally approaching the Laurentian Mountains. He headed toward Mont Tremblant, which at its peak was over three thousand feet. Noir had studied the Laurentians with Nicolas and knew they were one of the oldest mountain ranges on earth, formed over 540 million years ago during the Precambrian period. From their studies, Noir knew the Laurentian Mountains had been worn down over a vast period of time by glaciers and were not nearly the height of the American or Canadian Rockies. It was a critically important fact to know. When he heard Dr. Burke talk about the location of the bush with the nutritious berries, Noir was confident he could make the flight—both in distance *and* altitude.

Once Mont Tremblant was in sight, he flew toward the summit, watching for where the pines and scrub gave way to snowcap. Gradually, he lowered in altitude so he could scan the snow-covered foliage for the bush with red berries. The moonlight was bright, reflecting on the snow. Even so, to find this particular bush would require the keenest eyesight; it was nighttime and the snow was deep. However, his exceptional vision in virtual blackness had already been proven. Without it, the key would never have been found. Noir flew low, scouring the undergrowth. Then he saw it, a large bush covered with snow, the red berries poking through. He landed on it, shaking the snow off the branches, and then surveyed the bush carefully. Using his powerful beak, he broke the stems of three branches with the most berries, and then rested before lifting off again.

With the branches snug in his beak, soaring high above snowy fields and forests and ice-covered lakes in the frigid Canadian night air, the tailwinds once again favorable, Noir returned to Dark Harbor the same way he had come.

It was after midnight when he landed on the conservatory roof.

Lights were out except for in Silver's bedroom. He flew to the conservatory door, dropped the branches, and then flew to her window, tapping on the glass with his beak. Silver opened the curtain. He flew back to the threshold, standing next to the branches, the bright moonlight illuminating the shiny blackness of his thick feathers and the ruby-red gloss of the berries.

In seconds, Silver opened the conservatory door and looked down. Her eyes filled with tears as she looked at the small figure standing guard next to three berry-laden branches. As exhausted as he was, Noir stood proudly at attention, looking more like a military officer delivering gold bars than a raven delivering berries to one very weak macaw. However, in truth, the berries were as precious as anything could possibly be. They held the only hope for saving a life. Overwhelmed by the distance he had flown and the selflessness and courage of what he had done, Silver reached down, picked him up, and held him as tears fell down her face.

"Merci beaucoup, Noir. Merci."

Her whispered voice was filled with love and gratitude as she stroked the black feathered wings that had worked so, so hard.

She gently picked up the branches and together they went back to her room and stood looking at Taco. If it were not for the shallow breaths that were barely discernible, he could be mistaken for dead. Silver laid the branches on the bed and immediately Noir flew to them. He carefully plucked one red berry in his beak and flew back to the edge of the cradle. Then he hopped down and stood next to Taco. Lowering his head, he gently dropped the berry and then made the softest raven call, *prruk-prruk-prruk*, close to Taco's ear. Taco was lying on his back, his head resting on a small pillow. One eye blinked open and then quickly closed again. Noir picked up the berry, putting it close to Taco's beak.

Very, very slowly the macaw opened his beak, as though it took every ounce of strength he had. Noir dropped the berry down his throat. Taco swallowed. Noir flew back for another and Taco again slowly opened his beak and took the berry. With the greatest effort, he swallowed three more berries and then fell back into a deep sleep.

"Plus de baies rouges demain matin."

The raven's tone of voice was noticeably different. Although weak from exhaustion, for the first time, the words held emotion. A gentleness and resolute vigilance resounded in the stillness of the room, filling the air with *hope*.

He nodded once to Silver and flew down the long hall and up the stairs to Nicolas's room.

RÉTABLISSEMENT (RECOVERY)

Nicolas had been very worried when there was no sign of Noir inside Chadwick Manor. He had gone outside to call him and only the sound of the wind answered his calls. He asked everyone if they had seen him, but no one had. They only remembered he had been at dinner and then was in the living room with them, at least for a while.

When he had gone upstairs to their room to look for him, Nicolas could see his cage was empty and it was clear Noir was not anywhere in the bedroom, nor was he in any of the other second-floor rooms. He had also checked Theo's room and the third floor thoroughly. It was later, when he returned to his room deeply worried, that he had walked over close to Noir's cage. To his complete astonishment, he saw a note lying in the bottom of the cage. It was written on a small scrap of paper, but very legible.

> *Nicolas,*
> *Ne t'inquiète pas. Je vais revenir avant minuit.*
> *Noir*

He read and reread the note: *Do not worry. I will return by midnight.*

How was it possible that he could write? Nicolas knew Noir understood spoken English and could read both English and French, but he had never known Noir could write. As he sat on his bed looking at the tattered piece of paper, he tried to visualize Noir holding a pen writing these words. He must have taught himself to hold a pen with one of his feet. When did he practice? The penmanship was very good. Nicolas knew ravens were unusually adept at using tools in the wild and could figure out ingenious ways to use sticks to retrieve what they wanted. Nevertheless, holding a pen and writing would require exceptional dexterity, and he shook his head in amazement. Of course, he had not known Noir could dive, or hold his breath, or see underwater better than a human. Noir was mysterious, even to the person who knew him the best.

Nicolas could not even guess where Noir had gone or why. There was no explanation he could think of. He was lying in bed, but not asleep, when Noir pushed open the bedroom door and flew to his cage after midnight.

Nicolas asked him where he had been, but there was no answer.

Noir was sound asleep in seconds.

* ◆ *

The next day, everyone was astounded, watching. Silver instructed them to stay back, away from the cradle, and not talk as Noir continued his ministrations. He looked like the parent, feeding his baby, just as is done in the wild. Only he was not the parent, this was a cradle and not a nest, and Taco was certainly not his baby. Yet that was what it looked like. He paid no attention to the people watching as he went through the routine.

The three branches loaded with berries were now in the conservatory standing in a bucket of water to preserve them as long as possible. He flew to the conservatory to get one berry, and then woke Taco with the soft raven calls, dropping the berry down his throat. Then more berries, one at a time, as many as Taco would eat. Every hour Noir fed him, and between feedings, he was on his perch, watching the cradle intently. Silver stopped trying to feed Taco the potions. She knew he was getting the best food possible.

Then Silver told them what Dr. Burke had told her about the berries and where they were found. It was nothing less than amazing, astonishing, as everyone realized Noir had flown to the Laurentian Mountains to retrieve what offered the best hope for saving Taco's life.

Nicolas was overwhelmed. He realized Noir had flown almost seven hundred miles in one night to bring back what was Taco's best hope for survival. He walked over to Noir on his perch and spoke to him softly. No one heard what he said, but everyone saw as he reached up and stroked Noir with tears in his eyes. Then Alexandra and Elisabeth went to him. Together they thanked him, tears spilling down their cheeks. Noir nodded and then spoke softly in the familiar monotone, but the words he spoke belied the tone.

"Taco est mon ami."

* ◆ *

By late Sunday afternoon, Taco was responding to the nutritious berries and was staying awake for short periods, eating close to twenty berries at a time. It seemed like he wanted to eat more, so Noir flew to the kitchen and asked Evelyn for pastèque, which she recognized as the French word for watermelon, and she placed a couple of chunks on the counter. Noir took one and flew back to Taco. He held the watermelon in his beak while Taco took a bite, and then dropped what was left down his throat. Then he went back for the second chunk, and it, too, was eaten.

Then Taco spoke for the first time, in a very hoarse whisper.

"Merci, Noir, mon ami."

A SECRET PASSAGE
AND THEO'S SECRET

With Taco's recovery now looking hopeful, everyone gathered in the library at Silver's request. It was Sunday evening and the next day was a school day. Alexandra felt like a year had passed since she was in Olivia's class, but it had only been a few days measured by Dark Harbor time.

Life-changing events had happened, and yet there had to be a return—to what, Alexandra wondered. The real world had been altered, changed forever. How would this work? How could her parents be reintroduced, eleven years later, and looking so much younger? Everyone in Dark Harbor knew they had died. She realized the grown-ups must have talked about it, but she had not been curious or concerned. It just seemed somehow it would work out. They were alive and that was all that mattered.

The library was the coziest room in Chadwick Manor other than the kitchen. It was smaller than any of the other rooms, and the books lining every wall from floor to ceiling added to the coziness, as did the plump peach velvet couches and chairs. This evening there was a fire in the small corner fireplace and the lamplights were low. It was a perfect place to read or take a nap. Almost from the moment they arrived, it quickly became the favorite haunt of Nicolas and Noir.

Silver directed Nicolas, Theo, Jaclyn, and Alexandra to sit on one couch, and opposite them, on the other couch, were Olivia, Elisabeth, Graham, and herself. Blackie and Evelyn sat in chairs angled toward the couches. Olivia and Elisabeth were sitting next to each other. They were identical, except for the age difference of eleven years. Alexandra had already realized Elisabeth looked too young to be her mother, more proof of how terribly complicated time travel was.

Then Alexandra looked at her grandmother, surrounded by books, and suddenly a memory materialized, buried until this moment. She was very young, four or five years old, and she was looking for her grandmother. When she did not find her in her bedroom or the conservatory, she had walked into the living room. It was empty, but the door to the library was open just a little, and she had walked over and peeked through the crack in the door. Her grandmother was looking at the top row of books, her back was to the door, and the rolling ladder was *next to her*. Alexandra felt herself smiling and was brought back to the present when she heard her grandmother's voice.

"I have asked all of you here this evening so that we may discuss everything. There is a great deal to talk about, obviously."

Until this moment, no one had spoken about what had happened or would happen now that they had returned. Everyone had been so focused on Taco and through so much emotionally, it seemed like no one wanted to talk. Alexandra just wanted to be with her parents, close to them, and they seemed to want the same. It was also true what had happened was so miraculous words were completely inadequate.

Silver looked around the room at everyone and continued.

"The recent events have been, well, it would be accurate to say, highly consequential. And like anything this serious, will take time to adjust to. Elisabeth and Graham will stay here at Chadwick, of course. However, for some time they will not venture off the property. No one is to speak of them to anyone at The Pine School or in town. We need time to assess what is best. This will not be simple—it is complicated and quite challenging. So we need to have your promise nothing will be said about this to anyone else. Is that understood?"

All heads nodded. Alexandra knew very well that sometimes secrets were necessary.

"Very good. Now, the next subject is school. As Elisabeth, Graham, and Olivia all agree, it is most important for you to return to school with a focus on your studies and the good grades we know you are all capable of. You are coming to the close of this school year, and next for Nicolas will be the test for university, or preparatory school, as it is called in the United States."

She paused, looking directly at Nicolas.

"There are decisions that will have to be made about your future, Nicolas, and they will be, in good time. And of course, these discussions will include your father."

Then she looked at Theo.

"Theo, my dear boy, I want you to know I consider you my own. You are a member of this family and I will be funding your education. I feel fortunate, privileged, to be able to do this for you, my dear. Goodness knows you may be our next brilliant astrophysicist who discovers *the science*, not the magic, of time travel."

Her blue eyes twinkled as she looked lovingly at Theo, who swallowed, turned noticeably pink, and pushed his glasses up, reflecting tear-filled eyes.

"Thank you. I can never thank you enough, Miss Silver, for all that you have done for me." Theo's voice cracked with emotion.

"You are very welcome, my dear, and Theo, as you are very much a part of this family, please call me Grand Mama."

Theo just nodded. It was obvious he was too emotional even to speak.

"Now Graham has some things he wants to say."

Alexandra's father leaned forward with his hands clasped. He looked at each one of them and then began to speak. Alexandra loved hearing his voice. It really was like butterscotch, warm and soothing.

"There is no way Elisabeth and I can thank each one of you enough. Your bravery, determination, and resourcefulness are beyond remarkable. No adult could have handled this with the courage and fortitude you have shown. We apologize for being less than appreciative at first. We did not understand, could not even comprehend, what you were telling us. When we slowly came out of our shock and began to accept the truth, we both could not believe how hard you all worked to save us. Your efforts were heroic, as were those of Noir and Taco. Without all of you, we would not be sitting here right now."

He wiped his eyes and paused, again looking at each of them individually.

"Elisabeth and I love each of you, and Taco and Noir, very much."

Then he stood, as did everyone, and there were hugs and tears all around.

As they were leaving the library, Graham turned to Alexandra, Theo, Nicolas, and Jaclyn with a mysterious smile on his face.

"Meet me here in the library about fifteen minutes before you usually leave for school tomorrow morning. Blackie, you have the morning off. I will see that they get to school."

"Very good, Graham. Max and I will enjoy sleeping in a bit."

Blackie smiled and winked at all of them.

Surprised looks were exchanged. How could he take them to school without being seen by Headmaster Green?

Before going upstairs to get ready for bed, Alexandra went to check on Taco, who was asleep, but Noir reported he had eaten "vingt baies rouges et un gros morceau d'ananas" at his last feeding. Her grandmother was standing behind her and, hearing his report, interpreted, "Taco ate twenty red berries and a big chunk of pineapple."

Silver looked at Noir with approval and very apparent affection. "Très excellent, Docteur Noir."

Noir slowly bowed his head at the compliment and then resumed watching over his patient from his perch. Alexandra kissed her grandmother and walked down the long hallway toward her room.

It really felt like she floated down the hall and up the stairs . . . on pure happiness.

* ◆ *

Alexandra did not mind putting on the drab school uniform and ugly black shoes in the morning. In fact, she was not thinking about her clothes at all. She dressed quickly, hopped on the pole, and ran to her grandmother's rooms. Just as she arrived at the door, she heard her name.

"Come in, Alexandra."

Walking in, she was overwhelmed with a feeling of déjà vu. It was the first day of school in the fall, the beginning of her sixth year, and she had come to say good-bye. She was the only child and her grandmother was her only family. That day, which now seemed like a long time ago, she had dreaded going to school. Today everything was different; so much had changed in her life.

"Come, my dear. Come and see. Taco's eyes are open. Noir has taken wonderful care of him. The berries are helping him greatly."

Noir was sitting on his perch, intently watching the cradle. Alexandra wondered if he ever slept, he was so vigilant. She walked over to the cradle and peered in. Taco was lying on his back, the quilt pulled up to just below his beak. She knew he recognized her when she saw his eyes brighten and lock onto hers.

"Taco, you're awake! Noir has been taking wonderful care of you and he went a great distance to get the berries you've been eating. You look *so much better*, Taco, and every day you will be stronger!"

Stroking his head and running her fingers over the opalescent patch on his forehead, she remembered how furrowed it had been, how impossibly hard it had been to watch him in so much pain. He was blinking softly and then, to her amazement, opened his beak to speak. It was a hoarse whisper, but very clear.

"Taco beaucoup mieux."

"He said he feels much better," her grandmother interpreted.

Alexandra looked up at her grandmother and then at Noir, grinning.

"That is so wonderful to hear, Taco! I love you so much! Now rest and I'll check on you as soon as I get home from school."

She leaned into the cradle, kissing him right on the opalescent patch, and he slowly closed his eyes. He had not forgotten his French, and she knew he was speaking it for Noir. As she studied him, Alexandra knew she had witnessed something rare and exceptional. He cared more for others than for himself, expecting nothing in return. He had been willing to die so they could live. Alexandra knew that few people would be as selfless and brave. That few would ever have a heart as big as the one beating inside his small feathered body.

"Now off to breakfast, my dear. I don't know what your father has planned, but he promised you would not be late for school. So hurry along."

Alexandra smiled at her grandmother with tears in her eyes and gave her a hug, and then she turned to Noir. She walked over to him and looked into the dark eyes that were now so different. She could still see the intelligence and the intensity, but the blackness was no longer opaque, ruthless, and forbidding—now his eyes looked like black velvet. She said nothing, but she knew he understood the deep gratefulness in her heart, and he slowly bowed his head.

* ◆ *

They quickly ate a delicious breakfast—homemade waffles with strawberries and whipped cream—thanked Evelyn, grabbed their books, and ran to the library. Graham was waiting for them with the same twinkle in his eye as the night before.

"Well, I thought it would be fun to share a secret with you. Your mother told me about this . . . she discovered it when she was about your age, Alexandra, and showed me after we were married. One day she was pulling out some books and happened to pull out this book right here. Alexandra, come over and pull it down from the top, not all the way out."

Alexandra walked over to where he was pointing. The book was *A Little Princess* by Frances Hodgson Burnett. She had never read it. There were so many books to choose from she had never even noticed this one, but the title intrigued her. It reminded her of Taco, of what he had called her since she could remember. Somewhat tentatively, she placed one finger on the top of the book and then looked at her father, who was smiling and nodding. As she tipped the book down, the entire section of the wall and the floor she was standing on began to turn and she was transported around to the other side.

There were gasps all round.

Nicolas, Theo, and Jaclyn were now looking at a wall of books that looked the same, but as Graham ran his hand along the spines it was obvious the books could not be removed—they just looked like real books.

"Now pull it down again, Alexandra, and you'll come back around!"

There she was again, standing in the same place, wide-eyed, with her mouth open.

"What is on the other side, Alexandra?!" Jaclyn asked breathlessly.

Alexandra just stared at her father, unable to speak.

"It's a tunnel and leads all the way to The Pine School. It must have been built by the ship captain who also owned this house and the mansion used for The Pine School. There is something quite amazing you will see when we get to the end, which is why the tunnel was built, or at least that's my assumption. So do you want to go to school via the underground route?" he asked, grinning broadly.

The question did not need to be asked.

The section of wood floor in front of the bookcase was narrow and partially covered by a large area rug. The rug covered most of the circular cut in the floor, which was why Alexandra had never noticed it. The floor that was exposed was about two feet wide by about four feet long, enough room for two people. First, Alexandra and Jaclyn went around. On the other side, they stepped off the wooden floor onto some kind of platform. Alexandra reached for the book, tipped it, and the wall spun around to the library side. Then Theo and Nicolas came around, did the same thing, and then Graham arrived. They were now standing on the platform looking at a steep flight of stairs that went down so far you could not see where the stairs ended because the lighting was so dim.

"I know where this leads to. I have been there many times."

Everyone turned to Theo, staring at him, shocked by what he had just said. However, Graham seemed more curious than surprised.

"That is most interesting, Theo. I didn't think anyone except Elisabeth and I knew about it. You will have to tell us more when we get there. Now, let's go, I will lead. The tunnel is not that long, and it's a direct path to the school, much shorter than taking the coast road. So, tally-ho, follow me!"

With that, Graham started down the stairs with the others following, one by one. It was about the distance of two flights of stairs, dimly lit by some kind of old-fashioned lighting, which reminded Alexandra of the oil lamps in Chadwick Cottage and the street lamps in Dark Harbor—there were real flames, enclosed in glass. It felt spooky, even a little scary. When they got to the bottom, they were looking down a shadowy tunnel lit with the same glass lamps, spaced maybe twelve feet apart on both walls of the tunnel, so there was enough light to see.

"Come along, we'll be there in no time!"

Graham led the way, his voice echoing in the hollowness of the tunnel. Alexandra felt one wall. It was made of rock or stone and was cold and damp to the touch. She could not imagine how it had been dug so many years ago—or why.

The tunnel was straight. There were no turns or dips, and the air was musty. They were walking one by one—first Graham, followed by Alexandra, Jaclyn, Theo, and Nicolas. No one spoke. Graham was walking at a fast clip and everyone had to walk quickly to keep up with him. Their footsteps were the only sound and made a loud echo, magnified by the hollowness of the tunnel and the rock walls surrounding them. It seemed like only minutes later when Graham stopped and turned to them.

"We have arrived, ladies and gents! This will be something that will amaze you, assuming nothing has changed in eleven years."

Graham grinned and looked knowingly at Theo, who showed no expression. Alexandra could see what appeared to be the door to a vault right behind her father. The gray metal door had a small wheel in the center, and her father began turning it with obvious effort. It sounded like it had not been opened in centuries, creaking and groaning. Very slowly, he pulled the door open. He walked through first. In seconds, they were all standing on a stone ledge and looking at a sight so unexpected it almost did not seem real.

They were looking at a small lagoon.

Unlike the navy blue of the Atlantic, the water was the color of aquamarine, soft turquoise and iridescent green, swirled together like a tropical confection. Off to their left, where the current was coming in, daylight was streaming through breaks in the cliffs; even parts of the sky were visible. It looked like they were standing inside a fantastical diamond mine: the cave walls were entirely covered with crystals, sparkling in the rays of sunlight and reflecting in the water like silver stardust. The reflection made the surface of the lagoon look like a distant nebula of stars suspended in water instead of the vacuum of space. Here and there, frothy effervescent bubbles were rising to the surface from the depths of the lagoon. A good-sized path encircled the lagoon. Across the water from where they were standing, they could see a stone staircase leading up and then out of sight.

"This is a very old quartz quarry. You are looking at quartz crystals that form on the walls of the cave—they look like diamonds, but they're not. Miners have found diamonds in quartz mines; however, that is very rare and to extract them requires a great deal of work. What is most special about this place will surprise you, and it's not the sparkling walls. There are natural thermal jets at the bottom of the lagoon, coming up from deep within the earth, so even with the frigid ocean water continually coming in with the tides, the water temperature holds at a steady ninety degrees. The warmth turns the water this beautiful aquamarine color, and at night, bioluminescence in the thermal jets provides natural illumination. So even in the winter, and at night, you can swim here!" Graham said, grinning as he surveyed the beautiful vista.

"Elisabeth and I swam here many times in the winter when it was below zero outside!"

Theo was looking at everything seriously, but unlike the others, clearly not in amazement.

"I didn't think anyone else could possibly know about this, but Theo, you have been here before?" Graham asked, his expression now serious.

Theo nodded and pushed his glasses up. He looked sad as his eyes swept over the scene.

"Yes, I have. I was the only boarder who stayed during the summer months. Headmaster Green was certain, convinced actually, there were proper diamonds amidst the crystals, so he had me work down here with a pick, going along the walls and putting what I could hammer out into bags he would look through. I don't know if he ever found any diamonds. He never told me. I never got to swim . . . I had to work. I spent a lot of time here, alone."

No one could believe it. Theo had never told Alexandra, and she now understood why he always looked so pale and tired after every summer. Then she remembered something else. The first day of school in Classroom #6 and the puff of silvery dust that rose around him as he sat down.

Graham's expression had changed completely. From being so happy to frowning, with anger in his eyes, something Alexandra had not seen in the brief time she had been with him. He walked over to Theo, and holding one of Theo's shoulders with his hand, he looked straight into his eyes.

"I can assure you, Theo, no boarding student at The Pine School will ever have that happen again. It sounds like it's time I claim my office back, and I can promise all of you that *will* happen."

It was the moment they knew The Pine School would be changing.

The spell, or whatever it was that had fallen over the school after their deaths, was about to be broken.

"Now let's get you to class before the morning announcements. This is the fun part! You need to go up the stairs over there. As Theo knows, at the top is a trapdoor. When you open it, you'll be in the middle of the grove of large pine trees, actually under one of them, on the front lawn of the school. Follow me!"

Graham led the way down the steps from the platform. It could not be seen from where they had been standing, but they could now see a rowboat tied up to a small dock. It was not very far across the water to the other side where the stone staircase led up to the trapdoor.

"You can walk the perimeter of the lagoon to get to the staircase, but this is much faster and more fun! So hop in! Theo to the bow, Nicolas can row, and the girls sit on the seat in the stern. When you get across, Theo, just tie the boat to the post over there. The seawater will obviously be changing with the tides—but it's never so low that you can walk across, so you'll always need the rowboat. Shall I tell Blackie I will take care of your return trip today?"

They all grinned, even Theo.

"I'll have your grandmother call the school and tell them you were allowed to walk to and from school today. She doesn't know about the tunnel, at least I don't think so."

As he said this, Alexandra was certain her grandmother knew.

"And be sure the headmaster, or I should say the soon-to-be-former headmaster, doesn't see you coming out from underneath the pine tree. You might slip between the pines down to the front gate and then double back up the drive—but I have no doubt this will be a piece of cake for time travelers!"

He grinned at them.

"I'll be having a cup of tea in the library later today. Give me a holler so I know you've arrived!"

They set off across the tidal pool to the other side. Graham watched as they tied up the boat and made their way up the stairs. Alexandra was the last in line. As she approached the top of the stairs, she stopped and looked back at her father and waved. A mist was rising from the surface of the lagoon, and the crystals from the cave wall cast a sparkling aura around him as he waved back. Her father gradually disappeared from view, vanishing behind a white cloud. Soon, thick white mist filled the entire cave and then began to shimmer with silver dust.

Alexandra stood perfectly still, mesmerized. The silvery mist began swirling and rotating, forming tightly wound spiral arms. Then the motion ceased. Suspended above the lagoon was a miniature spiral galaxy. From deep within one of the spidery arms, a single star grew larger and brighter, soon eclipsing all others. It filled the cave, hovering like a golden disc over the lagoon, and within its sphere, faces began to appear.

Olivia's face and her grandmother's, both illuminated by magical crystals . . . her parents, as she woke from the ocean's powerful sleep . . . and then, like the pages of a book being turned in a gentle wind, she saw the faces of everyone she loved.

The last face was Taco's, his magnificent painted face gazing into hers.

As his face disappeared, the gold disc vanished in a brilliant starburst, and a waterfall of sparkling fireworks fell into the aquamarine lagoon.

When the last sparkle had slipped beneath the surface, Alexandra turned and began walking up the stairs. From above, she could see them looking down at her, Jaclyn, Theo, and Nicolas, grinning. Smiling back, she felt an excitement in the unknown and an anticipation of all that was ahead. A new journey was about to begin.

CHAPTER SIXTY-FOUR

And within her heart she felt a deep happiness and gratefulness.

Alexandra knew there was nothing more wonderful than being able to look into the faces of those you love the most.

EPILOGUE

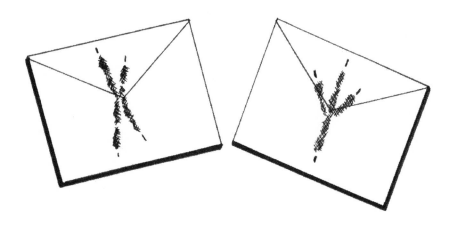

It was early fall in Dark Harbor.

The summer had ended all too quickly as it always seemed to. Nicolas had left with Noir to attend the same boarding school in England as Nicole. Theo was accepted at a private school called Choate in Connecticut and left early for orientation. Olivia had sent Theo's transcripts and test scores to a number of preparatory schools unbeknownst to him. One evening before dinner, Olivia had announced, with great pride in her voice, that Choate had accepted Theodore Arthur Eddington on a full scholarship. The acceptance letter said he would be entering the third form, which meant his ninth year, and Olivia explained that he would be skipping years seven and eight. Everyone had clapped and cheered, and Theo had turned many shades of pink. Olivia said it would be entirely his choice whether to stay at The Pine School as a seventh-year student or transfer to Choate, known for its outstanding math and science programs.

Alexandra knew there was no choice. They all understood it was what had to happen, "the next chapter," as Silver reminded everyone, trying to sound cheerful. However, everyone knew it was also an ending.

A special time in their lives was ending and would never come again.

Two bedrooms were once again empty in Chadwick Manor, as was one perch in the kitchen and one in the conservatory.

It was hardest of all on Taco.

He and Noir said their good-byes privately in the conservatory just before Noir and Nicolas left. When the long black touring car pulled away from Chadwick heading to Boston, Taco was not with the group tearfully waving good-bye. He had stayed in the conservatory, his back to the door, not moving when Alexandra called him to come see them off.

Something was lost when Noir left.

Taco did not speak for many days. His appetite was almost nonexistent and he spent most of his time alone in the conservatory, looking out toward the ocean. Taco knew Noir had gone in that direction, across the ocean to England. And he also believed that somewhere out there, where the sky and ocean meet, was the *back of beyond*, a place no one, not even a powerful raven, was supposed to return from—and live.

Over the course of many weeks, there were some small signs that his deep melancholy was gradually lifting. However, what came in the mail one day was what helped the heaviness in his heart the most. The letter, addressed to "Monsieur Taco," was written in very good handwriting. On the sealed back flap was a single footprint in black ink. The distinctive imprint of a common raven.

The extraordinary efforts by one macaw parrot to learn to hold a pen with one foot and write in French were most incredible, culminating in an envelope addressed to "Monsieur Noir," sent in care of Nicolas at the English boarding school. The envelope was delivered with great fanfare to Evelyn, who had beamed and promised she would be sure it had the proper airmail postage. On the back flap was the footprint of a South American macaw parrot, *the most distinctive of all.* Two toes facing forward, one larger and one smaller, and two toes facing backward, one also larger than the other, necessary for the strength needed to grasp and perch securely (called an oppositional grip because the long toes go both forward and backward). And Taco had never fallen, not even from the most precarious perch. Occasionally he would even hang upside down from his perch, holding on by one foot with his wings open—something he liked to do for fun (but also for the humorous reaction).

Over the summer months, Graham and Elisabeth had very gradually aged. By early September, it was as though eleven years had passed in the space of one summer. Elisabeth now looked identical to Olivia, and Graham looked older and more distinguished, more like a headmaster. It was never understood or explained, but they had begun going into town during the summer and everyone knew them and greeted them as though they had always been there. The fact that they had died in a storm years ago seemed to have vanished from everyone's memory.

As hard and bittersweet as the good-byes were, they were a little less painful because the summer had been wonderful. The halls of Chadwick were once again filled with voices, the *Windswept* was again hard-a-lee, and each night a young girl went to bed with a smile on her face.

✳ ◆ ✳

One summer day her father had asked if they wanted to drive to Chatham. There had been stunned silence at first, and then total excitement. They had not asked about the cottage, if it was still there, or like a mirage had vanished, now lost in time. It was better not to know. So when the invitation came they knew Chadwick Cottage was *still there*, which was the happiest news of all. Then her father had winked at Alexandra and said, "If I am not mistaken, someone is having a birthday next week, and I don't think there could be a better place to celebrate than Chatham."

Graham drove Blackie's car and they made the long trip in one day, leaving very early in the morning and arriving by midafternoon. The birds stayed behind with Silver, Evelyn, and Blackie and were told they would get a full report upon returning. Olivia was attending some kind of class for teachers in Boston.

They were too excited to talk very much during the trip. When they arrived, they parked and slowly walked out to the familiar beach. This felt very strange—they had never before driven to Chatham Beach. As they walked, they were all looking toward the sand dune. Then they saw it—the white picket fence and gate—*it was still there*. Chadwick Cottage looked exactly the same, but of course, Sam Adams was not sitting in the window. (He, too, had aged over the summer and had become an old cat almost overnight. His black face now had traces of white and he spent most of his days sleeping on Alexandra's bed, which never bothered Taco at all.)

The Snack Shack looked just as they remembered, with a line of people waiting for food, as always. They walked in silence toward the small wood building, and had just rounded the corner when they all heard the familiar voice. Then they saw him, wearing the same starched white cap and blue apron. His twinkling blue eyes had not changed (and still looked like Blackie's) and lit up when he saw them.

Brownie came out to greet them and warmly shook Graham and Elisabeth's hands, then the boys', and hugged the girls. He greeted them as though everything was entirely normal and told them the cottage was ready for their visit. With a meaningful look in his eye, he asked Nicolas about Noir and Alexandra about Taco. He was very happy to hear all was well with both birds. Then, smiling, he said he was sure he would be seeing a lot of them during their visit. (And he did. Elisabeth and Theo both wanted a strawberry milkshake every single day.)

Theo, always thinking, had silently pointed to the calendar on the back wall of The Snack Shack, grinning. No one else had thought to look at it. At last, it was *exactly correct*—the current month, day, *and* year. However, the agonizing battle with that calendar would never be forgotten by any of them.

Next, they climbed up the sand dune to look at the gate more closely. As with the painted gate in her room, there was no longer a keyhole. Alexandra ran her fingers over the place it had been, now just some peeling paint. They stood in silence, each lost in thought about that night . . . the night the sands of time came raining down and the hands of time unwound.

Then they walked to Chadwick Cottage. It was so familiar yet so strange to walk through the front door again. It was exactly as they remembered, even the faint aroma of Graham's pipe tobacco. They had walked around in silence, going into each room, remembering everything. The first night they were too excited to sleep. After Elisabeth and Graham went to bed, they dragged their pillows and blankets into the living room, lit the oil lamps, and stayed up talking for most of the night.

There were so many memories for each of them.

Alexandra saw Nicolas walk to the end of the dock and sit down, staring into the distance. She had wondered how Noir found the key in the pitch-black depths of the ocean—what had actually happened. But because Nicolas never talked about it, she felt she should not ask. Her parents also walked to the end of the dock, holding hands and looking out to sea. They each walked to the gate alone and sat near it, remembering, many times.

They had only been to the beach before, so it was fun to explore the town of Chatham. It was a quaint village with gift shops, ice cream parlors, art galleries, and many restaurants. They bought matching Chatham T-shirts and had lunch at the Chatham Squire Restaurant more than once. Alexandra found out her father *loved* clam chowder and steamers.

One night they had a fancy dinner at the Chatham Bars Inn, a very large inn facing the ocean. "White tablecloth," her mother had said, using the familiar expression, and it was a special occasion, her thirteenth birthday. Alexandra was so relieved it was not her fifteenth birthday and often wondered what would happen when that birthday arrived, as did Jaclyn. Would either of them receive a letter, and if they did, what would the letter say?

This night, happily, there was only celebration.

The Chatham Bars Inn looked like a palace at night. Large blue hydrangea bushes illuminated by elegant lighting flanked the steep staircase leading to the front entrance. As they walked up the stairs, her mother told her blue hydrangea flowers were her favorite, but lilacs and peonies were very close behind. Then she said, "Roses are already taken," with a big smile as she put her arm around her daughter. Alexandra had been learning little things about her mother all summer and this was yet another.

It was true. The little things are the most important of all.

The dining room was the size of a ballroom, but with all the candles lit, it felt cozy and inviting and reminded Alexandra of The Claw & Tail. Each table had a flower arrangement made from blue hydrangeas *and* pink roses. Mother and daughter had noticed this and their eyes met, smiling. As she looked at the flowers, Alexandra thought of her grandmother and could almost smell her rose perfume. She wondered, had her grandmother chosen roses as her favorite flower or—had they chosen her? A magical image floated into her mind as she imagined her grandmother surrounded by hundreds of long-stemmed pink roses, *the flowers choosing her*. It made her smile, and she decided that was what had to have happened.

Nicolas ordered lobster, as did her parents. When it came time for her to order, she asked for the same. Everyone had been surprised, but most of all Alexandra, who actually felt like someone else had ordered for her. Nicolas was expert at using the lobster crackers and helped her when she could not crack the very hard, thick claws. As she dipped the first chunk of lobster meat into the melted butter, Theo had called for a drum roll and everyone watched expectantly as the first piece of lobster went into her mouth. She immediately understood what they had all been raving about. Everyone cheered and she could almost hear her grandmother whispering, "I told you, my dear, that in time you would acquire a taste for lobster."

At the end of dinner, a beautiful birthday cake with thirteen candles was placed in front of her. It was decorated with seashells and starfish made from glistening, creamy white frosting. She heard the voices of her family singing "Happy Birthday," and looked around the table at each face aglow in the candlelight, then closed her eyes and felt warm tears on her face. The most amazing, miraculous wish had come true. At that moment, she knew on every birthday, for the rest of her life, she would never make a wish again. *Nevermore*. Instead, like the sound of the sea in a seashell pressed to her ear, she would hear and say the words "thank you," over and over again.

On their last night in Chatham, they went to a band concert on the town green. They arrived in the late afternoon. The grass was dotted with blankets, colorful balloons, and children holding puffy watercolor swirls of cotton candy. Breathing in the smell of fresh cut grass, they ran barefoot, throwing a football, still feeling the warmth of the sun on their skin from their last day at Chatham Beach. As evening fell, the band played under a large gazebo decorated with red, white, and blue crepe paper and balloons. The musicians were dressed in formal red blazers with gold cords and brass buttons, reminding Alexandra of the Duke's Christmas jacket. The last song was a waltz. Many couples got up to dance under the star-filled night sky, and one couple was still dancing even after the last note was played.

When they said good-bye to Brownie, it was not terribly sad because they knew they would be back the next summer, and the summer after that and the one after that, as her father had said with a twinkle in his eye. His words had made it so much easier to say good-bye, knowing they would return. As they waved good-bye to Brownie, it seemed like they were waving good-bye to summer as well.

And suddenly it was gone.

Once again, it was the first day of a new school year at The Pine School.

Blackie drove Alexandra and Jaclyn, with Max riding along, as always. They were still admiring their new school uniforms. It had been almost shocking to have a choice of *color* and styles. Alexandra had chosen the green and white plaid kilt skirt with a white blouse and a green bow tie. Jaclyn had chosen the same in blue. Graham and Elisabeth had left much earlier that morning, as they needed to arrive before all the students. Over the summer, her parents had gone to the school many times but never spoke about it upon their return—there were just mysterious smiles.

As they approached The Pine School, they could see the tarnished gold *P* was now shiny and the gate was painted hunter green. The ominous black shutters that had always been latched shut across the windows, like eyes closed tight, were now open, framing windows sparkling in the morning sunlight. It looked like the school was now awake, with eyes wide open, gazing out into the world. Over the summer, they had seen the drab gray color change to buttery yellow as painters worked on ladders all around the building, and the black shutters were painted a shiny hunter green. It was hard to believe it was the same school. When they drove up to the familiar portico, *her father* was standing where Headmaster Green had always been, but her father was standing outside, not peering from behind grimy glass. He was wearing a dark green blazer, white shirt, navy slacks, a navy-blue tie with tiny pine trees, and new penny loafers with shiny copper pennies. Grinning, he pulled open the door, now gleaming wood and glass.

And they walked into . . . a new school.

Under their feet, the black and white tiles were now highly polished and when they looked up, the chandeliers were glistening. Every bulb was lit, and there was not a cobweb in sight. The door to her father's office had no trace of Headmaster Green's name. (She inspected it closely.) And where she had seen the faint outline of her father's name was now "Headmaster St. Germaine" in shiny gold letters. Painted on the glass underneath his name was a large pine tree.

The teachers standing outside Classrooms #1 through #4 were all *normal looking*. Alexandra slowly studied each one. It was amazing. She could see they were each the same person as before, but all the odd colors were gone from their skin, eyes, hair, and clothes. Their names were the same, but there was only a trace of their former monochromatic color on a scarf, shoes, or sweater. Alexandra was also peeking into the classrooms and could see flashes of bright color, mobiles, and decorations. Miss Pomegranate suddenly emerged from the headmaster's office and greeted both Alexandra and Jaclyn. Her hair was still reddish orange but much more natural looking. She was wearing a white dress with orange scarf, belt, and matching orange shoes. Suddenly she sneezed and Alexandra studied her face. Her nose did not turn orange. She looked completely normal.

The next door down from the Headmaster's Office was open and the heavy curtain was gone. On the glass door in gold lettering it read:

~ The Pine School Library ~
All Who Enter Must Leave With One New Book
No Exceptions

It was as if a magic wand had swept over the room. Now immaculate, the shelves were filled with new books. The room even smelled new. There was no scent of mildew and not a speck of dust. As her gaze traveled around the room, Alexandra suddenly gasped loudly.

Next to the large desk, now cleaned and organized, was a tall perch—and who was standing on it and looking back at her but Taco?

Her father explained that he asked Taco if he wanted to spend his days in the library with the children and had barely asked the question when the enthusiastic response came, "Oui!" Then, without missing a beat, Taco had volunteered to teach French. Her father said it was obvious Taco had already thought about this in some detail. He told Graham he would take his nap during the lunch break after eating his lunch—assorted fruit Evelyn would prepare that he would take to school in a small satchel—and he said he would ride to and from school with the girls because he thought it best the students not see their French teacher flying to school.

So the headmaster of The Pine School had retained a French teacher.

(By the end of the first week of school, the routine was well established. Every day, beginning with Classroom #1 and ending with Classroom #8, the library would fill with eager students wanting to learn French. At the start of each class, Taco would ring one of the bells hanging from his perch and in a most authoritative voice, with a very authentic French accent for a South American macaw, announce, "Étudiants, votre attention! Je suis Professeur Taco!" The students in Classroom #7 did have an advantage, however. Jaclyn had agreed to assist the professeur and tutor anyone who needed extra help.)

Before leaving the library, her father led Alexandra to the large book open on the library desk. The last entry in faded ink was still there, but the dust was gone from the pages. Next to the faded entry, under the column "Returned By," in vivid blue ink she read, "Returned by Headmaster St. Germaine, upon safe passage home." As she blinked back tears, he led her to the aisle that said "L-P Fiction," and in seconds, she found it. It was the same book, *Moby-Dick* by Herman Melville, obviously worn and older, surrounded by all new books. She touched the spine of the book, remembering seeing it held tightly to her father's chest. He put his arm around her and whispered, "*Upon safe passage home.*"

Next they went into what had been the prison-like lunchroom. Now transformed, it was a real gymnasium with shiny wood floors and basketball hoops at either end of the large room. Sports equipment was organized and stored in containers and wall shelving. Shutters no longer covered the large windows and sunlight streamed in. Her father pointed outside and they could see picnic tables and wooden towers with slides and swings. He told them the students would have their lunch *outdoors* on the porch or the picnic tables, al fresco. In the winter, lunch would be in the gym, "picnic-style" with blankets on the floor. There would be Make Your Own Sundaes every Friday and hot chocolate in the winter from someone called a "caterer" who would bring in food carts every day.

Then they ran up the stairs to the second floor and stood in the hallway, taking everything in. Standing outside Classroom #5 was Miss Rhubarb. Jaclyn could not stop staring. Her eyes were still green but with no sign of being bloodshot, and her cheeks were pink, not blotchy red. She was wearing an ivory-colored dress with a red and green scarf, and her shoes were red (but not glittery). She was smiling, and actually looked quite pretty.

Mr. Gingerroot was standing outside Classroom #8. He was wearing brown slacks, a green sweater, a white shirt, and the same necktie as her father. His face was normal looking, no longer misshapen like some kind of root vegetable, and his hair was much less wiry and rootlike. It appeared to have been slicked down by some kind of shiny hair gel.

Then they looked down the hall. Olivia was standing outside Classroom #7, and Elisabeth was standing outside their old room, Classroom #6.

So this was how it was going to work. They would still have Olivia as their teacher. Olivia was wearing her "Taco-colored" dress, and her mother was wearing a red dress with a white silk flower and a white belt. Her mother's dress reminded Alexandra of Olivia's first day in Classroom #6 when she wore a white dress with a red flower. Alexandra loved looking at them, standing within feet of each other across a hallway, and she thought about all the vast distances that had been between them. Separated at birth, then by the Atlantic Ocean, and again by the ocean on that fateful summer day, and now they were just a few steps from each other.

Then their eyes fell on the two doors no one had ever wanted to go through. The grimy wood door that had said "To the Turret" was painted blue and covered in yellow stars and faraway galaxies. A large moon was in the upper right corner, shining down on the words "Stairway to the Stars." The other forbidding door Theo had known so well, for "Boarders Only," was now painted to look like a full-size red English telephone booth. On the panes of glass was written, "Artists and Musicians Enter Here," and after the word "Here" there were two unusual exclamation points—a paintbrush and musical treble clef.

Olivia and Elisabeth nodded as the girls headed to the door that led to the turret. Along with other students, they made their way up the narrow spiral staircase to the roof of the school and the widow's walk where two ghostly figures were walking on that cold November night. (Alexandra knew with absolute certainty they would *never* be seen again.) Telescopes of all sizes were mounted on tripods along the walk, pointing to the sky. Both Alexandra and Jaclyn looked at each other, grinning and thinking the same thing. Maybe they would be able to find the darkest spot in the night sky where there are no stars, where Taco had flown into the time tunnel.

* ◆ *

(Or more correctly, "wormhole." During the summer, Theo told them this was the correct scientific term, not time tunnel, and had tried to explain why it was called a wormhole. Nevertheless, even after hearing the complicated explanation, Jaclyn told him "time tunnel" was a much better description and he should change it when he became a famous astrophysicist—since *even she* knew there were no worms crawling into holes in space. Alexandra had immediately corrected Jaclyn and said Theo was going to become a famous doctor or veterinarian, *not* an astrophysicist, but Theo had just smiled, not revealing what he was thinking.)

The truth was, Theo had become even more engrossed with the study of astrophysics over the summer and Nicolas had become interested as well. And it was not unusual to hear Theo proclaim, with great enthusiasm, "Three quarks for Muster Mark!" upon mastering some complicated mathematical formula. Even Taco seemed interested and often sat on Theo's bed, watching and listening to their discussions. He tried very hard to follow what they were saying, but most of the time looked extremely perplexed. Once he brought them a ball of string from the wrapping closet—he had heard them talking so much about strings he thought it might be helpful. It had taken all the control they could muster not to burst out laughing, and luckily, were able to hold straight faces as they thanked him. Many nights were spent in Theo's room poring over thick books and then writing long formulas in Greek letters on a large blackboard they had found on the third floor. Just looking at the blackboard filled with their scribbling made Alexandra nauseous. Unlike Taco, she was definitely *not* interested.

Nicolas was convinced that if anyone could solve the science of time travel it was Theo. Theo would just need "plus de temps pour comprendre le temps"—more time to figure out time, he had said, smiling. Nicolas told them the author of "The Raven," Edgar Allan Poe, had also written about space, time, and the universe in a nonfiction work called *Eureka*, which he said even Einstein had called "a very beautiful achievement of an unusually independent mind." He said he found the book in the Chadwick library and was surprised, because he thought he had read everything written by Edgar Allan Poe. So every now and then, when Theo had written something that looked promising on the blackboard, Nicolas would exclaim "Eureka!" and Taco would echo, followed by a lot of laughter. It was interesting, as both Theo and Nicolas observed, how differently Noir behaved in their brainstorming sessions. He was always quiet, never saying anything, but it was very clear he *understood* what was written on the board, and occasionally would fly to the blackboard with the chalk in his beak and write something of significance that was helpful—in Greek letters—while suspended by his powerful wings. Taco was obviously impressed and not at all jealous of Noir's amazing comprehension, and the first to shout "Eureka!" when Noir had finished writing. Taco's enthusiasm and belief were completely genuine. However, whether there was any real merit to what Noir had written, well, it could be fairly said Taco did not have a clue.

With all of this attention, Theo had remarked (turning a little pink), "Maybe with a bit of luck, and a stint at Oxford someday, who knows . . ." Apparently, Oxford was a rather prestigious British school for very smart math and science students. Another thought that made Alexandra's stomach queasy. However, Theo had looked blissfully happy just thinking about it. He told them he had done some research and found out there was a famous astrophysicist who taught classes at Oxford, who had recently proven the universe was *flat*. "Bloody amazing," he had said, grinning, and pushing up his glasses.

* ◆ *

They came back down the "Stairway to the Stars" and then went through the red telephone booth door and up to the third floor where Theo had been alone for so long. There was not a single bed in sight. This was the moment they realized there would no longer be any boarders at The Pine School. The large third-floor attic room had been made into two rooms, one for art and the other for music. The art room was full of art supplies with colorful artwork displayed on the walls. There were round tables with brightly painted stools and art smocks hanging on wall pegs. The music room had all kinds of musical instruments stored on large shelves along one wall and a large piano against another wall. Chairs were set up in rows with music stands holding sheet music. It was like being in a different school altogether, so much had changed.

"Theo would have died and gone to heaven," Jaclyn whispered to Alexandra as they walked through the rooms. Alexandra nodded in complete agreement and hoped Choate had something similar. He would need a break from all those Greek formulas, and he was a very good artist.

It had taken a few weeks to believe all the wonderful changes were permanent and not some dream that would end. Morning announcements were *amazing*. Her father's voice was vibrant and enthusiastic, and there was no raspy, wheezing voice breathing into the microphone saying "Testing one, two, three" ever again. But the very best part was Taco began delivering some of the morning announcements. Each day he would announce the lunch menu and then the weather, all in French. (It was astonishing how fast the youngest students were learning French. First- and second-year students were learning faster than some of the older students.) There was never once any mention of "The Code of Behavior," and although she never asked, Alexandra was certain *The Infraction Record Book* had also been locked away by her father, never to record another student's name again.

And the hallways and classrooms of The Pine School were often filled with laughter.

Alexandra had been watching for any sign of Headmaster Green, afraid to ask her parents what happened to him. After a few weeks she was certain he was gone. He had simply disappeared.

Soon the leaves were turning colors and began fluttering to the ground.

Fall had arrived again in Dark Harbor and winter would be close behind. The tiny post office in town was delivering more mail to and from Chadwick Manor than ever before. There were letters going to and from England, some with the most unusual footprints imprinted on the back seal, and others going between Connecticut, Dark Harbor, and England. Among the mail going from Dark Harbor to Connecticut were postcards. Because he had become so focused on cosmology (another word he began using over the summer), Alexandra felt Theo needed to be reminded about becoming a veterinarian and began sending him postcards from Weston's Market. There was not a big selection. Most of the animal photos were of lobsters, seagulls, or moose; Alexandra never found any with ravens or macaws. She told Mr. Weston he needed to get some postcards with birds other than seagulls. He told her they would never sell to the tourists.

As a result, Theo received many lobster, seagull, and moose postcards, all addressed to "Dr. Theodore Arthur Eddington, Future Veterinarian."

Then another Halloween parade was upon them.

They all dressed up, the adults in their usual costumes, and after some prolonged conversations, Alexandra, Jaclyn, and Taco reached an agreement about what they would wear. In the end, the girls agreed to go along with Professeur Taco, who had obviously made up his mind and was *not* open to other suggestions. (He had quickly vetoed the mummy costume). Taco would go as the famous French artist Monet, wearing a beret and smock (with the name Monet embroidered by Evelyn, so everyone would know *which* famous French painter he was), and he would carry a paintbrush clasped in his beak. The two girls would be his art students, also dressed in smocks with berets, holding paint palettes and brushes. They sprayed their hair all different colors. (This was fun, but made Evelyn very nervous. What if it didn't come out?) They also put splotches of paint all over their faces. (That part was fun, too, but they heard, "Blimey, let's hope your peaches-and-cream complexions won't turn red and blue, my mouses!" Evelyn was an excellent worrier.)

There was something else to think about during the Halloween preparations and planning this year, which added to the air of mystery and excitement that always blew in with the falling leaves and cold night air. How would her parents dress? And Olivia? With mysterious smiles, they said it was a secret, and until All Hallows' Eve, when everyone assembled in the Chadwick foyer, it was. They were standing in the foyer, waiting, when three figures appeared at the center banister on the second floor.

There was only awed silence at first.

In the dim light of the sconces, three magical figures appeared. Her father was in the middle with Elisabeth on one side and Olivia on the other. Graham was dressed in white robes and carried a long white cane taller than he was. At the top of the cane was a giant pearl nautilus shell. His face was painted silvery white as was his hair, and he wore a crown encrusted with sparkling white seashells and starfish of all shapes and sizes, which instantly reminded Alexandra of her birthday cake. Elisabeth and Olivia were identical mermaids. Their black hair was woven with blue and green sparkling seaweed and small seashells, and they each wore a long dress made from shimmering aquamarine scales that clung tightly to their arms and bodies. The scales resembled real fish scales, smooth and glistening—almost wet looking. As they walked down the stairs, everyone could see the large mermaid fishtails trailing behind them and seashell-encrusted slippers on their feet. They each wore a nautilus shell necklace; the shell had been split in half, revealing a spiral swirl of mother-of-pearl chambers. Very long earrings made from tiny seashells hung down from their ears. Their eyes looked green or blue depending on the light, and their faces, necks, and hands were painted glittery blue-green, and sparkled in the dim light, blending into the iridescent scales. If not for their feet, you would have believed they were real mermaids.

Her father told them he was Triton, the god of Greek mythology who rules the sea, and Elisabeth and Olivia were his court, twin mermaids. They looked completely authentic, as though they had just emerged from the sea and could slip back in as easily, and there were gasps and oohs and aahs as people came to see their costumes and makeup more closely after the parade. As she watched her parents during the parade and thought more about their costumes, Alexandra realized this choice was intentional—and symbolic. Her parents had gone to watery graves and returned like mythological sea creatures that live forever.

Another mystery was solved on All Hallows' Eve in Dark Harbor.

Alexandra and Jaclyn had gone from shop to shop for their treats after the parade, but they stood outside The Book Nook for a while, debating whether to go in. Jaclyn wanted to; Alexandra did not. The Book Nook had actually closed sometime during the summer. A sign on the door read, "Under Renovation, Will Reopen at Halloween." Alexandra had been curious when she read the sign, but also relieved. She last saw Miss Ima at The Snack Shack and hoped the creepy old woman would never come back to Dark Harbor. (She had never even told Theo or Jaclyn about the one time Miss Ima had mysteriously appeared on Chatham Beach.) So Alexandra shook her head "no" and tried to pull Jaclyn on to the next shop, not wanting to know whether the bizarre Miss Ima (who was very likely some kind of witch) had returned. However, Jaclyn was not budging—*The Book Nook was the only bookstore for miles and miles, and they would need to buy books.* With some prodding, Alexandra very reluctantly agreed to go in. Jaclyn went through the door first.

The same dry paper smell met their nostrils as they entered, and they immediately swiveled to look where Miss Ima was always standing. Twin mermaids were behind the counter, smiling rather mysteriously. Jaclyn and Alexandra were speechless. What did this mean? Where was Miss Ima? They slowly walked over to the counter and that was when Olivia told them—twin sisters now owned The Book Nook. She said they would hire a manager for weekdays, but take turns working on weekends when they would need help from her two nieces, who would probably enjoy some spending money for . . . hmm, makeup and clothes? It was all so astonishing it had taken a few minutes to absorb.

Then Alexandra asked *the* question with apprehension, even fear.

"Where is Miss Ima?"

The answer came quickly. They did not know. She had simply disappeared, but she had left a letter on the shop counter addressed to "The Chadwick Twins." The letter said The Book Nook was her gift to them and to please keep it well stocked, especially with books about space for Theo. The letter was signed, "Your Friend Always, Miss Ima."

As Alexandra was absorbing this most unexpected development, Olivia said they should go upstairs, and pointed to the back of the shop and the dreaded door leading to the second floor. Jaclyn immediately pulled her cousin to the back of the shop. However, they both stopped as they approached the door. In silver lettering painted on the frosty glass it now read, "To the Second Floor—Where the Mind Takes Flight." Painted above the words was a pair of wings, but they were not identical. The left wing was layered hues of brilliant turquoise blue. The right wing was glossy black with traces of opalescence. They met in the center, wingtip to wingtip, the feathers intertwined, like the interlacing fingers of two hands. Alexandra stood in silence in front of the image, and as she studied the painting, she understood something for the first time. What words could never adequately express had been told, fully and completely, by an artist's brush strokes.

In that moment, Alexandra glimpsed a profound truth. She had felt and understood the transcendent power of art.

Jaclyn opened the door, gently pulling Alexandra with her, and they began to climb. The stairs were now completely normal, leading quickly to the second floor, which was entirely different—well lit and with lots of space between the bookshelves. In the center of the room, there was a round table with comfortable chairs, and on the table was a sign that said, *"Excellent Selections* from The Book Nook," along with some books about space, time travel, the universe, and physics. One title caught their eyes, *Open, Closed or Flat: The Mystery of the Universe Finally Solved.* They realized it had to be one of the books Theo was reading over the summer.

As they picked up some of the green and red chocolate eyeballs from the counter on their way out, Elisabeth called after them.

"Don't forget the books upstairs. Christmas is coming!"

* ◆ *

It was early December when they found out Theo, Nicolas, Noir, and Nicole would be returning to Dark Harbor on December 20th.

It was surprising how the time had flown by, faster than anyone would have expected, but mostly for Taco, because he was so busy teaching and grading papers. (Learning to write to Noir in French had been excellent preparation for teaching French.) As they left school each day, he *always* carried a folder of papers in his curved beak. (This was a sight that *always* brought smiles to tired faces at the end of a long school day . . . a most professional macaw parrot, holding a file of papers in his beak, sitting next to a border collie in the front seat of an antique touring car.) After having a snack, he would spread out the papers on the kitchen table and with great care (and his English-to-French pocket dictionary) begin grading the papers with a red pen. Her father had told Alexandra privately that Taco was an easy grader, but he said that was fine with him because The Pine School students were not required to learn a foreign language (not until the next level, preparatory school), so they were all getting a head start. However, Taco took his responsibilities very seriously, as did his students—they wanted to impress their most unusual teacher.

When they heard the date they were coming home, Jaclyn and Alexandra had the exact same thought. Nicolas would be turning sixteen a couple of days after arriving home. Would a letter come this year? They both felt it would because he was completely transformed—surely he had passed probation. No longer worried, they both thought Nicolas *should* receive a letter.

The days seemed to crawl by as they waited for the 20th to come.

Theo had recently written to Alexandra that Choate had some kind of special class in astrophysics, and he was accepted for the next term after taking more tests, and that he had a "bit of knees up" when he heard the news. She knew there had to be holiday parties at this time of year, but Alexandra was certain no one other than Theo would have a party because they got into a very hard science class.

Finally, December 20th arrived.

They were all waiting for Blackie's car to swing into the driveway around seven o'clock. He had picked Theo up from a bus station in

Boston and then went to the airport for Nicolas, Nicole, and Noir. Blackie had allowed plenty of time because Noir had to go through all kinds of red tape, from customs and airport security to animal control. Just like the time he had first arrived, getting through the gauntlet of being poked and thoroughly prodded was not fun. What did they think he had under each wing? His answer was a curt "non" when asked if he had anything to declare. What possessions would a raven have other than some shiny, cheap trinkets? The entire process had annoyed Noir terribly, and he made impolite remarks to everyone but because they were in French no one knew what he was saying, thank goodness.

At last, headlights flashed in the darkness, and minutes later, they were all standing in the foyer. Alexandra was suddenly overwhelmed with another feeling of déjà vu. She was standing in the same place the night she met her cousins for the first time. Now she was looking at Theo, Nicolas, and Nicole. They all looked so much older, yet it had only been about four months, and they all looked *so happy*. Alexandra realized Nicolas was holding Nicole's hand and let go to open Noir's cage, which he was holding in the other hand.

The raven lifted off and flew upward toward the center banister where Taco was waiting. As he flew, the foyer echoed with the powerful sound of one long raven caw, followed by three short caws, and then it repeated. Alexandra felt tears slip from her eyes as he landed gracefully next to Taco and slowly closed his black finger-tipped wings. They looked intently at each other for a moment and then, very slowly, the blue head with the shimmering opalescent patch bowed to the raven. Then the black head with traces of purple and green opalescence did the same to the macaw.

The best of friends—now and forever equals, both the most uncommon of birds—whose bravery and loyalty would be unmatched by most humans.

Whether Nicolas received his letter at midnight on December 23rd is not known.

However, there was something no one noticed the night they arrived. It happened so quickly that it was not observed. As Nicolas walked through the door, it appeared two pairs of emerald eyes became real, blinked once, and then instantly returned to gemstones. But what happens in a blink of an eye can *never* be proven to be true.

One secret that had been kept by Silver Chadwick and the Duke and Duchess of Devonshire will be shared. On the evening of the annual Christmas skating party there was a surprise announcement. They were told that a new preparatory school had been built on the coast road, just a short distance to the north of Dark Harbor. Funded by Silver Chadwick and the Duke and Duchess, the school was named "The Pine Preparatory School." Theo, Nicolas, and Nicole would attend beginning in January, as would Alexandra and Jaclyn in the future. For one semester, Graham would be in charge of both schools, but Silver told them beginning with the fall term, the new Headmistress of The Pine Preparatory School would be . . . Olivia.

When Silver's gaze had fallen on Nicolas and Jaclyn, she told them The Pine Preparatory School would have a Professor Emeritus of French, Professeur Noir. Then, her gaze directed at Theo, she said there would be another, yet-to-be-named, Professor Emeritus of Astrophysics.

Lastly, she had turned and looked at Alexandra.

Dr. Burke, who was retiring from his veterinary practice, would be teaching pre-veterinarian classes and would hold the third Emeritus position—with a special emphasis on *avian medicine*. Then, looking deeply into her granddaughter's eyes, she said in a tone of voice that held both a command and a challenge, "More young women are needed in the field of veterinary medicine. Especially those with a love of birds."

Just before they left to board the sleighs, with Napoleon and Chestnut stomping the snowy ground anxious to be off, Silver Chadwick had some last words.

"There will be some work required of each of you over this holiday. . . . We will need to prepare the third floor of Chadwick Manor for twelve boarders who will be arriving from England after Christmas. They will attend The Pine School for the second semester. Theo, I hope a second-floor bedroom will be all right. You are now family, my dear. Many years ago, the English boarding students stayed with us at Chadwick. It is time to put those rooms to their proper use again, and Evelyn will be hiring an assistant." Silver paused, looking at each of them, her blue eyes twinkling.

"*Welcome home*, all my dears."

If you happened to be in a rowboat passing close by the shore-line of Dark Harbor, Maine, on New Year's Eve, you most certainly would have been astonished to hear the sounds of children laughing and shouting and water splashing. And if you paddled into one small inlet through a break in the rocky cliffs, the tide would have swept you into a sparkling cave filled with aquamarine water illuminated by frothy jets of bioluminescence, and the sight would have amazed you.

On a frigid cold Maine night, two birds sitting on a large perch were refereeing a water volleyball game . . . with whistles blowing.

POSTSCRIPT

In the apartment above Weston's Market, a manila folder stuffed with newspaper clippings sits on the small kitchen table.

The file label reads, "THE ORION PROJECT."

A single photographic image lies on top of the newspaper articles. It appears to be an astronomical map or chart, with just a few words written in elegant handwriting.

It looks like this.

Through a cosmic gate . . .
to a future in the stars.

Olivia White studies the image while absently rubbing the small gold disc of her necklace. Then she looks out the window at the winter night sky. Her gaze quickly settles on a glittering constellation. In the center there are three stars in a row. A cloudy but luminous formation can be seen directly south of the triad of stars. Made of interstellar gas and dust, it is a vast cosmic nursery, a place where stars and planets are born . . . the Orion Nebula.

Still rubbing the gold disc she whispers one word.

"Orpheous."

THE END
OF
THE BEGINNING

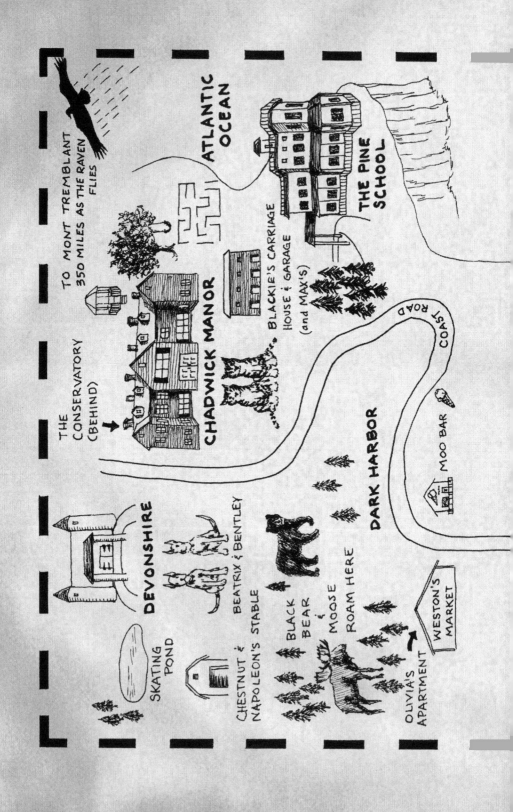

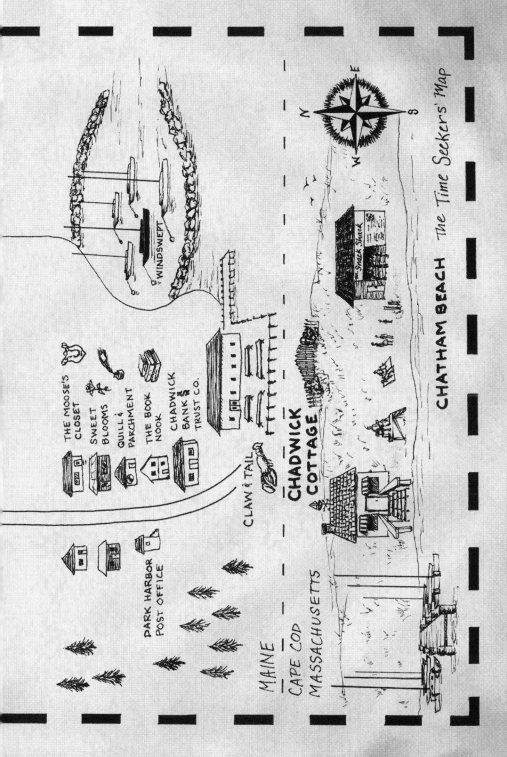

THE MOOSE'S CLOSET

SWEET BLOOMS

QUILL & PARCHMENT

THE BOOK NOOK

CHADWICK BANK & TRUST CO.

PARK HARBOR POST OFFICE

CLAW & TAIL

CHADWICK COTTAGE

MAINE

CAPE COD

MASSACHUSETTS

WINDSWEPT

Snack Shack

CHATHAM BEACH *The Time Seekers' Map*

N E
W S

AUTHOR'S NOTE

The Time Seekers is a work of fiction. The birds (and people) in this story are fictional characters. Exotic and wild birds are best suited to live in their natural habitats, and this book is not intended to suggest they are appropriate as pets. In fact, it is sadly not uncommon for macaw parrots to be in less than optimal and even inhumane conditions when privately owned. Macaws and other exotic birds are intelligent and sensitive, and when not properly cared for, can injure themselves due to depression, anxiety, and stress. The lifespan of exotic birds can outlast their owners', so this commitment is long and guardianship must also be considered.

A portion of the sale of this book will be donated to an exotic bird sanctuary devoted to the care and nurturing of exotic birds whose owners can no longer care for them. Located in Florida, this non-profit avian sanctuary provides housing for the birds in expansive flight cages, as well as the proper nutrition and veterinary care they will need for their lifetimes.

ABOUT THE AUTHOR

D. A. Squires began writing this story many years ago. The early chapters were set aside as she raised her two children and worked in various corporate jobs. However, the inspiration for this story was never forgotten . . . a blue and gold macaw parrot named Taco who steadfastly watched over her daughter's crib (sadly, a silent sentinel).

Fifteen years later she was astonished when, one summer day, a blue and gold macaw named Taco and a common raven named Noir landed on her shoulders and *insisted* their story be written.

So she wrote.

A graduate of the University of Connecticut with a Bachelor of Arts in English, *magna cum laude*, and elected to Phi Beta Kappa, Ms. Squires grew up in Connecticut and now lives in Florida with her husband, two cats (one named Samuel Adams), a dapple dachshund named Mr. Chips, and a slightly faded blue and gold macaw parrot who remains ever vigilant.

DASquires.com

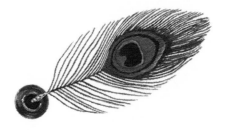

ABOUT THE ILLUSTRATOR

Kelly Arnold is an artist who specializes in commissioned portraits painted in oils. Her artwork covers a spectrum of mediums including drawing, painting, sculpting, and computer graphics, and continues to grow.

Working in the printing graphics industry earlier in her career, she was responsible for running a production department for a multimillion-dollar company. She began teaching art in the early 1990s, which led to creating and teaching art full time. Instructing students from as young as age four to their late nineties has been one of her greatest achievements. Many of her students have won awards and developed into professional artists. Giving back to them, she created The Arts Enrichment Club in Stuart, Florida, which is the longest running community service program of its kind.

The Time Seekers is the first book she has illustrated. The front and back cover artwork was done in oil, the sketches in pen and ink, and as a graphic and web designer, she was also responsible for the graphic design of the book and the author's website.

KellyArnold.com

ACKNOWLEDGMENTS

Kelly Arnold, whose magical art is the musical score
of *The Time Seekers*.
The lyrics are deeply honored to be accompanied by
such beautiful art.

Taco and Noir, for carrying me on their wings in a
flight traversing time and space.

And always and forever, my family, for everything.

51817014R00321

Made in the USA
Charleston, SC
04 February 2016